I0719780

# UNSEEN SERVANT

## R. G. Bisig

Copyright © 2020 R. G. Bisig

All rights reserved.


Print ISBN-13: 978-1-7324524-2-8
ePub ISBN-13: 978-1-7324524-3-5


UNSEEN SERVANT is a work of fiction. Names, characters, places, planes, and incidents either are the product of the author's imagination or are used fictitiously. Any resemblance to actual persons, living or dead, events, or locales is entirely coincidental.

Text Copyright © 2020 R. G. Bisig
Cover by Claire Lucas

All rights reserved. No part of this book may be reproduced, scanned, or distributed in any printed or electronic form without permission. Please do not participate in or encourage piracy of copyrighted materials in violation of the author's rights. Purchase only authorized editions.

To Calhoun, Taffin, Fiera, and others who fell victim as I learned
how to twist and turn a story.


Hope I did it right.

With exception of flashback scenes, all scenes are in
chronological order.
References to time of day match the location within that day.

*Tuesday, April 16*
*Day of the Explosion*

"President Taylor's on her way."

Leelee sighed at her husband's announcement from somewhere in the house. It was inevitable; the President coming to the house to pick him up. Damn woman couldn't just send a car to pick him up, she'd have to come herself. Grandeur at its fullest. He was the reason she was in Ann Arbor. Well, that and the conference.

She pulled the empty cardboard box down from the shelf in the garage and carried it into the house. Zach had scrawled the word *Easter* on five sides in his lousy handwriting. A university professor's handwriting, slightly more legible than a physician's.

Leelee placed the box on the dining room table next to the stack of wicker baskets and wreaths decorated with pastel plastic eggs. Earlier, she gathered them from their seasonal spots on bookcases and tables throughout the house. The corner of the cardboard box caught on the sleeve of her sweater. The temperature outside was in the forties, warm for Michigan, but she was used to something twice that in her native hometown on Oahu. The hunt for Easter eggs among the coconuts was much more challenging.

Zach bustled past her several times, roaming through the kitchen, living room, bedroom, and office. She stood out of his way, waiting for him to ask for help. Two months shy of their twenty-eighth anniversary, Leelee knew when to let her husband be and when to step in. He'd been at it for several minutes. She looked up and smiled as he stopped to stare at the ceiling for a moment. She'd give him another minute.

As she waited, Leelee wrinkled her nose at his pale blue shirt and navy-blue jacket with matching tie and belt. It was a throwback to his twenty-plus years in the Air Force. The suit had no flowers, palm trees, or ocean waves on it. No color on it at all. Still, it fit his trim, six-foot-three build. In his fifties, his sandy-blond hair was streaked with gray.

Leelee shook her head, recalling the grays she plucked from her chocolate brown hair that morning. Too soon to start dying her hair, but it was inevitable.

"Argh!" Zach stomped, pausing at the dining room table.

Leelee stopped him as he passed through the kitchen again. "What are you looking for, dear?"

Zach startled. He turned toward her, eyes wide. "Oh, there you are. I can't find my reading glasses."

He wore half-lens glasses for over two years. It started when he had to hold the restaurant menu farther out to read the page. Too proud to admit he was getting old, it was as if they had taken away his manhood. When the university student's—the women mostly—said it made him look more *professor-ly*, he capitulated.

Leelee nuzzled close to him, reached up to kiss him, and pulled his glasses off the top of his head. "Well, here. Use these instead."

Zach sank a little, blushing at his embarrassment. "Thank you, my love." He stuffed them in his jacket breast pocket and kissed her again. "Don't know what I'd do without you."

"You know you're over-reacting. There's nothing to worry about. Think of her as just a woman visiting the university to see your engineering project."

"Just a woman." Zach rolled his eyes. "Just President of the United States, leader of the free world… that kind of thing."

Leelee reached up, grabbed his firm chin, and turned his face toward hers. "And you've met with Holly many times before. Stop making a big deal out of this."

She insisted on using the President's first name instead of the honorific. It often relieved tension in him. Today, it wasn't working.

"This is a big deal," Zach said. "If today doesn't go well, it will be more than an embarrassment. It will reflect on the University. And what if she shows the suppressors to the audience? There will be humans and mutants at this second conference, not to mention all the national media outlets."

"The halos? You mean your top-secret project with the devices that block a mutant from using their powers?" Leelee grinned. "The one you've been working on for over two years now."

Zach relaxed, nodding. "Yes, that top-secret project."

There was a more technical name for the metallic headband—genetic mutation suppressor—but it got the nickname 'halo' for the shape and placement.

It was a topic he rarely talked about at home, not because of the top-secret status, but for the implications. He said he didn't want to bore her with the technical stuff of his work, but Leelee understood more than she let on.

She hid her frown as best she could. Their children were mutants, her son being able to do the very thing his device would do. Leelee hated the idea of her husband being recognized as the man who hindered mutant-kind, possibly their own children someday. He tried to explain the law enforcement aspect of the device, to control the criminal mutant, not the law-abiding mutant. Still, knowing how governments have a way of subverting anything, she was fearful.

Leelee brushed his shoulders and straightened his tie inside his jacket. "If you get all jittery, something could go wrong. Where would you be then? Relax and be your charming and confident self. But not too charming." She winked. "I don't care if she is the president. You're mine."

A warm smile came across Zach's face. He leaned down and kissed her forehead. "Now and always."

She patted him again, stepping away. "Good. Remember that."

Behind her, Leelee heard the television narrator discussing the brief history of mutants. She glanced at the TV as the hosts of Worldview argued.

The moderator faced a man to his right, an older gentleman, with white hair and a goatee beard. "Let's turn now to our network historian. Hiro, tell us the significance of this conference."

"Blake, the history of mutants began with a few people bending spoons or knowing the playing card hidden behind a screen. When a few mutants used their powers for illegal activities, fear rose across the nation and the world. Distrust of people who displayed unique abilities, even those without the mutation, became a national issue."

"And by a national issue?"

"Law enforcement agencies found they could not hold mutants in jail without placing them in drug-induced comas. Civil rights groups protested this act as cruel and unusual punishment. Soon, state governments outlawed vigilante groups of superhuman, and then Congress followed suit, encouraging them to join legal organizations and not work outside the law."

"This conference is termed as the 'second' mutant and human relations conference. Why the second?"

"This meeting came about after the horrendous event three

years ago, the death of four hundred ninety-two people from a radiation blast in Houston, allegedly caused by the mutant Carlos Rodriguez. President Taylor followed that declaring martial law for ten days, followed by her Executive Order revoking civil rights for all persons known to be mutants."

"The Supreme Court later blocked her Executive Order." Blake interjected.

"Yes." Hiro replied. "Then during last year's Independence Day holiday, the *Million Mutant March* took place on the National Mall in Washington DC. The mutant advocacy group Mutant Defense Foundation sponsored it. The march turned bloody as the protests by mutant humans met up with protests by non-mutant humans. Three months later, President Holly Taylor held a private, unannounced meeting at UC Berkeley with James Seaton and Heather Lovett, leaders of the group, Mutant Defense Foundation. Out of that meeting came the commitment to create the Cabinet-level position, Department of Mutant Affairs and this second conference."

"So, we have here today on the campus of the University of Michigan an auditorium filled with humans and mutants."

The moderator spun his seat around to face a woman to his left. "Melissa, the President has mutants on staff, in the Secret Service that can block another mutant's powers. Rumors surfaced that she has a group of scientists working on a device to do that sort of thing. Could such a device may be introduced today."

"It's possible, Blake. It is very possible."

A tingle ran down Leelee's spine as the hairs on her arms raised. "Go get your briefcase. She's here." She gave her husband a quick kiss before walking through the living room to open the front door. Two Secret Service agents approached the house, and three black sedans sat at the curb, along with a pair of motorcycle police in front and back. Leelee smirked, knowing the neighborhood wives would chatter about this for weeks.

"Come in, gentlemen," Leelee held the door for them, waiting for them to enter.

"Thank you, ma'am. We'll wait out here." The lead agent stood at the top step, his partner two paces away.

"Like hell you will. I'll not have you stand outside my door, nor am I leaving it open."

"Better do what she says," Zach shouted from his office.

The lead agent glanced over his shoulder at the sedan, his expression impossible to read behind his black sunglasses. Apparently he received a transmission because he nodded, turn back to Leelee, and say, "Thank you for inviting us in, ma'am."

The two men stepped inside, barely far enough for her to close the door. She beamed; they reminded her of her son, Adam. They were both tall and broad-shouldered, wearing black suits, white shirts, and clear plastic spirals running from under their collar to their right ear. Adam was also an agent, now working on Vice-President Antonio Mendoza's detail.

"May I offer you gentlemen something to drink?"

"No, thank you," the lead agent replied, holding a hand out to stop her from offering more.

Leelee smiled and stepped backward into the dining room, leaning to look down the hallway toward the office. Zach was in the hall, looking at photos of their children—Adam and Lani— each picture taken at ages six, ten, and thirteen. Above them were pictures of Zach and Leelee at age six.

Adam had his father's chin with black hair and a lighter version of Leelee's Hawaiian complexion. Their daughter's skin tone was darker, like her mother. Dark purple at birth, Lani's hair turned brown before reaching puberty, though her eyes kept their violet tint.

"Ready to go, guys," he said. He wore a weak smile as he exited the hall and walked toward the door briefcase in hand.

The lead agent pointed to the briefcase, flicking his index finger. "May I, sir?"

"Oh, yes. Gotta check for bombs." Zach flipped it around and popped open the latches. Papers slid around as he tilted it open. A silver circlet sat on top. About an inch wide, the brushed titanium had a series of LED lights in four spots around its outer circumference.

"We prefer the term *contraband*," the agent said, nodding his acceptance of its contents.

The second agent reached for the doorknob, but Leelee already had her hand on it. He did a double-take, looking to the dining room where she was moments ago, then back to her. She opened the door, and the agents stepped outside. Leelee reached up and kissed her husband one more time.

"I forgot to pick up a few items from the grocery store last night," Leelee patted him on the arm. "I'll pick up your dry cleaning while I'm out so you'll have suits for the rest of the week."

Zach kissed her again. "As you wish. I'll be on all the news channels, if you want to watch her speech."

She stood on the step outside the door and watched as he got into the limo. Leelee couldn't see who else was in the car, but she caught sight of a pair of legs crossed at the shins. Leelee frowned at the knees extending from under a bright red skirt. Zach had a broad smile on his face as the agent closed the door behind him. Arms crossed tight across her chest, she tapped her foot on the concrete and watched the caravan leave the cul-de-sac.

She finished packing the Easter decorations and carried the box out to the garage, mulling over the coming events of the afternoon. Collecting her purse, she dropped her phone inside, then rummaged around inside for her car keys. Small sheet of notepaper in hand listing the several stops to make besides the dry cleaners and the grocery store, she headed out into the city.

Half the town under the age of forty would be at the University, circling outside if not seated inside the hall. Traffic would be a hassle around the campus. It would add twenty minutes to her trip across town. Time enough to call the kids. She knew Adam would watch, being with Vice-President Mendoza in Washington. As she got out of the driveway, she pushed the hands-free call button.

"Call Lani."

The phone rang twice before her daughter answered. "Hello?"

Leelee counted, knowing the Air Force Academy was two time zones behind. "Good morning, dear."

"Three times thirty-two, squared… hi Mom… divided by five?"

"Have you talked with your father today?"

"No. Why?"

Leelee glanced at the clock on the dashboard. "Wanted to remind you he would be on TV soon."

"Right, the conference. No, that's not right."

"Oh, I'm sure. The news has been talking about it all morning."

"Nah, sorry, Mom. I was doing math. Sir, that's not possible."

Leelee pursed her lips as she waited for her daughter's attention. She must have caught her in the middle of a class.

"Sir," Lani said, "with that angle in the turn, the G-force would be more than the plane could take, let alone the pilot."

Leelee tried to interject. "I'm sorry to bother you, dear. I'll talk with you afterward?"

"No, sir. Doubt if I could either." Lani's voice became less formal. "Yeah, sounds good, Mom. I'll talk to you then."

Leelee frowned when the call disconnected. She sighed, not having time to say their usual "Aloha, I love you" before hanging up.

She drove by the dry cleaner, but the red flashing open sign was dark and all the lights were off. She frowned, but knew why. The owner, Mr. Han, was a mutant who could mend and restore colors to materials. He had become very discrete after a visit from the Fire Department's Hazardous Chemicals division found none of the usual dry cleaning chemicals.

Han had been open to answering Zach's friendly inquiries about the range of his abilities. He had canvassed a lot of mutants in town. Not that there were a lot. Most were attending the university, which as a professor, he had easy access to. Many were accepting of his testing; getting paid a few dollars an hour to sit in a chair with electrodes attached to their head was quick pizza money.

The parking lot at Mercer's Produce wasn't as bare as she expected. She circled the lot twice before finding a spot close to the door. Before getting out of the car, her phone chimed. With the time being close to noon, she expected a text or call from Zach. No doubt he'd tell her everything was going as planned, or it was complete chaos. With him, it was one or the other.

Instead, it was a brief message from Billy, one of Adam's friends from the University. Something about dropping off a package. Billy helped her around the house a lot. With Adam and Lani away from home and Zach working for the University, or President Taylor, Billy had been a godsend. Her latest project for him was repairing the broken bird bath. It seems ice and porcelain don't mix very well.

Feeling bad for interrupting Lani, she sent a text to Adam instead of calling.

**Leelee:** *Have you talked with your father today?*

Expecting it would be several minutes before Adam would reply, Leelee reached for several canvas bags from the back seat. She made her way into the store and began wiping down the shopping cart handle with a disinfectant cloth. As she finished, her phone chimed. It was quicker than she expected.

**Adam:** *No, but waiting for his speech. Was he nervous this morning?*

**Leelee:** *Of course.*

**Adam:** *President come to the door?*

**Leelee:** *No, she stayed in the car.*

**Adam:** *Sounds like her. Best to text Lani. She's probably in class.*

**Leelee:** *Good idea. Aloha, I love you.*

**Adam:** *A. Love ya 2.*

A yearning to see her baby boy welled briefly inside her chest. She saw Lani often, even though she was in Colorado Springs at the Air Force Academy because of her ability to fly without an airplane. But Adam was always busy working for the Secret Service, and Leelee rarely got to see him these days.

As she passed the fresh fruit displays, Leelee's phone chimed again. A banner at the top of the screen read: Conference at University.

Several televisions hung from the ceiling; the store used them for advertising specials, but they had been tuned for the day to show the live news feed of the conference. The camera view focused on a podium with six seats extending to one side. The scene reminded her more of a graduation ceremony. The announcers listed the speaker, naming Zach as the BioMed professor and emcee for the keynote, along with President Taylor, the secretary of the newly created Department of Mutant Affairs, and two students from the university representing Mutant Defense Foundation.

As she picked out a few avocados, Zach's voice sounded over the speakers as he introduced President Taylor. A loud round of applause from the audience followed. Leelee wasn't too concerned about catching every word. Zach had scheduled two hours of keynote speeches before the president even said a word. The pundits would analyze the president's speech all afternoon and evening, which left plenty of time for Leelee to catch the highlights before Zach came to pick her up for dinner.

Leelee stopped at the meat counter, looking over the selection. Another of Adam's university buddies stood behind the counter, staring at a TV monitor above aisle six. She cleared her throat, grabbing his attention.

"Oh, Mrs. K. Didn't see you standing there." The young man pulled off the clear latex gloves and tossed them into a trash bin. "How's the Professor? Big day today, huh?"

Leelee turned to look over her shoulder to see the monitor. "Yes. It's finally here. Been waiting quite a while for this moment." She pulled out her phone and searched for her grocery app.

"What can I do for you?" The man fished a fresh pair of gloves from a box.

Leelee looked up from her phone, stashing it back in her purse. "I'm fixing laulau for tomorrow, in case he survives the conference. What do you have for pork shoulder back there?"

"Well, we've got—"

A boom shook the building. Display signs over the ends of the aisle swayed. Some heavier items on the shelves fell to the floor, shattering or splattering their contents across the aisles. In the distance, car alarms sounded.

White-noise static filled every television screen she could see. Leelee barely noticed her hand slipping from the cart as the nearest screen seemed to pull her toward it like a magnet.

The pit in her stomach grew heavier. "Come back, tell us what's happened…"

The screen flickered, switching to a newsroom with three commentators sitting behind a curved desk. All were silent, their fingers to their earpieces. Their eyes went wide, jaws dropping open.

Her forehead furrowed, Leelee glanced out the floor-to-ceiling windows at the store's front. An immense column of smoke rose in the University's direction.

Keeping her eyes on the column of smoke, she made her way outside, ignoring the crunching of shattered glass under her shoes. Another patron bumped into her, and she realized others had come outside, too, all staring at the huge, thick charcoal cloud ascending into the sky, rolling around itself as it climbed. Police and Fire Department sirens blared, more noticeable as the car alarms silenced.

Leelee's stomach churned as she swallowed bile. Her head swam, and she realized she'd been holding her breath. When she allowed herself to breathe, the muffled sounds crashed in around her. Someone was crying in the crowd, and several people were shouting. Still others stood as though frozen, hands on their mouths or phones held up to record the scene before them.

A man nearby shushed the crowd, reading from the banner on his phone. "An explosion has occurred at the University, centered on the BioMed building." The man paused, looking away from his phone. "No word on the President."

Leelee held a hand against her chest. Tears blurred her vision. She dredged up what little strength and courage she could muster and fished out her phone.

"I need to call the kids."

*Tuesday, June 20*
*Present Day*

Sweat ran down Adam's back as he walked down 15th Street toward the Washington Monument and crossed at Madison. Carrying his brown paper bag, he skirted the side of the sidewalk, trying to grab any piece of shade he could. The trees lining the National Mall comforted little, the heat and humidity were both in the mid-nineties. He recalled the radio calling it sweltering hot —average for the first day of summer. Blistering hot would come around in a few weeks during Independence Day. The summer heat was coming on earlier each year. Adam chuckled at the thought of the President gathering a bunch of weather controlling mutants together. Mother Nature would probably have something to say about it though.

He took the cool bottle of water he picked up from the street vendor and held it to his neck. The water outside of the bottle mixed with his sweat on his neck, soaking his white collar even more.

The chorus of an anti-mutant protest chant rose up to Adam's left, grabbing his attention. A diverse group of people gathered along the path in the mall. The leader of the group held a bullhorn to her face. Signs on poles thrust up and down out of tune with the chant.

Adam smirked at the signs, calling for the end of mutants, jailing them for being 'abominations', 'criminals against nature', and worse. Clearly, they didn't know who the criminals really were.

As the protest marchers approached, a family of four packed up and moved from a shaded park bench. Adam took the opportunity and sat down on the vacated bench, bottle between his legs and lunch bag to his side.

Behind him, shouts of children and an occasional adult sparked his interest. A school bus sat at the curb, children streaming onto the sidewalk, adults attempting to corral them together. As the line of children and teachers headed toward the crosswalk, Adam's mutant ability triggered. Everything blurred—the buildings, the school bus, and the humans. Only the XZ-positive remained in razor-sharp focus.

Studying each one individually, an aura appeared around the child. He could interrupt that aura, letting him know what ability would manifest in the child at puberty. Adam chuckled at the boy with an ornery smirk who would develop x-ray vision. Glimpsing the aura around a woman in the group's rear, he understood why the children were behaving so well.

He could tell she was pushing out signals, mentally directing them. That would be a good thing to have when the next White House tour group gets off in the wrong areas.

He reached into his brown paper bag and pulled out a sandwich. Sliced ham and cheese, with mayo, the same lunch he made every morning this month. He frowned at himself, deciding to pick out a different lunch meat this weekend.

A gust of wind pushed against him as he brought the sandwich to his mouth. His teeth bit into nothing, the sandwich disappearing from his hand. He slammed his legs tight together, hoping to catch the lunch that slipped from his fingers. Looking down, there was nothing on his lap, the bench, or the ground.

A heavily accented voice sounded from beside him, from a spot that was previously vacant. "Agent Knight, so nice to see you again."

Adam shook, his arms trembled as his lungs sucked in air. A Russian man sat next to him, wearing a short-sleeve shirt, blue jeans, and brand new running shoes. Dark hair, cut shoulder length with bangs, partially hid a scar around his left eye. He held up Adam's sandwich.

Adam's entire body tensed. "Nikolai Demidov."

The Russian held up Adam's sandwich and winked, taking a large bite out of it. Adam had last encountered Nikolai in St. Petersburg during the Mutant Uprising last October. A band of Russian mutants attacked the leaders of the G9 nations, including President Mendoza, during a discussion of the United Nations Genetic Registration Accord. Mutant revolutions against governments took place around the globe, but only two coup d'états were successful.

"I am surprised to see you in America," Adam said. "As I recall, I left you sprawled on the streets of St. Petersburg, bleeding from the bone shard I stabbed you with."

"Yes, with my super-speed comes fast healing. You added rather ugly scar to my collection. Would you like to see?" Nikolai tugged at the hem of his shirt.

Adam's eyes went wide as he held a hand out to stop him. "No, thank you."

"I had expected something spicier," Nikolai said, handing the sandwich back to Adam. "You are Mexican, no?" Nikolai wiped the mayonnaise from the corner of his mouth.

"The President is Hispanic. I'm Hawaiian."

Adam reached for the sandwich, but a wave of vertigo overwhelmed him. He grasped the slats of the seat and pressed his back against the bench to keep himself from tumbling to the ground.

"It is disorientation that comes with the halo when it finds your power center and attacks it," Nikolai said, taking another bite of the sandwich. "It took longer than I expected."

The vertigo eased off a bit, and Adam put a hand to his head. His fingers met with a cold, thin metal band. It was so light he hadn't noticed it.

Nikolai casually slapped Adam's hand away from the band. "No, don't remove until it is off. If you do, you'll have migraine the size of Siberia and stomach cramps worse than from eating your Taco Bell."

"A halo? Where did you get one of these?"

Nikolai shrugged. "From a Russian soldier. He tried putting it on me. I kill him instead."

"What do you want?" The vertigo was wearing off, but his stomach still lurched when he tried to sit straighter. Blocking a mutant's ability was something he did to others, but never had done to himself.

"Fatima sent me. She has information she would like to share with you."

"Tell her to send me a postcard," Adam spat his words.

His memories of Fatima Gorshkov weren't exactly pleasant. She was a co-conspirator in St. Petersburg with the power of telepathy. She could listen to a person's thoughts or implant thoughts of her own, creating illusions.

"Is not that easy, getting information out of a Russian prison. Especially one designed for mutants. Visit her." Nikolai held out the sandwich again, raising an eyebrow as if impatiently waiting for Adam to take it.

Adam tossed it into the bag and grabbed the bottle of water he had tucked between his legs. "And why would I go to Russia and listen to her?"

"Because the information is about your father and his murder."

Adam's grip on the flimsy plastic bottle tightened, splashing water onto his pant legs. "They determined the explosion that killed my father and President Taylor was an accident."

"That is what your government wants everyone to believe. A safe choice. Otherwise, you would have mutants blaming humans, humans blaming mutants. It would be World War III."

"I thought it was something you wanted when you and the Russian President attacked the other seven world leaders in St. Petersburg."

"No, that was President Andreyev, and Fatima's husband, Iskander." Nikolai spat on the ground. "The fool. Me and Fatima, not so much. We wanted a fair deal for mutants. Instead, we got those things stuck on our heads as we shivered in hole five hundred feet underground."

"So hard to tell the good guys from the bad guys these days." Adam scoffed.

"That is good point. I'll tell Fatima you will come to visit. Goodbye, Agent Knight." Nikolai stood and pointed at the circlet. "The switch is on the left."

Another gust of wind blew at Adam as Nikolai ran down the gravel path in a blur.

"I can hear Lani now. 'I told you so.'"


It was barely there, but Antonio was sure he could see it, the heat rising up off of the White House lawn. Standing in the center of the Oval Office, he gazed out the iconic windows overlooking the Rose Garden. He twitched and muscles tightened. A nerve in his back screamed as a pair of hands ran across his button-down shirt.

"Good god, Antonio," Lauren said, her supple fingers stroking his spine. "How long has it been since you've had an adjustment?"

Antonio rolled his head in circles as her thumbs pressed against his shoulders and up his neck. The grinding gravel noise he heard dissipated as she touched his skin, healing energy flowing into him.

"I'd have to say it was you left the Surgeon General position to join the Eric Pope Research Institute." He tapped with his fingers, counting the months. "That was what, April of last year?"

He regretted her decision to leave the post that his predecessor, President Holly Taylor, appointed her to. It was a good move for her—to further the cause of mutant-kind—but it meant not seeing her at the occasional Cabinet meetings or other reasons he could gather to see her. To meet in private with her.

Lauren's hands moved down his spine, her thumbs pressing as each vertebra. He could feel a tingling as energy flowed into him as each point, moving the tissue and bone, aligning itself. A moment of pain shot through him, replaced by a relaxing minute of relief.

She reached his waistline, moving her hands out toward his kidneys. "I see you've been drinking more water, no more kidney stones."

"Following doctor's orders." He glanced over her shoulder and saw a hint of a blue aura around her, visually confirming the emotion he had sensed coming from her. One that matched his own—desire. He caught a flicker of green on the edge of her aura, curiosity, as her hands curved around his abdomen, reaching his navel. Her fingers found the top of his slacks, prompting him to bring his hands up to hers. A tingling probed from his skin inward, tickling him.

"And no more signs of the hernia I had to repair back then."

Her breath was warm on his neck as she leaned in closer to him. Her aura was becoming a deep purple. He took in a deep breath as her hands moved over his belt.

A chime came from a speaker on his desk.

"Sir, Agent Knight is here to see you." The sweet southern voice of Ms. Ferrell, the White House secretary, flowed from the speaker.

A long sigh stretched out of him. His fingers grabbed at Lauren's, pulling them away.

"Lauren." He whispered her name.

She sighed as she released her hold on him. He spun around on the carpet, his hands grasping at her as she stepped back. The brilliant blue aura around her faded into a frosty white. She sighed again as she reached for his suit jacket, laying on the sofa beside them. All he could do was shrug his shoulders. "Send him in."

The door leading out to his secretary's desk opened and Adam stepped into the room. He stood as he closed the door behind him, keeping a respectful distance. Antonio blinked, catching a greenish aura around the Secret Service agent.

"Adam! What's up? Am I late for something?" Antonio slid his arms into his jacket as Lauren pulled it up over his shoulders. Antonio pulled at the lapels as she brushed the wrinkles out of it.

"Dr. Thornburg. My apologies for interrupting." Adam turned his gaze to the windows. "No, sir. I wanted to report an interesting meeting I had."

Lauren lowered her hands, tugging at the bottom hem of his jacket. She patted him on the butt. He spun around, swatting at her hand.

"Lauren, thank you again. Maybe we can have dinner next week."

"Tonight is Taco Tuesday," Adam said, grinning.

"You, hush." Antonio pointed a finger at him as he walked Dr. Thornburg to the door. When they were alone, the president approached Adam with an energetic bounce in his step.

"All right, Agent Knight. What have you got for me? Tell me about this meeting."

Adam reached into his suit jacket and pulled out the metal circlet. Antonio took a step back, his face paling and his body tensing. He swallowed hard, stared at the suppressor, then moved to look closer at the ring. "That's not one of ours, is it?" he asked.

"No, sir. Russian."

He took the suppressor from Adam, turning it about. "Who did you get it from?"

"Nikolai Demidov."

Antonio looked up at Adam and met his eyes. "What? How the hell did he…"

Adam shrugged. "How did he escape from the Russian prison for mutants? He didn't say. Not sure if they ever captured him after the Uprising. CIA and NSA never could confirm who was in their prisons. All we know are the names the Russians provided to us."

Antonio moved to his massive desk and leaned against the front edge, still going over the design of the suppressor. "Not as crude as I would have expected. Same three lights as ours, switch is harder to get to. Does it work?"

"All too well." Adam nodded. "It was weird, as if losing feeling in your arm or leg."

"You've never had your abilities blocked?"

"No, I've always been the blocker."

"Did Demidov say what he wanted, other than to share this piece of tech?"

"Only to tell me that Fatima Gorshkov had information to

share. About my father's murder."

Antonio's gaze turned icy. He reached behind him and laid the suppressor on his desk. "That explosion was an accident."

Adam crossed his arms, widening his stance. "Yes, that is what they told us at the hearings."

"No, no," Antonio waved his finger at Adam. He rounded his desk to stand on the other side, facing Adam with jaw set. "Don't be throwing that conspiracy crap around. You were there for all the hearings. You heard the testimonies. I told you to attend. For nine months, I barely left this building so you could be there."

Adam stepped forward, eye to eye with the president, the desk between them. "And I appreciate the support you gave to Lani and me. All the same, sir, I'd like permission to travel to Russia and talk with Fatima. If she has something, I need to know."

"Well, whatever she has, there's no bargaining for it. Hell, I don't know if the Russians will even let you visit with her, wherever their prison is."

"A few hours east of Moscow, according to Deputy Secretary Nesbitt over at Department of Mutant Affairs," Adam said.

"Sounds like you've done some research." Antonio sat down and leaned forward, his hands clasped, resting on the desk blotter.

"I made some phone calls. It's a long walk back from the Mall." Adam crossed his arms.

Antonio's face softened. "Your sister never trusted Chief Justice Addison and the Commission. I suppose she will want to go with you, too."

Adam nodded. "I haven't told her yet, but yes, she will want to."

Antonio tried to discern Adam's aura, his emotional state, but there was no glow around him. He took a deep breath and broke eye contact. "You're blocking me, aren't you?"

"I didn't want you to change my mind on this." Adam crossed

his arms, a smirk easing into place.

Antonio leaned back in his chair and unbuttoned his suit jacket. "All right, let me get a hold of Secretary Wright and see if the State Department can arrange for a visa for the two of you."

Adam grinned. "Thank you, sir." Adam grabbed the suppressor and headed for the exit. "I'll send this out to Langley."

"Just do nothing stupid and let her escape," Antonio said, tapping on the intercom.

"Not planning on it, sir."

Seeing the green aura around Adam flash brightly, Antonio knew better.

The Hampton Roads Foodservice van turned a corner in the center of Norfolk Naval Base and pulled into a parking lot across from the ten-story Atlantic Fleet Headquarters. Lani stepped out of the driver's side, carrying two orange cones. After placing them on the back corners of the NSA surveillance van, she opened the back doors and climbed in.

The small ventilation fan blowing in the back from the van wasn't enough to fight the summer sun. The heat from the video monitors and other equipment made it worse. She popped three pills for the headache, washing them down with her bottle of orange-flavored power drink. For a mutant who could detect electronic and cellular signals, the buzz from the equipment was slowly grinding away at her.

Sitting beside Army Captain Troy Thornburg, they watched the four screens, each split into quadrants. Video from security feeds from inside the ten-story Atlantic Fleet Headquarters fed into all but two sections. The last two displayed video from the hidden camera on Navy Lieutenant Samira Haylom and from the one placed on top of the van.

Walking down the sidewalk, Samira turned and headed toward the headquarters entrance. Troy zoomed the camera on her backside.

"How's the view from the van, Army?" Samira asked, her voice carried by the microphone on her camera.

"Watching your every move, Navy," Troy said, his tone playful.

"He's watching my ass, isn't he?" Samira asked.

"Yep," Lani said.

Samira held a hand behind her at her waist, her middle finger sticking out. Troy chuckled and glanced at Lani. "Anything on audio?"

"You mean cellular?" Lani shook her head. "No, not that I can tell."

Troy raised an eyebrow. "What do you mean, not that you can tell?"

Lani scoffed. "There are literally hundreds of cell phone conversations going on in that building alone. It's rather difficult to isolate just one phone."

"Samira, you still have eyes on Shaffer?" Troy adjusted the control, widening the view on her.

She slowly nodded. "Five ahead of me."

Samira flashed her National Security Agency badge. The two marines at the main entrance saluted her as she walked past them, disappearing from the van camera's purview.

Lani turned her focus to the hidden camera on Samira's lapel. The lieutenant walked up to a set of elevators. Samira settled behind three people, their conversation coming through the mic. Two of them were in Navy dress uniforms. The third was in civilian clothing.

Samira's mic picked up the two officers discussing the commanding officer of the USS South Carolina, whether he was ready for the command. The senior officer expressed confidence in the man. The elevator doors opened, and the four stepped inside. Samira stood closest to the doors.

"What floors they punch?" Troy asked, adjusting the zoom on the US flag pin—Samira's lapel camera—reflected on the elevator door. Samira turned ever so slightly. Seven and ten stood out.

The ding of the elevator sounded through Samira's audio feed, and the elevator doors opened. Two of the people in the back stepped past her. When the doors closed, the golden reflection of Samira stood next to the senior officer.

Troy tapped at the screen, zooming in on the man's left breast pocket, which read: VADM. V. R. Shaffer, COMSUBLANT.

"Vice Admiral, commander of the Atlantic submarine fleet," Troy announced. "That's our man."

The officer reached into his pant pocket and pulled out a phone. "Hello?"

"Bingo!" Lani focused on the admiral's voice and then triggered her abilities, sifting through the cellphone conversations until she found the right one.

"Well," Troy said. "That was lucky."

Lani transcribed the conversation on the computer in front of her. "The caller is asking if he's there yet."

"No, not yet," the Admiral said. He looked at the floor indicator over the doors.

The elevator dinged again, and the cab doors opened. The admiral held his hand out, offering for Samira to go first. She stepped into the foyer, then paused. The camera jiggled slightly as someone bumped her from behind.

"Can I help you?" the Admiral asked.

Samira's voice followed, the tone light and cheery. "Oh, I think I missed my floor."

The monitor showed Admiral Shaffer walking away from Samira, phone to his ear.

"The caller is asking what the holdup is." Lani reported.

The Admiral walked down a hallway, passing several doors for stopping. He tapped a number on a keypad above the doorknob, then opened it. The view turned back to the elevator lobby.

"Thornburg, you get the passcode?" Samira asked.

"He's too far away."

"One seven, nine three, oh four, eight six." Lani spouted off.

Troy did a slow head turn to Lani. "And how did..."

Lani shrugged. "The signal came through his phone."

"Hey, you have a video feed for this floor, right?" Samira paused at the elevator lobby.

"Should have. Let me cycle through the feeds." Troy tapped on the video controls. Views of rooms and hallways flashed on the monitors until one of Samira came on. "Gotcha. Tenth floor elevator lobby."

Samira's camera caught the view of men and women entering or exiting the twin elevator cabs. The scene whizzed past as she swung around, apparently pacing.

Troy swung his head around. "Hey, slow down on those turns. You're giving me vertigo."

"Sorry." Samira whispered as she meandered down a corridor.

Troy looked over his shoulder at Lani and pointed to the computer controls in front of her. "Air Force, can you put the call on the speaker?"

"Yeah, but you won't be able to understand it. It's scrambled." Lani moved the mouse around on her computer and changed the frequency on the signal receiver. A squelch came out of the speakers along with garbled words. It sounded like the disguised voices on fake courtroom shows.

"Wait, you understand that?"

"Better than I understand you sometimes."

Lani wrinkled her brow as the sound changed slightly, sounding like the phone was on speaker. "Admiral Shaffer asked what the other guy wanted. The caller said he needed to pull up the deployment dates for submarine squadron six for the rest of the year."

"Can you tell who he's talking to?" Troy asked.

Lani shushed him, staring at the screen. "I don't know. He has a Middle Eastern accent."

She continued typing what she heard. "Shaffer says it is not exactly something he can send in an email. Plus, it changes frequently. Caller said it won't be necessary."

Lani heard a click then a soft thud as the door to the Admiral's office opened and closed. She turned to look at Troy. "Did someone just walk into his office?"

"Ah, hell. I was watching you." Troy switched the security camera feeds, trying to find the Tenth floor.

"Shit, Thornburg!" Samira shouted.

Lani heard someone struggling, choking, then a heavy thump. "That can't be good."

Troy turned his head slightly toward Lani. "What happened?"

"Sounded like a body hitting the ground," Lani said. "Haylom, get down there. I think someone just iced Admiral Shaffer."

"Damn it." Samira's video feed bounced as she ran into a crowd of people. "I was afraid of that."

Lani heard the clicking of a keyboard and the unfamiliar voice again. "The new guy's talking to the caller. Also, middle eastern. He's saying he's got ship names, crew rosters, ranks, and personal data." Lani looked at Troy. "He said something about having enough to begin recruitment."

Troy's eyes went wide.

"Out of the way." Samira's voice boomed over the speaker.

"Now the caller is saying to copy the info to a flash drive. He called the new guy Nazim." Lani wrinkled her nose. "And he wants Nazim to leave their calling card."

"Okay, I don't like that." Troy reached for his cell phone.

"All right. Nazim said 'Allah Akbar' and ended the call," Lani sat upright and spun her chair toward Troy. "We've got to get this guy."

The view from Samira's camera bounced around too much for Lani to get an unobstructed view of where she was in the building. She skimmed the security feeds for the Tenth floor, looking for the assailant or for Samira.

"There!" Troy pointed to a video square where Samira sped down the corridor. An unidentified naval officer slipped out of the office and started toward Samira.

"Stop! You're under arrest!" Samira shouted at the officer. Her arms and handgun blocked the view of the man she was facing off against.

Lani heard screams from Samira's audio. The hallway ceiling came on the video screen, then a glass wall, then floor. Over the speaker came the sound of shattering glass as Samira stopped tumbling. There was a forced exhalation as she fell to the floor. Lani's breath caught in her throat as she bolted to her feet. "Samira!"

"I'm okay... mostly," Samira groaned. "I'm going after him." The sound of Samira's voice brought both relief and urgency.

"I can't let her face him alone. He's a damned mutant." Lani shouted. She pulled the van's side door open. Light blasted into the back of the van, momentarily blinding her.

"Damn it, Air Force," Troy said, reaching for her. "Get back in here and close the door."

"I don't think so." Lani leapt into the air, flying toward the building's entrance in a shallow arc.

"Knight! What are you doing?" Troy's voice was loud and clear through her mutant ability.

Lani ignored Troy's frustration. "Eyes and ears, Army."

"Fine." Lani heard Troy's angry exhale. "Central stairs. No

cameras in the stairs, so I don't know up or down."

The marines standing guard withdrew their sidearms as Lani landed at the entrance doors, bursting in. She flashed her badge, knowing she would not give them time to look at it.

"Two X-ray Zulu! Lock down the building." She ran to the stairway next to the elevators. "And call for some ambulances! Lots of them." Lani slammed the door open, the noise reverberating through the stairway.

"Great," Troy said. "Now he knows you're coming."

"Just let me know what floor he gets off on." Lani leapt from landing to landing, not wanting to fly past a floor Nazim might have taken. She had on her game face, focused in the moment. A purple aura formed around her as she drew in cosmic energy, joining with the adrenaline flowing.

"Haylom, stay down." Troy's voice shouted in Lani's head. "Knight's on her way."

"Sorry, I'm not sanctioned for that," Samira replied.

A stairwell door slammed open above Lani. A flash of sunlight broke into the dim lighting of the stairwell and then vanished.

"NSA! Drop to the flo—" A garbled gasp sounded over the comm system.

"He's taking her toward the roof." Lani cleared the landing between the Twelfth floor and the roof. She pushed the door, but it didn't budge. Lani took a step back and aimed her fists toward it. A bright beam of light blasted forward, sending the door tumbling off the frame.

Lani stepped into the daylight, a thin gravel layer on the rooftop crunching beneath her shoes. She spun, looking for Samira and the mutant. She cautiously leapt into the air, hovering over the ventilation units on the roof. She caught sight of two figures and drifted toward them.

A man with olive skin and a full beard adjusted the jacket of his gray pinstripe suit as he walked toward the edge of the building. Samira floated three feet in the air, her body seemingly on an invisible tether, a leash that Nazim controlled. She clutched her throat, gasping for air.

"There's nowhere to go, Nazim."

Lani positioned herself closer to the roof, her feet hovering just above the rooftop. She drifted toward Nazim and Samira. Drawing in more cosmic energy, a purple aura surrounded her, Lani's fists glowed the brightest. She steeled herself for the combat she knew was about to happen.

Her eyes stayed on him, but kept Samira in her peripheral vision. Her fellow agent continued to kick her feet, struggling at the force holding her aloft by her neck. Lani's face grew more tense as she continued toward them. Samira won't hold out much longer.

Nazim met Lani's eyes, and without breaking eye contact, he waved an open palm toward Samira, causing her to float over the edge of the building. "You're too late," he said as he spread his other hand open and pushed downward. He rose off of the gravel, matching Lani. Then he smiled. "You won't be able to catch both of us."

He shoved down toward the rooftop with both hands. Waves of energy pushed into the pea gravel, spreading it with hurricane force. Then the building gave way.

The entire building rocked under them. The rooftop heaved upward, a cloud of black and gray rocketing into the sky in front of Lani. She released the energy she had stored in her, creating a protective bubble. Chunks of concrete and steel surrounded her, clouding her vision. She flew toward where Nazim had stood. Missing. And so was Samira.

"Hell…" Lani dove for the edge, searching for Samira. Her colleague tumbled through the air among the debris. She winced as Samira's body slammed into a chunk of the wall that broke away at exactly the wrong moment.

Lani willed herself to go faster, and her fingers brushed Samira's jacket. She grasped the clothing and pulled her to her chest. Lani embraced Samira tightly and swooped away from the collapsing building.

The moment she turned toward the street, she saw the surveillance van. A chunk of concrete half its size lodged in it, right where Troy should have been sitting.

"Troy!" Lani shouted, her voice lost in the chaos and destruction. Her throat felt raw and constricted, and her entire body was trembling with a mixture of rage, adrenaline, and fear for her friends. She landed in the grass just beyond the van, intending to lay Samira somewhere safe and then go back to pry Troy out of the van.

"Hey, Air Force!"

Lani, with Samira still in her arms, turned to see Troy running up to her.

"I thought…" Lani cleared her throat. "Are you okay?"

Troy waved it off. "Yeah, sure. The feeds all went dark when the building exploded. I stepped outside just in time."

Lani nodded, allowing a moment of relief to interrupt the tension. She gently laid Samira in the grass. "Watch her," Lani said. "I've got a damned mutant to find."

"Wait," Troy said.

"What?" Lani raised her eyebrows. "I have to go."

"Screw him. Go rescue someone."

Troy pointed to the building where the top corner was missing. Steel girders stood like bent plastic straws from what was the Ninth and Tenth floors. Paper flittered through the dust cloud surrounding the structure. Flames flickered in a few places, electricity sparking in others.

Lani stumbled back a step as she took in the destruction fully for the first time. Her mouth gaped open. "Holy…"

She leapt into the air, heading for the damaged building.

The two electronic deadbolts unlocked as Lani plodded up the stairs of her apartment. The second lock was a safety precaution Adam insisted on. Dropping her purse and keys on the kitchen table, Lani activated the locks. She let the metal chain hang loose, as always. If two deadbolts didn't stop an invader, neither would a little metal chain. This she knew from experience.

She rolled her shoulders and tried to release some tension in her muscles. Her transfer from the US Air Force Office of Special Investigations into the National Security Agency was a huge step forward in her career, but the job was more intense and emotionally draining. Lani did her best to unwind and leave work at work. Mom seemed very proud of her, not having to chase down those Air Force criminals any more. Lani didn't even try to explain what the NSA does, rather just leaving it at 'surveillance'.

Lani sighed as she sat her purse on the shelves to the right of the door, clipping her name tag on the strap. She knew it was going to be difficult to clear her mind. Images of the injured and dead flashed in her mind's eye with every blink. She'd done everything she could, acting as a rescue chopper, flying EMTs and equipment into hard-to-reach corners of the damaged building and carrying the wounded to the ambulances at street level.

Lani hadn't realized they took Samira to the hospital until hours after the ambulance had left. Troy had been keeping tabs on her situation at the hospital, and by the time Lani had finished at ground zero, Samira had already gone through surgery, meaning no visitors allowed for the rest of the day. Troy insisted they return to Fort Meade and sleep before the debriefing with their supervisor in the morning. It didn't seem right, leaving the hospital, but she had followed Troy's lead. He was the senior agent on the team and a good friend, letting her sleep during the four-hour drive north.

As she walked to the bedroom, she pulled the hair clips out of her long brown hair and ran her fingers through it, fluffing it up.

Lani untied and kicked her boots toward the closet before stripping out of her fatigues. Her favorite Air Force Academy t-shirt and sweatpants fit like a glove, comfortable. She rushed through her social media feeds as she meandered toward the kitchen, skipping the dog and cat photos along with the political jokes about President Mendoza and Congress. She had already read through those as a part of her job at the NSA.

Her phone buzzed as she reached the kitchen, the screen displaying her brother's goofy face. She slid the phone into her pocket and connected to the call with her ability.

"Hey, bro."

"It's been forever since we talked."

"We talked two days ago." Lani shook her head, smiling.

"Two days too long," Adam said.

"True," Lani said.

"You home tonight?" Adam asked. She could hear voices talking on the car radio. Most likely NPR news, one of his favorite stations.

"Yeah, why?" Lani opened the refrigerator door and frowned.

The fridge was mostly empty, and her stomach growled at the discovery.

"We need to talk. I got a visit from an old friend today."

As Lani reached in to grab a bottle of pineapple juice, her breast bumped against the butter tray lid on the fridge door. "Ouch! Damn it." She held the juice bottle against her breast. The coolness felt good.

"What's wrong?"

"Bumped my boob." Lani opened the bottle and took a swig from it.

"Jeez, Lani."

"Well, it was as if the door jumped out to hit them. It's not like they are huge, but they feel that way today."

"Wait, wait. Do I really need to know this?"

"Oh, don't be an ass. You used to listen to me and Mom all the time." She opened the refrigerator door wider and put the bottle back on the shelf.

"Ah, no, I didn't."

Her stomach growled at the juice, reminding her she hadn't eaten since before the surveillance on the Atlantic Fleet Headquarters. "Hey, if you're coming over, bring food. I'm starving."

"Don't you ever buy your own food?"

"Why would I do that?" Lani asked sweetly. "I have you."

"What do you want this time?"

"Stop by that Korean place on Williams, right off the interstate." She closed the refrigerator door and headed for the living room.

"Let me guess. Bulgogi and rice."

"Thanks. Love you, bro."

"Love you, too, sis."

Lani felt the connection break as she plopped down on the

couch. She yawned, stretched her arms above her head, and then pulled the blanket off the back of the couch, spreading it over her legs.

The quiet in the room was deafening. The signals from cell phones and Wi-Fi routers in her building buzzed incessantly. Lani eyed the television. At this hour, all the news would be about the explosion, and she didn't want to relive that.

Before they could overwhelm her again, she blocked out any thoughts of the events of the day. She grabbed her phone, her boyfriend's face smiled just under the time display. A mutant, Marc could move through objects or become invisible. That didn't affect his ability to warm her in his arms or the sweet, slightly musky scent of his skin. Just thinking about him made Lani more content.

This time of day, he'd be in day-end meeting with his crew, or in the locker room. Her stomach fluttered as she thought about him climbing out of his jumpsuit uniform. This weekend was too far away. That's really the only time she saw him anymore—on the weekends. She would like to visit him more often at Andrews Air Force Base, but he preferred to get away. She was happy to oblige. Her place was more comfortable, anyway.

Sighing, she set the phone down on the coffee table, used her ability to scan the radio waves for her favorite radio station, and snuggled into the couch cushions.


*The blue sky stretched endlessly above her. The controls for the F-15G Storm Eagle were right where they belonged—in her hands. One hand on the control stick, the other on the throttle, she tilted the stick to the left, putting the jet into a roller coaster spiral. Her smile grew wide, and her heart beat at a steady pace. Relaxed, she was at home.*

*Her muscles tensed as a male voice came over the comm system.*

*"Having fun, Indigo?"*

He had used her call sign. She recognized the voice belonging to her boyfriend, Major Marc Black—call sign Ghost. She steadied out to level flight and looked to her right. A sleek, black F-128 Dark Phantom eased up alongside the pilot wearing a black helmet with a cartoon ghost on the side.

"Enjoying the clear sky, Ghost. How about you?"

"Oh, you know the drill, caught between the Scylla and Charybdis."

"Copy that." It was his favorite phrase about being stuck between two poor decisions.

"So, ready for another air combat lesson?"

"Ready to kick some major ass. If you know what I mean."

Marc saluted, tapping the front of his helmet with two fingers. Then he and his jet vanished.

"Oh, we're using our abilities, are we? Challenge accepted."

She yanked the control stick and went into a steep climb. Lani spun around, flying inverted. Reaching out with her mind, she searched for electronic signatures. Their two jets would be the only thing electronic within thousands of miles.

Lani found his jet flying on a diagonal line below, heading in her direction. Locked on to it, she twisted around and flew toward him. Marc caught sight of her approaching and out-maneuvered her.

The Dark Phantom wasn't hard to follow at first, but his moves were getting the best of her. He gave up on the invisibility, banking into a storm cloud. She lost sight of him again. Diving in after him and switching to instruments, she spotted him on radar. Lani tracked the blip on the screen until they cleared the cloud bank. He gave up on his evasive maneuvers, giving her a moment to get a target lock on him, then applied his air brakes and ghosted. Her Storm Eagle flew right into and through him.

For a split second, she could feel him as their two bodies occupied the same space. She gasped at the rush of being intertwined. It passed as fast as he did. He was now behind her.

"Damn him."

Lani banked to the left, up, down, right, right, up. She followed several moves she had used before, but did not find him until the blip appeared at the bottom of the screen, behind her once more.

"I thought you liked me behind you."

"As if screwing is what you had in mind right now."

"No, not really." There was a three second pause, then the target lock alarm sounded in the cockpit.

The instruments on the panels in front of her lit up as the craft detected a Sidewinder air-to-air missile coming at her. She ran through a series of evasive maneuvers, and the missile barely missed her. Lani swore she could hear metal scraping on metal as it flew by.

"What the hell was that for?" She tried to evade another target lock, but Marc easily kept up.

"Just keeping it interesting. You're getting slow, Indigo. Too damn easy. Target lock."

The panel lit up again as Marc launched another missile at her. She tried to maneuver away, but this time, the Sidewinder stayed on course. Alarms erupted all around the cockpit.

"Screw you."

She reached for the eject handle between her legs and tugged. The explosive bolts on the canopy ignited, exposing her to the air. The rocket under the seat tossed her clear of the jet. Lani released herself from the seat and flew under her own power. The pilot seat tumbled away, getting smaller as it headed for the blue ocean below.

Lani's abilities again helped her locate Marc's Dark Phantom, flying toward her pilot's seat. Sparks ignited where a stream of bullets riddled the chair. A string of curses left her lips as she shot through the air after him, fists forward, a deep purple glow surrounding her. Finding his radio transmitter signal, she connected with it.

"What the hell was that for, Ghost?"

"Indigo! You're alive! Oh well. Try again." The Dark Phantom nosed up and pointed toward Lani. "Say hello to your father for me."

*A stream of bullets launched from the cannons on the wings of the F-128. Lani projected a circular shield of energy in front of her, deflecting the projectiles.*

*"This relationship is over." Lani's arms glowed with a brilliant indigo. Two beams of energy discharged toward the jet and sliced through the metal of the wings and then the tail structure, finally centering on the cockpit itself.*

*A sphere of red-orange flame engulfed the pilot as Lani and the fighter jet collided.*

The room lit up with a purple glow as an energy aura surrounded Lani. She leapt into the air, barely missing her head from slamming into the ceiling. Her heart raced, pounding against her chest. One hand thrust outward defensively while readying a cosmic blast of energy with the other.

"Lani?" Her brother's voice came through her front door.

Shaking her head to clear away the fading imagery of her dream, she released the energy, taking a deep breath. She still clung to the blanket tight in her hand, so she let it drop on the couch as she lowered herself from the ceiling.

"Coming," she said as she smoothed back her hair. Lani floated across her apartment, her feet touching down on the floor mat as she unlocked the door and opened it.

Adam filled the doorway, holding two plastic bags with foam containers inside. "I think your dinner leaked soy sauce all over my passenger seat."

He pushed passed her toward the kitchen countertop. Lani closed the door and locked it again before joining him.

"What's so urgent, anyway?" she asked, walking around him to grab paper towels, glasses, and silverware.

"Remember me telling you about Nikolai Demidov, the speedster from St. Petersburg?"

"Is he the one that killed your partner?"

"No, the one I stabbed in the parking lot," Adam said. "The muscular man killed Janice."

"Okay, what about him?" Lani sat an empty wine glass and a fork on the counter for him. Her stomach growled as she caught the aroma of her Korean beef dish. She grabbed the container marked with a B and sat at her little two-person kitchen table. She dove into the meal, not waiting for Adam to join her.

"He came to visit me during lunch." Adam went to the sink to wash the soy sauce from his hands.

Lani swallowed her bite a little too quickly, almost choking. "No way! I thought you killed him."

"Well, that's what I get for not checking for a pulse." Adam popped open his three-portion container and poked through the noodles. "Damn, can't they get anything right at this place?"

"Hey, it's not like Mom's so just deal with it," Lani said as she shoveled more meat into her mouth.

"Well, you seem to like it."

Lani pointed her fork at her brother. "Yeah, well, you don't have office bunnies giving you that look every time you put something tasty in your mouth."

"What look?"

"The one that says I'll gain a pound for every bite. I've been starving myself all week just to avoid their drama, plus this new job stress at the NSA is making my abilities all wonky. I think it's because the sunspot activity has reached a low point. The auroras haven't been recharging me as usual."

Adam went to the refrigerator and pulled out a bottle of red wine. He uncorked it and poured himself a glass before sitting across from her.

Lani raised an eyebrow. "So, what did Nikolai say?"

"You ready for this?" Adam asked, taking a drink.

"Probably not."

"He said Fatima had information about, get this, Dad's murder."

Lani coughed, spitting rice and beef pieces into the container.

"Ha! Told you so." She dropped her fork into the rice and sat back in her chair. Her head tilted to one side as she scrutinized his words. "Dad's murder? Why would anyone want to kill Dad? Granted, he was with the President and those pro-mutant activists... the... ahh."

"Mutant Defense Foundation."

"Right. I hated how they played both sides, saying they were political but supporting violent protests by mutants around the nation." Lani closed up the container of food and pushed it away. "Hell, they supported those protests worldwide, right? They started in England."

Lani floated up off of the chair to stand, walking to the fridge for more juice. She brought the bottle of wine back with her for Adam.

"So, what are you going to do?" Lani sat facing Adam.

He just sat staring across the room at the blank television screen.

"Mendoza said I could go if Secretary Wright could get me a visa."

"Did you tell Mom?"

"Not yet. Wasn't sure if I should."

"You know the rule. Call her before you leave the country." Lani took a drink of her pineapple juice, then looked to her brother again. "Did you call her? Alex?"

"Alexandrova? No, not yet. I wanted to see if you would come with me first."

"Ah, so you could stay at her place. Got it."

Adam threw Lani a glare.

"What? She was hot, right? You liked her. She even called you after you got back from St. Petersburg." Lani grinned at him, watching her brother blush at the reference to the Russian shapeshifter who had fought by their side during the October Mutant Uprising.

"No. I mean, yes, she called. But it was only to inform us that the Russian President was in a drug-induced coma in a secured holding cell."

"He's a nasty son of a bitch." Lani shuddered at the memory of the mastermind behind the Uprising. "I wouldn't mind seeing him one more time… alone."

Adam didn't answer. He was staring down at his hands, his mind somewhere else. "You okay?" she asked.

"Huh?" Adam shook his head as if clearing his thoughts. "Yeah. Anyway, you coming?"

"Hell yes!" Lani narrowed her eyes. "Well, I mean, my boss damn well better give me permission to go. I don't have any leave saved up yet."

Adam laughed. "Give him that look, and we'll be leaving in no time."

*Wednesday, June 21*
*Present Day*

The big, black-windowed buildings cast foreboding shadows over the parking lot of the National Security Agency. Lani circled the lot in her Dad's midnight-blue pickup, finding the last spot in the lot. She glanced at her watch. She was going to be late. Again.

Lani reached over the center console and grabbed her purse. She didn't bring a lunch, opting instead to grab something off site. The cafeteria in the building was nice, but it was Wednesday. That meant something heavy with mashed potatoes. Maybe she'd fly home to Mom in Hawaii and still make it back in the allotted sixty minutes for lunch. Mom would wake up around then.

She made quick time to the building entrance, flying with her feet just inches off the pavement. It reminded her of the first Halloween in Ann Arbor after discovering her ability to fly. Dad took an old carpet, stiffened it with wires and wood, then attached it to her crossed legs so it looked like a real flying carpet. Mom made her an Arabian princess outfit to wear. She got a lot of candy that year.

Catching up with other people arriving for work, the lobby was bustling with employees. Lani passed the Starbucks kiosk, the line already five people deep with only one barista behind the counter. She squeezed in the elevator with six other people, caught a whiff of someone's latte. Chocolate and cinnamon. She wrinkled her nose at the thought, tapping the bottle of apple-grape juice in her bag.

She mentally activated the button for the fifth floor. The usual buzz of electronic *chatter* filled her mind. The woman next to her was listening to an audiobook through bluetooth ear pieces while the man in front of her had a talk radio show blaring in his.

There was a refreshing quiet over the fifth floor. Mutant Central, as they called it, was alive and working by 7:35 every morning. Some employees came in as early as four. This morning, the usual loud chatter was missing.

Lani navigated the low-wall cube farm toward her own desk. Glass-walled offices and conference rooms ran around the perimeter. She reached her cubicle and nodded at Troy, whose desk was across the aisle from hers.

"Anything from Harris yet?" Lani dropped her purse on her desk, glancing across the room at the Assistant Deputy Director's office.

"Nah, nuthin' yet. Still selecting which set of flails to use on us."

"How about the hospital?" Lani glanced at Troy as she tapped on the keyboard to wake up her computer. His eyes were focused on his monitor.

"Samira's banged up, but she's in stable condition. They feel she'll be released by the end of next week."

Lani sat down and stuffed her purse in a desk drawer. "I'm going to see her tonight. You want to come with?"

Troy nodded, but didn't look away from his monitor. "Ah, yeah. Sounds good."

Lani rolled her chair across the aisle to find Troy clicking through a series of faces.

"What are you working on?"

"Going through the database for foreign mutants, first name Nazim. I need to find out where else he's been and what he's been involved in."

His fingers tapped the right arrow on the keyboard in a rhythmic beat, each profile gone before Lani could gather all the information.

"Any luck?" she asked.

He kept his eyes on the screen. "Got two hits, but they're right name and wrong power, or right power and wrong name."

"Abilities."

Troy looked up at her. "Right."

Lani sighed. She glanced inside the plastic grocery bag on his desk. A can of tomato soup, crackers, and an apple. An obvious bachelor.

A chime sounded when a message popped up in the bottom right corner of Troy's screen. He ignored it, continuing to run through the faces. A chime came from her cubicle, too, so she pushed on the floor with her feet and rolled back into her own cubicle.

"Who's the IM from?" Troy asked.

"Harris."

"He ready for our whipping?"

"Yep."

She studied him for a minute as photos flew past on the screen, leaning in, his eyes running over the information. He was one of the most stubborn guys she'd ever met.

"Slow down. We have the rest of the week to find this guy."

"I do. You don't."

"What?" Lani leaned back in her chair and crossed her arms. "Do you know something I don't? Am I getting reassigned?"

Troy stopped pounding the keyboard, but the faces continued to slide by for several seconds. He rolled his chair back to look at her.

"Seems your *friend* in the White House has a mission for you starting tonight."

"No shit!" Lani let out a whoop. "I'm cleared to go to Russia?"

"Knight! Thornburg!"

Lani turned to see Harris, hands on his hips, standing in the doorway.

"Get in here. Both of you."

Mitchel Harris' broad shoulders and graying flattop haircut gave him a bulldog figure, a Marine bulldog.

Lani swallowed hard, stood, and walked down the aisle toward his office, watching through the glass wall as Harris returned to his desk, tapping a pencil on its surface impatiently. Troy followed close behind her and closed the door when they were both in the room.

Lani perched on the edge of the metal chair, the faux leather creaking like plastic. She glanced at Troy, who seemed relaxed.

"Norfolk. Eighty-two dead, three hundred twenty-seven injured. Twelve missing." Harris paused, letting that soak in. "So much for what went wrong. What went right?"

Lani looked at Troy. She wasn't sure anything went right.

"Well, sir, we identified…" Troy paused.

Lani glanced back to Harris just in time to see him throw a dart toward her and Troy. It landed with a loud *thunk* behind them.

Two more darts sat neatly on the desk in front of Harris. He twisted a third in one in his hand. Lani glanced over her shoulder at the dartboard. A fourth dart stuck out of the red dot at the center.

"Go on." Harris stared at Troy, twirling the dart, the vanes whirling around it.

Troy locked eyes on Harris before continuing. "We identified Tarif Khoury, American-born Iranian, mutant powers—" Troy glanced at Lani. "—abilities… include telekinesis and force energy, level four. The explosion was not from a device. He exerted his energies downward. Had he been over a vertical shaft or staircase, the damage would have been much worse."

Lani's head snapped to look at Troy. She bit the inside of her cheek and reined in her frustration.

"And what of the person he was speaking to?" Harris studied the tip of the dart.

Lani took a breath before speaking. "Sir, we haven't traced—" She flinched as Harris launched the dart past her head. The dartboard wobbled as the impact of the dart caused it to bounce off the fabric covered wall behind it.

"Yusef Assaf," Troy announced.

Lani narrowed her eyes at Troy.

He continued sharing what he'd failed to mention to her. "Also an American-born Iranian. No exhibited mutant activity, XZ status unknown. Both grew up in New York and moved to Libya at twenty-one after completing a liberal arts degree in World Politics."

"Okay. Thornburg, you have the lead on researching these two. Find out who they work for, where they—"

"I will need the Major's help in Russia."

Both men turned to look at Lani.

"Excuse me?" Harris leaned forward in his chair, the two remaining darts twirling like crazy between his fingertips.

"Troy has experience in dealing with Russian officials. His father is the American ambassador in Moscow. Myself? I've only spent a few hours in St. Petersburg. My brother's time in Russia was momentary, and he was always at the President's side. I need Troy."

Harris turned his bulging eyes on Thornburg.

Troy threw up his hands in defense. "News to me, too, sir."

"I'm not sure I agree, Knight," Harris said, his voice striking a contrary tone as he narrowed his eyes at Lani.

"This isn't just a personal matter," Lani said, her voice on point. "This trip is being sponsored by the Department of Mutant Affairs, disguised as an international inspection of the treatment of mutants held in custody."

"Last I looked, Agent," Harris blurted out the word, his face turning red, "The sign out front didn't say M.A.D., although I'm not too sure it shouldn't."

"They prefer DoMA, sir." Troy mumbled, avoiding eye contact with Harris.

Lani stared at her supervisor, unflinching. She knew she had the upper-hand. All it would take was a phone call to either Mutant Affairs, the State department, or the White House. She didn't want to play that card if she didn't have to.

Harris leaned back in his chair and launched the third dart. It made a muffled sound as it sunk deep into the fabric of the wall.

"Forty-eight hours. I want you two back in the office Friday with a finished report."

Satisfied, Lani stood up and followed Troy out of the room. As soon as they made it back to Troy's desk, Lani swung a right jab at his bicep. The punch hit hard, causing him to flinch when she pulled back for another.

"What the hell was that?" Lani whisper-shouted.

"Damn, Air Force. Where d'you learn to punch like that?" Troy rubbed his arm.

"I have an older brother, remember?"

"Seriously." He sat down, rolling away from her as far as the cube would let him.

She leaned over him, then glimpsed other agents on the floor, watching. She ignored them. "Now, what about Nazim?"

"We thought Nazim was the guy on the roof. That was Tafir."

Lani crossed her arms. "So then, who is Nazim? That's the name the caller used."

Troy grabbed the mouse, and the screen saver turned off. He tapped at the keyboard and a series of faces appeared.

"This is Tafir. Recognize him?"

It was the mutant on the rooftop who had held Samira over the edge, then caused the building to explode.

"So, who was Nazim?"

Troy whizzed the mouse across the screen and clicked on an icon for a video. A window filled the monitor, showing the front entrance of the Atlantic Fleet Headquarters. The first few seconds showed Lani flying away from the camera view and into the building. The scene crept forward sixty seconds. The video showed a Naval officer exiting the building, suitcase in hand. Troy tapped a finger on the screen at the man's face.

Lani's eyes went wide and her mouth dropped open. "Wait," she squinted at the screen. "That's the admiral. I thought he was dead."

"And he is. Just wait."

Admiral Shaffer walked toward the street. Just as he stepped up to a car parked at the curb, the image of the admiral changed to a dark-skinned man wearing a ghutrah, a headdress worn by Arabian men.

Lani sighed. "Oh, great. A shape changer."

"The fact we only had audio in Shaffer's office predicated his escape. I checked the video feeds. There wasn't any camera pointed at his door." Troy moved the cursor over the long list of videos in the folder.

"Both entered Shaffer's office, one of them iced him, and then Tafir was a distraction to allow Nazim to escape."

Lani tilted her head and furrowed her brow. "Why didn't you tell Harris about Nazim?"

"So we would have something to do when we got back from Russia."

Lani pulled her head back, gazing at the smug look on his face. "Oh, you knew you'd be going?"

"Hey, a guy can hope."

The sunlight burned through the upper portion of the window, warming the office room. The brilliant white rectangle slowly traced along the sun-washed carpet as the morning dragged on. Erin Murphy sat uncomfortably at her desk in the Supreme Court Building, wishing the air conditioning could keep up with the summer heat. She didn't mind the heat so much, the humidity of Washington actually helped a person with DNA which allowed her to control water. However, the AC wasn't helping with that either.

The chime of another instant message annoyed Erin. Work-related phone calls or messages interrupted her web search for child-friendly summer vacation spots multiple times this morning. It was as if people expected her to work when she was at work in the offices for the Supreme Court.

She clicked on the notification, and the window enlarged. It was a link to a news article, sent by an intern.

*Mendoza to travel to home in New Mexico for the weekend.*

She clicked in the reply button.

**Erin:** *How is this important?*

**Aubrey:** *You said you wanted to know what the President's schedule was.*

**Erin:** *I was hoping for the next few weeks.*

**Aubrey:** *That's all I could get. Besides, I'm out of here in an hour. See ya in September.*

**Erin:** *Great. Thanks for your help this session. Have fun in Savannah.*

She sighed. Three months off. She hadn't had a summer off since college.

College. The thought reminded her of a task to do from earlier that morning. Erin closed the message window and went in search of her personal calendar. She nervously tapped on the desk, gazing at an appointment three weeks away. The information was simple, but the context was very complex: *MDF DoMA 10AM.*

Nodding to herself, she grabbed her phone and tapped the name at the top of her favorites.

"DK. Hey, who is the datalink guy we have on file?"

A male answered, his voice casting an East Asian accent. "Why? What do you want to know?"

"I need to look something up that would be on a private network. It's for work."

"Work, as in the Chief Justice's office?"

"Daiki, just give me the damn number."

"Nicholson." He rattled off a phone number.

"Thanks. Also, get us plane tickets to Albuquerque for Friday morning. And a hotel in Los Alamos."

There was a pause on the line. "We've got tickets to Friday's ballgame. Why there?"

"Mutant Affairs just cancelled out meeting next month. We need to go to the President and give it to him."

"Nobody called me. Why do we need—"

"Just make it happen, DK. Call Thandi, she'll arrange the

funding."

Erin hung up on him and counted to ten. At fifteen, she knew Daiki wasn't calling her back.

With the calendar page still open, she typed out a list of calls to make:

- White House
- Mutant Affairs
- Adam

Adam sat in what had to be the most uncomfortable chair ever. Leaning forward with his elbows on his knees, he waited as patiently as he could. Three people had come and gone out of the Secretary of State's office. Probably not lobbyists since they were carrying briefcases with handcuffs around their wrists. Adam smirked at the old school security—easily defeated with a pocket laser to the chain or flesh.

His phone buzzed, letting him know he got a voice mail. He reached for his phone, but Secretary Wright and an assistant stepped out, closing the door behind them. The assistant breezed past Adam, but Wright stood at the desk. Seeing he wasn't approaching, Adam stood.

"It took some doing, but I got you and your team visas into Russia." Wright crossed his arms. "Had to pull a few favors. Favors that don't come cheap."

"Thank you, sir. Lani and I appreciate it."

Wright leaned backward ever so slightly, his chin raised. "You're going on a diplomatic mission to Moscow, for DoMA. Inspection of the facility. We had to agree to the Russians coming to inspect our ultra-max facility at Florence, Colorado."

"I understand. Thank you again, Secretary Wright." Adam reached out to shake hands with the man, but Wright kept his hands crossed.

"Tell Mendoza he can deal with President Yegorov next time he wants to send someone to Russia."

"Yes, sir." Adam nodded, pulled back his hand, and walked away. At the elevator lobby, he glanced at the voicemail transcription.

*Adam, this is Erin. Erin Murphy. Hey, just wanted to say hi. I, ah, was going to be out at Los Alamos at the end of the week and was curious if you were still on the President's detail. Anyway, um, sorry to bother. Bye.*

A smile came slowly to his face.

Paperwork took up the rest of Lani's morning—updating vaccinations and checking passport information. Adam was working on the diplomatic visa requests. Troy took responsibility for arranging the plane, pilots, and gear. The flight to Moscow would be longer than the time on the ground. If they were lucky.

She called Marc as soon as she got in the truck.

"Hey, babe."

She cringed at this week's nickname.

"Marc, hey," she said, hoping that not using nicknames in return would eventually get the message across. "I'm going to Norfolk to visit Samira. The hospital said she was well enough for visitors."

"Are you driving? Long way there and back."

"Me? Hell no. Flying. Figured I'd buzz down the bay, over the water. Less intrusive that way."

"You mean less visible."

"Keeping the skies clear, yes. Everyone is still on high alert after the event in Norfolk." Lani said, looking out the truck's window to the skies. "I wanted to see her before going to Russia."

"Russia?" Marc sounded surprised.

"Yes, sorry. I forgot to tell you. Adam got a visit from Nikolai yesterday who said Fatima has info on the Ann Arbor explosion."

"Are those the terrorists from St. Petersburg?"

"Yes," Lani said. "He's the speedster, and she's the mind worm."

"And this isn't a ploy to escape from detention?"

"Oh, it very well could be. But we have to find out."

"Still chasing ghosts?"

A pain shot through Lani's chest. Marc convinced her to throw away the wall poster of pictures and sticky notes with names and dates. She'd never believed it was an accident. It just didn't add up.

"You are the only ghost I chase after. Who knows, maybe we'll find a lead that pans out."

"Lani, we've been over this. Why do you still think the Commission would lie?"

Lani shrugged. "I don't know. Guess it's part of the spy business. You know the NSA's motto; always suspicious."

"You need to let it go one of these days."

"Yeah, I know." Lani sighed. She forced a smile and intentionally used a cheery tone. "But hey, I get a Russia stamp in my passport this time."

Silence was her only response from Marc. She listened in vain for background noise, anything to give her a clue as to his reaction.

"So," Lani said into the quiet, "do you want to go with me?"

"You know how I am about you carrying me, flying at high speeds."

"I have dropped no one yet. Well, not since that time in high school. But he deserved it." She laughed, but then felt awkward when Marc didn't laugh with her.

"Thanks, but I have work to do on base. I can't just up and

leave like I used to at Thayer."

Lani bit her lip. That was bullshit. He had the same job as in Alaska, pilot training.

"You sure?" she asked, giving him another chance. "Maybe I'll see you tonight. We're leaving out of Andrews."

A few seconds of silence pass before he spoke. "When are you leaving for Russia?"

"Around nine tonight. I have to sit and ride this time. Troy is going with Adam and me."

"Troy? Your partner at the NSA?"

"I need him. He's got more experience dealing with foreign diplomats than me or Adam. We'll be lost there without him."

"Can't have that. Well, I guess I'll wait for your report when you get back."

Lani tried to keep the disappointment out of her voice. "Okay. Maybe we can go to a ball game. The Nationals are in town this weekend, right?"

"Yeah, good idea. I'll get us tickets."

"Great," Lani said with feigned enthusiasm. "Well, I've got to go."

"Same here. Later."

The call disconnected, and Lani rested her forehead on the steering wheel, wishing she'd never called.

The blue water of the Chesapeake Bay rushed a few dozen feet below Lani, the air currents around her causing a wave to form behind as she headed south to Norfolk. The freedom of flight so close to the earth was as calming as flying at the edge of space. The quiet here allowed her time to think.

*The Addison Commission hearings. Chief Justice Addison, senators, representatives, others. Senior year in the Air Force Academy, couldn't attend. Adam was there, though. Nine months of talk, all just to blame a natural gas leak in furnace room two floors down. Yeah, sure. That could happen. Happens all the time.*

*If it was intentional, then it was an assassination of the President. Surely not targeting Dad. Can't imagine a student wanting to kill Dad over a poor grade. Hell, he never gave out failures, didn't believe in them.*

*And how would the Russians know about it? Especially Gorshkov. Maybe she overheard something when she was in prison. Telepaths do that all the time.*

*Marc. Something's going on, but can't quite tell. Nah, that's not true. Hell, not the first time I broke up with a guy. Travis, back at the Academy. That was the hardest. Human-mutant thing again. Marc's a mutant. Was hoping it would be different this time. Just not sure if I'm going to do it or if Marc was.*

Lani swerved in her flight path to avoid a fishing trawler. She giggled at the looks on the fisherman's faces as she passed over them, pointing up at her, reaching for something to record her. The number of flying mutants were becoming more prevalent, but still an oddity for many humans. It was rather ironic to have flying people before flying cars.

Closing in on Chesapeake Bay Bridge/Tunnel, she keyed a button on the satellite phone in her hip pocket.

"Chesapeake Central, Knight Seven Three Four Personal."

"Go ahead, Knight."

Lani smiled, recognizing the voice. "Hey Tim, I'm flying one sixty degrees at one hundred up. Coming up on Bay Bridge, heading for Norfolk General."

"Copy that, Lani. Nothing in or out right now, you're clear across town at fifteen hundred, slow vertical descent."

"Copy, fifteen hundred, slow vertical. Thanks."

When she arrived, no one was near the helipads outside Emergency. Lani breathed a sigh of relief as she descended. No long-winded explanations to authorities would be necessary. She touched down unseen near a line of trees between the helipads and the main entrance. She preferred a rapid descent, fast enough that even if someone had eyes on her, they'd lose her until she slowed to float down the last fifty feet. Troy described it as angelic, which always made Lani cringe. But being a military city, anything fast flying would set off alarms all around the area. She didn't need that.

She brushed off her special-made Air Force-blue and white camo fatigues and checked for bugs in her hair as she walked down the sidewalk toward the main entrance of the facility. Passing the lobby gift shop, Lani paused. She caught sight of a small brown teddy bear dressed in a sailor's uniform with a sign in the shape of a balloon that read, "Get Well!"

She purchased the bear and headed for the elevators, stopping to study the floor listings. Lani ran her finger down the list.

Lani watched the numbers above the doors count down from seven as a man walked up, carrying a young girl. He put the child down as they waited. The little girl stepped toward Lani, pointing up at the listing.

"Which floor are you looking for?" Lani asked.

"I have a new brother." The girl's long, black curls bounced as she turned to look at Lani.

"That would be on the third floor." Lani pointed at the number three next to the word Maternity. She looked up at the gentleman as the child moved back to him and grabbed a hand. His day-old stubble and halfway untucked button-down shirt fit with the dark circles under his eyes. All the signs of a late-night delivery.

"He came last night. Mommy had to have a see… see…"

"C-section." Her dad corrected her. He glanced at Lani. "Her little brother came a month early."

Lani leaned over to catch the child's eyes. "My brother was

about your age when I was born."

The doors opened, and Lani held out a hand, offering for the father and daughter to enter first. She selected the second floor and settled in the back corner of the cab. The child tried to push the number three but couldn't reach it. Lani was about to push the button for her when the child grew in size, doubling her height.

"Shanelle, not here." The man spoke in a soft but scolding voice. The girl pushed the button before shrinking to her original size.

"I'm sorry. We're doing the best we can to teach her…" The man put a hand on the back of his neck, his eyes drifting to the floor.

Lani smiled at the man and touched his shoulder. "I understand. My dad would get furious with me for wanting to fly instead of learning to ride a bicycle like the rest of my friends."

His shoulders dropped as he relaxed. "They told us she wouldn't be doing anything until puberty."

"Well, you know what they say. Kids grow up fast." Lani giggled. "But not like that."

"Right." The dad snickered.

The doors opened at the third floor and Lani waved politely at the family as they exited the cab. She shuddered and swallowed the lump in her throat as she stepped onto the fifth floor. Her nose wrinkled at the sterile smell of disinfectant. She felt a tightening in her stomach. There were some terrible memories of hospitals, though she couldn't recall them exactly.

"Excuse me?" Lani's voice squeaked as she approached the nurse's station.

A nurse sat behind the counter, eyes on the monitor in front of her. The reflection of a news feed scrolled on her glasses. Lani noted the name on her badge. She cleared her throat to grab the nurse's attention. "Vickie, excuse me. I'm looking for Samira Haylom. She was in the explosion on the navy base yesterday."

The nurse looked up from the screen. "Family?"

Lani shook her head. "Co-worker. I was on the rescue team. I helped fly in several of the patients from the scene." She wanted to kick herself. Didn't have to mention flying.

Vickie looked long at Lani before glancing at the name stenciled on Lani's uniform. "She was very lucky," she said with a half-smile forming. "I understand someone threw her off of the roof."

"Yeah, I heard that too," Lani said, returning a bitter smile as her skin prickled from the way the nurse looked at her.

"I heard a mutant caused the explosion."

"I can't say," Lani bit at her lower lip. "Have they released any official findings on what caused it?"

"I also heard they saw two mutants flying away from the scene." Vickie stood, crossing her arms.

Lani sighed. "I heard it was a mutant who helped rescue many of the victims."

"A lot of good men and women died." Vickie continued to glare at Lani.

Lani suppressed another sigh. "Sorry if you knew someone who died."

Vickie tilted her head, the lines around her eyes softening a bit.

Lani pointed down the hallway. "Can I see my friend?"

The nurse sat back in her chair and waved her hand toward the hall. "Room 535, Captain Knight. Keep it under fifteen minutes if you can."

"Thanks," Lani said as she turned from the nurse's station and navigated the halls to the right room.

Samira was asleep. Her dark arms contrasted with the off-white blanket, covering her up to her chest. The blood pressure cuff inflated, and the monitor beeped as it deflated. Lani glanced at Samira's vitals—heart rate, respiration rate, blood pressure, oxygen. Lani knew that a mutant's statistics ran ten to fifteen points higher. Samira's numbers seemed normal for a human. At least they weren't trending up or down since she walked in.

An oxygen tube hung from Samira's ears and tucked under her nose. They wrapped bandages around her shoulder and arm.

Lani winced at the sight of the bandages. Under each wrap was a wound that would become a scar. She reached out to brush away a few strands of hair that had fallen over Samira's eyes, but she hesitated and pulled her hand back.

She hugged herself, rocking back on her heels. "I'm sorry I didn't get up to the roof faster. I caught you in mid-flight, though. From the tenth floor, no less. That's something I wouldn't have tried from a much taller building last year."

Lani sat the bear down on the tray table at the foot of the bed, using the empty water pitcher to prop it up. "Sammy the sailor. Corny, I know. I picked it up downstairs. I didn't bring anything with me. Flew here via the Mutant Express."

She glanced around the hospital room. They turned the TV to a news channel; the volume turned down. A reporter was interviewing the Secretary of Defense. A view of the Atlantic Fleet Headquarters came on. They made the damages look worse by the shaking camera view from a news chopper. Finding the electronic controls with her ability, Lani turned the TV off before sitting in a chair close to the bedside.

"Anyway, Troy and I are going to Russia tomorrow. My brother's going with us. You should meet my brother. He's a nice guy. Too big for his shoes sometimes." Lani rolled her eyes. Then she scolded herself for sounding like her mother, trying to find him a girlfriend.

"You remember my boyfriend, Marc? I asked him if he wanted

to come with me to see you, but he was busy. I don't think he likes hospitals that much. Something about his mom being in a hospital for a long time. Cancer, I think." Lani looked away, finding the blank TV Screen to stare at. "He doesn't talk about his family much. All I know is his dad was Mendoza's chief of staff for a while."

She sat in silence, the inflating blood pressure cuff being the only sound in the room. Lani watched the numbers as they counted down, then settled on a value as the cuff deflated the rest of the way. She leaned back in her chair, listening to Samira's breathing, wondering why she was doing there.

"I don't think Marc enjoys living down here. Can't be the weather, damn warmer than Alaska. Maybe the proximity to Washington. Probably Washington—dealing with a father who works for politicians. He doesn't talk about it. About anything, really. Always asking me about my work. Which I can't talk about."

Lani saw Vickie glance in the room as she passed by the open door, pushing a cart of some sort. Probably checking up on her, making sure she wasn't sucking the life out of her patient. Mutants do that, you know.

"He probably thinks I'm jealous of him being around the Dark Phantoms and being airborne. Me, I can fly without a jet. Why would I need a plane? Not jealous of him working with the women in his unit. I mean, no reason for him to be jealous of Troy either."

The scene from yesterday came to mind, staring at the back of his head while he kept his eyes on the monitors. Noticing the three gray strands trickling down through his unkept hair. Lani blinked twice, then looked up at the monitor, the colored lines bouncing up and down with each heartbeat, each breath. The hum from the electronics filled her senses, reminding her of sitting in the van before the explosion. The image of Samira floating over the edge of the building, Nazim's ability gripping her around the neck. She looked away, finding a distant corner of the room to stare at while she bit at her bottom lip.

"Not too sure if I want to go to Russia. I mean, going to Russia would be okay. But it's the whole conspiracy theory again. I want so much to know what happened and why my dad had to die that day. Then again, like Marc said, why can't I let it go? Just another thread, more smoke and mirrors. More sleepless nights."

The nurse walked into the room with a tray of small vials of meds to inject into Samira's IV. Lani glanced at her watch, then stood. She touched Samira on the arm.

"Looks like the nurse has goodies here for you. Better get back and pack for the trip. I'll come see you when we get back Friday."

She watched Vickie as she measured out a dose of something and injected it into the line, going into Samira's arm. Lani shivered.

"Um, you'll let her know I stopped by?"

"Sure," Vickie said.

"Great. Thanks." Lani left the nurse to do her job, her steps quickening once she was in the hall.

Outside, the sky turned darker as Lani walked across the tarmac at Andrews Air Force Base. Hoping to catch sight of Marc, she glanced over her shoulder several times as she approached the private jet that would take them to Moscow. One foot on the stairs, she sighed. Looking at sunset for a man that could turn invisible was futile. She hefted her duffel bag up on her shoulders again and climbed aboard.

The interior of the jet was narrow. It reminded Lani of Mom's old van with the two captain's chairs for her and Adam in the second row seats.

Lani fidgeted in her seat. She passed the time using her ability to listen to the pilot, co-pilot, and tower converse before taxi and take-off. Tempted to interject a comment or two, she let out a sigh and stared out the window, wishing she was out there instead of in here.

"Settle down, will you?" Adam said. He pulled his laptop out of his briefcase and sat it on the table in front of him. The pilot had just signaled that they were at elevation and were clear to start up electronics.

"I can't. I'm not used to being a passenger in an airplane. I'd rather be the pilot."

"Might as well get used to it," Troy said. "We have an eight-hour flight to Mildenhall Air Force Base in England."

Lani leaned forward and looked at him. "It'd be less than half an hour if I flew us there."

Troy scooted down in his chair and closed his eyes. "Yes, well, I believe Deputy Director Hinkley said no self-propelled flights during this trip."

"She said no use of any mutant abilities except under dire need." Lani pouted. "Being bored and trapped inside this thing comes close."

Troy scoffed. "Hinkley also said we were to report to the US Embassy and check in where a Marine squad was to escort us at all times. Are you going to buck against that, too?"

Adam turned to her. "Doesn't she realize you have more power in your little finger than they have in their assault rifles?"

"Right, you know," Lani laughed. "She does, but she said something about Russia still being in turmoil over the events in St. Petersburg. they may consider us persona non grata."

"Well, there is that." Adam returned his attentions to his laptop.

Lani glanced at Troy, arms crossed, shifting constantly in his seat.

He stopped moving and opened his eyes. "What?"

"Marc does the same thing. Like a dog walking around in circles, looking for the right place to plop down on the cushion."

"And I guess you fall asleep the instant your head hits the pillow?" Troy closed his eyes. "Weren't you going to meet up with him before we left?"

"I was going to stop by the base, but I didn't have time."

"Does this jet have cell phone service?" Adam asked.

"Of course, it's an NSA plane. There's a satellite feed." Lani shrugged. "Why, should I call him."

"No, I wondered if you told Mom we were going to Russia?" Adam asked.

Lani winced. "I forgot." Then she sat up straight. "Wait, didn't you call her? We're both going out of country, Adam. The rule applies to us both, you know."

Adam shrugged. "I thought you were doing it."

"What, I gotta do everything?"

"Better do it now." Adam shook his head. "Unless you want the wrath of Mom coming down both of us."

"Okay, fine. What time is it in Honolulu?" Lani looked at her watch and subtracted six hours. "You know she will ask where we're going."

Lani reached over to the seat next to her and grabbed her purse. She rifled through the bag and found her phone. Mom was first on the list of favorites. Tapping on the screen, she connected with the phone before tossing it back into her purse.

"Hello?" Leelee answered.

"Hi, Mom. I was just calling to let you know me and Adam are going out of country."

"Are you flying? Where are you going this time?"

"Not on my own. We're in a jet."

"Oh, okay. Tell him I said hi."

Lani looked at her brother and smirked. "Sure, Mom. Just a second." Lani grabbed her phone again.

Adam's cell phone buzzed, and he pulled it out of his jacket pocket. He glared at his sister as he raised it to his ear. "Hi, Mom."

"Adam!" Leelee said. "How are you? You should call me more often."

"Sorry. I'm kind of busy lately."

"Where are you flying to this time, or can you tell me?"

"Russia," Adam said, his fingers scrolling on his mouse pad

with his free hand, his eyes back on his screen.

"Back there already? Are you with the President?"

"No, not this time."

A loud rumbling snore reverberated throughout the cabin. Lani raised her eyebrows at Troy, his head leaning against the window, mouth gaping wide open.

"How's Marc? Is he there?" Mom asked.

"No, that's someone else," Lani said. "Marc's okay. He completed his transfer to Andrews Air Force Base, so I'll be able to see him more often without having to fly across the country."

"Adam, how about you? Any dates?"

"No, Mom. Nothing. Been busy with the President's schedule." Adam turned to look at Lani again. "Hey, I got more stuff to go over before we land in Moscow. Aloha, love you. Here's Lani back."

He stuck his tongue out at his sister as he tucked his phone back in his pocket.

"You've got to find that boy a girlfriend, dear. Maybe a normal girl, with no super-powers."

"Abilities, Mom. We prefer to call them abilities."

"Moscow, huh? I hope it's not too dangerous. I know you can't tell me what it's about, but I wish you could."

"Sorry, Mom. We're just going to talk with some Russians we met last year."

"Oh, okay. Well, you two be careful. Love you. Aloha."

"Love you too, Mom. Talk to you when we get back to the States."

The sound of the ocean waves rolling up onto the beach soothed Leelee. She stood in the grassy patch of land between her house and the beach. The afternoon sun beamed down on her back, and the cool breeze blowing off the ocean cooled her face. The neighbor children played in the surf, reminding her of the time before the Air Force transferred her husband off the island and onto the mainland. Before she and the kids left Hawaii for Florida.

She lowered the phone and pressed the button to disconnect the call. Watching the waves roll up onto the sand, the faint buzzing sound of an electrical discharge emanated behind Leelee. She glanced over her shoulder, undisturbed by the sound. A large oval encircled with streaks of purple electricity stood five feet behind her. Inside the oval, her kitchen came into view with the living room just beyond. A baseball game played on the wide screen television mounted on the wall.

A young man moved into view, carrying two glasses of fruit juice. He stepped through the portal and stood beside her, offering a glass. The oval shrank in size, the purplish electrical streaks closing the portal back into a golf-ball sized circle before disappearing.

"Who called?" He stood beside her, sipping from the juice.

The sweet smell of alcohol rose from the pineapple juice as she took a drink. Over the rim of the glass, his youthful face stared out at the surf. She enjoyed having someone younger around her. Leelee felt she should probably feel ashamed that he was the same age as Lani. But his presence gave her a feeling of youthfulness as well.

"It was Lani."

HIs eyes widened. "She on her way here? Do I need to leave?" A buzzing sound came from where the portal had appeared.

"No, no. Relax." Leelee turned and placed a hand lightly on his chest. "She's traveling with Adam, to Russia. But if you don't mind, I need to make another phone call."

"Sure." He leaned forward and gave Leelee a peck on the cheek.

The buzzing sounded as a portal appeared, a bedroom inside within the oval shape this time.

She watched him as he stepped through the portal, diminishing behind him. Leelee dreamed at how carefree in his stride was. She wished they could relax her like that, but with two mutant children who liked to gallivant around the world, being carefree wasn't an option. She looked at her phone, scrolling through the names on her contact list. Finding the one she wanted, she pushed the button to make the call.

"Doris, hi. What the hell do you have up your sleeve this time?"

The phone beeped when the connection dropped. Naked under a bedsheet, Doris Kutcher sighed and twirled her long, gray hair as she frowned, her thoughts troubled. She had not expected that call from that person.

She tossed the phone on the carpeted floor and rolled over to the center of the bed. A telepath, able to send thoughts and images into the minds of others, she secured her image of woman thirty years younger in the mind of the man she laid next to. Doris snaked her arm across his hairy chest. Inhaling the scent of his sweat and cologne, she flicked his nipple to wake him.

"Ouch." Marc flinched and grabbed her hand, rolling onto his side, their noses bumping.

"What am I going to do with that woman?" Doris asked.

"What woman are you referring to this time?" Marc asked.

"That was Lani's mother. Seems she's going to Moscow. Now I have to go."

"Easy enough for you." Marc yawned. "You can just teleport there in the blink of an eye. She won't get there until tomorrow morning our time, so you'll be able to stay the night and sleep in."

Doris ran her hand along his back, stopping to squeeze his

tight butt cheek. Marc reacted, pushing his hips closer to her. She smiled their flesh touched.

Marc furrowed his forehead. "Wait, why would Leelee be going to Russia with Lani and Adam?"

"No, not the Mom. Wait. You knew Lani was going. What is she up to, Marc?"

"Lani said she was meeting with some mutants from last year's Uprising. Someone named Fatima has information on Ann Arbor."

Doris sat up in bed, pulling the sheet with her. "That BITCH!" One arm holding her up, the other holding the sheet, she twisted around to glare at Marc.

His eyes flew wide as he rolled to his back, trying to slide away from her. "Who, Fatima? I understand she's a telepath as well."

Doris' nostrils flared as her face reddened. *"No, not her. Lani."* She planted an image of an unattractive Lani into Marc's mind.

Marc pulled his head back, reacting to mental shout. "Hey, she's not a bitch."

Doris snorted a laugh. She fluffed the sheet upward, rolling on top of him. *"Forget her. Think only of me."* Her eyes bored into his, her mind piercing into his, implanting the image of a voluptuous blonde over the gray-haired elderly woman that she was. *"Lani is nothing. I am everything."*

Marc wrapped his arms around her, pulling her into a kiss. His eyes dilated, staring at an image quite different from reality.

"Come here, beautiful."

*Thursday, June 22*
*Present Day*

The business jet circled for an hour before given approval to land at Moscow's Sheremetyevo International Airport.

"I don't think they want us here," Lani said as the plane descended. "Why else keep us waiting so long just to land?"

"I don't know," Adam said. "It is a major airport."

A loud snore emanated from Troy. Lani rolled her eyes. "Oh, good grief, Army." He continued to snore.

As soon as the jet touched down, the pilot announced on the speaker. "We're being directed to a location away from the main terminal."

Lani pointed to the speaker. "Told you."

"That means nothing," Adam said, dismissing her concern with a wave of his hand. "Private jets don't park at the main terminal, anyway."

Lani looked out the window as the plane rolled to a stop. A squad of eight Russian soldiers ran in formation toward the jet, assault rifles in hand. A small airport cart closed in behind the soldiers. The passenger in front wore a black uniform, black epaulettes trimmed with gold, a single red strip and four silver stars on the shoulder. Her black hat had a red strip in front with a stylized Russian eagle in the center above the bill. Several ribbons were pinned over her left breast.

"Military escorts outside. I was right." She looked at Troy. "Major. We're here." Lani kicked at Troy's foot, but he moved it at the last second.

"Good," Troy said.

"Sorry. Thought you were still asleep."

He peeked out under closed eyes and mumbled. "How could I with you two bickering?" Troy stood and stretched in the small cabin, then made his way to the exit. Just as the door swung open, and the stairs deployed, he raised his hands and stepped backward.

Lani snapped to her feet, her body tensing as she took a step in Troy's direction.

"Stop," a voice shouted from outside the plane, their English choppy. "Do not exit plane."

"No problem." Troy moved back to his seat. Looking at Lani, "Welcome to Russia."

Lani stayed standing, stepping between Troy's chair and the entrance.

Adam looked out a window before turning to Lani and smiling. "I know who's here to meet us. I think we should go say hello."

Lani nodded. "Let's go, then." She led the way to the doorway, Adam on her heels.

Three soldiers stood ready at the bottom of the stairs, their rifles pointed at them.

Adam raised his hands and stepped to the forefront. "Whoa, whoa. Hang on now."

"Let me know if we need to escape," Lani whispered from behind him. "I can do Mach one in a second." She snapped her fingers.

"We won't need to," he whispered back. "It's Stepanida."

The airport cart pulled up behind the three soldiers, and the passenger stepped off. The vehicle pulled away, and she walked up to the squad leader. They talked, then she stepped passed them and climbed the stairs.

"Captain, excuse me, Major Alexandrova," Adam said, holding a hand out in greeting.

The Russian soldier didn't return the gesture. Instead, she pointed to the interior of the plane. "Please step inside."

Lani stepped back along with Adam to let the Major on board. Standing eye-to-eye with Adam, her broad shoulders filled her uniform. She took her peaked hat off and tucked it under her arm, shaking out her chocolate-brown hair. Back to the cockpit door, she faced the trio.

"Alex! What's up?" Lani said, leaning against the back of a seat. "What's the goon squad for?"

"We do not clear you to enter our country." Her tone was authoritarian, her expression cold.

"Our request to enter was sent two days ago," Adam said, hands on his hips. "We received confirmation before leaving Washington."

"Told you this wouldn't be easy," Troy said, still sitting in his seat.

"This is true, but there are some…" she took a breath, eyes flicking briefly toward the ceiling as if fishing for the right words. "… requirements you must know before exiting this plane."

Lani stepped forward to stand beside her brother. "Requirements? Like what?"

Stepanida held her hand out. "Before I can allow you to touch Russian soil, you must surrender passports."

Lani scuffed at that. "Easy enough." She went back to the seats and grabbed her purse.

"Also," Stepanida continued, "You must wear halo devices."

"Ah." Lani spun around, her body tensing as her hands curled into fists. "That's not going to happen."

"Lani." Adam took a step nearer to her and held out his hand, palm open. "Hang on now."

Lani crossed her arms. "But, Adam—"

"If you do not wear halos," Stepanida said, "you must wear tracking devices on ankles and be escorted at all times."

Adam glared at Stepanida, pointing a finger at her with his other hand. "Now, that I expected. I'm fine with an escort. But tracking anklets? Really?"

"It was a requirement by my superior."

Troy stood. "I'm not a mutant. I shouldn't need a tracker."

Stepanida remained silent for a moment. "No, you will not, though you must surrender your passport."

Troy sighed. "Fine, I got others back home."

Adam looked at Lani and shrugged. "We may not have much of a choice."

"You'd better hope they're satellite-based trackers," Lani said, sitting down hard in her seat, thrusting her leg into the aisle. "They'll be useless otherwise."

Stepanida waved through the doorway and shouted something in Russian before stepping further into the cabin toward Adam.

"I noticed you have a few more dangles on your uniform," Adam said, pointing at the medals hanging over her breast pocket.

"And that she has a uniform." Lani cocked an eyebrow and pursed her lips.

"Lani," Adam said, scolding her. Lani crossed her arms and slouched further into her seat, her leg jutting even further into the aisle.

"Hell, I'm surprised she's not nearly naked so she can pull her quick-change into a bear without ripping her uniform."

Stepanida ignored her. "Yes, I have received a few

commendations following October Uprising. And I am no longer commander in Federal Protective Service. They promoted me to Major with assignment in Federal Security Service."

"FSB. Bold move. And a promotion." Lani nodded at the advancement. "Capturing a rogue president worked out pretty well for you, didn't it?"

"Much like your rescue of your president." Stepanida stared at Lani.

"Something tells me this visit isn't going to be much fun." Lani turned to stare out the window.

"Okay, ladies," Adam said. "Let's get on with it. We have to check in at the American embassy."

Stepanida nodded. "I will allow this."

The doorway darkened, and two soldiers appeared. They hesitated, waiting for someone to invite them on board. Adam nodded, and Stepanida waved them in. Each of the men held hard plastic cases.

Lani balked as one of them approached her. "Damn, how big are these things?"

"Settle down, Lani," Adam said as the other soldier knelt before him, setting the box on the floor.

The soldier in front of Lani followed suit. Inside the foam-padded case was a small hinged circlet. Also in the case was a device resembling a thin rectangular whiskey bottle with a little screen and number pad. Stepanida tapped one of her men on the shoulder and spoke to him in Russian. Something about one controller and both trackers.

"Da, Major," the soldier replied.

Troy whistled. "Damn things look like home arrest trackers." Stepanida glared at him; so did Lani and Adam.

"These aren't halos, right?" Lani asked, pulling her leg back before the soldier could wrap it around her leg.

"These will not impair your mutant abilities, I assure you," Stepanida said.

"No, but he can," Adam said, pointing at someone in the doorway.

A young Russian, as tall as Stepanida but not as broad-shouldered, joined the group. He wore a military uniform, but it differed from the others. Similar in style to hers, it was a deeper purple with no epaulettes or ribbons.

"This is Lieutenant Oleg Bazhenov." Stepanida indicated the newcomer with a nod of her head. "He will be one of your escorts."

"I like the uniform," Lani said. "Nice colors. Not as military, though."

Stepanida glanced at Oleg, then back to Lani. "He is an officer of FSB, assigned to Mutant Quarantine Services."

"Quarantine," Troy said. "Pseudo-political for prison."

"And he's just like me," Adam said.

"If you are referring to his mutant abilities, yes," Stepanida said, "He can block yours. Locating more blockers was one of the first orders from our new President, Thaddeus Yegorov."

Lani stood up and shook her foot a little, swinging the tracking ring around her ankle. "Well, not bad, but it'll have to come off if we go dancing."

"I suppose you know why we're here," Adam said as a soldier placed a tracker on his leg.

Stepanida nodded. "Your message said Nikolai Demidov visited you. Hard to believe."

"He placed a Russian-made halo device on my head before he ran away."

"Ah, that must be why he could escape." Stepanida followed her soldiers toward the front of the plane "I can take you to our detention facility, but I don't know if you can meet with Mrs.

Gorshkov."

"Then this trip may be for naught," Lani said, pointing to the exit. "Why don't we talk in your car while we go to the embassy. I'm hungry, tired of being on this plane, and I have to pee."

"I'm with the lady on that one," Troy said.

"Very well," Stepanida said. "You will ride with me."


The line at the Starbucks in Terminal F wasn't that long, but Doris was getting anxious. Wearing jeans and a blue knit blouse, she stood behind a man reading a folded copy of a Russian newspaper in his hand. In front of him was an Asian woman in a khaki pantsuit. The barista behind the counter was having difficulty understanding the woman's thick Chinese accent.

Sparky, Doris' small golden-brown toy poodle, followed a few sharp barks with a long growl.

"Shut up, fleabag." Doris narrowed her eyes at the woman behind the register. "I'll see what I can do."

The barista blinked as Doris telepathically helped him understand the complex drink being requested. He rang up the order and began mixing the drink while the customer dealt with the credit card device.

The poodle whimpered in Doris' arms. She squeezed the dog. "We won't be late."

She got her grande mocha and a biscuit for the dog, then headed down the corridor to Gate 48. Doris walked up to the floor-to-ceiling windows and watched the Russian soldiers surrounding a small business jet. Several people exited the plane, including three Americans led by a female Russian officer.

Doris dropped the biscuit on the floor and sat the poodle down. The dog latched onto the snack while she pulled a cell phone from her pocket and made a call.

"Did they make it to Russia?" The person on the phone was

male, a deep radio-announcer voice.

"Yeah, they're here." Doris sipped at her drink.

The man grunted. "Did you find out why they were there?"

Her grip tightened on the paper cup. "How the hell should I know? No, I didn't go digging."

She heard the man growl. "You mean you woke me up just to say you watched a plane land?"

"I don't have time to babysit the wonder twins." Doris realized several people were staring at her. "You want play-by-play, get someone else." She snapped her fingers at Sparky, then walked out into the concourse. The poodle dodged between several legs to catch up with Doris.

"Sorry," the man on the phone sighed.

"I gotta go, the dog's gotta pee." Doris ended the call, then slid the phone back in the pocket of her jeans.

*"Come on, Michael. Time to go home."*


The large sheet of paper crinkled as Lani wadded up the hamburger wrapper. She tossed it over her shoulder, aiming for Adam's chest. Grinning, she watched in the rearview mirror as he tried to give it to the Russian soldier next to him. The soldier looked at Adam, then faced forward again. Adam shrugged, then dropped it to the floorboard.

"Feeling better?" Troy sat shoulder-to-shoulder with her in the middle and Bazhenov on the other side.

"At least my stomach isn't growling anymore."

"Good," Troy said. "Glad you didn't get too Hangry."

"I don't get Hangry," Lani said, "just irritable."

"And then some," Adam said.

"You shut up back there." Lani turned around to glare at her brother just as the vehicle came to a stop.

Lani looked out the right-side window and saw an American

soldier standing at the lowered gate arm. Another soldier stepped out of the small guard shack to join him.

Stepanida got out of the front passenger seat and opened the rear sliding door. Bazhenov stepped out and walked around to the back of the van.

"Finally," Lani said, rolling her shoulders. "Oleg was rubbing me the wrong way, literally."

She climbed out, glancing at the dimming, late afternoon sky. Troy followed her out, along with Adam and the other Russian soldier.

"We will wait here for you." Stepanida stood in a parade-rest position, her eyes focused on Adam.

Lani kicked her ankle out and pointed. "You have trackers on us. Can't you tell us where to meet you?"

"No, that will not be possible."

Lani tilted her head, staring at her. After several moments, Stepanida's brow furrowed. Lani, satisfied at the small display of discomfort, straightened her head and smiled.

"Right. Well, hang around then. We'll be right back with a few of our own grunts."

Troy led the way up to the soldiers at the Embassy gate. "NSA, here to see the Ambassador."

"Passports," the guard replied.

"She's got them." Lani pointed a thumb over her shoulder. "But I have my library card."

The guard looked over Lani's head and glared at Stepanida before looking back at Lani. Troy handed over his government ID, and the guard passed it under a scanner. He gave a satisfied nod and handed it back. Lani waited for him to do the same for her ID and Adam's.

When he finished, the guard gestured toward the smaller entrance gate.

"Welcome to the American Embassy. The ambassador is waiting for you."

Lani followed Adam and Troy into the compound. The guard saluted, standing stone-faced as they passed him. Inside the front doors of the building, they approached the security post. Dropping her purse in a white plastic bin on a conveyor belt for the x-ray device, she stepped through the metal detector portal. An audible alarm sounded, prompting an embassy guard to hold her hand out as another joined her.

"Excuse me." The guard said. "Please step back through and remove all of your metal items."

Troy pointed down at Lani's ankle. "Trackers must have set off the detectors."

"Trackers, sir?" The guard asked. "We can't allow position trackers in the building."

Lani waved her hand at the guard. "Don't worry. They aren't working, anyway."

Troy raised an eyebrow. "Excuse me?"

She tapped her temple. "Electronics expert. The trackers think we're still in the van out on the street."

Troy chuckled. "Awesome."

A second embassy guard joined the other with a metal-detector wand in hand. He waved it all around Lani and Adam, concluding they were metal-free except for the anklets.

Fifty feet across the huge Seal of the United States inlaid on the floor stood a man looking very American in his blue suit, white shirt, and red tie. His thin white hair matched his goatee. Lani raised an eyebrow after studying his face. Uncle Sam, with his top hat and finger pointed at her, came to mind.

Moving ahead of her and Adam, Troy reached out to shake hands with the man. "Good to see you, sir."

"Troy. Good to see you, too." The man moved in closer and

they hugged.

Troy turned and waved a hand at his companions. "Lani, Adam, this is Ambassador Charles Thornburg. My father."

Adam stepped forward and shook his hand. "A pleasure to meet you, sir."

Lani stood next to Troy as she shook hands with the Ambassador. "So, I finally get to meet the Dad."

Ambassador Thornburg tugged on his goatee as he threw Troy a questioning look.

Troy sighed. "Lani and I are partners at the Agency."

"Oh, yes," the ambassador said with a half-grin. "The goof ball he keeps telling us about."

"Goof ball?" Lani stepped back, glancing at Troy over her shoulder, eyebrow raised.

"I understand you're on your way to one of the mutant detention facilities," the Ambassador said.

"Yes, sir," Adam said. "We got a tip that someone in the facility may have important information about an investigation."

"And this involves the Secret Service?" The ambassador crossed his arms.

"Potential impact on the death of President Taylor," Adam said.

The ambassador shook his head slightly. "Still chasing rabbits?"

Lani forced a bright smile. "Down every rabbit hole until we find Wonderland."

The ambassador pursed his lips and then turned to Troy. "Son, the President sent a few guys from Germany this morning to go with you. I have briefed them on their mission: Escort you to the facility, through it, and back out. They're not to leave your side. I've checked their records. They are top-notch."

"Thank you, sir." Lani said.

Ambassador Thornburg led them to a side door, then down a

corridor to a parking garage.

"So, Ambassador," Lani said. "I don't recall Troy saying much about his family. How long have you been in Russia?"

Troy spoke up before his father could. "President Mendoza selected him soon after the Uprising."

"But," the ambassador said, "I'm looking to retire at the end of President Mendoza's term."

"So, home for the holidays then." Lani glanced at Troy, grinning. He touched his forehead with the palm of his hand.

"Yes, I suppose so," the Ambassador said.

Ambassador Thornburg touched Troy on the shoulder. "A word with you in private, if I may."

"Sure," he replied. He pointed to Lani. "Hang on a sec. I'll be right back."

The Ambassador led Troy away from the others. His dad pulled a key out of his pocket after reaching the second door down one of many corridors. A plate on the door had his name etched in gold lettering. He unlocked the door, and Troy followed his dad inside the office.

"Have a seat." His dad rounded the large wooden desk, sat, and waved to a chair on the other side.

Troy shook his head. "Don't have much daylight left. What's up?"

"To the point," his father said. "what the hell are you doing here? And I don't mean here in this room, if you were thinking of being sarcastic."

Troy sighed and slipped his hands in his pockets. "Thanks, Dad. Love you too."

"Seriously, son." He pointed at Troy. "You, meaning all of you, have no place going to that facility."

Troy frowned. "We're following a lead Adam and Lani

received."

"By unreliable sources. My God, son. A *clue*—" he used air-quotes, talking down to Troy as usual "—given by mutants to mutants, leading you into a prison designed for mutants. And you're just tagging along."

"This has to do with Mom?" Troy stepped in front of the desk, crossing his arms as he glared at his father. "Because Mom is a mutant?"

His dad drew back and shook his head. "Your mother is an excellent surgeon. Lauren's skills are remarkable."

"She's a healer, Dad. Her mutant ability helps her look at a person and recognize what their ailment is and how to fix it. And you rejected her as soon as you found out she was XZ. Not too sure you wouldn't reject me if I was as well."

"We never had you tested because we didn't need to." His dad sighed. "I'll say it again; you and your team have no place going to that facility." The ambassador sat, placing his hands on the desk blotter in front of him. "The Russian government is still reeling from the discovery that their President was a mutant. They do not understand who is and who isn't a mutant. The tension is high."

"What does that have to do with us following up on this lead?" Troy crossed his arms. "We've got to investigate this, Dad. We have a chance to find out if the explosion was an accident or an assassination."

"The Commission already decided that, son. Let it go. Apparently, Knight's children can't. They'll be dragging you across the globe, chasing after shadows and ghosts, making up stories just to prove someone killed their dad."

"And what if it was you?" Troy threw up his hands in exasperation. "What would you have me do? Would you want me to sit back, cross my heels and say, 'yep, an accident,' and give up chasing your murderer?"

"Son," his dad shook his head, "my soul would be at rest. I would expect yours to be the same."

"Well, maybe Professor Knight's soul isn't at rest. And he has two children to continue the search. And a good friend in me to help." Troy gave his father a half-assed salute as he turned to go. With one foot out the door, he stopped. "Don't wait up to hear from me." He glanced over his shoulder. "Not that you ever did."

He slammed the door and quickened his pace to get back to Adam and Lani.

She cocked her head, dabbing his chest when he stood before her. "You okay?" Lani asked.

"Just another pep talk from dear old Dad." Troy huffed, then stuffed his frustrations back where they belonged, buried deep inside. He smiled and pointed toward the garage. "Shall we?"

Three black Suburban SUVs acted as a backdrop to four Marines decked out in olive green camouflage fatigues, rucksacks for equipment, and weapons. Each carried a 45-caliber handgun and an M16 rifle. Lani whistled as they walked up to their escorts.

"Cool, a complete fire team." Lani walked to the middle vehicle and waved her hands over their gear. "Your electronics won't be of any use inside the facility."

The squad leader, a gunnery sergeant, lowered his eyebrows and glanced at Lani. "Ma'am?"

"The place we are going scrubs all signals except the ones they want. Nothing gets in or out unless it is Russian and scrambled."

"Hope that doesn't apply to the people," the marine replied, hand on his chest. "Gunnery Sergeant Gillis, ma'am. I got Sergeant Morrison, Corporal Hardy, and Corporal Ortiz." He looked to each as he introduced them.

Lani went through her own introductions. "Captain Lani

Knight, Air Force. Captain Troy Thornburg, Army. Don't hold it against him." Lani smiled at Troy. Troy rolled his eyes. "My big brother here is Adam Knight, White House."

"What, no Navy?" Morrison's voice was deep and gravelly for a woman but still maintained an air of femininity.

Lani smirked. "Not this trip. Where are you out of?"

"Camp Pendleton, ma'am," Gunny said. "Assigned to the cyber unit in Estonia for a year now."

Lani turned to Adam and gave him a thumbs up. "Okay, let Operation Starry Night begin."

Adam coughed into his hand, but his laugh still came through. "Starry night? Where did you come up with that one?"

"Every incursion into hostile territory needs a mission name." Lani looked at the marines. "Right?"

They all shouted in unison. "Oorah, Captain."

The driver slammed on the brakes of the SUV, tossing Lani forward in her seat.

"Damn, dude. You drive worse than my brother." She reached beside her for the seat belt latch, then stepped out of the Suburban along with Troy and two Marines. Adam and the other two Marines got out of second SUV. Their entourage of five vehicles parked in Moscow's Red Square. Waiting a few yards away sat a large olive-green transport helicopter with a red star painted on its side. The blades already spun at speed. A fence of soldiers on the opposite side of the helicopter kept the few dozen tourists and locals from getting too close.

Stepanida and Oleg climbed out of the lead SUV. Four Russian soldiers waited by the helicopter. At Stepanida's signal, Lani headed toward the helicopter. Two Marines walked ahead of Lani, Adam, and Troy while two walked behind.

"Look at that architecture," Troy said, whistling between his teeth at the buildings towering over the Red Square.

"We don't have time for sightseeing." Lani nudged him along, nearly dragging him on board the helicopter with everyone else.

With the two groups inside, the four Russian soldiers climbed in last and closed the doors as the transport lifted off and headed east out of Moscow.

Flying inside a vehicle and not in control dug at Lani. The space inside was open, but the tension inside pressed in on her as if everyone piled on top of each other.

Seats were staged with two rows facing each other, another set behind the front. Stepanida and Oleg sat facing Adam, Lani, and Troy. In the back, four Marines stared down four equally intense Russian soldiers; all eight of them wore full combat gear.

Lani kept her body ready to move. If the wrong person so much as sneezed, she was out of there with Adam and Troy in tow.

"That was a nice touch, lifting off from the middle of Red Square," Troy said over the headphones and mics worn by those free of an assault rifle.

"True, it was for show," Stepanida said. "For such high-level trip, I needed to give assurance of who was going."

"Assurance to your President?" Troy sat leaning forward, elbows on his knees. "As if parading us through town wasn't enough?"

"This is Moscow," Stepanida shrugged. "Everyone loves a parade."

"True," Troy said, "and with all of you, plenty of firepower to show off."

Lani elbowed Adam's arm. "Do you have those files? Alex probably needs to see them."

"Oh, right." Adam pulled his messenger bag out from under the seat and opened it. He rifled through and pulled out some folders. "Since this visit is on the guise of an information-sharing visit for mutant detention, here's what I have," he said as he handed them across to Stepanida. "Fill in the blanks, starting with the name."

Stepanida looked through the papers and photos. The images

were military-grade satellite imagery of an area that would have resembled an orchard if not for the steel piping sticking out of the ground at regular intervals. And the raised guard shacks and military arms and vehicles staged around the perimeter.

She furrowed her brow, then closed the folder and handed it back to Adam.

"Cherenkov Detention Facility. I know of similar locations within the United States."

"Ours are not below ground," Lani said.

Stepanida shrugged. "We felt it easier to control population if they knew escape was not as easy as going through wall."

Adam opened the folder, his eyes scanning the pages. "Regular shipments of food, fuel, and other supplies. Enough food to serve over three hundred people. Estimated one hundred and ninety detainees."

"Two hundred five," Stepanida corrected him. "More were delivered last week."

Lani craned her neck to see the page. "You seem to know about the facility."

"Mutant criminals have been a major part of my job since the October Uprising." Stepanida's icy stare sent a chill down Lani's back. "I have been to this facility and others many times."

Lani returned her blank look, remembering her from the combat that took place on Air Force One in St. Petersburg during the Uprising. Stepanida seemed friendly, more alive back then. Maybe it was because she was using her abilities to protect President Mendoza and subsequently take down President Andreyev. Now, the burden of bureaucracy seemed to weigh her down.

Adam pulled an ink pen from his jacket pocket and scratched the new number on the page. "Two hundred and five detainees," Adam said, "housed in cells stacked in vertical tubes one to two hundred feet below the surface."

Stepanida nodded. "I was told the facility was re-purposed from old missile silos. A part of the Moscow defense battery."

"Now you have satellites for defense," Troy said.

Stepanida shrugged her shoulders. "What is phrase your politicians like to use? I cannot confirm or deny."

Troy chuckled. "Ah, an oldie, but goodie."

"They keep thirty-four detainees in drug-induced comas for safety reasons," she continued. "The ones that could do the most damage or could escape through the rock."

"The rest?" Adam asked.

"With support from your President, we duplicated your father's mutation suppression device."

"Just call them halos. The technical name is a mouthful," Lani said, her eyes closed and arms crossed. The claustrophobia of sorts—being in flight and not being in control—wore on her.

"A rather ironic name for a device placed on people not exactly holy, wouldn't you say, Major?" Troy piped up. Lani held her fist out and they fist-bumped.

Adam shook his head again. "What about Nikolai Demidov? Was he a detainee here?"

"Demidov was not captured on the night of Uprising," Stepanida said. "We search where you said you encountered him, but did not find him."

"Somehow," Adam said, "Demidov can communicate with Fatima."

Stepanida leaned forward, resting her elbows on her knees. "I do not know how," she said. "She is one of thirty-four we maintain in coma."

Over an hour passed as Lani watched the Russian countryside slide under the helicopter. Green pastures covered the landscape with only small towns dotting the thin concrete lines connecting them. The roads she did see were sparsely traveled. She had seen this before, flying back and forth between Maryland and Hawaii. So peaceful, distant from the politics of Moscow, or Washington.

She spotted the apple orchard from Adam's satellite photo. Lani grabbed Troy's attention and pointed out the large circular grassy areas among the rows of apple trees. The only structures above ground included two barns inside the five-hundred-acre plot and guard shacks stationed every two hundred yards along the razor wire fence. The bare spots resembled a double-five domino.

The helicopter circled once around the orchard and hovered over it as four men exited a barn and pulled a canvas tarp off an asphalt helipad with a white, encircled H at the center. Three armed soldiers and an officer stepped out of the second barn and approached, but hung back as the dust from the landing site created a cloud. The loose dirt blew away, and the soldiers positioned themselves at a safe distance from the whirling blades.

Stepanida opened the door of the helicopter and stepped out,

Oleg following behind her. The four soldiers riding along from Red Square finished the Russian contingent.

Lani threw out a leg to stand up but felt a hand on her shoulder. She looked up over her shoulder. The working end of a rifle slid passed her.

"We've got this, ma'am." Sgt. Morrison hunched over, squeezing past her. Gunny and the other marines followed. They had rifles raised, forming a perimeter for the Americans.

Lani climbed out and waited for Troy and Adam to join her in the semi-circle of marine protection. The Russian soldiers held their rifles aimed toward them. Stepanida had pushed between them, heading straight for the facility officer. His arms were waving all about. Stepanida's shoulders hunched up.

"Ahh, guys." Lani tapped Adam on the shoulder with her fist. "Think something's going on."

"Eww, cat fight." Troy chuckled. So did Lani.

The whirl from the helicopter's blades blocked Lani from hearing the argument between Stepanida and the facility officer, but she could tell who won when he tossed his arms outward, then turned and strutted off. The soldiers lowered their weapons and followed behind him. Stepanida waved them toward the barn.

"That didn't take long." Troy said.

"She can be a bear when she needs to be." Adam commented, nodding to Gunny that it was clear to step away from the helicopter.

"Literally." Lani smirked.

The interior of the barn was quite the opposite from the rustic exterior—drywall and tiled floors all accented with wooden trim. Low cubicle walls separated a few office workers, not in uniforms. In the back of the barn, a semi-circular control console with a half-dozen solider and technicians stood under a second story. Cheering came from the second floor, men wearing t-shirts and blue jeans, watching what was probably a soccer game.

The officer led them to a large conference room in the back of the barn. A polished wooden table stretched down the center of the room, a dozen black leather chairs encircling the table.

The officer stood behind the chair at the end of the table. A photo of Russian President Yegorov hung on the wall behind him, staring over his shoulder. Stepanida stood beside the officer, Oleg and the Russian soldiers lined up beside her. Lani, Troy, Adam and four marines took up the opposite side.

"This is Director Tychonoff, supervisor for this facility and two others." Stepanida turned to gaze to Lani. "These are the representatives from the American president, here to inspect the facility for human rights."

Lani raised an eyebrow at the contempt in Stepanida's words.

"I will not let armed Americans into my facility." The pudgy man waved his hand at the marines standing behind Lani and Troy.

"We have the authorizations, Director," Stepanida said. "It comes straight from President Yegorov."

"I don't care if you have authorization from Lenin himself, Major," Tychonoff said.

Stepanida glared at Tychonoff, then pushed past him to a desk phone on a corner table. She dialed a number and held the receiver out to Tychonoff. "If you doubt me, you can talk to the Kremlin."

"Hello?" A man's voice emanated from the phone's speaker, clearly audible.

Tychonoff stepped forward and grabbed the receiver out of Stepanida's hand and hung up. "Very well, Major. But I want guards on the Americans at all times."

"You have soldiers throughout the facility." Stepanida said, "However, I will take two of mine."

Troy mumbled, counting on his fingers, then raised his hand. "Knight, party of twelve."

Adam rolled his eyes. "Why did you have to bring him, again?"

Lani grinned. "Comic relief."

Tychonoff pushed through the crowd on the Russian side of the table toward a set of double doors. The sound of a dozen footsteps echoed up and down the corridor. It ended at an elevator.

Lani shuddered as they entered a wide, dimly lit concrete corridor. She folded her arms across her chest, her hands rubbing her biceps.

"You okay?" His head tilted more to her face.

"Yeah, just not a place I want to stay in very long." She shot out a weak smile, but it quickly faded.

"I know what you mean." Adam said. He wrapped an arm around her, pulling her close.

"We will have to go in two groups," Tychonoff said, pressing the single down-arrow button. "The single elevator is not big enough for twelve."

The elevator door opened, and Tychonoff stepped in. Lani entered next and Troy tagged along. Sergeant Morrison and the two Russian soldiers filled the cab. Adam winked at Lani just before the door closed. It was his way of reassuring her, something he started back in high school.

"There's only one level underground?" Lani asked, pointing at the two buttons on the panel. The top left button had a staple-looking symbol—ground floor—with the number one on the button below it.

"Five floors, actually. Sub-level One is one hundred feet below ground with fifty feet between each of the other underground levels," Tychonoff explained. "There is no direct elevator from top to bottom. We will have to cross to another elevator to get to

Sub-level Two, then again down to Three. That is where the sleepers are at; those maintained in comas."

"So, not everyone is sleeping?" Troy asked.

"The mutants not in comas wear suppressors." He turned to face Troy. "They cannot remove them."

"Must have taken some time," Troy bounced on his toes. "Building such a massive underground facility for so many prisoners."

Tychonoff had a look to kill as he glared at Troy. "The facility was originally eight converted ICBM missile tubes, with two central chambers built for medical, security, and dining for those detainees who are free to move about on Levels One and Two."

The cab stopped at Sub-level One, and the door opened into a tube-shaped corridor cut through stone with a narrow deck plate to walk on. The corridor ended with a spaceship-style airlock system. Lani studied the mechanisms as a ten-foot wide wheel rolled away, pulled and pushed from the wheel's axle.

"The double-door lock system is designed such that only one door is opened at a time, slowing any mutant with super-speed in the middle of a lock as the doors cycle closed. The ventilation ductwork has no direct path from top to bottom to slow down any mutants that can become gaseous. We bring fresh oxygen down in compressed cylinders." He pushed a button to close the outer door, then moved across to another control panel to open to the inner door.

"Bottled air, fresh. What's on Sub-level Four?" Troy asked.

Tychonoff scrunched his forehead. "What is word where dead are kept. Morgue?" He shook his head. "Da. Power systems and other equipment are on Five."

"Morgue?" Lani asked. "You don't bury the dead?"

"No, we use them for research." Tychonoff spoke with a coldness. Coldness that dug at Lani.

They walked past several niches with guards standing, waiting. Lani paid attention to how the Russians reacted to seeing Marines in the facility. Some stared straight ahead, like stone statues. Others shifted their weight from one foot to another. A few curled their lip or muttered a curse. Out of the corner of her eye, she saw Morrison monitoring the guards as well.

"A rifle, taser, and a baton." Lani pointed out the guards' weaponry.

"You missed the laser tag rifles," Troy said.

"It delivers a high-energy blast," Tychonoff said. "It is not toy."

"Why the variety of weaponry?" Morrison asked.

"Each detainee comes with a unique method of being subdued."

Troy pointed at the silver metal nozzles placed around the airlocks. "Not your normal sprinkler heads for putting out fires."

Tychonoff nodded. "Very observant. Throughout the facility, we have Novichok nerve gas canisters staged in the walls."

"Novichok. Freaking deadly stuff, dude," Morrison said. "Inhalation or absorption, it slows the heart and restricts the airways, leading to death by asphyxiation. Acts within thirty seconds, two minutes tops."

"I don't see any detainees around." Lani said. "Surely you didn't lock them away just for us?"

Tychonoff kept his gaze forward. "It is dinner time. They are all in dining hall."

On Sub-level Three, Tychonoff led them to an auditorium big enough to seat fifty people. Adam, Stepanida and the others arrived a minute later. Those not carrying weapons took seats in the first two rows. Those with weapons stood against the outer wall, the Americans boxed in by the Russians.

"Why do you need an auditorium if you don't get many

guests?" Troy asked.

"Being so close to Moscow, we get frequent visits from our leaders, wanting updates on any rehabilitation taking place," Tychonoff said. "We have little success in rehabilitation, but we are… *trying*." The corner of his mouth turned up at the last word.

He walked to a speaker on the wall and pressed a call button. "Doctor, if you'd care to join us."

An older man, in his sixties, his hair and beard graying, came into the room. His assistant, dark-skinned with tightly curled, shiny black hair, seemed to be only a few years younger than him. Both wore lab coats. The older man stopped a few paces into the room when he caught sight of the marines. Stepanida stepped forward and waved him into the room. "It is okay, Doctor Zarkov. Our American counterparts would like to ask you some questions." She grabbed him lightly on an arm and pulled him in further. "Doctor Zarkov is lead scientist for this facility."

"Good evening. This is my assistant, Nurse Galkin." Zarkov said, turning to show the woman behind him.

"Doctor," Stepanida motioned toward Lani and Adam as his audience. "Tell us about Sub-level Three."

Zarkov stepped to the podium on the right of the auditorium. He tapped at something and the two wide-screen monitors at the corners of the stage lit up. Each monitor showed four room resembling hospital rooms. The lighting in each was dim, a brighter light shining down on the patient, arms above blankets, IV tubes extending down to each arm, oxygen line stretched under noses. Screens with multiple colored lines ran across, showing the patient's biometrics stood off to one side. The monitor cycled through several sets of rooms. Lani counted on her fingers each time the view changed, losing count at twenty.

"Not every mutant can be controlled by the suppressor worn around the head or neck. We maintain those who cannot be suppressed in a drug-induced coma. These mutants typically have enhanced strength, dexterity, or charisma. We even have one detainee who appeared to cast magical spells, though I believe the words and phrases were stage-show theatrics to disguise everything from teleporting objects to manipulate cosmic energy."

"How many detainees do you have that are drugged?" Troy asked.

Zarkov chuckled. "We have over two dozen sleeping dragons, as we like to call them."

"Fatima Gorshkov, is she one of your *dragons*?" Lani asked.

"Yes, she is," the assistant stepped in. "She is a very powerful telepath and illusionist, overcoming our strongest suppressors. Coma was the only method we had to control her."

"And even that was not enough," Adam said. "She contacted another mutant outside of this facility who contacted me earlier this week. Which is why we are here."

"I assure you, young man," Zarkov said, "That is impossible. With the chemicals given to her, she is medically brain-dead."

"Regardless, we need to see her." Adam's tone was firm.

Zarkov's eyes widened. He blinked several times. "I'm sorry? Did I hear you correctly?"

He turned to Tychonoff, who looked to Stepanida. She nodded agreement. Zarkov frowned. "Very well then." He whispered something to his assistant, who left the room first. "Right this way, please."

Lani stood, her heartbeat racing at the anticipation. It was time.

"Are you ready?" Adam stood beside her, putting his arm across her shoulder.

"Oh, hell yes." Lani reached around his waist. "Came this far, no turning back now."

She followed the doctor with Adam by her side and Troy just behind. The Marines and Russian guards kept close. She wrinkled her nose as they stepped through the auditorium's back door. The maze of bland tubes changed into a dimly lit medical facility, including the smell of disinfectant. They approached a nurses' station where the hallway split in two, each lined with hospital rooms. Along with the medical staff wearing white shirts and slacks, detainees wearing dirty gray jumpsuits and neckband suppressors.

Zarkov stopped and pointed to the men with rifles. "They will have to remain here."

Adam paused, unsure, but Lani didn't have any reservations. She shrugged and took a step down the hall.

Gillis stepped forward to stop her. "Ma'am? Are you sure?"

"Don't worry, Gunny," Troy said, patting the Marine on the shoulder. "Where she's going, I doubt if even your rifle will protect her."

Stepanida held up her hand. "Doctor, I insist Bazhenov to go with them," she said. "The rest of us can stay here."

"What?" Lani put a hand on her hips. "If he's coming, then one of our Marines are coming."

Adam touched her on the arm and whispered in her ear. "There is nothing he can do that we can't stop from happening."

Lani sighed. "But…"

"It's okay," Adam said.

Their eyes met, and Adam winked again. Lani nodded and accepted the unwanted tag-along.

Lani, with Adam by her side, followed Zarkov and Nurse Galkin down the hallway. With every step, her heart seemed to beat harder.

*I want so much to learn something, even if going back to Marc and say 'we found this'. But if I learn nothing new, I just need to know that that is the case.*

Adam's hand grabbed hers, and she pulled himself out of her thoughts. Zarkov had stopped in front of Room 416. Adam squeezed Lani's hand and let it go, casting her a sidelong smile.

The doctor hesitated at the door, but when his assistant touched his arm and nodded slightly, he opened it and walked in.

The assistant stepped back and gestured for Adam and Lani to go first, so Adam led the way into the hospital room. Bazhenov followed. The assistant was the last to enter, closing the door behind her.

The lighting in the room was dim. A soft beeping from the monitors repeated in a steady rhythm. Lani's eyes went to the woman lying in the hospital bed. She paused and looked at Adam. He turned to meet her eyes at the same time. Lani saw the same thought in his eyes. It was not the same woman from the October Uprising. She looked back at the woman. The patient's richly dark complexion was the first giveaway. Fatima was from Afghanistan with an olive-brown skin tone.

Lani's fingernails dug into her palms as she squeezed her fists tight. An intensity rose in her voice. "What the… Adam."

"Um, Lani…" Adam tugged at her sleeve and pointed to the other side of the bed where the doctor and assistant waited.

Lani looked up from the patient. Bazhenov stood motionless, his eyes glazed over. Doctor Zarkov and his assistant shimmered from head to toe until that of Nikolai Demidov and Fatima Gorshkov replaced their likeness.

Lani stepped back, her heart jumping into her throat. "Oh, hell no."

Fatima's long wavy chocolate brown hair framed her full, round face, cascading down the front of her nurse's uniform. She looked different without her headdress, beautiful even.

"Please, do not sound an alarm," Fatima said, briefly meeting Adam's eyes with her own. She looked away quickly, tucking her hair behind her ear.

Nikolai looked from Fatima to Lani and Adam, his expression, his jaw jutting forward.

"I'm guessing that's the assistant." Adam pointed to the sleeping woman.

Lani looked back to the woman in the bed. Her hair was longer, and she wore no makeup, but Adam was right. She was the spitting image of the woman Fatima had disguised herself as.

"So where's Zarkov?" Lani asked.

"Still in his house in town," Nikolai said.

"It took a month for me to add to the illusion of the chemical drip so I could move." Fatima stepped to the side of the bed and looked at the woman. "Then I had to wait and watch her routine so I wouldn't raise Zarkov's suspicions. In four months, I learned a lot about medications."

"If she's the assistant, why are you here, now?" Lani asked.

"And if escape was your intention," Adam said, "Why did you bring us into it?"

"If escape were my intention, Mr. Knight, I would have delivered the message myself instead of asking Nikolai to do it."

"What is the message? What do you know about our father?"

Fatima faced the siblings. "My message is two-fold. First, to show you the fate of mutants in Russia. While probing the nurse's mind, I saw what they are doing in here."

"I can assure you some mutants in the United States are treated equally bad, forced into comas as well," Adam said.

"Not all the detainees are mutant," Nikolai said, placing an arm around Fatima. "Some are sympathizers. Humans held captive because they helped mutants escape detection or detainment. They place mutants who refuse to be coerced or forced to support the government in facilities like this. This is what we were fighting against in October."

Fatima grabbed tight onto Nikolai's arm. "And what they were doing to the dead down below. Cutting them apart and testing their organs."

A flood of emotions hit Lani in the chest. She used her training to keep her composure, to keep her expression neutral. *This is every mutant's worst nightmare… and it's definitely a breach of human rights… but this is Russia, not the United States. Mendoza would never allow something like that.*

"I'm sorry. There is nothing I can do about this facility or Russian politics," Adam said. "I will get the word to President Mendoza, but I can't guarantee anything."

"This is not what we came here for." Lani gritted her teeth. "What about our father?"

"I do not know details of your father's death," Fatima said. "I mean, nothing more than what the report said."

"WHAT?" Lani shouted. Her hands gripped the railing on the hospital bed. A purplish glow began to surround her. The lights over the bed flickered but remained lit.

"I mean the cause of his death," Fatima said, "the explosion caused by a natural gas leak. All I know is that it was a murder, and not just an assassination of the President. There is an unseen servant, one that plotted against your president, one that wanted your father to die. One that could go places and open doors without notice."

Lani's facial muscles tightened as she stared at the telepath. The bed railing radiated a red glow, white light shining through her hands. Her increasing glow offset the darkness, making shadows appear behind Fatima and Nikolai. Fatima raised a hand to cover her eyes.

"Who was it!" Lani shouted, leaning over the bed, causing Fatima to back away.

"Lani, calm down." Adam grabbed her by the shoulders and shook her.

Lani could feel Adam reaching inside of her mind, trying to block her abilities. But she wasn't having any of it. Her father was murdered, and she needed to know more.

The electricity blinked off, and the medical monitors went blank. Silence prevailed until shouting sounded in the hallway, followed by alarms. Lani blinked twice, coming out of her angry trance. Power restored to the room, at first the red lighting from emergency generators, then switching back to white.

"That is all I can tell you. You must go now." Fatima held her hand to the side of her head, as if stabbed with pain, then looked to Nikolai. His eyes shot wide open, horror appearing on his face.

The door knob rattled as someone tried to enter the room and then banged on the door.

"Agent Knight!" Stepanida shouted. "Open the door!"

"Shit." Lani shouted. She looked to Adam, wide-eyed. "What'd I do?"

The likenesses of Dr. Zarkov and Nurse Galkin shimmered back into existence, concealing Nikolai and Fatima. Oleg shook his head and wobbled. Adam reached out a hand and steadied him.

The door burst open as a huge brown bear fell into the room. The creature stood up on its hind legs, its head brushing against the ceiling tile. The brown fur drew inward, revealing pink flesh and stretched underclothes. Her extended snout melted into her strong nose and lips. Back into the form of Major Alexandrova, she grabbed her jacket from the floor.

"We have an issue," she said. "Come."

The alarms blared in the hallway as she led them down the hall and past the vacant nurse's station.

"We must hurry," Stepanida said as they reached the auditorium. "The power of the building cut out. The backup generators started up, but not in time."

"Not in time for what?" Lani asked, barely keeping up with Stepanida. Ahead, the effects of a combat were clear. Three detainees and two Russian soldiers laid dead on the floor at an airlock.

"The system lost power to the controls for the suppressors," Stepanida smashed the button to open the airlock. "It turned them off."

Lani's heart skipped a beat, and her palms sweat. "Wait, you tied the halos to that Wi-Fi system that's been buzzing in my head?"

"It is microwave energy field—Tesla coils in the ceilings. It eliminates need for batteries for the suppressors."

Lani glanced at Adam, whose face was turning paler by the second.

"This isn't good," Adam said. "This really isn't good."

"Where are the others?" Lani stepped out of the airlock into the sixty-foot square center intersection of the former missile silo.

Stepanida pointed up. "They have gone to Level Two."

They crossed the intersection and into the airlock to reach the elevator. Out of the elevator and airlock on Sub-Level Two, they came upon a mass of people. Troy and three of the marines joined with two Russian soldiers firing around the corner, then ducking back as the detainees returned fire with their own mutant weaponry. One marine, Ortiz, sat against the wall. Black scorching covered his chest armor, his face and neck red with blood. Two Russian soldiers lay in the hallway, unmoving.

"Gunny! Report." Lani shouted.

"Lobby's full of mutants, ma'am. We're holding them off as best we can." He turned to Lani, an apologetic look on his face. "Sorry, ma'am. Detainees."

"Don't worry." Lani nodded. "Call them what they are."

"We could use some mutant blockers up here, if you don't mind." Troy moved back from the corner as a lightning bolt struck the concrete wall across from him in the hallway. Chunks of stone sprayed everyone.

Adam moved passed Lani, dragging Oleg with him. Lani followed. "Adam! You two block, I'll blast."

"I can block two at most." Oleg said.

Lani's shoulders dropped. "I guess you have the rest, bro."

Adam nodded in agreement. "Ready? Now."

Lani counted to three then stepped into the twenty-foot corridor. Several detainees held their arms outward, trying to unleash their mutant abilities with no effect. Lani did the same, with better results. A brilliant flash of light and energy flooded the intersection ahead of her. Screams echoed all around as mutants fell victim to the blast. As the light dimmed, bullets came streaming toward Lani. She dove for cover in the hallway.

"We could be at this all night." Troy said, checking the clip in his handgun. Morrison did the same with her rifle. "And we're getting low on ammo."

Gunny and Morrison prepared for another round when Zarkov's assistant walked up to them and put an arm over their weapons, motioning for them to lower them.

Gunny resisted, then paused. His mouth gaped open slightly as three detainees walked across the hallway opening in single file. They stopped at the closed airlock and waited as the doors opened.

"Ma'am, what's going on?" Gunny asked.

Lani's eyes narrowed as she stepped into the corridor. A dozen detainees stood in line, waiting for the airlocks to cycle open and closed.

"Ah, Adam. Come here." Lani motioned for him to join her.

Adam peeked around the corner, then joined her. Troy stepped out as well.

"Did they go zombie on us?" Troy asked.

"Could be why they aren't bothering you." Lani snickered.

When the last detainee entered the airlock and the door closed, Tychonoff pushed passed Lani, Stepanida and Oleg following.

"I wasn't aware of any preconditioning, Director." Stepanida walked shoulder to shoulder with Tychonoff. He stopped at the hallway to the elevator and raised a handgun at Zarkov.

"There isn't any."

With one eyebrow raised, Stepanida looked at Adam, then at Zarkov and Galkin. She reached for her sidearm. Adam touched her on the wrist.

"Let it go," he said.

Stepanida jerked her arm away from Adam, her eyes narrowing tight. "Agent, I do not think you understand."

"Oh, we do," Lani said. "Completely. Now let's go." She pointed into the elevator.

Stepanida moved quickly toward Nurse Galkin. She grabbed her neck and shoved her hard against the concrete wall. Withdrawing her handgun, Stepanida held it against the nurse's forehead. Long brown hairs pushed out of the Major's clothing and down her arms, her nose elongated slightly.

"Damn it, Stepanida!" Adam shouted, "Stop it. Now!"

"Bazhenov!" Stepanida growled. "Come here."

Oleg sheepishly obeyed, coming within arm's reach, close enough for Stepanida to land a blow to his chest with her free hand, knocking him backward. The Russian mutant's head bounced off the tile floor as he slid five feet away from her.

"Did you not know who she was?" Stepanida asked.

Oleg groaned and raised up on an elbow. "No, Major."

The illusion around Nikolai and Fatima vanished. Nikolai moved to Fatima's side, grasping her hand.

"You..." Stepanida huffed, cupping her handgun with both hands, aimed at Fatima's forehead. "You will not make it out of this facility."

"Afraid so," Adam whispered, his chest pushing against Stepanida's shoulder blade. "You saw what she did to those mutants, controlling them. She could make us join them if she wanted."

"Your visit here just was a cover." She flashed a sideways glance at Adam. "To allow them to escape."

"Alex, she escaped weeks ago. She's been walking in and out of this facility daily. How do you think I got the report I showed you earlier?"

Stepanida shoved back with her shoulder, pushing Adam backward. Her lips pulled tight, she pulled the handgun back, holstering it. "When you leave, Agent, you will never set foot in Russia again." Her eyes met Adam's, then Lani's. "Neither of you."

"Okay by me," Lani said. "Can we continue now?"

Tychonoff pointed down the hallway to the elevator to Sub-Level One. "Major Alexandrova, we should go." He nodded to the Russian soldiers. They raised their weapons and blocked the airlock entrance. The Marine squad took aim also, stepping in front of the agents. Stepanida and the director stepped into the enclosure, then the soldiers filled the rest of the space.

Lani stood with her mouth gaping open as the wheel closed in front of her.

"Well, hell." Lani looked at her NSA partner.

"I guess you've never been back stabbed by a Russian before," Troy said.

"It will be okay." Fatima said.

Lani threw her a questioning look, then watched through the small window in the door as the outer door rolled open. A soldier stepped into the hallway and fell from an energy blast from the hallway to the right. Stepanida shifted into a giant brown bear again and bounded out of sight, followed by the remaining guard.

Tychonoff stepped out of the lock and looked back at Lani and Adam.

"Come on, close the door." Lani mumbled.

Tychonoff pulled a pistol out of his holster and aimed at the control panel. He looked at the door controls, then back at them.

"Don't you dare." Lani shouted.

As Director Tychonoff looked at the buttons one last time, a long bone-white spear struck him in the chest, tossing him into the lock. The outer door closed as he rolled in pain on the floor.

"You do that?" Lani asked.

"In his mind," Fatima whispered, "he fired his handgun three times."

Lani pressed the control again when it turned green. Adam stepped in front of her before she could release any of the cosmic energy she was gathering around her fists. He grabbed Tychonoff by the chest and yanked him to his feet. Morrison grabbed him from behind and led him down the airlock, shoving him out into the larger corridor.

The wheel closed with the Americans inside as Tychonoff got to his feet.

"Welcome to the new Level Five," Troy said, waving at him through the window.

Lani stepped out of the airlock and into Sub-level One's center intersection. Two Russian soldiers were dead, along with several detainees. Blood smeared the wall above two of the detainees, with Stepanida's uniform on the floor near one of them.

Lani kicked at the ripped slacks. "Looks like she went *full bear.*"

Stepping out of the elevator and into a corridor, Lani breathed a sigh of relief at having made it out of the underground at last. That quickly changed as she got an unobstructed view of the scene before her.

Ahead appeared to be the last gauntlet from the elevators to the exit into the barn. Burnt marks on the floor, walls and ceiling from energy discharges. Lighting fixtures dangled from the ceiling by their cords, some blinking from the occasional electrical connection. Bodies of soldiers and detainees littered the hallway, blood pooling under some.

"Looks like we missed a party." Troy muttered as they watched Hardy and Morrison checked the bodies. Lani stood at the last corner while they waited for the remaining six to make the long elevator trip from Sub-level One.

"I can only sense Stepanida and Oleg," Adam reported. "No one else upstairs or within fifty yards."

Lani nodded, a purple glow surrounding her hand, as she peeked around the corner. "Copy, two other soldiers. They're all standing at the console."

"Sir, wait." Morrison called out as Adam moved passed Lani and entered the open area of the barn.

"Shit." Lani muttered, following him.

The scene in the barn reflected that of the corridor. Dead bodies were strewn about the large open room. A hole in the structure's ceiling exposed the night sky above. The barn doors laid out on the ground, allowing a breeze to blow in, distributing the loose papers off of desks not covered by dead workers.

Lani created two bright beams of light from her hands as she joined Troy and the two Marines outside. They did a quick search of the empty field between the barn and the orchard. They found several more bodies, including a dead pilot where the helicopter had sat.

"Major!" Adam shouted out, stepping onto the raised platform of the control center. Oleg stood closest to Adam, holding a three-ring binder, reading and pointing at controls that Stepanida was operating.

"Not now, Agent," Stepanida kept her attention to the information Oleg gave out.

Lani heard the click of the switches, then felt the electronics as signals were being sent from the console down into the facility below. She ran back into the barn. "Adam, what did she just do?"

"I'm releasing the nerve gas, Captain."

"We still have people in there, bitch." The glow around Lani flared as she ran to get a clear shot at her. She raised both of her arms, pointed at Stepanida, but no energy released. A force clamped around Lani's head and arms, cast out by Oleg as he blocked her. Lani dropped her hands and reached for a handgun at her waist.

The two soldiers raised their rifles, one pointed at Lani, the other at Adam. Morrison and Hardy moved into positions, aim centered on the Russians.

Oleg lowered his hand and went back to reading from the book. Lani understood some Russian words, but the technical ones slipped passed her.

Behind her, Lani heard Fatima's voice.

*"She plans to blow up the facility."*

Lani turned toward the elevator corridor. She, Nikolai, and the other two Marines had entered the room. Gillis and Ortiz took up positions to flank the Russian soldiers.

Oleg read a few more lines from the book when Adam shoved him aside. He grabbed Stepanida's arm, pulling her away from the controls. She used the motion to toss him backward. He regained his balance and approached her again. "What are you doing?"

"I am doing my job, Agent Knight."

Adam put both of his hands on his head, running his fingers through his hair. "You're going to kill them, aren't you? Is that your job? Killing mutants? People just like you and me?"

Stepanida turned to face him, taking two or three aggressive steps toward him that pushed him farther from the control panel. Oleg took her place at the controls. Her movement caught the attention of the Marines, who moved inside, keeping Troy and Lani behind them.

"No." Hands clasped behind her back, shoulders tense, Stepanida kept stepping forward, pushing Adam back. "Not mutants. Terrorists and criminals. Something I could classify you as if Fatima leaves this facility."

Adam looked over his shoulder. Fatima and Nikolai stood off to the side, apart from both the Marines and the Russian soldiers. Their eyes were wide, almost pleading when Adam met their gazes. He sighed and turned back to Stepanida.

"If you don't want her to get away," Adam said, "I recommend you arrest her now while you can."

In a rapid motion, Stepanida pulled a handgun from her holster, aimed at Fatima and Nikolai, and fired. The bullets struck the center mass, tossing them backward sightly as they fell to the ground. Then she pointed the gun at Adam's throat.

The Marines closed the distance to the control area, weapons trained on the two Russian soldiers. Gillis motioned, and the Russians lowered their weapons. Morrison collected the weapons and ejected the clip as she passed from one to the other.

Troy took a step toward Fatima when Lani grabbed his arm, shaking her head.

Adam glared at Stepanida, unsure of what to do. Even with her mutant power blocked, she would have a slight advantage in hand-to-hand. She counted off the distance between her and Oleg when a signal came to her from outside.

*"Knight Seven Three Four, this is Wanamaker Three One Four."*
*"Copy Wanamaker. Just in time."*
*"Aim to please, Knight. Approaching three three five at two hundred."*
*"Understood. Touch down and make visual. We'll be right out. Make*

*room for seven seats."*

*"Copy that. Got plenty of room."*

"Adam, our ride is here." Lani shouted as a warm breeze that blew in from outside picked up, stirring dust around their legs. The soft thumping sound of helicopter blades filled the interior of the barn.

"Ah, Lani? Is that…" Troy placed a hand on her shoulder.

She glanced behind her. A military helicopter with American markings shimmered into existence just outside the barn.

"No, it isn't Marc. Asshole wouldn't come." She cupped her hands over her mouth. "Hey bro! I don't think she's going to kiss and make up. Let's go."

Adam held out his hand. "If you don't mind, we'd like our passports back."

Handgun still trained on him, Stepanida reached into her back pocket and pulled out the three document holders. Adam took them and backed away, stepping from the control platform and joining Lani and Troy. The Marines moved to create a barrier between Americans and Russians.

Stepanida shrugged. "I do not have the equipment for removing your tracking devices."

Lani laughed. "As if they were ever actually an issue." The anklet on Adam's leg beeped, then fell to the ground. Lani unhooked the one on her leg and tossed it at Stepanida. "It's all right," she said. "People underestimate me all the time." She winked at her.

"As they do me, Captain." Stepanida said, emotionless.

Once Adam joined Lani and Troy just outside the destroyed barn, she motioned to Gillis. "Gunny, I'm going to fly these two straight to the airport."

"Copy that. We'll be right behind you."

She watched as they loaded Ortiz onto the helicopter, then

each of the Marines joined him. The door slid closed, and she nodded to the pilot.

Just as the wind from the chopper increased, lifting it off the ground, Lani swayed. She thought it was the transport until a rumbling rose out of the ground.

The ground shook with the power of an earthquake. The walls of the barn swayed. Adam held both arms out to keep his balance, his eyes wide at the scene beyond the barn. Troy pointed to the orchard, his mouth open, speechless. The earth swallowed row after row of apple trees, replacing the orchard with an immense cloud of dust.

"I can't believe she would do that," Adam whispered as he came to stand beside his sister. He turned to stare at the two Russian mutants, Stepanida on the phone and Oleg at the control panel.

Troy said, "It's all she knows."

Lani moved to stand between Adam and Troy, sliding her arms under theirs. The ground fell away from them, rising hundreds of feet into the air. The five-hundred-acre chasm was still visible for minutes after that.

"Adam, remember that guy," Lani said, "the one who would always play the paladin in Donny's fantasy game. He would always kill the orcs, even the ones who gave us clues."

Adam nodded. "Lawful good. What does that make us?"

"I prefer to think we're neutral good, myself."

*Friday, June 23*
*Present Day*

Gray skies threatened to unload a deluge of water on the Beltway. A steady drizzle was already falling as Lani pulled off the highway and around to Fort Meade's gate. She presented her ID to the Marine, who saluted and waved her through to the NSA grounds.

Lani searched for Troy's vehicle as she cruised the lot, looking for a spot of her own. She had showered, put on a fresh ivory pantsuit, rolled her brunette hair into a bun, and walked out the door. Only a ninety minutes had come and gone. She could never understand how Troy could take two hours getting ready for the day.

As she expected, the light rain turned into a full-fledged downpour by the time Lani found a spot to her liking. She reached to the back seat of her truck, searching for the umbrella which always ended up in the darkest regions of her vehicle. It was moments like this she wished she could stretch her body like Iskander Gorshkov, Fatima's husband and fellow October Uprising conspirator.

Her hand finally found the handle of the umbrella. Lani popped it open as she exited her truck. Walking toward the NSA building, she caught up with a pair of women in short dresses and high heels. As she got closer, she heard one lady complaining about the rain.

"It would be nice if a mutant on the fifth floor could stop the rain for a few minutes."

Lani smiled. They were practically begging for a response.

"It would be nice," Lani said, "if taxpayers could build us a covered parking garage."

The ladies startled at the sound of her voice and watched her with open mouths as she glided past them, her feet kicked back as she drifted clear of the puddles collecting on the asphalt.

Once inside the building, Lani tossed her purse and umbrella onto the x-ray machine, then stepped through the explosives and metal detectors. She didn't need the caffeine, but Lani took a side route and swung by the Starbucks kiosk before heading to the bank of elevators across the lobby. If the day is going to be hell, she was going to start it with a good drink.

Mutant Central was already abuzz with conversation when she stepped off the elevator. She wasn't sure if it had to do with her fiasco at the detention facility or if some other part of the world was in chaos. Lani tried to catch some conversations as she made her way to her desk, but they hushed voices as she approached. Lani discarded her purse on her chair in the low-wall cubicle and took one last drink before sitting the paper cup beside the keyboard.

"So, we heard there was a collapse in Russia this morning," said a voice behind her. The deep baritone was unmistakable. Damian Nicholson. Lani held back a groan.

She looked over her shoulder to find her fellow mutant standing just outside her cubicle. He was handsome—tall, fit, with a nice, russet-brown complexion—but he was also annoying as hell.

"Well, being a datalink, I imagine you hear a lot of things," Lani said, hanging her thin jacket inside the locker beside the desk. "Which collapse would this be?"

"The detention center you and Troy went to yesterday, along with your brother. Seems they lost around fifty detainees before they could stop the bleeding."

Lani looked at him and shrugged her shoulders. "I'm not sure what you want me to say, Nicholson."

He quirked an eyebrow, and Lani thought she saw a satisfied glimmer in his eyes. "Harris is pissed, you know, losing our only contact in the Russian mutant military."

Lani drew in a quick breath, the hair on her arms standing on end, a pit forming in her stomach. "Our only contact? Major Alexandrova?"

Nicholson shrugged. "Yeah. From what I heard, her head was rolling along with some doctor named Zarkov. Literally." He twirled his index finger in a circle.

Lani sat hard in her chair, forgetting that her purse was still there. A crack sounded beneath her, but she only barely noticed. She imagined a sword swinging across Stepanida's shoulders, severing her neck.

"Nicholson, buddy," Troy said, walking toward them from the elevators. "What's happening?"

Nicholson smiled widely. "Hey, man. Just telling your partner what you all might be in for today with the boss."

"Whatever it is, we can handle it." Troy stopped in front of Nicholson. "Have a nice day."

"Yeah, you too," Nicholson said. He patted Troy's head, which only came up to his shoulder. "See you later, little guy."

Lani scowled as he walked away. "What's with that guy?"

"He's not so bad," Troy said. "Anyway, what'd I miss? And what's that smell?"

Lani stood and unzipped her purse, grimacing at the onslaught of flowery perfume. "I sat on my perfume," she said as she quickly threw away the plastic bottle, the liquid dripping from a crack all over her hand, chair, and the floor. She grabbed a tissue and soaked up the liquid in the purse before throwing it into the short locker. Lani plopped into her chair and leaned her head back.

"So," Troy said, "what did Nicholson say?"

"They killed Alexandrova."

Troy's head jerked back. "Damn."

"They blamed her for losing over fifty mutants."

"That many got away?"

Lani looked up at Troy, raising an eyebrow. "To them, losing fifty means the fifty we killed trying to get out. More than that probably escaped up the elevators."

A buzzing came from Troy's pocket. He pulled out his phone and looked at the screen. His eyes immediately shot up to Harris' office.

Lani followed Troy's gaze to where Harris stood in the doorway of his office, eyes narrowed at them both. As usual, he wore a matching tie and suspenders. Today, they complimented a pale green shirt and drab olive slacks.

"Harris is ready for debriefing," Troy said.

"Let's get this over so I can pack before lunch." Lani finished the mocha and tossed the paper cup in the trash can.

Lani followed Troy into Harris' office where their boss sat behind his desk, his expression dark. Lani closed the door behind her.

She cleared her throat, fighting off a bout of nausea. "Green day today?" she said, offering a small smile and a nervous chuckle. "Must have missed the memo." She pointed at Troy's clover green polo and Harris' shirt.

"Cute." Harris crossed his arms. "I'm not sure which I'm more pissed at—Gorshkov and Demidov getting away or that

Alexandrova is dead, along with any chance of going back for more inspections."

Troy's eyes bulged, and his mouth fell open. He looked at Lani. "They got away? I saw her shoot them."

Lani smirked. "Demidov can run faster than the bullet she fired at them. And Fatima is a mentalist. What we saw was an illusion to make us think they were dead."

"So Stepanida would let us go." Troy smiled. "Cool. But you could have told me."

"Sorry," Lani said, shrugging. "I forgot to mention it."

"Yeah, well, not cool is that Alexandrova is dead. That's not an illusion," Harris said, glaring at Lani. "She's dead, along with several other top officials in the Russian mutant army division. President Yegorov cleaned house during your flight back."

"Damn." Troy's voice was just above a whisper. He folded his arms and stared at his shoes.

"Sir," Lani said, her cheeks flushing. "I want to say—"

Harris held up his hand to cut her off. "Nothing to say, Knight, except case closed. And not just your father's case." Harris leaned back in his chair. He pointed the pencil in his hand at Lani. She flinched, then glanced to see if the dartboard was there. It wasn't.

"The State Department is up in arms over you being there during the prison riot." Harris threw his hands up. "Yeah, that's what it's being called. After your presence couldn't be denied, your involvement is being downplayed as much as possible. But we got word Russia has plans to go to the UN and The Hague over the destruction of the detention facility."

"The International Court of Justice?" Troy asked. He ran his fingers through his hair. "That's serious shit, there."

"Damn straight," Harris pointed the pencil at Troy. "You're lucky to still have your badges. As it is, you're on administrative leave. Trackers on both of you, especially you, Knight. Do not even think about leaving the country."

Lani sat in her chair and stared at Harris. "I understand, sir. Case closed."

Harris continued pointing at her. "Don't give me that blatant acceptance. I've seen that look on too many agents that went off on their own and continued an investigation. Always ends up bad for them, the Agency, or both."

Lani gave him her best innocent look. "No. Digging up my father's death is not something I enjoy. He was a wonderful man and father. But, he went behind my back and that of my brother when he developed a device that can make me as worthless in a firefight as this schmuck." Lani pointed toward Troy, who huffed at her comment. "But that's okay. It's for the greater good."

She really didn't feel that way, that Dad had betrayed her or her brother. She knew Dad was doing some experiments on Adam to find the source of his abilities. Lots of scientists did that, even the Military. They must have thought Dad had an insight because of Adam that the others didn't. Mom had bitched several times about Dad's travels that summer before the explosion, going to Atlanta or Boston to share notes, or to Washington to update the President. Lani understood the reason for the devices, but also knew Mom's distrust of the government was not all that misguided.

"Whatever." Harris waved the pencil between them. "I mean it. No lone wolf stuff."

"Yes, sir." Lani nodded. "For how long?"

"At least until this Russia mutant prison thing blows over," Harris said, leaning forward, elbows on the desk. He dropped the pencil and folded his fingers together.

"It didn't blow over," Troy said. "It kind of sunk into the ground."

"I don't care, Thornburg. Look, go home. Take the weekend

off. Next week, too. Spend time with your families."

Troy shrugged. "Dad's in Moscow, so probably won't go see him."

"Whatever, Thornburg. Just go home. Come back after the Fourth. We should know something by then."

"Thank you, sir. Have a safe weekend." Lani stood and headed toward the door. She turned and looked at Troy, who was still sitting in his chair, looking at her. "You coming?" she asked.

Troy stood. "Right," he said, nodding to Harris. "Vacation. Thanks."

Lani shrugged and walked out of the office toward her cubicle. She heard Harris' door shut behind her. It only took a few moments for Troy to catch up to her.

"So, what are you going to do?"

Lani raised an eyebrow. "What do you mean?"

"I know you, Lani. You've got a plan."

She put a hand to her chest. "Me? What? Probably go to Mom's, spend some time on the beach, work on my tan."

"The hell…" Troy shook his head. "You're gonna go James Bond or something."

Lani stared at him. "What, go rogue? Besides, James Bond was a fictional character."

He opened his mouth to say something else, but Lani held up a finger. He closed his mouth and narrowed his eyes at her. Lani pursed her lips as she followed the approach of a woman entering Mutant Central. A young woman, mid-Twenties, with short blonde hair. She walked with a bit of a bounce. Lani recognized her and felt a heat flushing through her body.

Out of the corner of her eye, she could see Troy adjust his shirt and puff out his chest. *Good god, he's preening.* Lani's jaws clinched.

The young woman stopped in front of them and held out her

hand to Troy. "Hi. Janice Steinke."

He took her hand and squeezed. "Major Troy Thornburg, US Army." Troy cocked his head to one side. "Have we met before?"

Janice shook her head. "No, I don't believe so. Do you watch a lot of porno?"

"Ah, no." Troy's face turned red.

Lani cleared her throat. "Troy, can I have a moment? I'll call you if I leave town."

He looked at Lani, blinking rapidly. "Nothing stupid, got it?"

Lani shrugged her shoulders, mouthing *whatever* at him.

After Troy walked away from them, the guise of Janice faded away, revealing Fatima Gorshkov.

Lani whispered, "Fatima, you're risking a lot coming here like this." Lani cleared a stack of papers off the guest chair in her cubicle.

"I had to come and tell you. You are in danger." Fatima sat down.

"Oh, really? Like you aren't in danger now, walking in amongst a group of mutants, disguising yourself as a dead Secret Service agent."

"Except for Troy, no one in here knew Janice. I checked." Fatima leaned in close to Lani. "You do not understand the chain reaction you and your brother started. A reaction you will need to follow to the end."

"What we started? You had a hand in it also, you know. Alexandrova is dead because of you and your boyfriend."

"Nikolai is not my boyfriend." Fatima scoffed, sitting back in her chair.

Lani smirked. "Right. I saw how you two looked at each other."

"That is irrelevant." Fatima looked away from Lani, a gaze that seemed to travel for miles.

Lani sat back in her chair. "Whatever. Just tell me what the hell you're talking about."

"That's what I'm talking about." Fatima pointed to Harris' office.

Lani's eyes followed Fatima's lead. Harris was walking out of his office with a bottle-blonde woman wearing a dark blue pantsuit and a white button-down shirt. She walked with an air of authority, which came regardless of her position.

"I believe that is Theresa Hinckley, your Deputy Director," Fatima said.

Lani looked away, trying not to be too obvious. "She never comes down to the fifth floor." Hinckley and Lani had spent little time together, even though there was only one layer of bureaucracy between them. Pleasant enough, Lani could tell there was always something on this woman's mind. She shrugged it off as political posturing.

Lani and Fatima watched as Hinckley and Harris walked to the outer aisle and headed out of the section, Hinckley in the lead and Harris doing his best to keep up behind her.

"They are on their way to talk with someone about you and about your President."

"Did you get the name of who they're meeting?" Lani asked.

"No, only where they were meeting. A bar in a hotel someplace near what they called the D.C. Border."

Lani grabbed her purse and umbrella from under her desk. "Sounds like it's time for a mid-morning drink."

She stood up, waiting for Fatima to stand and step out of the cube first. "You hungry? Wait, how did you get here?" Lani waved her hand in front of her. "No, never mind. You probably flew with us in the back of the plane."

Fatima grinned. "As a matter of fact…"

The rain had no effect on the traffic on Interstate 495. Blizzards were the only thing that slowed traffic on the Beltway. Fatima sat without disguise in the passenger seat of Lani's pickup truck, white knuckles holding on to the oh-shit handle over the door. She pointed with her left hand at the blue sedan they had been following seven to ten cars behind.

"They are pulling off here," Fatima said, showing the off-ramp just ahead.

"I see it." Lani glanced over her shoulder and saw the opportunity to shift two lanes to the off-ramp. She eased into one lane and then the other, avoiding the brakes.

"I hope you fly better than you drive." Fatima grabbed at the armrest, her foot reaching for an imaginary brake.

"I'm an excellent driver, I'll have you know. Better than my brother."

"That is for sure," Fatima said. Her eyes went wide as if she realized she'd slipped.

Lani gave Fatima a long stare after merging into the southbound traffic headed into the city. "You've ridden with Adam? When?"

"I was a student at Ann Arbor, a year behind him." Fatima released her grip and settled back into the seat. "I dated his friend, Billy Watson."

"This web of yours, girl, goes everywhere." Lani shook her head.

The blue sedan pulled off of the street and under the entrance canopy of a multi-story hotel. Lani drove past them and turned into the parking lot beside the hotel.

"This the place?" Lani asked.

Fatima stared straight ahead, then nodded. "Yes, I can see the entrance. He is taking a piece of paper from someone, then walking into the hotel."

"You can see what they see, and you can make them see what

you want." Lani turned to Fatima, arm on the back of the seat.

"Yes. Your agency has labeled me as a telepath and an illusionist. I don't create illusions. It's more like implanting visions."

Lani had dealt with several types of telepaths in her various jobs since leaving the Air Force Academy. Fatima was, by far, the strongest. "Kind of the same thing, isn't it?"

Fatima's hijab dissolved away, her tunic faded into a white button-down blouse. She became a mirror image of Lani—hair in a tight bun, her skin tanned and smooth. The blouse she wore gaped between the second and third button, Lani's beige bra and breasts peeking through.

"My boobs aren't that big." Lani glanced down. Her shirt opened wide between buttons. She sighed, pulling at the fabric until the gap closed.

"To everyone else," Fatima said, "I look like myself. Only you see yourself. If I created illusions, everyone would see two of you right now. In the facility, you and Adam saw me and Nikolai. Everyone else saw the nurse and the doctor."

Lani gave her a nod, understanding her example. "And how everyone watched you die upstairs."

Lani gave Fatima the umbrella and created a shield of shimmering light above her to block the rain as they dashed down the sidewalk to the hotel's street entrance. Inside the lobby, Lani shook off some water that made its way around the shield and into her arms. She was glad she wore her ankle boots this morning; she'd forgotten to drift over the wet concrete as she had in the NSA parking lot.

"Do we need, you know, disguises?" Lani whispered to Fatima.

Fatima nodded, pointing to a mirrored steel wall across the way. Two older women in conservative clothing stared back at them. They reminded Lani of her grandmother.

"*You're welcome,*" Fatima said, her mouth unmoving.

Lani pointed at her. "*Let's be careful with the mind reading, okay?*"

Fatima shrugged. "*You have no concern when you listen in on phone conversations.*"

Lani opened her mouth to reply, but realized she was right. "*Okay, fine. Let's go find Harris and Hinckley.*"

Fatima led the way through the lobby and around the tables set up for incoming visitors for a cosmetology convention. Women of all ages, shapes, and sizes gathered around the area, all chatting about fashion, products, and people. Lani was careful not to bump into anyone, fearful of losing the illusion.

Deputy Director Hinckley and Assistant Deputy Director Harris sat on the cushioned semi-circular sofa in the center of the lounge. Both had drinks in hand, Hinckley with a pink-colored daiquiri and Harris with an amber-colored liquor. The server brought a plate of appetizers to the table.

Lani led Fatima to a table just outside of the center sofas. After a few moments, the server approached them and took their drink orders—a glass of red wine for both of them.

Lani and Fatima monitored the women in the lobby and even commented on make-up styles in Russia to complete their cover, all while focusing on Hinckley and Harris.

"*Anything of interest in their brains? And don't go stealing nuclear launch codes while you're at it.*" She went for a light, humorous tone, but the thought made her shudder. With Fort Meade so close, Fatima could have all the secrets of the government as bathroom reading material.

"*They aren't talking much, as you can hear for yourself,*" Fatima said, "*But I am getting visions of a woman pouring water from a container.*"

She shared the image with Lani, who recognized it as the image for a constellation.

"Aquarius," she said, verbally. "A friend of mine at the Air

Force Academy was an Aquarius. A real bitch when she wanted to be."

Fatima put a finger to her lips and then tapped her temple, continuing the conversation through thought. *It seems connected with the name of a group. Aquarius Group, I think."*

*"Never heard of it."*

*"She's here."* Fatima discreetly nodded toward Harris. *"He recognizes the woman approaching them."*

An older woman in a tight-fitting red dress and red high heels joined Harris and Hinckley. Her graying hair wrapped in a bun, she carried a small, golden brown toy poodle in her left arm.

*"Kutcher."* Lani almost said the name out loud.

Doris Kutcher was Lani's neighbor when she lived on the south side of D.C., back when she worked for the Air Force's internal criminal investigation group. Mrs. Kutcher usually wore a sundress or a robe that hung from her like a sack, walking like someone from the "Thriller" music video. And she always carried that dog of hers, Sparky, wherever she went.

Fatima connected with Lani's mind, allowing her to hear the conversation over the background noise of women at the cosmetology convention.

"I suppose we are here about what the wonder twins did in Russia," Doris sat Sparky on the floor at her feet, then picked an hors d'oeuvre from Harris' plate and fed it to the poodle.

"So, you've heard already. We're concerned what will happen if it gets to the President," Hinckley said.

"Oh, it's too late to worry about that," Doris said. "He was the one that told me."

"Damn," Harris blurted. Hinckley put her hand on Harris' knee, and he quieted down.

"You forget," Doris said. "Adam is Antonio's personal bodyguard. Antonio even arranged for them to go to Russia."

Lani glanced at Fatima. *"She's calling the president by his first name."*

"We put Captain Knight on administrative leave," Harris said.

"You gave her a vacation? Instead of another assignment in a different part of the world. How wonderful!" Doris' smile clearly feigned. "Now she can continue her investigation."

"Your recommendations, then?" Hinckley asked.

"Just walk away," Doris said. "It's in our hands now. I have surveillance on the girl, and Antonio has the boy on a leash. Just keep an eye out on what President Yegorov does. We quelled World War III once already. We don't need this flare-up to rekindle the flames of war."

Lani wiggled in her chair. *"We? Where the hell were you in St. Petersburg?"*

"Fine with me, she's all yours. If she comes back after the Fourth, then we'll assume you're done with her." Hinckley said. She downed the last of her daiquiri and stood up. "Thanks for the drinks. Have a good day."

She stood, nearly pulled Harris to his feet, put a hand on his back and pushed him out of the lounge area.

Lani looked to Fatima, eyes wide. *"Wow. Talk about control issues."*

Fatima shrugged. *"Are you really surprised?"*

Lani nodded. In the few things she had seen Director Hinkley in action, the men and women around her whimpered like dogs.

Doris picked up Sparky and stood gracefully. Lani shook her head and smiled. When they were neighbors, she acted frail, going to the extreme of using a walker.

Doris walked up to the bar and handed the bartender a credit card. The bartender waved it off, and she tucked it back in her purse.

Lani watched as Doris headed for the lobby. Sparky looked at Lani and growled; he had always hated her, growling every time

Lani came within ten feet of Mrs. Kutcher. Lani frowned at the dog.

*"Tell your mother I said Aloha."* Doris grinned as she gave Lani a *jazz finger* wave.

Lani looked at Fatima. "Did you hear that?" She asked in a whisper.

Fatima shrugged her shoulders. "Hear what?"

Lani jumped from the chair and ran for the lobby. She weaved her way through the crowd to the rotating doors. Fatima shouted for her to slow down. Lani stepped outside into the rain and looked up and down the street. There was no sight of her.

Lani entered the hotel lobby again, dripping wet from the rain. The group of women at the cosmetology sign-in booth gawked at her. She looked down at her arms and realized the illusion had vanished.

"You didn't hear her tell me to tell my mother, Aloha?" Lani asked aloud, not sure where Fatima was at.

*"No."*

Lani spun around, facing the rotating doors again, her shoulders drooping. Fatima wasn't there. "She's a telepath. That bitch."

"Can I help you, ma'am?"

Lani turned again to see a hotel concierge standing behind her.

"Fatima?"

"No, ma'am. Franklin." He pointed to his nameplate. "Can I get you an umbrella?"

"No, thanks. Too late for that." She smiled as politely as she could, shaking the water off her arms. Lani walked back to the lounge to get the umbrella, only to find it missing along with the rest of her wine.

"Damn," Lani said, stomping her foot.

*"Sorry,"* Fatima said from wherever she was, *"but you are on your*

*own now."*

"No kidding." Lani threw up her hands, ignoring the people staring at her for her outburst.

*"Nikolai and I are returning to St. Petersburg,"* Fatima said.

*"What about Iskander?"* Lani asked. *"Did your husband make it out?"*

*"I never saw him in Cherenkov."*

Lani felt a sadness come over her. She could feel Fatima's loss through their connection.

*"Thank you, Fatima, for all you have done. I'm sorry I couldn't do more."*

Lani waited, but there was no reply.

The rain had died off by the time Lani made it back to her apartment. She didn't feel like opening the window and tapping in the code for the gate, so she mentally touched the circuits and made it raise the reinforced metal pole. Lani wheeled her truck around and parked in the spot designated for her.

Caught between the exhaustion of jet lag and the hype over Mrs. Kutcher mentioning her Mom, Lani floated up the four flights of stairs instead of walk. As she turned on the landing between the second and the third floor, a two-year-old boy gawked at her from the top of the stairs. She touched down just before the child's mother joined him. Her hands were full—a raincoat, purse, and a few other mom-bags.

"The rain is letting up," Lani said, running her hand through the boy's hair. The woman pulled the boy back a little, letting Lani step past.

"She was floating," the child said, looking over his shoulder as his mom tugged him down the stairs.

Lani gave the boy a childish wave, then floated up to the fourth floor. She stripped out of her wet clothes as soon as she locked her apartment door behind her, draping them over the hamper in the closet to dry.

Mrs. Kutcher's words continued to run through her mind as she flopped down on the bed. "Tell your mother I said Aloha," Lani said out loud, letting the words echo back from the ceiling fan. The coolness of the breeze relaxed her. She let out a sigh, grabbed the comforter, and draped it over herself before drifting off to sleep.

The great room of the thirtieth-floor condo was void of color—white walls, white couch, white loveseat, white wood-laminate flooring, white vertical window shades. Doris' red dress and Sparky's golden fur were the only color in the room.

Adding to the void of color was Michael Clarke, his pasty white body held up by a brushed aluminum brace of a glossy, white wheelchair. He wore white cotton pajamas. His thin white hair and the age spots dotting his skin didn't represent the man that she knew for nearly fifty years.

She stared at him, unmoving in the wheelchair, not reacting to her sudden appearance five feet from him. Only his blinking eyes gave away any life in his body. Life that existed only from neck up.

Sparky wiggled in her arms. She sat him down as she slipped her shoes off. "There, ya fleabag. Go sit on your lap."

The poodle bounced across the floor and leapt into his lap. Sparky put its front paws on Michael's chest and licked his chin. She could feel Michael's consciousness drifting back to his own body. The dog shook its head and circled twice on the white blanket covering Michael's legs before sitting down.

Doris headed toward the kitchen, decorated in brushed

stainless steel. Holding up a wineglass to check for water spots, she sat it down and reached in the refrigerator for the opened bottle of red wine.

She walked past Michael and tapped the first of two buttons to open the drapes to the balcony door. She prized the view from their Miami Beach condo. The Florida Strait stretched out toward the horizon and the southern sky. South Point Beach laid below Speed boats pulling paragliders cut white-foam waves along the shore as cargo ships with toy-size containers stacked a dozen high drifted into the port nearby.

Doris pulled pins out of her hair, letting her long greying hair flow down to the middle of her back. She unzipped her dress, letting it slip off of her shoulders and onto the floor. Nude, she tapped the second button to activate the motor to open the door. The wind blew into the condo, tossing the drapes and caressing her skin. Sparky barked at the breeze that blew in, interrupting the moment.

"Shut up, fleabag." She stepped out onto the balcony and took a long drink of the wine.

"I don't like it when you call him fleabag. He has a name."

Doris inhaled, as if smelling the fragrance of a flower. The man's Cockney British accent used to be an aphrodisiac to Doris. Of late, it resembled stale bread.

"Yes, Michael, I know. And it is a fleabag."

"Sparky is well behaved. There was only that one time when I had… he had to poo in Central Park."

"Yeah, and I almost had to pay a fine because I didn't have a poop bag." She took another deep drink from the glass. "I had to *convince* the police officer it was just a brown rock."

Doris turned and saw the wheelchair rolling across the room toward her. His chin moved away from the control, stopping the chair before rolling over her dress and shoes. She watched

Michael's eyes run up and down her skinny frame, her aged skin, her gravity-stricken breasts.

"I look old to you." She leaned back against the railing, her glass dangling in her hand.

"I did not say that."

Doris leaned her head to the right. "No, but I know your thoughts. Even the ones you aren't thinking."

Michael nudged the control for the chair, looking for a way to maneuver around her clothes. "You are just as beautiful now as when we first met."

"Fifty years ago? Bullshit. If that's true, I must have been damn ugly back then, too."

"When I had my choice of any southern California woman, it was your charm that drew me to you."

"Ah, so I am ugly." Doris turned away from him, thrusting her ass toward him as she propped her elbows on the railing, taking another sip of wine.

"You still have the figure of the eighteen-year-old woman I met fifty years ago."

"Hardly. My tits didn't droop like this back then. Not to mention my ass."

Michael raised an eyebrow. Doris didn't see him do it, but she could sense it. She could feel every neuron firing his brain. Being paralyzed below his neck, there weren't that many.

"Perhaps. I wasn't in a wheelchair either."

"Another pity party, Michael? Is that what this is? Pity for each other?"

Doris downed the last of the wine in her glass. This conversation was going where it always goes. She turned and looked at him. Once a tall, proud Englishman now held captive by the cords attached to his body. But today was not the time to discuss health care. She had a young woman to deal with.

Michael backed the chair away from the balcony door. "So what did you learn from the NSA?"

"You were there, or at least your mind was." She waved the empty glass at the poodle as she stepped back inside, heading for the refrigerator.

"I can't hear what others are thinking as you can, only mind swap with them. I know what they said. What did you learn while you were inside their heads?"

She heard the chair spin around and follow her. Doris scoffed as she poured another glass.

"And what makes you think—"

"Doris, please. I know you. Fifty years, remember? You can't help but go probing other people's brains, looking inside for any secrets they may hide. It is as if everyone's mind is a new playground to explore."

She took another drink of wine.

"And why was that young girl there? Didn't we see her in Russia just yesterday?"

"Yes, that was her and her brother. They flew back this morning, after letting several hundred escape. According to Harris' pee brain." Doris put a finger up to her chin. "I think I have to talk with her boyfriend. He'll know. She can't keep anything from him."

"Did he have something for you when you talked yesterday?"

"Oh, he had something for me, yes." A smile flashed across her lips.

Michael's eyes narrowed. "You had sex with him, didn't you?"

Doris ignored his comment. "Marc has to convince that girl to drop her investigation of the explosion. Maybe take a vacation someplace. I must convince his commanding officer to give him some time off."

"Who was the woman she was with?"

Doris tilted her head. "What woman?"

"There were two women sitting at the table across the room. One was the girl, the other was someone new. I had not smelled her before."

"What are you talking about? Lani was by herself."

"No, there was another person next to her. Maybe another telepath, blocking you from seeing her."

"No one has ever hidden from me."

Michael smirked. "Not that you know of, anyway."

Doris splashed the red wine on his pajama top as she strutted past him. Surprised, Sparky jumped from his lap and skittered to his bed by the balcony window.

*"Screw you, Michael. If there was someone else there, you should have said something."*

*"If you were expecting her to be alone, you should have said something."*

In the bedroom, she sat her wineglass on her bedroom dresser and opened a drawer. She sighed at the sight of Michael wheeling through the great room toward her. Doris stepped into her enormous closet, shoving clothes aside as she searched for what to wear next. A few minutes passed before she strutted out of the closet, buttoning the blouse of an Air Force officer's uniform. The rank insignia of Colonel stitched on the collar and a black, plastic nameplate with Kutcher on it over her left breast pocket completed the outfit. It was tight-fitting around her thin frame. She ran her hands along the seams over her hips, enjoying the sensation.

She stepped for the door, but Michael's wheelchair blocked the way. The red wine had soaked into his white pajamas, giving it a rose-colored stain. She pointed past Michael, toward Sparky. "Are you coming with me?"

"No, not this time. You know how cranky he gets when he teleports with you so much."

"Just as well, an Air Force base isn't the place for a poodle, anyway."

She watched as his eyes ran up and down her body.

"Nor is his bedroom."

Doris wanted to slap him across the face, the only place he might feel it. Then again, she wasn't sure if he would feel even that. Tilting her head to one side, hands on her hips, she waited for him to move. Instead, Michael remained defiant. Doris reached for the wineglass, took a step forward, and teleported into the kitchen. Pouring another sip of wine, she heard the powered wheelchair as he chased after her.

"Close the balcony door before you leave, please."

"Close it yourself," she whispered as she envisioned her next location and vanished.

*Tuesday, April 16*
*Day of the Explosion*

The sands of Miami's South Beach were full of Spring Break visitors at nine in the morning, many left over from last night. The high-powered boats skimmed up and down the coast, pulling kite-riders, dodging the huge cruise liners and cargo ships leaving the Port of Miami.

Phone pressed against her ear, Doris paced across the living room of her condo. Stepping through the open floor-to-ceiling windows overlooking the Miami South Beach area, the morning sun warmed her through her lacy pink nightie. Michael sat in his usual morning spot—sipping breakfast tea on the 37th floor balcony while reading the news on his tablet. She could read the headlines across the top of the screen. *President Taylor To Meet With Mutants In Michigan Today.*

"Mr. Williams, please. Don't worry. This is what Aquarius Group does. We find mutants that are rising stars looking for help in their climb up the ladder—corporate or political. Just like you."

The caller whispered. "I think Bill—"

"Please, Larry. You need to do two things. First, let us handle your campaign manager." Doris stopped to take a drink of wine. "And second, and most important, don't reveal your abilities.

Okay?"

Larry's nervous voice came through quietly. "Okay, but what about—?"

"Mr. Williams, listen. Under no circumstances do you let slip your ability to levitate. I don't care how fast or how far. No more floating up to save Frisky from the tree or whatever, understood?"

Doris swapped hands. She was lecturing him; she knew that. It was something she's had to do with every client. At least the ones she didn't mentally *adjust*.

"I will talk with your campaign manager, and we will work out the details of your election to the US Senate. You need to focus on keeping your abilities under wraps."

Michael stared at her. Actually, at her hips. Doris snapped her fingers, shaking her head. He lifted his gaze to her eyes, smiling. She sighed and walked away from his view.

"Okay. Mr. Williams? Listen, I have to go now. I have another client waiting just outside. We will talk again later this week. How about Friday? We can go over your schedule for the rest of April."

"Yeah, okay. Friday's good."

"Okay. Good day, Mr. Williams. Good bye."

She tapped the button to end the call and tossed the phone onto the couch. "Why are they all the same?" she asked herself.

"So, what was Williams' deal?" Michael sat the tablet next to his teacup on the table.

"Paranoid, as usual." Doris shouted from the kitchen, setting the glass in the sink. "How many years have we been doing this? Nearly forty-five years, placing mutants into positions of power." She turned on the water and rinsed her hands. "And each one of them not ready to give their lives over to us so we can improve their chance of doing something with themselves that helps them deal with their powers."

"I know, I know." Michael came into the kitchen and stood behind her. He wrapped his arms around her and nuzzled her on the neck. "And in all those years, we've had twice that many successes. Not one of them has exposed us for the power brokers that we are."

Doris spun in his arms, soaking up the heat from his white silk pajamas. "None have exposed us, but not all of our clients have kept their powers hidden."

"True, but you yourself know how difficult it is to keep such *power* in check."

Looking into his eyes, Doris could feel herself being drawn into him. Her vision narrowed into a tunnel, seeing only his eyes. He was trying to mind swap with her. She pushed out with her own powers, mentally finding him and stopping him, kicking him out of her consciousness.

"Michael, stop." She teleported out from his arms to a spot three feet away from him. "Now's not the time. Go get dressed."

"Killjoy." He turned to face her. "Just looking to practice my skills before we leave for Michigan."

Doris shook a finger at him. "Nah, ah. I know what you want. Same thing you always do when you're in a woman's body."

Michael shrugged his shoulder, palms turned upward. "I can't help myself."

"Because you're a pervert." She teleported away from him. Through the closed bedroom door, his English accent boomed. "You still love me."

Doris fell back against the door. She wasn't so sure about that.

Dressed in a black pantsuit and white button-down shirt, Doris fidgeted with the earpiece and clear spiral cord that stuck out from the back of her collar. Getting it to stay in her ear, she stepped out of the bathroom and walked past the king-size bed. She put a hand on the white comforter to steady herself while she slipped on the black, low-heel shoes. Standing upright, she glimpsed herself in the full-length mirror by the bedroom door.

"Black, ugh. Makes agents look so ordinary." She wrinkled her nose in disgust.

She smoothed her hand print out of the bedspread and walked into the living room. Michael was standing there, arms crossed, a smile on his face. He wore the same Secret Service agent outfit.

"Ready to go play good guys for a change?" He rose on his tiptoes twice.

Doris frowned at him. "You didn't shave."

"I don't need to shave." He ran a hand across his chin. The two-day-old growth was coming through in a salt-and-pepper pattern, matching his hair.

"Yes, you need to shave. Secret Service agents are clean-shaven. Especially the ones on President Taylor's team." She stood, pointing to the second bathroom in the condo. His bathroom.

Michael let out a *humph* as he strode away from her. "Can't you give me the appearance of being clean-shaven?"

"No, it will take too much of my concentration away from everything else I have to project."

She walked up to the glass doors and opened them, stepping out onto the balcony of their thirtieth-floor condo. From this height, she could see the people moving along the beach, the waves rolling in, and the power boats pulling paragliders. Doris took in the view, waiting for Michael to shave. It wasn't long before he joined her side on the balcony.

She tucked an arm under his, moving in close. He placed his arm across her back, holding her tight.

"I so love this view, this location," Doris sighed.

"And it was so nice of the former owners to sell it to us for pennies on the dollar." Michael leaned his head over against hers.

"I recall you almost slipped up when you listed the price at the sale, in front of the banker." Doris snickered.

"Well, his wife kept grabbing at my leg."

A breeze brought the smell of the ocean salt, invigorating Doris. "You don't miss DC, do you?"

Michael released her to glance down at her. "Washington? Bloody hell. Glad to get away from there. I know you don't miss it."

"No, it was time to move on." Doris sighed. "We lost Antonio twelve years ago when he ran for Governor of New Mexico."

"A shame. Your boyfriend brought us many of the successes you mentioned." Michael stepped back from her, moving toward the wet bar. "Now, as Vice-President, he's still a pain in the arse."

Doris followed him, watching as he poured a double shot of bourbon. "What do you mean by that?"

"You know what I mean. We've been cleaning up his messes for twelve years now." He spoke into the glass. "Or at least I have."

Doris moved in front of him. "You?"

Michael swirled the liquid in the glass. "Yeah, me. He's the empath. He changes someone's emotions. You, you're the telepath. You mess around with people's thoughts. When he couldn't and you couldn't, you relied on me to make it happen."

Her eyes narrowed. "Each of us has our strengths and weaknesses."

"Partly right. You couldn't make Knight stop work on his device. Antonio couldn't convince Taylor to stop wanting the damn thing. Now you need me to go into the bitch's mind and use her voice. To announce to the world she's stopping work on the project to appease the rest of the mutant world from tearing apart the work we've been trying to do behind everyone's back."

"Because we were a team."

"Because you are weak and getting weaker."

Doris' hand flew up, moving across his cheek, knocking the glass from his hand as it moved to his lips. The glass shattered on the marble countertop. Her hand reflexed back to her face, covering her gasping mouth.

"Michael, I'm sorry." She couldn't believe she swung at him. In all the years they've been friends, it was the first time she had slapped him. Her hand quivered as it moved toward his face.

He jerked his head away, four red welts forming on his skin. "I suppose I had that one coming."

Michael grabbed for a white towel on the bar, picking up the shards of glass as he soaked up the amber liquid spreading on the counter. He went around the bar and dropped the glass pieces into the small trash can, then rinsed the cloth and his hands in the sink.

"Perhaps we best be on our way." He dried his hands on a different cloth, keeping his eyes away from her. "Don't want to be late for the conference."

Doris watched his eyes, trying to gauge what he was feeling. She couldn't tell. She always relied on Antonio to do that, then share with her. All she could do was hear Michael's thoughts, which were on the conference, the speech she had written for him to give after he swapped with President Taylor. He was throwing her off, blocking his true thoughts from her.

But his words gave away his feelings. She had no idea he felt like that. How could she not see it?

"Mutant-Human Conference." Michael rolled his eyes. "Bollocks! At least I get to play the American President this time instead of some stuffy corporate CEO."

"Ms. Holly Taylor, most powerful woman in the world. You're

gonna love that, aren't you?" She probed his mind again, seeing the mission, not the sting of her strike.

Doris held her hand out, slinking her fingers across his palm, and grabbed it tight. "Fine. Hang on so I can teleport us to Michigan." She focused her thoughts, envisioning a lecture hall in the University. In a second, a veil lowered over them and they vanished.

The siren from the motorcycle police in front of the Presidential motorcade whooped as it closed in on the University of Michigan campus. President Holly Taylor glanced out the front windshield of her armored vehicle and caught sight of a mass of police and the public between them and the building where the auditorium was at. Sitting on the broad seat in the back of the vehicle, she swayed back and forth as the car drove off the street and onto the driveway near the building.

She held her makeup mirror in front of her, checking to make sure her red lip gloss was picture perfect. She let out a sigh, then wiggled to sit higher in the seat. Today was not about the conference, not about mutants or humans. It was about her re-election campaign. But most of all, today was about the man sitting across from her, and the little gizmo he built for her.

Zach sat, eyes glazed over, with a humorless smile on his face. The briefcase on his lap slid off and fell onto the carpeted floor, leaving his hands to drop onto the seat cushion. He was a pathetic fool to her. She was certain he had no idea what he had created, all on her request. And her charm. She shook her head, hoping she had picked the right man for the job. After all, he had his son to experiment on. Now if he could only get the damn thing to work.

"Get the halo working. Today." She reached down to slip on her high heels. "I don't care what it takes. I want a demonstration today. If not at the keynote, then at the briefing after. Understood?" She snapped her fingers, releasing him from the influence of her charm.

Zach blinked several times, falling out of his stupor. "Yes, ma'am." He rubbed his eyes, clearing the sleep from them. He glanced out the thick shaded glass. "Are we here already?"

"Now be a good boy and smile for the cameras." She licked her thumb and wiped a red smudge off of his cheek. "But not too much. No need to raise any more suspicion than we need."

"Yes, ma'am." He looked at her and his euphoric appearance returned. She snapped her fingers again, forcing him to blink rapidly.

A Secret Service agent outside the vehicle reached for the door handle. He moved to block her from the cameras and public as she got out of the limousine. She brushed the wrinkles out of her bright red skirt, then threw her blonde hair back off of her shoulders. Satisfied at her appearance, the agent stepped aside and Holly headed toward the sidewalk leading to the two-story building.

A loud cheer went up as the crowd caught sight of her. She waved with her typical *Queen's* wave, her backhand toward the public, keeping her distance from the hands reaching out to touch her. A slightly louder cheer went up, and Holly paused. Behind her, Zach was walking along a line of students. Trying to not frown, she snapped her fingers for Zach to catch up with her.

She smiled and waved once more before walking up to the revolving door at the entrance. White House photographers and Secret Service agents cluttered the lobby. Stepping clear of the doors, searching through the people, she shouted for her Chief of

Staff.

"Carolyn!"

"Here, Madam President." Carolyn Sayers squeezed through the flashes of light from a photographer. "This way. We have a break room ready for us." Carolyn pointed down a hallway, then led the way, an entourage of interns and agents trailing behind them.

The vacant lecture hall Doris envisioned solidified around her and Michael as the veil lifted and the teleport was completed. Michael shivered, breaking the grip Doris had on his hand.

"Ah, what a rush," he whispered, rubbing his arms. "Always so cold when we do that."

"I never notice." Doris said. Being able to teleport since the age of 14, she didn't know the science behind her power, only the benefits. She never needed a driver's license, or a passport. The world, to her, was a heart-beat away.

Michael was first at the door, peaking through the thin vertical window in the door. "No one outside." He pulled the door open and stuck his head into the hall.

"Gee, that's not obvious," Doris grabbed him by the shoulder and pulled him out of the way. She walked out into the hallway, heading for the center of the building. "I put us on the second floor. The lecture hall the President will be speaking is on the first floor. Everyone will be down there."

"Know about a place before you teleport." Michael rushed to catch up with her. "How did you learn so much about this place?"

"That college student that approached us last year." She implanted a vision in Michael's mind of a young black woman, close-cut curly hair, black pantsuit.

Michael smirked. "Ah, yes. Asmara, the duplicator."

"I got her on the White House staff as an intern. Best I could do for her. But I put a tag in her mind. I can see everything she does. And right now, she is following along behind the President." Doris pointed downward, off to her right. "Right down there."

They walked down the wide central staircase, finding the lobby still full of Secret Service, directing reporters and civilians down a corridor to the left.

"All these people here because of the President?" Michael asked.

"Yep."

"Bloody hell."

Connecting with the minds of the crowd of reporters, White House staff, and Secret Service agents, Doris opened a path for them. Following the trail of the intern, she stopped at a door to a conference room. She sensed Michael's thoughts, ready to get this going, and opened the door.

Cabinet lined the break room over a double sink. Vending machines stood at one end, coffee maker at the other. Two small circular tables sat in the center of the room, one being filled with snacks, finger foods, chips, and dip, all available for the picking.

President Taylor sat, legs crossed at the second table, her hands holding a cup of coffee at her lips. The steam rising from the cup was a thin wisp of cotton. Taylor's chief of staff sat to her right, stylus in hand, pressed to a tablet on the table in mid-stroke of a word. Asmara stood at the sink, water flowing over her hands. To the three women, Doris' telepathy-induced mental paralysis made it appear as if Time had stopped moving.

Doris walked to the table and glared at the President. "What the hell do you have in mind today?"

"Do you think she's a mutant also?" Michael asked, pouring a glass of champagne. "Maybe that's why you couldn't change her mind, or Knight's?"

"It's possible. We won't know until you go in there." Doris pointed at Holly's forehead. She pulled a chair to the threesome's table for Michael to sit in.

"Don't worry. I'll be in your head the whole time." Doris tapped on her temple, then pointed at him.

"Nothing new there. Make sure *she* stays put for the duration." Michael sat across from President Taylor, who was still conversing with her entourage. "We don't need her wandering around in my body while I'm on stage inside hers."

"Holly will be asleep and these two ladies won't see you or me standing here." Doris looked around the room. "There's no closet in here, so I'll have one of the Secret Service agents carry you back to the room upstairs where we popped in."

Wiggling in his seat, elbows on the table, Michael looked into the President's eyes and concentrated. Although he had done this over a thousand times—send his consciousness into another person's mind and have theirs enter his—the act of mind swapping was exhilarating.

Everything around Holly's face faded from view. Her white hair vanished. The wrinkles around the temples of the sixty-seven-year-old woman went blurry. Everything other than her eyes disappeared. Soon, he was zooming into her eyes and her mind. He caught a flash of light, a blurred image of President Taylor, coming toward him, passing by him. Then there was darkness.

He blinked, and the view came into focus. He was staring at himself, his eyes closed, his head leaning to the left.

"Well, alright then. Let's check out the goods." He brought her hands up in front of her. Hands wrinkling, a plain gold band ring on her left hand. He recalled that her husband had passed away some years ago from cancer. Holly reached for her breasts and squeezed. He could feel the flesh, the nerves, the nipples. He searched through Holly's memories. "And a bonus prize, real tits."

"Michael, shush. Remember to use her American speech pattern, not your English accent." Doris stood behind Michael's body, holding him from falling out of the chair. "Get ready, I'm going to release them."

The two women beside her came back to life, returning to their conversation. Michael had no clue what it was about.

"—or we can go to Lansing, which I don't recommend. Personally." Carolyn continued her conversation. She looked to Holly, her eyes opening wide. "Ma'am?"

Holly lowered her hands and tugged at her dress slightly. "I'm sorry, Carolyn. You were saying?"

"I was asking about dinner tonight? Did you want to accept the Governor's invitation or not? It would be local instead of traveling to Lansing."

"Oh, here in Ann Arbor will be fine." Michael searched Holly's memories, learning that she grew up here. A great Italian restaurant came to mind. "At the Intermezzo. It has been a while since I've eaten in my hometown."

Michael had had the luxury of studying the President's speech for several days, getting down the phrases, the inflections. He didn't have to worry about mimicking her voice, just the way she talked and moved. She didn't use her hands to talk, but used her facial expressions to emphasize her words.

The door opened, and an agent entered. Doris pointed toward Michael's body. She and the agent walked over to him and helped stand him up. Doris pointed at Holly. "Don't go away."

Holly nodded as the other two women at the table continued going over who should be at the dinner tonight. They paid no attention to Michael's body, Doris, and the agent as they left the room.

The President stood up and walked to the food. She picked up a carrot stick and dipped it in the veggie spread. Just as she bit down on it, she felt a hunger pang for roast beef and mayonnaise. Frowning, he wasn't sure why that combination would taste good together. It wasn't anything he would eat. She moved to the end and grabbed the champagne bottle again. One clean glass remained, and she filled it.

"Madam President?" Carolyn asked, a confused look on her face.

"Yes?" Holly asked before taking a drink.

Carolyn stood up and walked to Holly, taking the glass from her hand. She offered a bottle of water instead.

"You know very well you should not drink any alcohol before going on stage."

"Yes, I suppose you are right."

Michael's consciousness explored his new host body. She differed from the other humans he had mind swapped with. It was like drinking water, but Holly was like sparkling water. Then he realized. *The president is a bloody mutant. The witch.*

He noticed nothing in particular, no special senses, no energy beam powers. He realized that when the Chief of Staff and assistant looked at the President; they smiled. It wasn't just a polite smile; it was a look of admiration, of love.

Her ability was enhanced charisma. She could make people love her without even trying. Her landslide election three years ago made sense now. Her memories told him everything. It was an aura about her. Whenever people came close to her, they fell into her power, and fell in love with her. It was something she could control, which was why he didn't fall for her when he walked into the room.

There was a knock at the door before it opened. A different agent stuck his head in.

"Zach Knight, ma'am."

*"Bloody hell."* The President smiled and motioned, waving to let him in.

Carolyn and the two assistants collected their papers from the table and walked to the door. "Madam President," Carolyn said. "We have just a few minutes before heading for the stage. Call if you need me."

Holly raised an eyebrow. Interesting that the President's Chief of Staff knew to leave the room when Knight is here. Inside of her mind, Michael scanned Holly's memories for her history with Zach. Her jaw dropped open. She has had sex with him. Several times. That's why he's working on the suppressors.

Zach entered the room and stepped aside for the women to leave. He nodded to them as they walked past him.

Holly stood against the table, pushing a tray of cookies back so nothing brushed against her dress. "Zach Knight. What do you have for me today?" She pointed to the briefcase he was carrying.

He moved to the small table and laid it down. "The working version of the suppressor, ma'am." He worked the number locks on the case and popped up the latches. Zach raised the top half and reached in, retrieving a thin silver headband, an inch and a half in height, three sets of LED lights on it.

"As I said in the limo, I should be able to make it smaller and thin out the emitters on the inside." Zach held it so Holly could see the pads attached to the inner side.

"Why don't you put that away and come here?" She looked at him and projected a charm toward him, a feeling of wanting, of desire. Being able to swap minds with a woman allowed him to experience sex from a woman's point of view, to feel the difference, knowing what it was like on the male and the woman.

Doris and he would have sex in the opposite bodies frequently until she caught him hacking her memories while humping himself.

A smile appeared on Zach's face. Without looking away from her, he dropped the suppressor inside the case and walked to her. He pushed up against her, his arms reaching across her hips, around to her lower back.

"I have missed you so much." His voice was low and loving, leaning in to kiss her.

Holly put her hands on his shoulders and pulled him closer. She kept her eyes on Zach's, making sure not to lose the hook she had on him.

"Maybe you can show me how much you missed me."

He pressed her lips to his, but there was no reaction from him. Holly leaned back and blinked, staring at Zach, waiting for it. Zach wasn't blinking.

*"What the hell do you think you are doing?"* Doris screamed in Michael's mind.

Holly looked over Zach's shoulders at Doris, standing at the door.

"What does it look like? She's a charmer."

"Nah. Hell no." Doris looked at Holly with discontent. She grabbed Zach by the shoulders and pulled him away.

"Oh, come on." Holly pouted. He could tell Doris was trying to wipe Zach's memory of this moment, maybe implanting a distinct memory.

"Now get ready. It's time to go on stage."

Holly walked to the small table and Zach's briefcase. Pulling the suppressor out and holding it up for Doris to see, he said, "This is the reason we are here."

"Fine. I'll make sure he brings it. Now go find your girls and get out there."

Doris led the way down the corridor full of people, half Secret Service, half University staff. President Taylor marched behind her, Zach in tow behind her. Doris mentally search for Asmara to get a sense of where to go. She found her standing next to Carolyn, waiting off stage. Carolyn stopped Holly, brushing off her shoulders and handing her a tissue to wipe the lipstick from her teeth. Doris stepped to the edge of curtain to check out the audience.

The seating in the auditorium curved, stairs splitting it into three sections with a wide passage cutting them in half. Cameras from the various media outlets filled the passage. Reporters with microphone raised to their face spoke to the lenses, probably talking to anchors at the news center. Clearly filled over capacity, Doris estimated a thousand people in the place. Many appeared as professionals—those dressed in a suit and tie—taking up one-third of those gathered up front. Students and the public took up the rest of the front and the whole of the back.

A single podium stood on the far side of the stage, a mass of microphones in front and two teleprompters screens at the front corners. The back of the stage was a gigantic screen, made up of small LED screens.

Standing off stage behind the curtains, Doris probed around those around her to learn the agenda for the day. Zach would emcee, followed by the President, who would talk for forty-five to sixty minutes. She hooked her head. Nothing worse than a politician who loved to hear his or her own voice. Mutants were introverts, hiding their superhuman powers. Politicians were just the opposite, having to speak to large groups of people, getting their positions on topics out to the voters. Who better to do that than someone who loved to talk.

She followed as the audience's attention spun to a group of

people being escorted to the reserved seating front and center of the audience. Cameras panned to the woman and two men entering from the outer hallway. Doris recognized each of them, either by reputation or as a client. Dressed in suit and tie, the lead man was Joshua Barnhill, Secretary of Mutant Affairs. He hired Aquarius Group four years ago, a mutant with telekinesis. Doris and Michael were able to get him a position as Deputy Secretary in the Department of Energy and became a darling to Holly when she was looking for someone to lead her new Mutant Affairs department.

The leaders of Mutant Defense Foundation, James Seaton and Heather Lovett, followed behind him. A pro-mutant organization, they led the Million Mutant March on Washington last July. If she was a Southerner, she would have spit on the ground. They were interlopers, promoting a peaceful existence between humans and mutant. Not that it was a bad idea, but not what Doris was ready for. Whereas their efforts were overt, Aquarius Group's plan to put mutants in power was more covert, and definitely illegal.

Doris mentally felt activity behind her. A man wearing a wireless headset had gotten Zach's attention. Zach stepped away from Holly and Carolyn, toward Doris. She tried to get a ping on Zach, casting the illusion around her as just another Secret Service agent.

He stopped shoulder to shoulder with her, a smirk on his face. "Hello, Doris."

Doris' eyes flew wide open, her mouth gaping slightly.

*"How does he know who I am? I should look like someone else to him."*

Without an answer, he strode out onto the stage.

The back half of the audience roared into cheers, whistles, and applause. Zach raised his hand to wave, pointing to someone in particular in the back of the audience. He stopped behind the podium and tapped on the microphones.

"Thank you, thank you. Welcome to the Second Mutant-Human Conference."

More applause interrupted him, many in the back behind the bank of media cameras standing. Zach waved for them to settle down, then spoke to today's series of speeches, meetings, and discussion panels.

Doris felt Michael's presence coming closer, being directed by Sayers.

"Hey, beautiful." Michael's British Cockney came through, strangely placed from the blonde woman.

"Midwest American, not North London." Doris reminded him.

Holly coughed, clearing her throat. "For forty-five bloody minutes. No guarantees after the first fifteen."

"If it sounds like you're drifting, I'll let you know."

She thought about telling him about Zach, what he had said, but that would distract him from the speech he was about to make, telling the world she was scrapping the halo project over complaints from the ACLU.

"… the President of the United States." Zach finished his introduction.

The audience stood, giving polite but not enthusiastic with their applause. Zach clapped as his eyes ventured to Doris and Holly.

Holly put her hands on her breast and pushed up. "Here goes nothing."

President Taylor stepped out from behind the curtain, waving to the crowd, making her way across the expanse. Zach met her halfway, reaching out to shake hands. Holly shook his hand, then made it to the podium.

A half-cocked smile came to Doris, pleased Michael practiced walking in high heels for several days prior to his moment. She recalled standing in his body, wincing each time her body took a step forward and twisting an ankle. Yet another time she regretted Michael and her swapping bodies.

"Thank you, thank you." Holly waved for everyone to take their seats. "It's good to be back at my alma mater, University of Michigan."

This time, the back half of the theatre lit up with whoops and hollers. Doris wondered how many of them she could shut up. She hated crowds, too many people to control mentally.

Zach stood beside her, an enormous smile on his face. Curious, she probed his mind, but was interrupted by a slamming door far back stage followed by shouting. She turned around in time to see Sayers and the intern back away from Secret Service Agent Michael Clarke.

Michael grabbed Carolyn at the elbows and shook her. "Carolyn, it's me, Holly!"

Carolyn screamed, her face contorted in fear.

"Oh, hell!" Doris mumbled. She spun toward the stage and the President. "Michael! Swap back!"

As she envisioned their condo in Miami, Doris' ears popped and a force shoved against her.

Sunday, August 4<br>Four Months After the Explosion

The buzzing of hedge clippers outside the study filtered inside the President's study at the Camp David compound. President Mendoza sat on the sofa, centered in the room, his feet kicked back on the coffee table as he watched one of the Sunday morning political talk shows. Sipping at the steaming cup of coffee, he was watching his Presidential candidate from the rival party comment on last week's nominating convention.

"He's a buffoon, Bill. The man barely carried his own state four years ago." A big, burly man, reddish brown beard that hung below his collar, moved in the tall chair, scooting himself back onto the cushion.

"Strong words, Senator Stephenson," the reporter said. "But he was only the VP on the ticket. You yourself said 'no one votes for the number two spot.'"

"What I said was that no one runs for the number two spot." Stephenson said.

Antonio stared at the wide-screen television from the sofa. *Can't wait to get on the debate stage with him.*

Stephenson continued. "Look, he got his party's nomination on a smile and a prayer. Maybe that should be his theme song— living on a prayer."

Antonio let go a humph and reached for the TV remote to mute the sound. "Bon Jovi. Not an awful choice, actually. Maybe a different song, though."

The past few months had been a whirlwind for him. Following President Taylor's death and the start of the investigating commission, led by the Chief Justice of the Supreme Court, Antonio had to pull the nation back from the brink of civil war while keeping his own party together as they fended off those from across the aisle.

He stood up and walked around the sofa, stopping to watch a pair of gardeners trimming hedges across the lawn. Antonio stretched his mind out toward the nearest man, sensing a pale yellow aura around him. The aura flashed to red as the gardener yanked his hand back, dropping the tool he was holding. The second gardener laughed, shouting something in Spanish. Antonio glimpsed a bluish aura around him, slowly shifting back to white.

Someone tapped on the open door to the study, pulling Antonio's attention back inside. He turned to see a tall man, balding across the top, standing at the door, a briefcase in one hand. "Good morning, Mr. President."

"Leonard!" Antonio walked back to the sofa for the remote and turned off the TV. "Come in. What are you doing up here?"

Supreme Court Chief Justice Leonard Addison took a step into the room and closed the door. "I found something you might be interested in. Mind if I close the door?"

Antonio waved him to join him at the sofa. They shook hands before sitting down. Leonard sat the briefcase on the coffee table in front of them, then leaned back, one elbow over the back of the chair.

"This have anything to do with the Harrison case?" Antonio asked, sensing a dark blue aura around the Chief Justice.

"No, sir. Ann Arbor." Leonard's aura was pure white, emotionless.

Antonio leaned his head to one side. "Oh shit. What did the Commission uncover?"

"Technically, they have uncovered nothing. Yet." Leonard turned back to the table and placed his thumb on the briefcase security lock. The latches popped open, and he raised it open. Inside sat a bent and mangled computer hard drive inside a gallon-size plastic bag. Large red letters read *Evidence. Do not open without proper authority.* Underneath was a digital tablet, a couple of cables, and battery power pack.

"The network used for the security videos was finally recovered. Sort of." Leonard inserted a finger under the tamper-proof seal on the bag and ran it across the words on the tape, unsealing it. He pulled the drive out of the bag and placed it next to the briefcase.

"This hard drive from the PC used for the video was delivered to me, to enter as evidence. The tech group told me that the drive was damaged beyond repair. It's an older model, still has a rotating disc inside. I arranged for a duplicate, undamaged, hard drive to be brought to me for comparison. In private, I restored the security hard drive."

Leonard waved his hand over the hard drive. The drive snapped and popped as it flexed and flattened. Antonio leaned back in the sofa, watching the hard drive become restored to its pre-explosion condition.

"Well, now." Antonio said.

"The surveillance camera had a motion detector associated with it, so it only took a snap when something in this hallway moved. It was a hallway directly under the auditorium."

Leonard connected the tablet to the hard drive, then connected the drive to the power pack. A series of folders appeared on the screen, each dated with a month and day. He double-tapped on the folder named Corridor 1B16. He pulled an index card from his jacket pocket with five file files as he handed the tablet to the President. Antonio double-tapped on the first file, launching a photo viewer app.

The camera view was from high on the wall, a hallway thirty feet long. A corner on the right wall close to the bottom of the photo showed another hallway to the right. A black oval filled the center of the hallway straight ahead, purple electrical sparked lining it. A man wearing a hoodie pushed a two-wheeled dolly with gas cylinders in front of the oval, his right leg is cut off, hidden inside the oval. The hoodie shades his face. The word Michigan is seen stenciled across the front of the hoodie. In the bottom left corner, the time *11:45 AM* stamped in orange.

"Okay, what am I looking at?"

"It appears someone has opened a portal and wheeled two bottles of hydrogen into the building. We know it is hydrogen because of the color of the cylinder and the symbol on its side." Leonard pointed at the bottles on the cart, then he pulled the photo from the stack.

"Two minutes later, the hooded man is pushing the bottle cart through a portal in front of the door to the furnace room."

"You're sure that's the furnace?" Antonio glanced at Leonard.

"I checked the camera location." Leonard pointed to orange numbers on another corner of the photo. "There's no question this caused the explosion, not a natural gas. I do not see this man leaving the room. My guess is that he created a portal while inside or died in the explosion."

"Which means he didn't know the layout of the room, just hallway." Antonio nodded, swiping across the screen to the next photo.

Time stamped at *12:01 PM*, the short white lines of static

covered the photo, making the view blurry. Half of a man's body —head, arm and shoulder, leg and hips—walked out of the wall on the right side of the hallway.

Antonio waved his hand across the photo. "Why the static?"

"The video was clear until he stepped through the wall," Leonard said. "After he clears the wall, the static stopped. That didn't happen with the first man, so I think it was a unique power that somehow messes with electronics."

The next photo was clear of static as the man turned to his left, toward the camera. Slightly taller and muscular than the man with the hydrogen bottles, he wore a waist-length jacket with US flag patches on the shoulders and another over the left breast.

"Not trying to hide." Antonio stabbed at the photo. "I think I know that man."

"Thought you might." A mischievous grin slowly came to Leonard's face.

The last photo, also static-covered, showed the same man walking through the door to the furnace room. The time in the corner read *12:10 PM*.

"No portal," Antonio said.

"The explosion occurred less than a minute later."

Antonio went back to the fourth photo. "Have you identified him?"

"Possibly, but I'd like to confirm it." Leonard disconnected the cable and closed the briefcase, hiding the evidence bag and the disc drive. "Is John here?"

"That's who." Antonio snapped his fingers. He pulled his phone from his shirt pocket and dialed up John Black, his Chief of Staff. "Can you come to the study, please? Thanks."

A minute passed before a double knock on the door. The door clicked and John stepped into the room. "Yes, Mr. President?"

Antonio and Leonard stood and approached, the President

lifting a leg to sit on the back of the sofa. Leonard held the tablet for John to see. "Can you identify this man?"

Antonio focused his eyes on John. He reached into his mind, feeling, searching for any emotion he was experiencing. A bluish aura encircled him, showing that John was relaxed. The aura changed to a pale yellow, flowing outward, but the calm remained.

John shrugged his shoulders, then looked up at them. "Clearly not his best side."

"John, I need confirmation." Antonio said. "Who is he?"

John waved, pointing a finger at the photo. "That's Mark, my son."

Leonard leaned against the sofa, crossing one leg over the other. "Where's your son right now?"

John stuffed his hands in his pant pockets. "He's stationed in Alaska. Thayer Air Force Base."

"Have you talked with him recently?" Leonard continued the questioning.

"Right before Independence Day." John gave a quick nod. "He said he had to go on flight ops over the holiday and wouldn't be able to talk that week." John shifted his weight from one leg to another. "So, what's he done know?"

Antonio noticed the aura around John turned to a deeper yellow, flowing faster outward. *He's curious, wanting for information.* The President squared up with his Chief of Staff. "I have to ask you a private question. You aren't under any obligation to answer."

John raised an eyebrow. "Yes, Mr. President, anything."

"Is Marc a mutant?"

The aura around John quickly switched to a charcoal gray, pulling in toward him. Antonio tried to control the change of emotion, pushing a blue calm into John. The aura lightens into a bluish gray, settling on a periwinkle.

John nodded. "Yes, sir. He can walk through walls and become invisible. He calls it being *intangible*."

"Has he registered his abilities with the Air Force?"

"Yes, sir." John crossed his arms over his chest. "Excuse me, but being a dad, I gotta ask why you're asking?"

Antonio smiled, pushing a deep calm into John. "Can't really disclose that right now. But let me get back to you later, if you don't mind."

John nodding, dropping his hands back to his pockets. "Yes, sir. If there's nothing else, I'll get back to my argument with reporters out at the fence. They've been asking if you have any replies about Stephenson's comments this morning."

Antonio laughed. "Other than he's a piece of shit, yeah, no comment. And you can quote me on that."

John laughed and turned toward the door. Before leaving, "I may paraphrase that a bit, sir."

They stood staring at the door for what Antonio estimated at four breaths before he looked at Leonard. "Recommendations?"

The Chief Justice shrugged his shoulders. "The drive must be returned and entered as evidence. It will have a 'Do Not Tamper' order on it, of course, meaning no one will do what we just did. Option 1 would be to reveal the information on the hard drive, which would prompt an investigation of these two potential suspects. And reveal me and your Chief of Staff's son as mutants. Option 2 would be to do the investigation outside of the Commission, and risk being accused of withholding information from Congress."

Antonio looked at Leonard, holding his hand out for the tablet. "Sure is a shame that it damaged the hard drive beyond all repair. It would have provided so much information."

"Agreed, Mr. President." Leonard opened the briefcase and

waved his hand. The device bent and twisted back into the warped state. He grabbed the drive and placed the drive back in the bag. He waved his hand once more, resealing the evidence seal.

As Leonard closed up his briefcase, Antonio took the tablet over to his desk. Swiping across the screen, he deleted the photos from its memory.

"I trust these photos were the only copies."

Leonard stood at the door, tapping on the briefcase. "Correct, sir."

Antonio reached out to shake hands. "Thank you, Leonard. Now if you will excuse me, I need to make a phone call."

Leonard clasped the President's hand. "You should call Doris. She says hi."

Antonio grimaced at the name. "I doubt that very much."

Leonard echoed the grimace. His voice went gruff. "Well, she did, damn it. She could have said go screw yourself."

Antonio's eyes went open wide, realizing he pushed his own anger into Leonard. He saw the deep red around him and pushed to shift it back to the other end of the spectrum. "Leonard, I'm sorry. Thank you for conveying her message. Tell her I'll try to contact her and Michael next month when I'm in Miami."

A pleasant smile came to Leonard's face, then disappeared. "Michael is paralyzed. From the neck down."

Antonio's head snapped back at the news. "Damn. What happened?"

"They were in Ann Arbor. Apparently he had mind swapped with Holly just prior to the explosion."

*Friday, June 23*
*Present Day*

The white SUV came to a stop in front of the Pajarito Hotel in downtown Los Alamos. Erin swung the passenger door open and gasped as the dry heat blasted inside through the remaining pieces of cool air conditioning. For a woman who could command liquids to take on any shape and turn her flesh into a liquid, the lack of humidity felt like needles to her skin.

She tucked her long, platinum-blonde hair behind her ears, then bent down to collect the empty snack bags and water bottles around her feet. The ride from Albuquerque to Los Alamos was longer than she had expected. The bathroom break at Santa Fe didn't help. A break that Thandi M'bombo, one of her associate in the back seat, claimed to desperately need.

Erin tried to reach for the seat belt buckle, but with full hands, she opted to slide under the shoulder strap instead, allowing the lap belt to move through her as her flesh turned to water and back to flesh. The belt pulled her sleeveless blouse out of her slacks, which she regretted.

"God, it's hot here," Erin said, shading her eyes as she walked toward the trash bin under the concourse. "And you had to park us in the sun."

"I got this." Thandi clasped her hands, then pulled them apart slowly. A sphere of shadow formed between her hands, expanding out around her and farther around the car. The shade was enough to block the sunlight, but not the heat.

"But it's a dry heat, DK." Daiki Kobayashi waved his hand toward Erin and the trash in her hands disintegrated, turning to dust that flittered away in the dry breeze.

"Which is why it hurts even more. Washington didn't feel this hot." Erin waved her hands to keep the dust cloud away from her, then went back to the car and grabbed her purse from under the seat.

"That's because you prefer the humidity." Diego Rojas, the fourth member of the group, shouted from the back of the car, pulling suitcases out. "I don't think it's so bad."

"Girl," Thandi said, "I don't care. Humid or not, the sun is hot." Beads of sweat were forming on her forehead.

Daiki went to help Diego as Erin and Thandi entered the hotel lobby, heading for the front desk. Erin wiped her hands together, trying to rid her fingers of the stickiness of the candy wrapper she had picked up. She wiped her hand on her pant leg, expecting the jeans material would remove it. It didn't.

She glanced around the lobby, locating the breakfast bar and lounge area, including a popcorn maker with a twelve-inch layer of yellow popcorn inside. A gentleman in a business suit paced around the room, phone held up to his ear. Just down from the lobby, a hallway led to the pool. There were no signs for it, only the sick feeling in Erin's stomach from the potent smell of chlorine. She ran a hand down her upper arm; the chemical making her skin itch.

A slender Latina woman stepped out from behind the wall and moved to the counter. Her uniform matched the colors of the hotel sign out front, and much of the decor inside. Her name tag read *Javiera*.

"Good afternoon, ladies. Checking in?"

"Yes, we have a reservation under Murphy." Erin sat her purse on the counter and reached inside for her wallet. Unzipping it, she pulled out a credit card.

Javiera tapped at the keyboard, then scrolled up and down on the screen. Her forehead furrowed slightly, dropping her hands back to the keyboard. "I'm not seeing anything under that name."

"Try Kobayashi." Erin spelled it out for her. Again, Javiera shook her head.

"DK, did you put the reservation in under my name or yours?" Erin turned and looked toward the two men guiding four floating suitcases behind them. Diego's ability over gravity made the bags drift like three-day-old helium-filled balloons.

"Neither. MDF. I wasn't sure who was coming at the time I made them."

Erin frowned. "I thought we talked about that in DC last week." She turned to Javiera. "Look for an organization called Mutant Defense Foundation."

"Mutant Defense Foundation? I don't recognize your group. Have you stayed with us before?"

"No, this is our first time in town."

"Here it is. Three rooms, non-smoking, two Queen-size beds for one night only."

"Three rooms?" Erin looked over her shoulder to Daiki, cozying up behind her.

"Yeah, One for Thandi, one for Diego." He wrapped his arm around her, nuzzling against her neck. "And one for us."

She shrugged her shoulder, pushing him off. "Ah, no." She turned back to the desk clerk and held up two fingers. "Two rooms."

"Good, that will give me a room for Mr. Powell there." She pointed to the man pacing in the break area.

Erin raised an eyebrow, and the clerk beamed.

"We always get an influx of reporters when the President is at his residence. The hotel he had a reservation for overbooked."

Erin handed her the credit card, then grabbed an ink pen from the cup. The clerk went about her business, swiping the card, handing Erin the paperwork to sign, then preparing four door keycards for the rooms.

"Rooms 402 and 404. They are adjoining rooms if you want to open the doors between."

Erin didn't plan for that to happen. Four hours on the plane, two more in the car, plus the time at the President's home. More than enough time with the guys. Plus, she had plans for tonight that didn't include them.

"What time is our appointment?" Daiki checked his watch.

"Two o'clock," Erin answered. Looking to the clerk, "How long does it take to drive up to the President's from here?"

"I'm told the drive is only twenty minutes. I've never been there myself."

"Then that will give us plenty of time to get ready."

"And a bite to eat," Thandi said. "Those donuts from that last stop are fading fast." She stepped up to the counter. "Any delivery service around here?"

The clerk rattled off several phone apps that worked in town, then recommended two sandwich shops.

"Mutant Defense Foundation?" the clerk asked. "If I may ask, who do you represent?"

"We are an advocacy group supporting the rights of mutants." Erin gave just enough information, waiting for a reaction from her.

"Oh." Javiera's eyes went wide open. "Never heard of it."

"We stay under the radar," Erin said. "Some hotels don't care to have mutants as guests."

Javiera leaned forward. "Don't worry. My boyfriend is one. He can control fire and stuff. Cool when we go camping."

She was grinning. Erin guessed there was a memory tied to the smile. Erin reached into her wallet again and pulled out a business card.

"Here. Maybe we can meet with him tonight or tomorrow in the morning."

The desk clerk studied the card, then stuck it in her back pocket. "Thanks."

Erin passed out the door keycards, then latched on to her suitcase and pulled the handle up. "All right, boys and girls. Meet down here in ninety minutes."

"Yes, Mom." Phone in hand, Thandi's thumb moved all around the screen, looking for one of the restaurant apps Javiera mentioned.

Room 402 was three doors down from the elevator, the last door in the hallway being the staircase. Erin pulled her suitcase into the room and headed straight for the bed closest to the air conditioner. She let go of the suitcase handle and ran to the window unit. The setting was down as far to the left as it would go.

"You want anything from this sandwich shop?" Thandi stood by the other bed, her nose deep in the phone, fingers swiping up and down the screen.

"Small club, if they have anything like that. No tomatoes."

Erin tossed her suitcase onto the bed and frowned when it didn't bounce off of the mattress. She knew it would be another night is a semi-liquid state. She tugged at the long TSA tag wrapped around the handle; the adhesive sticking to her fingers as she pulled at it.

"Just have DK dissolve it."

Erin stopped pulling and glared at her roommate. "No, thanks. He'll just want to snoop inside."

"So, what's this thing with you and DK?" Thandi tossed her phone onto the bed and grabbed her suitcase.

"Mr. Macho? We broke up two months ago."

"Again? What, this the third time, right?"

Erin wrinkled her nose. Thandi and Erin were co-workers in the organization, but not a best friends to share intimate detail with. Details like a three-year-old daughter that looks less like her father and more like the man she can't stop loving.

"Office relationships are such a bad thing. My ex-husband was a lawyer at the firm I worked at. Didn't end so well. He divorced me after a few years."

"That's cause he's human and didn't understand how mutants work."

"Not so sure DK does either." Erin gave up on the TSA strip and flipped open the suitcase. She grabbed her overnight bag and headed for the bathroom. Unbuttoning her blouse, she flapped it open and closed to cool herself.

"You think?" Thandi's voice dripped with sarcasm. "He's even president of our group. Supposedly started it too, you know."

"Yeah, the protest wing. Others formed the political wing." Erin rummaged through the bag, pulling out a hairbrush.

"You mean Seaton and Lovett, the two that died in Ann Arbor at the Conference?"

"Well, protesters have a habit of getting shot at as well." Erin mumbled, not caring if Thandi heard or not. She ran a hand between her breasts, her fingers outlining the scar from the surgery to remove the bullet that struck her during an anti-mutant protest. That was also in Ann Arbor, four years before the Conference.

Out of the corner of her eye, Erin saw Thandi stand at the

bathroom door, leaning against the frame. "You still running for president of this motley crew, against DK?"

"Hell yes. I think he's taken it too far to the right, too militant. This group needs a lawyer at the top, not a warrior. I learned a lot from my job in DC, got lots of connections. More than I did from the law firm in New York."

"Just have to fight off DK for the top position, you know."

Erin nodded at her reflection in the bathroom mirror. "In more ways than one."

Thandi tilted her head. "That's why you two broke up, ain't it?"

"Yeah. He didn't take well to the breakup, either." Erin turned the cold water on and reached for a washcloth.

"So, you going against him for a little revenge?"

Erin shook her head. "Nah. Strictly about the group. For me, anyway."

"Alright. Going down to get the food. Another bottle of water?"

"Yes. Two, please. There's a five-dollar bill in the side pocket of my purse."

"That's okay. As treasurer, I think I can pull a few dollars out of the budget." Thandi chuckled.

Erin listened as the door clicked closed. Soaking the washcloth, she wrung it out and held it against the back of her neck. Her body absorbed the water, the coolness sending chills down her spine. Goosebumps followed the cloth as she pulled it across her shoulder and down her arm.

Erin ran it under the water again, placing it on her upper chest this time. A small rivulet of water traveled down, disappearing into her skin before reaching the small bow on her bra. Just above the scar from the surgery, the bullet, the protest against mutants.

"Cooling off?"

Erin jumped at the male voice. She spun around, water from the faucet leaping into her hand in the shape of a knife. Relaxing when she saw Daiki standing in the bathroom doorway, she held the liquid over the basin, releasing it from her control.

"What the hell, DK? How'd you get in here?" Erin reached for the collar of her blouse and buttoned it.

"Adjoining rooms, remember? I *dusted* the latch." He put an elbow high on the door frame. "You know, there was a time you would get undressed for me."

"Long past." She hated the smug look on his face. Always so damned confident. She pushed past him and sat at the small table near the window. "What do you want?"

Daiki pushed her suitcase aside and sat on the bed. "I thought we'd go over today's agenda."

"We covered the meeting with the president on the flight, and on the drive up here."

"I don't mean that. I mean you and your boyfriend."

"What?" Erin shook her head. "I don't have a boyfriend, DK. I told you, that's not why I broke up with you."

"No, I mean your old boyfriend, from college."

"Who, Adam?"

"Yeah, the Secret Service guy."

"DK, I haven't spoken to him in years."

Daiki turned to study the contents of Erin's suitcase. He stretched over and snatched a pink nightshirt.

"Daiki Kobayashi, put those back." Erin stood up and reached for the underwear. He yanked his hand back, keeping them away from her.

"Cotton, nice. Doesn't take much to make cotton decompose." He plucked at a button on her blouse, causing her to step back. "Now plastic and polyester takes a bit, but easily done."

"DK, come on. What do you want?"

"What if he's there, Erin?"

"So what? I'm sure the President has lots of mutant blockers on his staff."

"He's the reason we're meeting with Mendoza, here at his residence."

"Secretary Saunders wasn't available. I wanted to get this report done."

"Bullshit, Erin." Daiki stood up, her nightshirt tight in his fist before her face. "I called her office. They said you cancelled the meeting. The meeting I sat up."

"Look, the report is mine as secretary to give per the Bylaws established years ago. You don't give the damn report. I do. And I'll do it when and to who I damn well please."

"Bah!" Daiki's fingers flew open, her underwear becoming a cloud of dust, floating around his hand.

"Damn it, DK." Erin slammed her hands into Daiki's chest, pushing him toward the door. "Get the hell out of here."

"Fine, bitch."

Daiki jabbed his hand toward the bed. Erin's suitcase dissolved like a sand castle surrounded by an ocean wave. A layer of multi-colored powder covered the white bedspread.

Erin stood in amazement, not hearing the two adjoining doors slam as Daiki returned to his room with Diego. She was still standing stunned when Thandi walked up to her, two sacks in her hand. She handed the sack of water bottles to her.

"So, we going shopping later?"

Erin finished lunch in relative quiet while Thandi scanned through her social media feeds. Glad for the silence, Erin wasn't about to go into any detail about why her suitcase was now a five-inch layer of colorful fibers and micro-plastic on the bed. She enjoyed the quiet whenever she could get it. It was something she got little at home, with a rambunctious three-year-old running about the house.

Thandi startled her by breaking the silence. She rattled off something about needing to print an email downstairs and dashed for the door. Erin cleaned up the collection of paper wrappers and napkins, then made her way for the hotel lobby.

Standing at the elevator, she heard a room door close. She peeked around the corner and saw Diego floating toward her. He pushed himself along, touching the carpeted floor with his tiptoes, gliding along on an invisible skate board. They both grinned as she reached out and grabbed his hand, pulling him toward the opening elevator doors.

"Why is being a mutant both so much fun yet so dangerous?" Diego asked. He stood flat-footed in the elevator as they descended.

"The *unknown* would be my answer." Erin tilted her head. "Being a mutant is like free climbing a mountain in Yosemite. It's exhilarating but deadly if something happens. It is rare, but mutants have died from their own abilities, and not because of the actions of a frightened human. I've seen many reports come through my office of just that."

"Like what?"

"For example, just because I can control water or make my body liquified doesn't mean I wouldn't drown if I fell unconscious in a pool."

Diego nodded. "Yeah, I see what you mean. I guess the same could happen if I became weightless in the wrong area."

"Like a hurricane, maybe."

Diego laughed. "Not too many hurricanes in Colorado, but we get some strong winds."

Before the elevator dinged for the first floor, Erin heard shouting coming from the lobby area. Thandi's voice. The doors opened and Diego held up a hand, holding Erin back as he stepped out first. She touched his ribcage, tickling him, making him move away so she could exit as well.

"You'd better think twice before you go dusting someone's clothes like that again. You understand me?"

Thandi was all up in Daiki's face, index finger waving around while Daiki stood back like a little boy, about to get a whipping from his mother. Erin put a hand over her mouth, holding back the snicker welling up inside of her.

Diego walked toward them, clearing his throat. Thandi heard him and snapped her head around, ready to take him on as well. Diego raised his hand in defense. Erin walked past Diego and between Thandi and Daiki.

"Daiki, I hope you have the car running to cool it off. I think she will need it more than I will."

*Hotel California* was playing in Adam's earphones when the seat belt indicator sounded. The pilot of Air Force One announced clear skies around Albuquerque, current temperature of 85°F and light winds. Adam put his phone away and stared out the window at the view of the city as they circled around to land on Runway 8. It may not have been the runway of choice by the pilot, but the President liked when Air Force One landed in clear view of the Sunport terminals. Purely political, but it was a quicker taxi to where the plane would be parked near the hangars for Kirtland Air Force Base.

He stood behind Secret Service Agent Joe Strickland at the open doorway, watching airport workers roll stairs over to the plane. Stairs in place, Adam rapped twice on the door to the President's quarters. The door unlocked and swung open. Antonio slipped on his jacket and stepped out, closing the door behind him.

"Everything's clear, sir. Chopper is waiting for you." Adam stepped away from the exterior door, allowing the President to exit first.

"Where's Shane?" Antonio asked.

"Still in the back." Adam pointed a thumb over his shoulder.

"Well, tell him he rides with me or rides with the press. We're not holding up air traffic any longer than I need to."

Joe nodded and headed for the rear of the plane. Adam followed down the stairs behind the President at a respectful distance. Taking in a deep breath, he was glad to be in the southwest. The humidity of Washington and of Russia wore on him. His native Hawaii wasn't as dry as New Mexico, but he rarely wore an armored suit when he visited his Mom.

It was a short walk to a waiting olive green helicopter to take them the rest of the way to the so-called *Western White House*. Others from the President's entourage would follow along in a private jet to Los Alamos and drive from there up the mountain to Cerro Grande. The press had to find their own way north, or stay in Albuquerque and report from there.

Inside the helicopter, everyone slipped on noise-cancelling headphones and buckled into the seats. A serviceman closed the chopper door, and the blades whirled. In flight, Adam watched the alternating green and brown landscape slide under them as they headed north. The scene reminded Adam of the landscapes he saw in Russia as they flew to the mutant detention facility. The one they escaped a short twenty-four hours ago, leaving it in disarray.

He hadn't fully resolved what happened in Russia. Fatima telling Lani and him the cryptic message about *unseen servants*, then Lani getting pissed and causing the suppressors on the prisoners to turn off. Some mutants escaped, Stepanida killed the rest. It was too much of a mix of emotions. He dozed lightly on the flight back from Moscow, not helping with the situation. Now was not the time to be distracted, time to be on the job.

The job made itself clear when Shane slapped him on the knee. "Agent Knight. Adam."

Adam turned to see Antonio and Shane looking at him.

"Yes, sir. Sorry. How can I help you?" He blinked several times, clearing his eyes.

"Shane here was telling me we have a meeting with a group soon after we reach the ranch," Antonio said. "I'd like for you to attend that meeting."

"Yes, sir. Who is the meeting with?" Adam leaned forward, the request grabbing his attention even more. It was rare for visitors to come to the President's home, even more rare for Adam's presence to be requested.

"A group of four people from Mutant Defense Foundation," Shane looked up from his tablet.

"The Mutant Defense Foundation group?" Adam asked. "Four mutants, I take it."

Shane went back to the tablet. "Time for their annual report."

Adam raised an eyebrow toward the President. "They are reporting to you instead of DoMA?"

"They insisted on meeting with me instead," Antonio said. "So I told them today in my home or next month in Washington. They settled on today."

"Understood." Adam nodded as well. He thought back to the voicemail from Erin, wondering if there was a connection. The trip to Russia had been fore-front on his mind. He forgot to call her back.

The helicopter swung around, revealing the main house and a few smaller outbuildings on the Mendoza Ranch in the window to Adam's right. Out the opposite window, a business jet approached from the south, descending toward the runway at Los Alamos. No doubt the rest of Mendoza's entourage or members of the press that could arrange for the additional air travel.

As soon as the chopper sat down at the estate, a Marine opened the helicopter door and saluted as Antonio stepped out. Shane climbed out next, following close on the heels of the

President as they entered the house. The lead Secret Service agent for the President's residence stood outside, waiting for Adam.

"Allyson." Adam nodded to her.

"Rough flight?" Allyson crossed her arms across her chest.

"Do I look that bad?" He stopped to talk with her, stuffing his hands in his pant pockets.

"You look like you could use a nap."

"Great." Adam sighed. "How's everything up here on the mountain top?"

"Nothing to report, sir." Allyson stuffed her hands in her pant pockets. "County reported no disturbances of recent. Seems all the politics are heading north to Salt Lake City."

"Senator Stephenson's rally. Good. Maybe it will be peaceful this weekend."

"We can only hope, sir."

Adam took a step back and headed for the front door. "Guess I'll go shower before the next tour comes through."

"Mutant Defense Foundation, sir?" Theresa asked.

"Right."

After a quick shower, Adam headed for the kitchen. His stomach was still on a jet lag time schedule. Not *officially* on duty, not until the meeting with the Mutant Defense Foundation members, Adam pulled a beer from the fridge along with a plate of tacos the cooks had ready and waiting for them.

Adam was wiping his mouth off when Antonio swung through the kitchen sporting a colorful shirt and khaki shorts. Adam snorted. Rarely did he see the President in relaxed attire.

"What, you a clothing critic now?" Antonio asked, grabbing a taco from Adam's plate. "What do you wear when you're on vacation?"

Adam pointed to the suit jacket he had on. "Vacation? If I

recall, it was before the mid-term elections two years ago when I got a vacation."

"Well, we must do something about that."

"Right," Adam said, a touch of sarcasm in his voice.

His senses picked up four mutant DNA signatures entering the mansion then walking back out of range. "They're here. I think they went into your office."

"I told Shane to bring them in." Antonio grabbed Adam's can of beer and downed a drink before handing it back. "You're back on duty. No drinking."

Adam laughed. "With you around, I'm always on duty."

Adam walked two steps behind Antonio as they moved through the house. It had been in the family since before New Mexico became a state. Antonio's grandfather, Cicerón Mendoza, was a US Senator, serving for multiple terms in various government offices. Antonio's father didn't follow the political path, but a circular path around a NASCAR track.

The President's office was about as large as the Oval Office and arranged in much the same fashion, but decorated differently. The carpeting was a mix of brown, orange and yellows, no seal of the presidency. There were several Native American artifacts staged around the room, a few tapestries with southwestern patterns, and a large stuffed bear. Adam's thoughts went to Stepanida when he glanced at the bear. Its stance—upright with its claws down at its side—was one that she took each time he saw her shift from human into bear form. He sighed, knowing he would not get to see that transformation occur again.

He detected the mutant signatures again before they got to the office. There was an interesting mix of abilities: molecular disintegration, gravity control, darkness control, and water control. The latter was one he experienced before.

Shane leaned against the President's desk, chatting with two men and two women seated on the facing sofas. They all stood as Antonio walked in.

"DK, good to see you." He shook hands with him, politician-style.

"Good afternoon, Mr. President. Thank you for seeing us." He pointed to the others. "Thandi M'bombo, our Treasurer; Diego Rojas, Special Project Manager; and new to our executive staff, Erin Murphy, Secretary."

"Ms. Murphy. Welcome to Cerro Grande." Adam noticed that Antonio held her hand a bit longer than the others. He could sense the President using his mutant ability, scanning each person's emotional state.

"Thank you, Mr. President." Erin nodded, almost a curtsey.

As he took a seat in an armchair positioned in front of his desk, Antonio pointed to Adam. "Some of you may have met Adam Knight, part of my White House staff."

Adam reached out to shake hands with the four.

"A mutant that can read a person's DNA and know if they are mutant," Erin said.

"Hello, Erin." Adam held on to her hand, not wanting to let go. Memories flooded him; *Erin laid in a hospital bed, breathing tube at her mouth, her father standing behind her mother as she pounded on his chest, weeping that he caused her injuries.*

"I take it you've met before," Antonio said.

Adam blushed, stuffing his hands in his pockets. "Erin and I dated back at Michigan."

Adam remembered his mom telling him that Erin had gotten married a few years back. He made a quick glance to her hands for a wedding ring. No rings on her left hand. Something sparkled on her, a necklace of diamonds in the shape of a water jug with several strings with sapphires hanging from the mouth of the jug. It was a gift he had given her for her nineteenth birthday—Aquarius.

They all stood until Antonio walked over to his chair and sat down. Shane sat in a chair off to Antonio's left. Adam stood to the right, arms crossed.

"Okay, so what do you have for me?" Antonio clapped his hands, then interlaced his fingers.

"Well, sir, as you know," Daiki started, "Mutant Defense Foundation has been working with Federal, State, and Local governments to find fresh ways to integrate mutants into the organizations. Bring Water Controller such as Erin here into fire…"

*Erin stood in the shower, pointing a finger at him. "You know I could make this water come after you," she pointed a finger at him through the clear section of the curtain. Water coalesced into a snake-shape, rising from the shower basin, waving like a viper next to her hand.*

*"Only if I let you." He pointed a finger back at her.*

"… with the next Appropriations bill, still to be passed and brought to you for a signature," Thandi flipped through a bundle of papers as she talked, "Mutant Defense Foundation can continue…"

*The server sat down the fake leather check holder on the table and picked up Erin's plate. Adam wiped his mouth with his napkin and placed it on his plate as the server lifted it. He reached around to his back pocket for his wallet. "Ah, Erin? You bring your purse?"*

*Her hand went for her forehead.*

Diego's hands swirled in front of him "… outreach programs are placing mutants into jobs where they could do the most with their abilities and not be drawn into gangs and other street crime groups…"

*Two men walked up alongside them. The bald, tattooed man beside Adam held a wooden bat, twirling it around in his hand. Hugging Erin closer, Adam pushed on across the street's five lanes. On the sidewalk, another man sporting a mohawk stepped in front of Erin. "Wait, wait, my friends. Aren't you going to join the party up on Huron?" The man to Adam's side centered in front of him. He touched Adam's chest bone with the business end of the bat. "Unless this isn't your kind of party?"*

Last, Erin talked of how they were trying to improve human–mutant relations from the community level on up to the national level. She glanced at him, but didn't lock eyes with him. Her opalescent skin shifted colors.

*The sun had crept around the Bell Tower and fell on Erin. Adam laid on his side, watching the skin on Erin's bare arm change color—lavenders, baby blues, and soft pinks—as the sun warmed her.*

*"You're staring." She raised her arm to cover her eyes to peek out at him.*

*"I'm watching."*

The President cleared his throat and shifted in his seat. Adam blinked twice, then looked away.

"So you can see, Mr. President," Daiki started his closing statement. "Mutant Defense Foundation is continuing to make strides forward in the efforts Ms. Taylor started four years ago. Although meeting like this doesn't get the global attention as a larger conference would."

Erin moved to the edge of her seat. "But we appreciate the time you are giving us."

Daiki threw his hand out in front of him, not letting his point get away. "Still, Mr. President, if I may, I wanted to express my disappointment that you have asked us to come to your residence up here in the mountains to have this meeting."

Adam noticed the President grabbing the arms of the chair and pushing himself upright.

Antonio stared at Daiki, his eyebrows dipping. "Your meaning, Mr. Kobayashi?"

"In the past, these meetings have been at Washington. The only time they were away, it was connected with other events, such as the dedication to President Taylor's Museum or the speech to the United Nations last year when you flew off to St. Petersburg." Daiki turned from facing the President to glaring at Erin. "I sense you may try to keep our meeting secret."

"I can assure you, keeping our meeting secret is not part of any agenda. As my chief of staff can attest," the President nodded to Shane. "Combining meetings at a single location is necessary to go through them all. And if you think bringing you here to keep you out of sight of the Press Corps, then you weren't watching when you turned in at the first gate at the bottom of the hill." Antonio leaned forward in his chair, waving his hand toward the road. "That broken-down blue Ford is not there because the county sheriff hasn't hauled it off. Watch for the glint of camera lenses when you leave."

"But sir, it would be..." Daiki motioned with an open palm toward Antonio as if to stop him from interrupting.

The President stood up. "Everyone, thank you for your insightful presentation. We will meet again." He glared at Daiki. "In Washington."

Shane stood and stepped between the four mutants, stopping at the door. Slowly, the other four stood as well. Adam stood back as Antonio and the Mutant Defense Foundation leadership left the room. He followed at a respectful distance when he saw Erin turn to look at him and wait for him to catch up. The others continued on.

"How have you been?" Erin looked up to him, her fingers interlaced in front of her.

Adam walked beside her as they walked through the corridors toward the exit. He pointed toward Antonio. "Busy working for him. Sorry I didn't return your call. I had to make a quick trip... out of the country."

"That's okay. Kind of forward of me to call like that. I'm sorry about your father. He was a good man."

"Thank you. That means a lot." He held the huge wooden door open, allowing her to step through.

"Lani still flying?"

"Oh yeah," Adam laughed. "She's in the Air Force, piloting fighter jets when she can't fly on her own." He knew he shouldn't mention the NSA. That would be another conversation, maybe.

"Erin!" Daiki shouted, slamming the door on the rental car.

She sighed. "This is what I get to work with. Like I said, we're staying overnight in Los Alamos before heading back to Washington tomorrow. Are you free for dinner tonight?"

"Damn straight he is," Antonio said as he walked past them back into the house. "Buy them all dinner tonight, Adam. My treat."

Adam rolled his eyes. "That would be great. I'd suggest the Pasta House, but wasn't sure how you felt about pasta after last time."

Erin giggled, then reached up and kissed him on the cheek. "See you there at six?"

"See you then."

He remained at the water fountain in the center of the circle drive as the sedan cleared the last checkpoint on the road. He tried to suppress the broad smile on his face as memories flooded his mind. The smile wouldn't go away.

*Friday, June 23*
*Present Day*

The kitchen of her Miami condo blurred, and the lobby of the Andrews Fitness Center came into focus. Instantly, Doris broadcasted a *you-don't-see-me* mental command to everyone around her. She knew enough to not look up in case security cameras were catching her popping into the scene. Standing next to the check-in counter, Doris waited until two service women passed by her. She didn't feel like saluting and all that crap, anyway.

A young man stood behind the counter, watching the two women as they walked away. Shaking her head, Doris positioned herself on the opposite side and coughed, clearing her throat. The man jumped in surprise, turning to face the noise.

"Good afternoon, Colonel," he stammered. "Can I help you?"

"I'm looking for Major Black."

"Oh, he's down playing racquetball with General Harcourt." The assistant looked down at the log sheet, running her finger down the list. "Here it is. Court number five."

"Is there a viewing booth above the court?"

The woman leaned over the counter and pointed down the main hallway. "Down the hall here, second left, then continue down."

Doris teleported into the small room, looking down at the back of the racquetball court. Two men were playing, an older, gray-haired man serving to a younger man with short-cut, sandy-brown hair. Both were wearing white athletic clothing with terry cloth sweatbands on their wrists and around their heads.

Doris watched the game play out for a while, then tired of it. She mentally whispered to Marc. *"Hello, lover."*

The ball came at him, and he stumbled, missing it. He looked up to the viewing booth. Doris stood, smiling. She waved at him, and he frowned.

"The hell, Black. That was an easy one." Harcourt said, retrieving the ball. "Game point."

He moved to the service line and bounced the ball, swinging at it. Marc swung at the return and stepped away. Harcourt returned the volley after it bounced off the back wall.

Marc stepped up to swing at the ball again, but Doris mentally whispered to him again. Marc's arm jerked, and he missed. The game was over.

"Hell, man. You had me dead. Didn't have to let me win, you know."

"Yes, sir. Think I may have pulled something in my shoulder." Marc twisted his right arm around.

*"I'll help you with that when he leaves."*

Marc glared up at Doris again.

"Pulled something, alright." Harcourt picked up the towel laying at the back of the court and wiped down his face. "Better get ready. Next time we play, I double cash value."

"Yes, sir." Marc sat the racquet down and grabbed his towel to wipe off his face.

Doris watched from above as Marc hid behind the towel, both of them waiting for Harcourt to leave. As soon as the General stepped out of her sight from the viewing booth, she teleported down to the court.

"Ready for another game?" Doris tugged at his towel.

Marc lowered it, nostrils flaring. "That one cost me $100. What are you going to cost me?" He rubbed the towel across the back of his neck.

"Oh, win or lose, I'm sure you'll come out ahead." She moved closer to him and put one hand on his chest, then took his free hand and moved it to her breast. Marc took a half-step back, jerking his hand away from her and swatting her other hand away in the same move.

Doris smacked him across the face. Welts formed on Marc's face. He balled up his right fist.

"Careful, now. Don't want to strike a senior officer."

"You'll never touch me again." Marc stepped through her. As he walked for the door, Doris reached out to grab him. Her hand found nothing solid to grab on to.

"Marc, wait," Doris shouted, running to catch up with him. "Let me take you somewhere we can talk."

"There's nothing I need to hear from you except goodbye."

At the door to the men's locker room, Marc phased through the door also. Doris stopped at the door and paused. She angered him as he was not one to blatantly use his ability in public. She let out a sigh, then pushed it open.

In the locker room, a half-dozen men stood in various stages of dressing or undressing. Several more were showering, including General Harcourt. Doris mentally replaced herself with an image of Michael in uniform in the minds of the six men in the room. She rounded the corner of his row of lockers and moved between two guys to get to Marc.

"Marc, I need your help."

Marc stared at the image of Michael, shook his head, then disrobed. "What now?" he whispered. "What radar component do you want me to steal this time?"

Doris leaned against the lockers. "You let her fall in love with you. That wasn't supposed to happen."

"Well, it did, and I kind of enjoy it." He pulled a clean towel from his locker and wrapped it around his waist.

"You don't love her, though." She stared up at him, admiring his chest muscles.

"Not your concern." He pulled off his underwear from under the towel and tossed it to the bottom of the locker. "And don't go messing with my head, making me think I'm in love with you again. It hurts, and it sucks."

"But her well-being will be your concern if you let her continue this investigation of her father's death."

"Are you threatening her?" Marc slammed the locker door closed. His fist went translucent.

Doris took a step back from him. In his angered state, he was less susceptible to her mental control. She wouldn't be able to prevent him from reaching inside of her and pull out any body part he wanted.

"No, I'm just saying she will not like what she finds if she keeps pulling that thread. You know what that will be. She has to stop before everything unravels."

"Fine. I'll talk with her. After I shower." He grabbed his shower bag off of the bench and walked away from Doris.

Doris watched him hang his towel from a hook, then step naked into the showers. She stood at the entrance to the locker room showers and admired his body for a second before teleporting out of the room.

The tires squealed as Marc's BMW wheeled around the cloverleaf exit off of I-95 North. An SUV ahead of him sat, blinkers flashing, waiting for an opening in the slow lane. Marc inhaled deeply and ghosted him and his car, sliding between the molecules of the SUV and two others, reaching the left lane and a gap between vehicles.

In the time it took him to travel around DC and halfway to Baltimore, heading for Lani's apartment, Marc had plenty of time to examine his relationship with Lani and with Doris.

Something about Doris coming to visit him at the fitness center set him off. She was a mind flayer, always messing with his head, even when she wasn't using her abilities. She came out of nowhere and started a relationship years ago while he was stationed at an Air Force base near Boston. Then they reassigned to Thayer Air Force Base in Alaska. He hated the cold. Boston was bad enough in the winter, but it was always winter in Alaska.

Then, out of the clear blue, Doris contacted him last October, asking for help. An Air Force Colonel—his base commander—was sending sensitive information to a Russian terrorist group. Information was about American mutants, data that the Colonel had stolen from Doris.

After Marc had stopped the dissemination of information, the Colonel contacted the Air Force's Office for Special Investigation, who sent Lani and a second agent to investigate and arrest Marc. Instead, Lani fell in love with him.

Doris played him, using him to spy on Lani, reporting out on her assignments at the NSA. Doris would visit Marc often whenever he had something to report, when she wanted to have sex with him, or both.

He tapped in the four-digit number he thought was the code to raise the gate arm, but it didn't move. He sat, wondering if he may have gotten the last two digits backwards. That wasn't it either. Seeing no one behind him, he waved his hand at the keypad. His hand ghosted through it, disrupting the electronics. The gate arm lifted, and he drove through, smiling.

A young mother carrying a two-year-old sleeping child was trying to reach for the door to Lani's building as Marc approached. She had the boy in one arm, an activity bag over the shoulder, and two grocery bags in the other hand. He offered to carry groceries, and the woman accepted.

Standing in the elevator, Marc glanced at the child as they went to the third floor. He was passing thirty-three and no serious relationship to speak of. He was dating Lani, though she wasn't a serious relationship. She was an assignment, a situation.

One that Doris was right about. He had let Lani fall in love with him. He had some feelings for Lani, but were they real or were they a defense against Doris? She could make him think he was in love with her, but the emotion was not there. Any thoughts of love for Doris were momentary, almost fleeting. Still, he enjoyed being around Lani. There was pleasure there, even after they parted. It wasn't love, not yet.

At the woman's apartment door, Marc sat the bags down on the floor and stepped back to the stairs as she fumbled for her keys. He climbed up to the fourth floor and walked down to Lani's door. He listened at the door to hear if she was awake. Nothing heard, he ghosted through the door.

Inside her apartment, the woman laid the sleeping child on his bed and returned to the kitchen and the groceries. With a jug of milk in her hand, she reached under her long brunette hair and tapped on her bluetooth earpiece.

"Mrs. Kutcher? He's here now."

*Lani tugged at the seat belt, tired of sitting. Dad was in front of her, driving Mom's SUV. Adam sat behind Mom. He had to sit behind her because Dad always moved his seat back too far for Adam's long legs.*

*She finished another book and tossed it over her shoulder onto the pile of suitcases and items Mom didn't want the movers to pack in the enormous truck. Lani looked at her teenage brother, drool creeping out of the corner of his mouth as he slept.*

*Out the window, she saw a highway sign advertising a nearby lake. Coldwater. A shiver ran over her body.*

*"Dad, can I ask you something?"*

*"We just crossed into Michigan, Lani. It will be another ninety minutes or longer."*

*"No, not that."*

*"What do you need?"*

*"We won't be near the ocean, will we?"*

*"Afraid not, baby girl. But there are two Great Lakes nearby."*

*"Will they be as warm as the gulf?"*

Lani's bladder tugged at her, waking her up. She rolled off the bed and wandered into the bathroom. Sitting down, she frowned at herself, forgetting to grab her cell phone. She sat on the toilet, waiting for nature to finish its course, her chin resting in her hands.

"Hey, sleepyhead."

Lani's hands flew up, pointing toward the bathroom door, a bright purple glow around them.

"Whoa, it's me," Marc said, becoming visible in the bathroom doorway.

"Damn it, Marc. Warn me next time you ghost in on me."

Marc stood with a smile on his face as she pulled up her panties and moved to the sink.

"I did. I left you two messages."

"I was napping."

"I saw."

She looked in the mirror at him, his eyes watching her breasts wiggle as she washed her hands. A grin flashed across her face.

"You probably snuck in the girl's bathroom after you got your abilities, didn't you?" She flicked water off her hands into the sink, then turned to him, wiping her hands off on his Air Force uniform.

"Maybe," he grunted, going insubstantial and letting her hands move through him.

Lani walked through him and into the bedroom. A chill ran through her, remembering the dream she had a few days ago.

Grabbing her bra from the foot of the bed, she put it on. She looked around for him as she reached in her dresser and pulled out a pair of ankle-high socks. She was about to call out to him when the toilet flushed, followed by the water faucet.

"I thought you had duty this weekend. New guy on base or something like that," Lani said. She leaned over the bed to straighten up the comforter.

"I got out of it." He walked up behind her and grabbed her by the hips. "The President flew to New Mexico, so they released me."

Lani giggled and stood up, trying to wiggle out of his grip. Unable to slip free, she looked over her shoulder, and they kissed.

"Mmm, you smell clean. Harcourt challenge you to racquetball again?" She reached up and behind, running her fingers through his hair.

"Yeah. Lost to him again. Just so I can kick his ass next time we play."

Marc moved his hands over her belly and up to her bra.

"Gently. The girls are feeling sensitive."

"Sounds like they've been missing me."

"I know I have."

She spun around in his arms and wrapped her arms around his shoulders. Up on her tiptoes, Lani pulled at him, bringing his lips down to hers. Marc leaned forward, bending her backwards. She used her power of flight, letting them drift softly down onto the bed.


The ceiling fan whirled slowly, almost hypnotizing Lani to sleep again. She rolled away from Marc's arm and crawled off the foot of the bed. A breeze blew across her backside as he swatted at her. Grabbing her underwear from the floor, she made her way to the bathroom. A minute later, she returned to the bedroom. She could feel Marc's eyes following her as she headed for the closet.

"Have I mentioned how gorgeous you are?"

"Not recently. You've been so distant." Lani looked over her shoulder. "It's almost as if I saw you more when you were still in Alaska."

"Andrews differs from Thayer. I've told you that. Too many politicians pretending to be military officers. Besides, you aren't in town every day either. Flying off to Russia on a whim."

"Being in the NSA is like Special Investigation. I mean, I'm doing the same stuff, almost. Investigation, either at a base or facility." Lani walked to the open closet door and leaned against the frame, arms crossed.

"Several days at a time." Marc patted the bed in front of him, inviting her back to bed. She shook her head and stepped back into the closet.

Hanging in the back of the closet, she reached for a jumpsuit. She held it in front of her and took it off of the hanger. From neck to toe, the thin material was various shades of deep blue, violet, and black. When it moved, it had a shimmering effect. Lani's mother called it her Ultraviolet costume. Lani preferred the term flight suit.

"Looks like we aren't going to the ball game," Marc frowned at her when he saw the suit.

"Oh, damn. The game's tonight. Sorry, I gotta go see Mom." She sat on the edge of the bed and slipped her feet into the suit.

"If you'd like, we can pack a bag and spend the holiday with her." The bed bounced as Marc crawled across to sit behind her. He caressed her shoulders, his fingers digging deep into the muscles. "After what happened in Norfolk and then Russia, you could use a vacation."

Lani huffed. "What's with this vacation stuff? Third time today."

Marc stopped, his hands at the base of her neck. "What do you mean?"

"Everyone's wanting me to go on vacation, as if they're trying to get me out of town or stop following this last lead on Dad's murder."

"Will it be the last lead? I've said it before, and I'll say it again. Let it go."

"Thanks for believing in me." Lani twisted her body, sloughing his hands off of her.

She stepped away from him. Pulling the suit over her shoulders, she tugged at the front zipper, hidden by an indigo ribbon of color.

"You need to take time off, Lani," Marc sat on the bed. "Someone attacked you in Norfolk one day, then you had to fight your way out of the Russian prison a day later. You need to relax."

"It has been a week from hell, Marc. But there are so many questions going through my mind right now. Even my nap was filled with dreams of Mom and Dad."

Lani moved to the balcony glass door and pulled the metal brace out of the track. Stepping outside, she saw Marc's legs ghosting through the mattress as he followed her outside.

"Better go cloudy there, mister, or put clothes on." She ran a finger across his bare waist line. He sauntered back to the bed and grabbed his underwear. Watching him hop on one leg, she keyed the satellite phone.

"Chesapeake Central, this is Knight Seven Three Four personal. Traffic check."

Her course would take her over the bulk of the nation at a high rate of speed. She followed the guidance given her by Space Force and contacted them with her plan. No need to send the military on high alert because she wanted to visit her mother.

She nodded as she got the clearance she needed. "Copy that. Climbing to angels fifty, tracking two eight two."

"Sure I can't talk you into waiting?" Marc joined her on the balcony again.

"Don't worry, I'll be right back. What time does the game start? Maybe I'll be back before the first pitch."

"Nineteen thirty hours."

Lani stepped to the railing, lifted her butt up to it and swung a leg over it. She looked around, seeing if anyone was in the area, watching her. Swinging her other leg over, she drifted into the air and blew a kiss to Marc.

"Be a sweetheart and lock the balcony door for me." She waited for him to nod, then launched herself into the overcast sky.

Marc followed her flight upward as much as he could, then stepped inside. Locking the door as she asked, he closed the drapes. As he turned away from the balcony, he bumped into something. Or someone.

"You could have tried harder." Doris stood inches from him, still in her Air Force uniform.

"What the hell are you doing here?" He ghosted and walked through her to the other side of the bed.

"Making sure you do what I asked." She spun around, hands on her hips. "You're a lousy negotiator."

"Then why didn't you do it?" Marc sat on the bed as he put his pants on. "You love mucking in people's head."

As he reached for his shirt, he saw Doris walk around the bed to stand in front of him. When he looked up, it was Lani standing there, naked.

"Lani? How'd you—?"

Lani pushed him backwards onto the bed and tugged at his pants.

Standing with her back to the wall, Doris watched as he reacted to the image she implanted in his mind.

*Mucking with people's minds is what I do best, love.*

*Friday, June 23*
*Present Day*

The miniature electronic altimeter and compass woven into Lani's suit told her when she reached an altitude of fifty thousand feet, traveling west. Traveling at fifteen times the speed of sound, her mutant ability created a force field around her with a bubble of air whenever she flew fast or high enough. It had tempted her a few times to cross the fifty-mile limit used to consider someone an astronaut. For now, nine and a half was high enough.

Before crossing into the Central Plains, Lani keyed the miniature satellite phone also woven into her suit. "Call Adam."

"Hey, sis." Adam's voice came in strong.

"Hey, bro. Just had an interesting situation a while ago. Remember my neighbor downstairs when I lived south of DC?"

"The older woman. Don't think I met her."

"Well, I just saw her earlier today. She wasn't that old and frail."

"Sure it was her?"

"Yep. Same damn dog. It even barked at me like it knew me."

"Interesting."

Lani could tell he didn't care.

"Anyway, she told me to 'tell Mom aloha.' So I thought I'd fly out to Mom and chat with her for a while. You want to go?"

"Um, I'd like to, but I also ran into an old friend."

"Not another Russian mutant, I hope."

"Erin, my girlfriend back in college."

"Cool. Going to have dinner with her?"

"Yeah, later tonight."

Lani smiled. "Good. Mom will be pleased."

"God, don't tell Mom. She'll call me right in the middle of it. I know she will."

"Alright. Well, if you're outside, wave at me."

"Waving."

As the blue of the Pacific came up under her, she rolled over to face the black of outer space. When she applied for the Air Force Academy, Dad told her he had considered applying for the astronaut corps, but being a Dad to two mutants was dangerous enough. The memory brought a smile to her, then reminded her of putting her initial path aside. Mendoza's offer to send her into criminal investigation kept her tied to the Earth. Maybe once an outpost was established on the Moon or Mars, she'd be able to fly into space. With space currently occupied by a dozen people and inside a series of tubes, there's not a lot of crime to investigate.

Once she got close to the Hawaiian islands, Lani slowed down so to not to break the speed of sound over the islands. She didn't need sonic booms announcing her arrival. Gravity did its thing, and she descended in an arch toward the north shore of Oahu, keeping the sun directly behind her to block her from being spotted.

Nobody was on the beach, so she could stop her descent twenty feet above the water and drift down to the ground. Memories of growing up on a Hawaiian beach came to her. The feel of the warm noon sun and the sound and smell of the ocean filled her senses. As she walked the distance from the sand through the grass and up to the house, she caught a whiff of her mom's flower garden. Lani had often told her family it was moments like this that made her wish she could move back to Hawaii.

Expecting her mom to be standing in the doorway, she hesitated at the door. There was no such thing as arriving unannounced. Mom always knew when she was at the door. A second passed, and the Mom had not appeared yet. Probably gone to the grocery store or the garden center, Lani mentally searched for the electronic door lock. It was not set. She frowned as she reached for the doorknob and opened the door.

The house was quiet, which confirmed her belief that Leelee was out. Her mom was always humming a tune or had music playing. Lani looked around the living room and didn't see a purse, but there was a set of car keys on the kitchen counter she didn't recognize. Mom's keys were just key fobs, no actual keys. This ring had car key and a key that was worn down along the jagged edge. Mom had visitors from time to time. Probably a friend's key ring.

She grabbed the lone banana out of the fruit bowl and headed for her room. Mom kept a bedroom open for whenever Adam or Lani came to visit. It was always Lani, since time away from the President was rare for Adam.

Lani unzipped her flight suit and pulled her arms out, then squeezed the end of the banana to peel it. The banana had a few spots on it, but wasn't quite to the leopard stage, just the way she liked it. She took a bite, then sat the fruit on the bedstand and continued undressing. She found a bikini top and bottom of hers in a dresser drawer and slipped them on.

As she walked into the living room, a splash sounded from the covered deck. Lani remembered that the house that President Mendoza purchased for her had a hot tub, but her Mom did not use it often. Especially in the middle of a warm summer day.

Stepping through the French doors to the deck, Lani spotted a man in the tub, his head laid back, arms on the railing. Mom wasn't back there, but there were two of Mom's aqua blue bath towels, a novel on the wicker table and two bottles of water. Lani reached for the door handle when the man sat up and stuck his hand out. His arm disappeared at his elbow, the rest of it appearing over the table, grabbing a water bottle.

"Ah, excuse me?"

The man's head spun, tossing his long, wet hair up over his face. He wiped the blond strands from his eyes and smiled.

"Lani? Hey, how's it going?"

"Billy Watson?" Lani smiled back. "I haven't seen you since Dad's service. What are you doing here?"

"He's helping with the house." Leelee walked out of the house behind her daughter. She was wearing a long flowery sundress, carrying a glass of tea. Lani stepped over to her mom and they kissed each other's cheek. Leelee sat in one of the aqua-colored wicker chairs and offered the other to her. Lani declined.

"What's wrong with the house?" Lani sat her phone on the table, then climbed into the bubbling water, sitting across from Billy. The warmth of the water grabbed at her muscles and relaxed them.

"That last big storm we had pushed waves up over the seawall. It damaged a part of the foundation."

"And here I am, putting my college education to work." Billy raised his arms over his head.

"But I thought you were a chemical engineer?"

"It wasn't all chemistry."

Lani giggled. Billy Watson and Adam were best friends when they were going through Engineering Studies at the University of Michigan. She and Billy dated for a brief time when Adam was spending a summer in London. Tall and scrawny, Billy was the definition of a Midwest farm boy.

"Adam will be sorry he missed you."

"How is big and burly nowadays? Still doing the cloak and dagger thing?" Billy took a long draw on the water bottle.

"Secret Service, which I always thought was an oxymoron. You see them there, surrounding the President. You can't miss them."

"Would you like a glass of tea?" Leelee asked after taking a drink of the glass she brought out. "How did your trip to Russia go? I know you can't tell me everything."

"It didn't go as planned. Adam and I learned a few things, though."

"That's too bad. Are you hungry? Is it too early for lunch, or is it dinner time yet for you?"

"Something to snack on would be nice. Thanks, Mom."

Leelee patted her daughter on the head as she went inside. Lani waited for a minute, then reached into the water and splashed Billy.

"Hey, saw an old girlfriend of yours this morning."

"Girlfriend? Who's that?" He wiped the water from his eyes and smiled at her. "You?"

"Ha, besides me. Fatima Gorshkov. I forgot her maiden name. Kotoyava, I think."

Billy's jaw dropped. "Where did you see her?"

"Over in Russia. She flew back with us to Washington, but had to go back."

"She still getting into people's heads?"

"Yes. She dropped us another clue about Dad."

Billy's head tilted. "A clue?"

"Something about an unseen servant that could go places and open doors without notice. I'm not sure what she meant by that."

Billy stared past Lani's head into the space behind her. That meant something. Billy never could keep a secret. She could always trick him into revealing what Adam had gotten her for

Christmas.

A smirk popped up on his face. "I was glad she went back to Russia after college. Between studies and her bouncing around inside my noggin, wow. You still working for one of those three-letter spy groups too?"

"Yeah, something like that." Lani let her arms float to the water's surface. "Say, I don't recall Mom saying anything about big storms. What are you doing here, really?" she asked.

A huge grin came across Billy's face. "I got a job working for an engineering firm in Honolulu right after New Year. Aerospace firm needed help in mixing propellant. I hadn't seen your mom since she moved out of Ann Arbor, so I thought I'd come say hello one day. Next thing I knew, she asked if I wanted to stay here."

"Oh, really? I've never known Mom to take in lost puppies. You aren't drugging her with your chemicals, are you?"

He offered a sheepish grin. "More like her tempting me with home-cooked meals. I've gained twenty pounds."

He moved in the water, repositioning his long legs. Lani felt a heel drift down on her lap. She frowned, a memory from last year coming to mind. Billy pulled his leg back, but Lani grabbed his foot and tugged on it. She ran her thumbs along the length of the sole of his foot. A second later, Billy's other foot was also in her lap.

"Lunch is ready. Come and get it." Leelee shouted from the kitchen.

Lani relinquished his feet and Billy stood up. Sitting on the edge of the tub, he opened a portal and reached for a towel. "Hey, don't tell Adam, okay? He'll kill me."

"What, for visiting Mom?" Lani nodded, holding a hand out for the other towel. Billy grabbed it and handed it over.

"You know how he gets about your Dad gone, him never

coming around. Me here will look bad."

"No problem, until it becomes one."

Billy nodded. "Don't worry."

Billy grabbed a plate and the napkin next to it, then went into the living room a few feet away. He fell into the cushiony couch and stretched out, feet up on the ottoman. He found the remote for the TV and turned it on. The noon news was on, talking about President Mendoza campaigning for the Vice-President's run for the office.

Lani climbed up onto a bar stool at the kitchen counter. She moved a small aloe vera plant, running her fingers over the big yellow Michigan M on the flowerpot.

"Are you here for the weekend?" Leelee asked as they walked into the kitchen. She filled a glass with ice from the refrigerator door, then reached inside for a jug of tea. Two small plates with ham sandwiches sat ready for them.

"No. I came to talk to you about something." She pulled the sandwich open, enjoying the aroma of the meat and mayo.

"What about, dear?" Leelee sat the glass of tea on the counter and reached for the sugar bowl. She scooped out a heaping spoonful to add for her daughter.

"Doris Kutcher said to tell you Aloha."

The spoon of sugar slipped out of Leelee's hand and bounced off the rim of the glass. The sugar spread across the counter as the spoon fell to the floor.

"I was just as surprised. She used to be my downstairs neighbor. I wasn't aware that you knew each other."

"When did you talk with her?" Leelee asked as she wiped the sugar off of the countertop.

"A few hours ago. Right after I heard her talking to my supervisor and the department manager. It seems Adam and I have been under surveillance for some time now. Any idea why?"

Lani took a bite from the sandwich, gazing over her hand at her mom, waiting for an answer.

"I'm not sure what you mean." Leelee stirred another spoon of sugar into the glass and handed it to Lani. She stared across the sink at her daughter, her face emotionless.

"Mom, ever since Dad died in that explosion—hell, even before that—someone has controlled Adam's life and mine, guided by some outside force or group. And whenever one of us gets a clue about who killed President Taylor and Dad, we get stopped by this force."

"Lani, your father's death was an accident. They involved hundreds of people in the investigation. The commission interviewed me. Even Billy was interviewed. Let it go."

Lani raised an eyebrow at Billy being interviewed. But that was a distraction. She leaned back in the chair and crossed her arms. "Regardless, how do you know Doris Kutcher?"

Having heard his name, Billy turned off the TV and walked through a portal to stand beside Lani. Her mother switched looks between her and him. Leelee stared down at the countertop and sighed.

"Mrs. Kutcher came to visit us several months after President Taylor approached your dad about the old Air Force project he ran. Doris had concerns about what the government would do with the device he was creating."

"The halos?"

Leelee ran her finger under her eyelid, wiping away a tear that was forming.

"Yes. Your dad assured her that his mandate was that they would use it for peaceful purposes. Doris pushed back, saying once when he finished, the government would warp it or the technology into whatever they wanted. And that was it. I think we talked one last time a few months before the explosion."

Leelee dabbed a tissue at the corner of her eye. Lani also teared up at the remembrance of her father's death. She was in her junior year in the Air Force Academy and almost dropped out. The national backlash against mutants and the protests against the treatment of mutants kept her in the military. She wanted to prove that mutants had a place in the world, such as it was.

Lani looked at the time and calculated what time it would be back in Washington. "Hey, I have to go. Marc wanted to take me out tonight. I think I can get back in time." She stood up and started for the bedroom.

"How is Marc?" Leelee asked. "Did he move to Washington?"

"Yes, earlier this month, Andrews Air Force Base," Lani said, leaving the door open so they could talk more. "I thought I told you."

"You should bring him out for the holiday," Leelee said. "I'm glad his invisibility didn't get him in trouble in Alaska. He's such a nice man."

Lani stepped out of the bedroom, back into her dark-colored flight suit. She slapped Billy's chest with the back of her hand as she passed by him. "Stay out of trouble." They laughed and hugged. Then she went to her mom and hugged her tight.

"Love you, Mom."

"Love you, too. You be careful going home."

Lani giggled. She always said that, no matter what the mode of transportation Lani was taking. She reached into one of her hip pockets and pulled out a small refrigerator magnet of a hula girl.

"I found this the other day when I was on assignment. It reminded me of when you made me take hula lessons in second grade."

Leelee smiled. "Yes, I remember. You looked so cute in the grass skirt." She walked to the door and held it open for her. Lani kissed her on the cheek and stepped outside, already floating off the ground.

"I'll see about Fourth of July. And I'll call first." Lani pointed at Billy, and they laughed a tentative laugh. They waved, and Lani shot up into the sky.

Before she cleared five hundred feet, she reached out with her senses and found the frequency of the listening device inside the hula girl.

*"Do you think she's suspicious?"* Billy's voice was distant, but getting louder.

*"She's her father's daughter. She's always suspicious. Especially after what Fatima said."* Mom's voice. Lani guessed she was by the sink.

*"Something about an unseen servant. Think she'll go find Doris now?"*

*"I'm counting on it. Ugh, your trunks are wet. Did you sit on my couch?"*

The purplish translucent bubble around Lani shimmered, darker ahead of her as it pushed against the thin air around her, lighter as it came to a point behind her. She cleared the Rockies, giving a salute to the land below her as she passed over her alma mater, the Air Force Academy. As she adjusted her flight path to the south to avoid a storm front rolling over the central plains, a buzz from her satellite phone tickled her leg. Probably Central Air Traffic Control.

"Knight Seven Three Four Personal."

"Hey, sweetie. Where are you?" Marc sounded cheerful.

Lani cringed. Another flipping name. "About to cross the Mississippi. What's up?"

"I was curious if you were going to make it back in time for the ball game. I haven't purchased any tickets yet. I was going to call Robbins in Maintenance to see if he had a pair for sale."

"Oh, right? The ball game. You know, I don't think I'm going to make it in time."

"The eastern half of the US? You should be able to clear that in a few minutes."

"Yeah, but I think I need to make another stop before coming home."

"Your mom has something for you?"

"Just some information about Doris Kutcher. I thought I'd see if she's still in her apartment at Kingwood."

There was a long pause in the conversation. Lani would have guessed it was a dropped signal, but she knew better. A long pause means he's sending a text to someone. But who?

"You sure you don't want to come on home first?"

"Oh, I'm pretty sure what I need to do now. Talk with you later tonight." An evil smirk rose across Lani's face. Kutcher was at the center of all this, after all.

She hovered directly over the Kingwood apartment complex according to the GPS system woven into her suit. Lani lived at the complex when she first moved to DC. Her first job out of the Academy was at the Air Force Office of Special Investigation, located to the south near Quantico, VA. Her apartment was on the second-floor, above whom she thought was a gentle elderly lady. Today, Lani realized Doris may have been older, but she was neither gentle nor elderly, and she had doubts about the *lady* aspect. Sparky was the same mutt Lani knew and disliked.

Lani touched down on the back side of building 401, hiding while a couple left the apartment across from her old apartment. She remembered them but had dealt little with them. She kept to what little shadow there was until the couple got in a car and pulled out of the lot.

She floated over to the door, finding it locked as she expected. "I know you're in there," Lani shouted, banging hard on the door. No movement inside. She banged again. "Mrs. Kutcher?" Not even a barking dog. Lani scanned the apartment for electronic signals. There was none. It had to be empty.

She had to know for certain. Either the woman she saw at the hotel bar was a doppelgänger and the old lady was sleeping or Kutcher was not who she believed she was the whole time.

Standing with her hands on her hips, it was time to go inside. If it was empty, then it's hardly breaking and entering. She could use her NSA credentials, but she was in her shiny flight suit, not in a normal civilian clothes.

She pointed between the door and frame at the single deadbolt with her index finger. A needle-thin laser beam sliced through the metal.

The apartment was vacant. There was the standard couch, a round dining table, and two bar stools at the kitchen counter. But that was it. No belongings. The place was ready for someone to move in.

"What do you want?" Doris said.

Lani spun around and saw Mrs. Kutcher across the room from her. She was wearing a gray t-shirt with a rock band logo splashed on it, skinny jeans, and black flats. Someone must have called her.

"A teleporter?" Lani asked. "No walker this time. Where's Sparky?"

"What are you doing here?" Doris stood with hands on her hips, her weight on one leg. Her graying hair was down. Lani picked up the smell of coconut suntan lotion around her. Definitely a fresh look for the old lady who lived downstairs.

She stepped up to Doris and got in her face. "Did you kill my dad?"

Doris took a step back, then scoffed at her. "Seriously? I don't have time for this."

As suddenly as she appeared, Doris disappeared. Lani reached around her, in case she had gone invisible like Marc. Lani and Marc had played enough cat-and-mouse games she felt she could guess which direction Doris could have moved.

"Come back here, you bitch." Lani cast an ultraviolet beam of light, trying to pick up any hidden figures. Catching the image of a body near where Doris stood, she narrowed the beam down to pencil-thin and amped up the intensity.

Doris reappeared, moving away from Lani's laser. "What the hell."

"Mom says Aloha." Lani pointed an open hand at Doris and released a broad blast. The energy beam knocked her off her feet and tossed her across the room. Bouncing off of the wall, Doris dropped to her knees, then slid over to her hip.

Doris laid there, the blast knocking the breath out of her. "Damn, that hurt. I'm getting too old for this shit."

"Did you cause the explosion that killed my father and President Taylor?"

Doris sat on her knees, holding a hand out for help standing. Lani balled her hands into tight fists, glowing deep purple, almost black.

"My dear, you do not understand what you are dealing with here."

"Answer my question, bitch. Did you—"

Lani stood motionless. Doris got to her feet with difficulty and stepped away from Lani's aim.

"Misguided little... Don't call *me* a bitch." Doris slapped Lani across her face.

"Ouch. Damn it." She flexed her fingers, the sting from the strike traveled deep into her thin flesh.

She studied the determination on Lani's face. Doris tapped Lani's forehead with a finger. "It would be so easy to reach in there and scramble your brain. If you weren't so damned important."

Noticing the intensity of the energy built up around Lani's hands, arms pointed at the outer wall. "Better not let that go off in here. Probably knock the entire building down."

Doris touched Lani on the arm and they disappeared.

The setting sun pushed the shadow of Doris' building far beyond the Miami beach. A large yacht passed the South Pointe Pier, people onboard already partying. Thirty stories up, no one would have noticed the sudden appearance of two women.

Lani stood under Doris' mental control, arms positioned outward, still glowing with a purple aura. Doris checked the skyline for any para-sailors who might trail behind speed boats up and down the coastline. Then she positioned Lani facing southeast, away from the populated areas.

Michael's electric wheelchair made a whining sound as it wheeled toward the balcony. He stopped a few feet from the glass door and watched. Perched on Michael's lap, Sparky barked at the women.

"Shut up, fleabag." Doris waved at the dog as she passed them by. She held a hand to her temple, a headache from Lani's energy attack made worse by Sparky's yapping.

"Who is this?"

"Marc's girlfriend."

"Oh, sweet. Can I play?"

"No."

With a full glass of wine in one hand and a towel full of ice in the other, Doris sat down on the plush loveseat, an ice pack against her graying hair. She released the mental block on her. Lani stepped forward and bumped against the balcony handrail. An energy blast flew out away from her hands, toward the Atlantic Ocean, traveling several yards before dissipating. She spun around, then found Doris and raised a fist.

"Blast me again, and I'll send you to the bottom of the ocean," Doris said, an index finger sticking out from the wineglass. "You can't fly through a thousand feet of water."

"Try me." Lani charged into the great room but stopped after two paces. She staggered as she walked the rest of the way to stand next to Michael in the middle of the great room. Doris furrowed her forehead, unsure why the young woman would be stumbling.

"Ah, it feels good to walk again." Lani spoke in a British accent. She moved her arms around, bending and twisting. "And arms as well."

"Damn it. Did you mind swap with her?" Doris asked, facing Lani. Or what was Lani's body.

"Well, yes. Of course. It looked like she would do whatever she did out there." Lani pointed outside. "And you weren't blocking her, like you usually do."

"Cause my head hurts. Michael, swap back right now."

Michael's eyes bounced back and forth. His voice rang out with a squeak. "Wait, what just happened?"

Sparky stood up from his lap and growl at his face, then jumped to the floor, barking at him.

Doris watched as *Michael* had full control of the young woman's body. Lani did two jumping jacks and ran in place for a few seconds. She tried to twirl ballerina style, but the white wood laminate floor wasn't slick enough. Lani stepped around in front of Michael's body, still in the wheelchair. His eyes stood wide open, darting left and right.

"So, love, what else can you do besides energy blasts?"

"Who the hell are you?" Michael turned his head back and forth, looking for Doris. "Kutcher, where are you?"

Lani's body stepped away from the wheelchair, then ran her hands up and down her body in unobstructed view of the man in the wheelchair. "It's been a long time since I've been in a body, let along a female."

Doris shook her head. "Michael," she said, in a scolding voice. "This is why I had to find a caretaker that could shield against you."

"Oh, this is…" Lani moved her hands across her breasts then down to her crotch. She roared. "This will be so much fun."

"No, damn it. Swap back." Doris mentally reached out to Michael's consciousness in Lani's body, trying to implant thoughts of a need to return to his body. The headache pain stabbed at her each time she tried to project at him.

She glanced at Michael's body with Lani's mind inside. His eyes tried to follow Lani as she moved around the room, not knowing how to manipulate the wheelchair controls. He watched her body do what Michael was making her do.

"Hey, make him stop!" Michael's voice shouted. He tossed his head side to side, trying to move his body. His chin bumped the lever for the chair, causing it to jerk sideways, then backwards.

"You do it." Doris said. "He won't listen to me."

Lani's consciousness floated in a different body and in a different brain. She had access to Michael's muscles, but couldn't make them work below his neck. All she could make work was his head, including his brain, his mind, and his memory.

*Doris dressing in an Air Force uniform. Colonel Kutcher on a name tag. A dog licking my face, the smell of dog biscuit breath. The dog walking in circles across my lap. Doris standing naked on the balcony, drinking wine. A red dress on the floor.*

*Memories from yesterday. No, this morning. Go back, farther.*

*The taste of meat and cheese, the smell of perfume, liquor, wet carpet. Hinkley and Harris. And two older women, my shampoo.*

*He must mind meld with the dog somehow.*

*Doris pacing back and forth, arguing over surgery. Michael wants a healer. Doris won't allow it. She teleports out. She comes back with someone. Marc! They go off to another room. Door is closed before Michael can get into the room.*

*The ceiling fan, twirling. The dog snoring to the left. The wheelchair to the right. A man in a red polo shirt flexing my legs, knees to my chest, then feet straight up. Focusing on the man's face, trying to catch his eyes. A brief blur, then the ceiling comes into focus again. I hear Doris' voice, 'No, no. Gotta stay where you are.' Eyes squinting, ears pounding. Michael cusses at her. 'Bitch'.*

*Doris standing at the balcony door, arms crossed. Chin pushing forward, the chair moving toward her. Michael demands to see Dr. Thornburg. Doris says no. Michael demands to be healed. Doris says he can't.*

*Pain! My head is on fire. But no pain below my neck. Bandages around my face, an airway at my nose. Doris is talking with someone wearing a white smock. Severed spinal cord, paralyzed from the neck down.*

*President Taylor on stage. Dad!*

"Michael, you'd better swap back."

"Screw you," Lani's voice said. "I have a body now. I don't need you anymore, or the dog." Michael moved Lani's body out of the great room and into the kitchen.

Doris heard the refrigerator door open and items being moved inside. She mentally sensed Michael's mind and saw the bottle of wine being lifted to her mouth, taking a long drink. She could feel Michael's mind enjoying the taste, the sensation as it flowed into

Lani's body.

Lani moved back into the great room, carrying the wine bottle. She knelt in front of the wheelchair, holding Michael's body. Squinting her eyes, Michael peered into his own eyes.

"You're on a quest. Unseen servant. You went to Russia yesterday, to talk with another telepath." Lani snapped her head around to face Doris. "She thinks you caused the explosion."

"Michael!" Doris winced as she shouted. "Mind swap back right now."

"Screw you, bitch," Michael's British accent replied. "This is the first time in five years I've had human legs to walk on, human arms to reach with." Michael pointed Lani's hand at Doris. "Your mental shields have always prevented me from swapping with you or anyone else. Trust me, I've tried."

"You wouldn't let him be healed," Michael's voice muttered. He leaned forward and activated the chair control, turning to face them.

"I had to keep you here, Michael. I didn't want to lose you like I did Antonio."

"You *pushed* him away. You were lovers until you got pregnant, Doris. He didn't want to raise a child. Instead, I had to be the father figure. A human child, at that. You couldn't even give birth to a child with powers."

Doris pushed a command into Lani's mind. *"You must mind swap back with him."*

Michael's eyes went wide open. *"I don't know how to do that!"*

Lani's face had a broad smile on it as she emptied the bottle into the glass. She walked past Doris, handing her the empty bottle. Lani's hands located the zipper of the flight suit and tugged at it as she strutted toward the balcony.

"You've kept me in that chair since that explosion in Michigan. You've kept me isolated from everyone. My only time out of this prison is in the body of that damn stupid dog. Now excuse me while I enjoy my freedom outside on the balcony."

Doris watched Lani walk away from her out to the balcony railing, head tossed back to bask in the last rays of sun. Then she looked at Michael's body, confined to the wheelchair, Lani unable to move his legs, his arms. She saw tears rolling down his face, Lani's reaction to the fear she was experiencing.

"I'm sorry." Lani's plea sounded strange in Michael's voice. "Make him stop. Please."

Holding the empty bottle by the neck, Doris walked up behind Lani's body and swung. The glass of the bottle shattered on the back of her head. Lani dropped to her knees, falling sideways into a wicker chair from the force of Doris' swing.

She turned and looked at Michael's body. He too was unconscious. Doris knelt down beside Lani and pulled the hair back from her face. There was a small gash on her head, but wasn't bleeding badly. She tried to put a smile on, but couldn't.

"Matching headaches now," she said. "But you forced my hand." She looked up at the man in the wheelchair. "Both of you did."

Doris picked up pieces of the broken wine bottle and carried it to the kitchen. Running water onto a washcloth, she returned to Lani and held it against the injury.

Sparky ran barking at Lani's face. Doris sneered at it.

"Shut the hell up." Doris pushed out mentally. The poodle froze in place, baring its teeth in a growl.

"Time to go, girl. Let's see what Marc can do for you." She grabbed Lani under her arms, pulled her up, and together, they vanished.

The slowly increasing rhythm of a pipe organ played as the roar from the crowd at the baseball game cheered on the home team. Marc stretched out on his couch in his apartment, the game between Washington and Philadelphia playing on the wall TV. Lani suggested going to the game. But after his racquetball loss to General Harcourt, he did not have the money, anyway. Staying at home and drinking less expensive beer was just as good. No hot dogs, though. Ballpark hotdogs are great. He realized why he was still single.

The leadoff batter for the Nationals hit a single, allowing the runner on third to make it home and taking the lead. The next batter walked out to the plate when a shimmer appeared between him and the TV.

"Damn it, Doris. Not now."

Two figures took shape in front of him, one he expected and another he didn't. Doris had an arm around Lani, holding her upright.

"What the hell did you do to her?" Marc jumped off the couch to grab the young woman as she slid out of the teleporter's grip.

"I didn't. Michael did."

"I thought I told you to stay away from her." Carrying Lani

into his bedroom, he laid her on the bed.

"She came after me, I'll have you know. She went banging on my door…"

"Lani doesn't know where you live."

"She went to the apartment in Fredericksburg, the one under where she used to live. Just like you said. I told you to make her stop snooping around. It's her own damn fault." Doris put a hand to her head. "Don't know why I even have that apartment still."

Marc glared at Doris, pointing to the blood on the pillowcase and in Lani's hair. "He do this, too?"

"Okay, that's on me. But Michael is to blame. He swapped with her and ranted about being free. I was afraid he would fly off in her body."

"He can do that? I mean, I knew he could swap minds but didn't realize he could use their powers."

"A mutant's DNA provides the power. It's the mind that controls it. When it's his mind, he can use it."

Marc went to the bathroom and grabbed a washcloth. Running it under the water to get it damp, he brought it out with a clean towel to lay her head on.

"How long has she been out?" He sat on the bed and dabbed at the cut on her head.

"Not more than a few minutes." Doris put a hand on Marc's shoulder.

"Does she have a concussion?"

"How the hell do I know? I'm a diplomat, not a doctor."

Marc laughed. "You, a diplomat? My ass." He opened one of Lani's eyelids to look at her pupils. "Oh, what the hell, neither am I."

"Stop worrying about her. She'll live, she's a mutant. Our healing factor is much stronger than humans."

Marc looked at Lani, her Hawaiian complexion, almond-shaped eyes. She was beautiful.

*"She's not your girlfriend, Marc."* Doris moved close to him and ran her fingers through his hair. *"I am."*

"Don't do that." A shiver went down his back as her fingernails ran across the back of his neck. His shoulders crunched up in response.

Doris pulled at him, turning his face toward her abdomen.

*"You love me. You love how I make you feel. Comfortable, aroused."*

He dropped the washcloth and wrapped his arms around her. He loved Doris, he just knew it. He didn't really feel any love for her. There were plenty of times he hated her, like earlier today. But here, now, he loved her. It was something he had always known. What he may have felt for Lani was different, but it would never last. His love for Doris was much more enduring, sustaining. He didn't always have this love for Doris, and she was pushing these thoughts into him. She had done it before. And she was just as irresistible now as she was then.

"You do this on purpose. Why?"

"If I can't get into your heart one way, I use the other."

Marc stood up and held on to her. Their lips met in a passionate kiss. He wanted to sink into her. Then he felt himself lifting upward.

His eyes opened and glimpsed the purplish glow around them as they smashed into the bedroom wall, his forehead bouncing against it over Doris' shoulder. The force was enough for their bodies to crush the drywall in several places.

"ASSHOLE!" Lani shouted.

Marc turned to see Lani crawling off of the bed. She held a hand to the back of her head. He could see she was still in some pain.

"Damn those hurt." Doris' voice was weak. She was still in his arms, but she was slipping to the floor.

"Lani!" Marc held tight onto Doris with one arm while holding the other out as if to block the next blast from her. "I can explain."

"Like hell, you can. I saw you, at her place. I saw what Michael saw."

"She must have… seen some of Michael's memories," Doris whispered.

Lani pushed out another broad blast. Prepared, Marc went translucent, allowing the force to go through Doris and him without effect, the bedroom wall taking the full brunt of the energy. A cacophony surrounded him, wood snapping, bathroom wall tiles cracking. A cloud of drywall dust filled the bedroom.

"Damn it, Lani. Stop!" Marc coughed at the powder floating around them as he returned to normal.

"Go to hell, Major." Lani stood up and stumbled past him.

Marc laid Doris on the bed where Lani had been. He heard another crashing noise as he rushed into the living room. The balcony glass door was shattered along with a large section of the outer wall missing. Sparks jumped from the missing lower right corner of his wide-screen TV. One of the mounting brackets gave way, and the television swung to the left and fell to the floor.

"Well, shit."

He took a step toward the opening in the wall, then heard Doris groan. Marc looked back at the bedroom and sighed.

"Should have gone to the stadium."

The ground rose to meet Lani as she tried to fly out the hole she made. Instead, her ability to fly only saved her from a hard landing among the broken bricks, twisted metal, and shattered glass. Hurt physically and emotionally, she laid on the warm grass, curling into a fetal position.

Glass doors on apartment balconies slid around her. Someone shouted about an explosion. Lani urged herself to get up. Still daylight, no NSA badge. Can't let the police find me. Got to hide somewhere.

Lani unclenched her arms from her legs and rolled to her hands and knees. Through her tangled hair, she saw a man approaching. She created a violet aura around her, hiding her features as she stood up. With a stream of purple light trailing behind her, Lani launched herself into the sky. She flew too fast to check for any air traffic going to any of the three nearby airports. Chesapeake Control was going to be pissed, she was sure of that. But at the moment, she didn't care.

The pain stabbing at her heart felt worse than the pain throbbing at the back of her head. Lani felt around in her hair, finding blood. She knew she would need to go higher.

What the connection was between Marc and Doris, Lani

couldn't tell. But they were kissing passionately. That man—whoever he was—was in her body. And she was in his, trapped in the wheelchair, paralyzed. She recalled some of his memories, of Marc and Doris, of him with President Taylor, seeing Dad on the stage. There were arguments between him and Doris, about his injuries and her refusing to heal him. It confined him to the wheelchair, his face being covered whenever a therapist came to visit. Lani still recalled seeing his attempts to mind swap with Doris, being stopped by her mental shield. Going through Michael's memories still lingering in her mind, she lost all thought of Marc.

Lani soared up to her usual altitude of fifty thousand feet, well above the city, the cloud cover, and airliner traffic, then turned southeast over the ocean so she could drop to a lower, more breathable altitude and drift with the winds. The sun filled the northwestern part of the sky, blocking any visible aurora, but she could feel the energy of the sun's solar wind interacting with the earth's magnetic force. The solar particles energized her, giving her strength, and relaxing her all at the same time. It also helped to heal the wound on her head.

Lani spread her arms outward, her head back. She wanted to float higher, to absorb more of the aurora, but the air was thinner, making it more difficult to breathe. She didn't have her protective bubble around her, filled with the air being pushed ahead of her. And she was in no shape to fly fast enough for very far.

Michael's mind swap was an unfamiliar experience for her—unique—but not all that strange for a mutant. Marc and Doris were a whole different thing. Through Michael, she saw them together. Then again, just now. She had to talk with someone about it. Samira's in the hospital. Adam's off with Mendoza. Mom's even farther away.

A smile grew across her face. Someone she talked with nearly every day.

Troy.


The airplane traffic wove an intricate pattern under Lani as she drifted just under the cloud cover over the apartment complex north of the DC beltway. She had to apologize profusely as she took a scolding from Chesapeake Central for her rapid ascent.

Drifting down to the balcony of her apartment, she manipulated the electronic lock before touching down on the concrete slab. Inside, she stared at the blanket that she and Marc had laid under earlier today. Grabbing it, Lani rolled it into a ball and tossed it to a corner. There was a clothing drop-off center not far away.

She tossed all of her electronics onto the bed, then stripped off the flight suit, dropping it to the floor. She reached around to unhook her bra, but stopped. Tiptoeing into the living room, hands charging up, she searched the place for any visitors. Half expecting Marc or Doris to be in the room, she really didn't want to blast a hole in these walls. Maybe just a targeted laser beam to the forehead.

Confident no one was in the apartment, Lani went back to the bedroom. She undressed the rest of the way, then grabbed her smartphone and tapped the screen.

"Call Troy."

The injury to her head throbbed as she mentally listened to the phone. The connection rang three times before someone answered.

"Air Force! Enjoying our vacation?"

Lani sighed. "Guess this one is on me, isn't it?"

"Nah, not my first disciplinary week-off."

"Interesting. I didn't know." She walked to the bathroom and turned on the water in the shower.

"There's a lot about me you don't know."

Lani raised an eyebrow. He was right; she knew little about him. Married once, single now, no kids. That was about all he'd ever shared about his past. Her, he knew everything about her past, including Boston.

She could hear the ball game playing in the background. "So, what's the score?"

"Ahead by two. Weren't you going to the game tonight?"

"Yeah, an old friend of Marc's came into town instead." Her fist glowed. Lani shook her hand, dispersing the energy. "Say, I could really use some company right now. You mind if I come over for a while?"

She heard a grunt and the sound of something bouncing around on the floor.

"Shit. Ah, yeah, sure. You have my address?"

"I got it. You okay?"

"Yeah, just dropped something." The TV noise faded, then she heard a grunt, bare footsteps over a tile floor, then a wooden door closing. "Come on over. I still have a few cold ones."

"Sounds great. See you in a few."

Lani stepped into the water and let the thoughts of Michael and of Marc wash away.

With the truck windows open, the hot summer wind blew Lani's hair all around. She ran her fingers through it occasionally, pulling the wet strands off of her face. The shower helped her clear her mind and her mutant DNA sped up the healing process on her skull, but a lingering ache remained.

Troy lived north of the NSA building, closer to BWI Airport, too close to fly to without dealing with the air traffic. Still, she packed her flight suit and electronics into a small duffel bag and tossed it in the truck. Just in case.

There was something about driving Dad's truck that centered her. It made her feel normal. For someone who wasn't a mutant, her dad was so damn cool about being a mutant. At least she didn't think he was. Neither he nor her mom talked about it if they were. Adam wouldn't say. Him and his damn 'don't ask, don't tell' philosophy.

Lani knew she was not normal, let alone living a normal life. Events as what happened yesterday and today were evidence of that. Seeing her body prancing around, under control of someone else, still shook her. But not as deep as seeing Marc kissing that hag. Lani felt a surge as she recalled the scene. She blinked several times, dismissing the image and dispersing the energy. Making the truck shutdown on the freeway now would be a bad thing.

Sliding out of the truck, she tugged at her pink v-neck top. Lani loved her Dad's truck, but her shirt always seemed to ride up in the back as she drove. She climbed back onto the running boards to reach across the seat for the bottle of wine she had pulled out of her refrigerator.

As she walked up to the front door, she heard a shout from inside, above the sound of the ballgame. More of a curse. She rapped on the door, and the TV volume decreased. Troy opened the front door and stepped back.

"Army." Lani smiled, holding up her bottle of wine.

"Air Force! Nice hairdo. Come on in." He was still wearing his clover green polo, but faded jeans instead of the khaki slacks.

"I'm guessing that wasn't a Nationals hit?" Lani walked past him, catching a whiff of fresh deodorant and minty toothpaste. She smirked at his attempt to hide the beer breath.

"Of course not. Damn pitcher. Gave up two runs already."

Lani pointed to the kitchen, and Troy nodded. "Yeah, help

yourself."

She sat the bottle down on the counter next to the wet dishcloth that smelled of beer. She opened cabinet doors, looking for a wine glass.

"Above the dishwasher." Troy said, sitting down on the couch.

She found the cabinet with glasses, but nothing resembling a wine glass. In fact, there wasn't much of anything in the kitchen that resembled a small appliance. The place was more of a bachelor pad than Adam's place. Or hers.

Commercials started up when Lani walked back into the living room. She looked around the room, noting the decorations. Lots of wood and natural colors, a bookcase of old musty books. No photos, which surprised her, but only slightly.

"Finally made it out of the inning," Troy said, pointing to the armchairs facing the TV. Lani sat in the chair closest to the couch where he was at. Both took long looks at their drinks, then their eyes met.

"But I'm guessing you aren't here for the baseball."

"You are a smart man, Troy Thornburg." She took a long sip of the red wine.

"So, brother or boyfriend?" He took a drink as well.

"Why would you think one of those?" Lani tucked her feet up under her and got comfortable.

"Okay, that rules out the brother."

"Did I mention what a smart man you are?"

"Well, I've been in a few relationships myself." Troy leaned back against the cushion and waved outwards. "I kept the house after the last one."

"Must be why there're no photos anywhere."

Troy took a drink from his beer can. "No photos, didn't happen. Right?"

Lani nodded, also drinking.

Troy rubbed his chin. "Guessing again, the 'friend from out of town' wasn't a guy."

"Three for three."

"And you're trying to figure out what to do about it?"

"Damn, you are good. You used to guess people's weight at the circus, didn't you?"

Troy turned and stared at the TV. "Yeah, that's me, a damn circus clown."

Lani wanted to kick herself. "Sorry, didn't mean to bring up a touchy subject."

"Nah, it's not your fault." He took the last drink from his can and sat it on the coffee table. "Now, let's get back to you. What did the guy do? Marc, right?"

She nodded at the correct name. "Before or after I blasted him against his bedroom wall?"

"Ouch. And this is the guy that can walk through walls, too."

"Not when I catch him off-guard." She took another long drink.

"What do you want to do with the guy?"

"Well, there's always Romero down on fourth floor."

"Ah, black ops to take him out. What about his ghost trick?"

"Like I said, just gotta catch him off guard."

"Could just do it the usual way. You know, 'Dear John' text message."

Lani wrinkled her nose. "Too simple."

Troy grabbed his beer can and stood up, reaching for her wineglass as he passed by her.

"So, how did you come to be single?" Lani winced when she said it, wanting to slap her forehead.

"Two missions too many."

Lani heard the refrigerator door open then close. Troy walked back to her, holding a full glass of wine in one hand, a beer can in the other. Lani looked up at him and saw his eyes glancing down to her cleavage, then back to her eyes. She shook her head and sighed.

The mention of NSA missions intrigued her. She finally learned a bit more about him. "Too many? How so?"

"Jackie—Jacelyn—and I were okay through my first few short missions. It was the longer ones that killed it." He popped his can open and took a drink. "Had a rather long mission over in the Middle East, came back pretty rough looking. Jackie didn't care for that so much. I guess you could say she was high maintenance, a nail polish and perfume kind of girl."

Lani knew plenty of women like that. She was too much of a *tomboy* growing up, trying to keep up with a brother three years older than her, playing in the ocean or later, in the air.

"Anyway, had another long mission in England." Troy continued. "Over a year in England. Had to stay deep cover, could only make three messages to her during that time. When I got back around Thanksgiving, there was nothing to give thanks for, except an empty house and a ton of utility bills to pay before I could flush the toilet."

"How long were you together?"

"Less than a week after our third anniversary. Missed all three of them."

They sat in silence for a long moment. Lani watched his eyes dart around the room, wanting to look, but not wanting to make eye contact. What was up with him, anyway? She wanted him to look up, but was glad he didn't. Kind of. The silence was becoming awkward.

"Dad's ambassador to Russia, huh? What's Lauren think of Moscow?"

"My mom? She's not there. Lives in Boston, runs a hospital there." Troy took a drink, then gazed at the top of the can. "She specializes in mutant anatomy, illnesses, and injuries."

Lani stared at the red wine for a moment. His mom's name? Her name wasn't mentioned when they met his father in Moscow. Michael, that's the connection. He wanted to see her, to heal him. Doris wouldn't let him.

Her stomach grumbled, reminding her she hadn't eaten since the banana at Mom's house. "Say, are you hungry?"

"May have some cheese and crackers. I haven't been shopping for a while."

"I was thinking about Mexican." Lani cocked her head to one side.

"Sounds good. There's a Mexican grill not too far way."

"I know a place near Los Alamos that serves excellent burritos 24/7."

"Los Alamos, as in New Mexico?"

"Yeah, a place called Cerro Grande."

Troy's head jerked back. "You want to crash the President's house. You don't mean…" Troy made an upward motion with his hand, mimicking a plane taking off.

"Sure. Only what, six o'clock there. Adam's bound to be eating by now. We can be there in fifteen minutes or less."

"Please. The three minutes it took to fly from the detention facility back to Moscow airport was bad enough." He walked back to the kitchen.

"This will be easier." Lani got up and followed him. "There won't be any surface-to-air missiles to avoid."

As she walked into the kitchen, Troy turned and they collided. Lani stood there for a moment, wanting to reach up and touch him, before Troy took a step back.

"Ah, awkward. Sorry about that." Troy mumbled.

"Oh, I don't know." She touched the side of his face with her hand. There was a longing inside of her she didn't understand.

Her focus flipped between his left eye and right, urging something to happen.

"That wine seems to hit you bad. Maybe you shouldn't go flying." Troy took a hold of her hand and lowered it.

She blinked repeatedly, clearing her focus. She sat her glass on the counter and stared at him. "Screw the wine. Flying is just what I need to clear my mind. We should try it. Put on jeans and pack a bag." Lani patted him on the chest, then headed for the door.

The heat and the setting sun hit Lani hard as she stepped outside. She held onto the doorknob, steadying herself. She wasn't sure if it was the wine or the blow to her head that almost caused her to lose her balance. Flying would help clear her mind, she told herself, again. Better than a slow walk in the park, as her Dad would say. Of course, her Mom would add in how hard it was to hold hands in a fighter jet.

She grabbed her duffel bag from the passenger side, slinging the strap over her shoulder. Inside Troy's house, she didn't see him around. The television was off, so she took that as his acceptance of the offer to go with her. Figuring out the floor plan of the spec home, Lani located the second bathroom and closed the door behind her.

Pulling her shirt over her head, Lani kept reminding herself this was just two co-workers going out for food and drinks. Nothing more. Okay, maybe the wine was hitting her hard, but that wouldn't explain why she thought Troy was hot. She'd sat across the aisle from him at NSA for five months, been out together on multiple missions. There wasn't a least bit of attraction before. Why now?

Pulling her flight suit up over her shoulders, she caught sight of herself in the small medicine cabinet mirror. Michael's face briefly flashed, replacing her own until she blinked again. Lani tried to shrug it off, lasting effect of the mind swap, maybe. Maybe a residual bit of Michael's consciousness remained because of the abrupt method of swapping back, thanks to the blow to the head. That could explain why she felt like she was flirting with Troy. One memory she experienced from Michael was his sexuality. Briefly, she wondered what memories he stole from her.

A couple of knocks sounded on the door. "Air Force. You in there?"

Lani reached for the zipper and pulled. "Yeah, just a sec." She stuffed her civilian clothes in the duffel and opened the door.

Troy was standing in the center of his living room, jeans and a Nats t-shirt with matching duffel hanging from his shoulder.

Lani pointed at him. "Good call. Mendoza gonna love that shirt."

He pointed back at her. "Well, my flight suit is at the cleaners right now."

She giggled, then led the way outside. After waiting for him to lock the door, she walked out to stand in front of her truck.

"Chesapeake Central, Knight seven-three-four personal. Traffic check." She pulled the strap of her duffel over her head and across her body, motioning for Troy to do the same. "Flying two six five at angels fifty, landing at Cerro Grande."

Troy crossed his arms, looking down at her. "Who are you talking to?"

*"Copy that, Lani. Standby five."*

"Space Command." Lani pointed upward.

"They keep track of you when you go flying?"

She nodded. "Especially around here. Anywhere else, they have a tracker on me, as do most of us."

"Most of who?"

"Mutants with high-speed flight ability."

"And just how fast…"

Lani smiled, wanting to brag. "Fastest I've done is Mach 15, just shy of ten thousand miles an hour, at an altitude of fifty thousand feet."

"And you know this how?"

*"Knight seven-three-four, ten-minute window. Contact Gulf Central at the Mississippi. Have a pleasant flight."*

*"Copy that, Tim. And apologies again for the unannounced earlier."*

*"It's okay, Lani. I got your back."*

Lani put an arm around Troy's back. "Another device relays the info via a signal I can sense."

"How is it you're just a wiretap for the NSA?" Troy brushed the tree branch aside as they floated upward. "You can out match any aircraft on the planet in speed and weaponry, yet all you do is listen in on telephone conversations."

"Guess I just haven't found my niche yet."

"You should go back to the Air Force and find other mutants like you. Start your own squadron or something."

"Trying to get rid of me?"

"Nah, no. I just see what you are good at and wonder why no one else has."

Lani looked around her as she cleared the one-thousand-foot elevation. "Cause I'm hard to follow."

Two sonic booms sounded as Lani launched them farther into the air.

*Friday, June 23*
*Present Day*

Adam stepped out of his room at the Western White House and sighed. He always packed blue jeans and casual shirts for dress-down occasions. However, when Adam was anywhere with the President, he always felt on duty and wore his standard black suit jacket and slacks.

He tugged at the short sleeves of his blue and gray shirt as he walked to the President's office. The office was dark. Smiling, Adam realized where he would be in front of the TV. He cleared the large foyer to the entertainment room. The Nationals/Phillies ball game played on the huge ceiling-to-floor television screen. Adam sat down on the arm of the empty chair next to the President, glad the man was at least pretending to relax.

"Any score yet?" Adam asked.

"Nats are ahead so far, one to nothing."

"I've told Barrett where I'll be, in case something should happen."

Antonio waved him off. "Nonsense. You aren't the only agent on the team, you know. I've got a ton of marines and other Secret Service agents here. We'll be fine."

"You know what I mean." Adam stared at him. "Okay, Barrett knows what to do. There are suppressors staged throughout the mansion, right?"

Antonio pointed to a table against the left wall. "Got one over there, the usual weekly battery checks done and everything. Now get out of here."

"Just checking."

"No one should have to wear the headbands. But just like handcuffs, they serve a purpose."

Adam sat, watching a Phillies player pop a fly out to center field. He was more of a football fan than baseball, so it felt strange that he should feel anticipation at the play. The outfielder caught the ball, and anticipation was replaced with relief.

He turned to the President, seeing him edge forward, then realized the emotion was coming from him, being pushed out by his mutant ability. Adam looked to the table against the wall, considering the ability suppressor.

"Mr. President."

Antonio leaned back in his chair, reaching for the beer can at his side. "What? Don't worry about me. I will call before I go launching any nuclear attack."

"I'm serious, sir. Just now, you—"

"Go. Have fun, damn it. You deserve it. And take one of the Marine's Humvees. Just in case you need to go off road."

"Thank you, sir. I think my Jeep will do just fine. Have a good night." Adam felt excitement, then saw that the commercial was over and the Nats were up to bat. He shook his head. Best to tell Strickland to keep a suppressor on hand. Just in case.

The drive to Los Alamos would be a thirty-minute drive. Adam walked outside and around to the garage area of the ranch. A black, nondescript four-door Jeep sans doors waited for him. Adam pulled the keys from the dashboard tray and headed down the hill past the two gates and into town.

Parking around the Pasta House was full, as Adam expected. Los Alamos was a small town. It didn't take much to fill up the restaurants on a Friday night. A small contingent of press corps stayed in town to report on any activity in or around the Mendoza residence, and a select few photographers stalked any visitor, celebrity or otherwise, who may find their way up the mountainside. Dressed in something other than a black suit and tie, he didn't expect any paparazzi to stalk him.

He found a spot half a block away and walked up to the restaurant. Four couples stood or sat near the *WAIT TO BE SEATED* sign at the entrance. Rubbing his sweaty hands against the pockets of his jeans, Adam stood on his tiptoes to get a view of the dining area. His phone buzzed.

**Unknown:** *At the bar.*

Adam spun his head around. Erin sat at the end, dressed in a white, spaghetti-strap top, white skirt, black high heels, and a matching clutch. He tugged at the collar of his button-down shirt, the air-conditioning vent he stood under not affecting the heat he felt right then. Adam pushed passed a couple of reporters he recognized from the flight on Air Force One and made his way to the bar. He climbed into the empty seat beside her.

"By the way, how did you get my number?" he asked, waving to get the bartender's attention.

"I have a few sources. I do work for a Mutant Defense Foundation group, remember?"

"Okay, true."

The bartender finally made it to their end of the bar. Adam ordered a single beer; Erin was only half-way through hers.

"This place is crazy busy." Erin brought the bottle to her lips. "Reminds me of homecoming night in Ann Arbor."

"Yeah, I remember the Field House used to be packed

shoulder to shoulder by this time of night, whether the game hadn't started or already ended."

"Hostess said it would be a half-hour wait to get a table. Hope you don't mind eating at the bar."

"Nah, it's good. You look fabulous, by the way."

Erin blushed, causing some opalescence of her skin coming to light. Her necklace seemed to sparkle more. She brushed her shoulder-length platinum blonde hair back over her ear. A natural blonde, as he recalled.

"Thank you. You've been working out more, I see."

"Yeah, my life as a bodyguard."

"Secret Service, huh?" Erin said. "That's a change from FBI."

"True. Once they found out what my abilities were, it wasn't long before they recruited me. President Taylor also had a Shield on her detail, so they placed me on Mendoza's detail."

"A shield?"

"A power blocker, like me." Adam said. "Anyway, when Mendoza took office after the explosion, he kept me on his detail."

"How's your mother?"

"Doing good, living back in Hawaii."

"I feel bad about having to break up with you after the protest. My parents pushed me to leave Michigan. Not like Harvard was any better. Anyway, after law school, I met a guy and fell in love. He was human."

Adam detected a bit of a sigh. "Not what you were expecting?"

"Turns out he wanted to date me for the novelty of being with a mutant."

"Lani used to talk about guys hitting her up just so she would take them flying. Thrill seekers. Me, I never had to worry about it."

The bartender dropped off a plate of small bread slices, then took their order—tortellini for Adam and manicotti for Erin.

"You mean no one hits on Secret Service agents?"

"Gotta keep that as low key as possible, you know. So, not a lot there. Did you get married?"

"I did, but it didn't last long. Office romance. He had a fear that someday our child might set him on fire during a tantrum. He filed for divorce—unreconcilable differences. Soon after, Mutant Defense Foundation contacted me, and I joined, steering clear of the protest marches and taking part in just the political arena."

They talked and laughed, sharing memories of funny events with family and friends. Erin mentioned St. Petersburg and the October Uprising. Adam went silent for a second, then told her about Janice, a fellow agent whose dying act was saving him.

"The powerful man threw her ten feet across the alley. Just before the guy could grab the President, Janice shot him, then collapsed. When I got to her, she was gone."

He paused, turning to look toward the bartender, away from her. He coughed to clear his throat, then took a drink from his beer. Erin reached out and touched him on the cheek.

"Adam, I'm so sorry." She leaned forward, touching his arm. In a stark reaction, Adam leaned back, his eyebrows furrowed deep.

"Kobay…" Adam started.

"Erin!" A voice shouted behind them. "There you are!"

"… ashi."

The mutant bumped against her, beer spilling from his mug. Erin reacted, turning the liquid into a rubbery gel that bounced off of her shirt and fell to the floor.

"DK!" Erin shouted. "What the hell are you doing?"

She grabbed the mug from his hands before he could slip any more. At a distance behind him, the other two members of the Mutant Defense Foundation group approached, not appearing as drunk.

"Screwin' 'round with President's butt boy?" Daiki slurred his words.

He put his hands on their shoulders. The strap of Erin's shirt dissolved, the remaining fabric falling down. The cotton threads in Adam's shirt became powder and fell off of him, creating a hole in the sleeve the size of his palm. The motion caught Adam off-guard, unable to do anything but watch. The decay spread down the sleeve and across the shirt, turning it into half of a muscle shirt. Adam pulled the rolled section of his sleeve off his wrist.

Daiki put his hand over his mouth as he faked a gasp. "Oops. Did I do that?"

Erin got off of the bar stool and into Daiki's face. Shorter than him, she glared hard at him, shoving a finger passed him while holding her shirt on with the other. "Damn it, DK. Outside, now." She looked behind him and saw Diego and Thandi, trying to back away. "All of you."

Erin pushed passed her friends, shoving her way toward the entrance. The few customers watching made a path for them.

Adam smiled to the bartender and laid a one hundred-dollar bill next to his beer glass.

"For the drinks and any damages that might occur in the next few minutes."

"Keep it," the bartender said. "In case you lose more than the shirt."

The sun had already dipped below the western mountain range, but the ambient light kept the tall street lights from turning on. Erin had walked past the *pasta to go* parking spots and the overflow of people waiting with buzzers in hand. Diego and Thandi followed behind with Daiki. At first, Adam thought he was walking pretty well, considering his slurred speech earlier, but noticed his toes were dragging the ground. Diego was levitating him, pulling him along.

"Hey, Erin, come on," Diego said, letting Daiki drift down to the asphalt. "You know he gets this way."

Erin stopped in an open section of the parking lot, in front of a closed store, a 'For Lease' sign hanging in the front window. She turned and closed the distance between them. Lips pursed, she pointed an index finger pointing at them. Adam had experienced the anger in her eyes before. It was not a pretty sight then, and won't be now either.

"Yeah, he gets jealous and scares people off," Erin shouted. "How in the hell are we supposed to convince people we aren't to be feared if he goes around making tires rot away on a car because the driver cut him off?"

Adam unbuttoned his shirt and pulled it off, leaving his white t-shirt on. Circling around the Mutant Defense Foundation members, he joined Erin at her side. He felt Daiki using his ability. Rapidly, he looked around at the cars, the people, the trees lining the building. A green aura flashed around Daiki, then faded inward. Adam recognized that the focus wasn't on the area around Daiki, but on himself. On the alcohol in his body. He was making himself sober.

"Impressive," Adam whispered. "Rapid decomposition of matter, organic or synthetic. Would have come in handy in Russia a few days ago."

"You're not helping." Erin replied.

"Splash," Daiki said, calling out to Erin. Awkwardly, he got to his knees and stood. "Come on, let's go home."

"Don't think so, DK," she said. "Not this time. Not again."

A frown came across his face that turned into a grimace. Daiki rolled his hands around each other, a dark green ball of energy forming between them. He thrust a hand toward a tree at the side of the restaurant. A two-foot section of the trunk dissolved, toppling the tree onto the pavement. Adam grabbed Erin and pulled her away from the limbs.

Green energy crackled around the fallen branches, and the wood fell apart into sawdust as Daiki walked through it. Another ball of energy formed.

Adam reached out with his mutant ability and snapped control of Thandi's shadow ability and cast a circular wall of darkness around them. Then he blocked Daiki, causing the weave of green and black to expand out, dissipating like whispers of smoke.

"Ah, a blocker." Daiki stepped closer to Adam. "Well, block this."

His right foot swung up at Adam's chin. He dodged the kick, grabbed his leg, and sent Daiki falling to the ground. On his back, Daiki tried to swing his legs around to knock Adam off his feet. Adam stepped backwards, clearing the motion.

As Daiki stood up, Diego ran and blocked him. "Dude, back down. You don't need this."

Daiki tried to shove him aside, but Diego increased the gravitational pull on him, making his arms heavier.

"Damn you," Daiki dropped to his knees from the weight he felt. "Siding with Erin?"

Diego pointed to the hands poking through the wall of darkness. "No, trying to keep you from damaging *the Foundation* more than we need."

Thandi ran over to Erin. "You better go, honey." She looked to Adam. "We got this."

Adam released control over Thandi's ability, dropping the wall of darkness. "Erin?"

"Yeah, let's go."

Adam motioned toward his Jeep. "Stay with me tonight, at the mansion."

Erin pulled back and looked at him. "At the President's estate? Will he mind?"

"He won't mind. He likes you. Hell, he gave me a lecture when I considered not showing up."

"You would stand me up?"

"Trust me, relationships for Secret Service agents do not last long. Especially for agents like me."

"Mutant Secret Service agents. How many are there?"

"Oh, I'm not the only one. Just the one Mendoza keeps close at hand."

Adam heard Erin let out a deep sigh. "Yes, I would love to stay with you tonight. Let me get my things from the hotel."

"Don't worry. I'll have an agent get them for you."

Erin tilted her head down as if looking over a pair of glasses. "I'm not having unknown men gathering up my things."

Adam smiled, helping her into the Jeep. "The Secret Service is not a men's only club. There are several women, plus some female staff members at the mansion we can send."

Daiki stood with his hands on his hips, watching Erin and Adam drive away.

"We done here?" Diego asked to both Daiki and Thandi.

Thandi nodded. "Just about."

"In that case," Diego stepped toward the restaurant. "I need another drink."

Adam stopped the jeep at the post across the entrance road and reached into his back pocket for his ID.

"Good evening, sir, ma'am." The soldier took a step from the guard shack and approached.

"Evening, Dave." Adam held his badge out. "This is Erin Murphy. She was here earlier today."

"Ms. Murphy," the soldier nodded as he waved the red beam of a scanner over Adam's badge. "ID, please."

Erin fished her wallet from her clutch, flipped it open and pulled out the plastic card. The soldier took the card, passed the scanner over it, then handed it to Adam.

"Thank you, sir. Have a nice evening." The soldier took a step backward and saluted. The post across the road raised and Adam drove on.

At the top of the hill, he drove around the fountain in the center of the drive and parked. A staff valet stepped out of a side door from the building and held out a hand to help Erin climb out. She greeted him and waited for Adam to come around from the driver's side before walking toward the front door.

"Must be nice to have service like that." She whispered to him as they entered the house.

"I'm told they are glad when the President is here. Otherwise, it's boring."

Adam heard a shout followed by a groan come from the great room across from the entryway. He smirked a little as he put his hand on Erin's lower back.

"Sounds like the Nationals aren't doing so well."

He escorted her into a large room, several reclining chairs and sofas set about, most facing the television screen with a baseball game playing.

"Adam! How was dinner?" Antonio waved, sitting in the center chair. He sat down his drink and stood up when he saw Adam was not alone.

"Ah, Erin, right?" He walked over to them and shook hands with her.

"Yes, Mr. President."

"Antonio, please. Come in." He looked at Adam's t-shirt and the missing strap on Erin's top. "Dinner must have been really something."

"We didn't eat. One of Erin's co-members of Mutant Defense Foundation interrupted us."

"Well, damn." He stepped back to his chair and picked up a small remote-looking device. Before he could rejoin them, a woman stepped into the room.

"Ms. Alvarez, do you think we have anything Ms. Murphy can wear? And alert the kitchen."

"Sir, with your permission," Adam interrupted. "I've offered Erin a room tonight, just in case."

Adam saw Antonio smile. "Plenty of room. Mi casa es su casa." He looked to the maid. "Have Allyson talk with Ms. Murphy so she can gather our guest's items from the hotel."

"What's left of it." Erin mumbled. She grabbed Adam's hand and squeezed, then went to join Ms. Alvarez.

"Thank you very much, sir." Adam nodded to the projector. "How's the game?"

"Oh, hell, you know the Nats. Lost 4-3. They left the pitcher in too long and let Philly get the lead." He looked at Adam's shirt. "So, what happened?"

"Seems Kobayashi has a crush on Erin. He caught me off guard and caused the cotton in my shirt to turn to ash. Then he tried to pick a fight with me in the parking lot."

"Were you able to handle it?"

"Yeah, the other guy from their group stepped in. Kobayashi could be a threat. That's why I thought it might be a good idea if Erin stays here for the night."

Antonio nodded, then smiled again. "Were you thinking the Rose Room or…?"

Adam smirked at the President. He could tell he was using his abilities, no doubt assessing Adam's emotional state. "Yes, sir. Thank you."

"No problem." Antonio patted him on the shoulder, then went back to the after-game show.

The Rose Room was large with two queen-size beds, next to Adam's adopted room. His king-size bed would be more than enough, larger than the bed he and Erin shared when they lived together at the University of Michigan. Still, there was much for them to talk about before that would happen. Like her relationship with DK.

He changed shirts before heading to the kitchen. Two cooks busy heating fajitas, hamburger, and refried beans. He went for the refrigerator and pulled out a cold bottle of soda. His phone buzzed as he twisted off the cap. The caller ID had the name of the lead agent assigned to the night shift.

"Knight here. Go ahead."

"Sir, Kirtland AFB reports in-bound airborne mutant. It's your sister."

"Understood. I'll meet her in the courtyard."

He took a drink from the bottle, then headed for the front door. On the way, he spotted Erin approaching with Allyson. Erin was now wearing a pastel yellow top with red trim, and a bright smile.

"You look nice." Adam noticed her skin glisten.

"Thank you. It's Allyson's."

"Anything else, sir, let me know." Allyson smiled and stepped back before walking away.

He stood and waited for her, holding out his hand. Her hand in his felt good, bringing back memories from ages ago. The whole evening tonight made him realize how much of his life had been focused around the President and the White House. He had socialized with only a few people other than his sister.

Adam reached around Erin and pulled her close. She responded, her hand stretching across his waist.

"Missed this," she whispered.

"Me too." He pointed toward the door. "I have to go out front. Lani's coming."

"Oh, God. I haven't seen her since the protest." Erin's face went serious, putting a hand to her chest.

Adam frowned, wanting to kick himself. "Sorry." He wasn't sure why he apologized. The protest and her injury was the reason Erin's parents forced her to move to another college, ending their relationship, until today.

Erin's smile returned as she squeezed him. "Don't worry. That was a long time ago."

They walked outside, Adam moving to the edge of the sidewalk close to the door. He acknowledged the two agents standing a distance off from the courtyard drive, nodding to each of them. One agent approached, handing him a set of binoculars.

Adam nodded, then reached into his pant pocket and pulled out his earpiece.

"He's online now, Captain." The agent said.

"Hey, bro."

"Hey, sis. What brings you this way?" He raised the binoculars and focused on a point of light, just visible in the darkening sky.

"Thornburg and I were hungry for Mexican."

"What, Taco Bell not open in DC?" Adam handed her the binoculars, pointing at the falling star coming toward them.

"Nah, you know I like the real stuff."

"You like free food."

"Well, there's that too. Say, Mendoza still has that flower room, right?"

Adam looked at Erin and raised an eyebrow. "Someone might take it tonight, but I think we can make arrangements. You said Thornburg with you?"

"Yeah, is that a problem?"

"Not for me. You are on an open channel, by the way."

"Oh, right. You'd answer your phone once in a while…"

Erin handed the binocs back. The falling star grew in size as Lani dropped from her cruising altitude. As she slowed, the purplish glow around her lessened in brightness, but remained as a slight aura. Adam saw she was wearing her specially made flight suit and a bag over one shoulder. Troy had an arm wrapped high on her back, also with a duffel bag.

"Incoming in sight. Stand down alert." Adam spoke to his comm link, then pulled the earpiece out and stuffed it in his jeans pocket.

Lani and Troy touched down in the circle drive between the fountain and the front door.

Adam walked up to them and held out his hand. "Troy. Didn't expect to see you so soon."

Troy took his hand and gripped hard. "Well, when the lady offers authentic Mexican food, I couldn't turn it down."

"Hi, Lani." Erin walked up to Adam's side, her hand down low, waving to Lani.

Lani smiled and dashed to her, arms open wide. Adam thought they were two long-lost sisters for a moment.

"Erin! God, it's so good to see you. How are you? Love your top."

Adam sighed, relieved. He patted Troy on his back. "Come on inside."

"Did I hear Lani's voice on the comms?" A voice boomed out from the house.

Antonio stood at the front door, fists on his hips. As soon as he got Adam's attention, he walked out to the edge of the sidewalk. Lani advanced, then snapped to and saluted him. Antonio waved off the salute and reached out to shake hands. Lani closed the distance and took his hand. She turned and pointed to Troy.

"Mr. President, this is Troy Thornburg, my partner at NSA."

"Sir." Troy reached out to shake hands.

"Troy. How are your parents?"

"Fine, sir. My father met us in Moscow. I don't see much of my mother these days."

Antonio crossed his arms. "You were lead on the Atlantic Fleet investigation."

Troy hung his head down. "Yes, sir. Sorry, sir. We weren't expecting the insider to be a mutant."

"Seems nowadays, we need to assume any threat to be a mutant." He looked at the group standing around him. "No offense."

"None taken, sir. We're all on your side." Lani said.

Adam smirked at the President's comment, knowing full well

that the President was a mutant. It was a secret he had to keep, and the secret from everyone else's mutant capability.

"Well, come on in." Antonio motioned toward the door. "I told Ms. Alvarez to fire up the second stove."

"Lani." Adam touched Lani on her arm, motioning for her to stay. She released her grip on Erin and waited as the others followed the President inside. When there was a distance, he crossed his arms and stared at Lani. "So, where's Marc?"

Lani's shoulders sunk as she looked up at him. "I left him."

"Something I need to know about?"

"Let's say it involved an older woman."

Adam sighed, wrapping his arm around her. "Ok. Let me know if I need to go beat him up."

"You haven't done that since high school."

"You haven't had a serious boyfriend since high school."

She let out a huff and smiled. "Doesn't matter now. I'm hungry."

Inside, they found Antonio sitting at the head of the dinner table, Erin and Troy sitting across from one another next to him. Each had a plate of beef fajitas along with refried beans and Mexican rice. Lani walked over to a cook, holding out a plate and motioning to the various dishes to choose from. Adam had the cook roll up two burritos, no rice.

"So, what'cha up to?" Lani asked of Erin.

"Well, my paying job is law clerk for Chief Justice Addison. The rest of my time is with Mutant Defense Foundation."

"Oh, so you're just down the street from the White House. Where Adam hangs out at."

Lani's glare at Adam didn't go unnoticed.

"You're not in the Air Force anymore?" Erin asked as Lani sat next to her.

"Well, kind of still am, just on assignment to NSA."

"Probably seen some strange stuff."

"Strange can hardly describe it, sometimes. Having bone daggers thrown at me, chasing invisible men. Even spent a few minutes today inside another man's body."

"Wait," Adam stopped her. "When did that happen?"

"After talking with Mom today, I went to see my old neighbor, Doris."

"Inside another man's body?" Erin asked. "Now that's strange stuff."

Adam felt Antonio use his empathic ability, but it was too quick to catch what the emotion was or who it was directed to.

Troy reached for a napkin, wiping his face. "How'd the Nationals' do tonight?"

"Lost." Antonio replied. "Nats struck out in the eighth and ninth."

"Speaking of striking out," Lani pushed her plate away from her. "What are we going to do next?"

"There's a wide range of movies in the theatre." Antonio offered.

"No, I mean with the investigation."

"What investigation?" Erin piped up.

"Someone hinted they knew who murdered Dad and President Taylor." Adam glanced over at Lani. "Despite what the Addison Commission determined."

"The one that investigated the explosion?" Erin asked. Adam nodded.

"You could start there." Antonio reached for his glass and finished it.

"Where?" Lani asked.

"Helena, Montana."

"Sir?"

"Chief Justice Addison. He lives just near Helena." Antonio

pulled out the remote from his pant pocket and pushed a button. "He went back home after the court closed, didn't he?"

Erin nodded. "Yes, sir."

"After they swore me into office, one of my first acts was to charge Addison with the formation of the Commission and a thorough investigation into the death of Taylor."

A frown came across Adam's face. Where could he being going with this? "But sir, with the Commission meetings being so open… I mean, Lani and I were there. What more is there to know?"

"The meetings were open to the public, but not the investigation. I'll call Leonard in the morning and let him know you were coming to visit." Antonio held his empty wine glass up when a maid came into the kitchen. "Maria, could I get a refill, please?"

"Yes, sir." She took the glass and plates from Lani and Erin off of the table.

Lani nudged Troy's elbow. "Wanna go? We have the weekend off?"

He shrugged his shoulders. "Sure this isn't what Harris said to not do?"

"Of course not. We're just up visiting a friend of the President." Lani pointed across the table. "And Erin's boss."

Erin nodded. "He enjoys visitors going fishing with him out on the Missouri River. He's offered to me and… my daughter several times."

"We'd have to fly by plane. I can't carry all of you." Lani wiped her hands off with her napkin after being relieved of the last of the food on the table. "We'll have to get a charter jet from Albuquerque." She looked across the table to her brother. "Uncle Allen flies down here all the time. Does he have an office nearby?"

Adam shook his head. "I don't think so. I think the closest ones are Las Vegas and Dallas. Looking to borrow one from him?"

Lani nodded. "Thought crossed my mind."

The parking lot of the Pajarito Hotel was still full of vehicles, despite most of its residents were still out to dinner. Diego pulled into the closest one to the door, still twenty cars away.

"Give me the keys." Daiki reached across as Diego pulled them from the ignition.

"No." Diego yanked his hand back, almost hitting the window.

"Ain't going there, DK." Thandi scolded him as she climbed out of the car.

Daiki grabbed at the seat belt, causing dust to fly around him as it dissolved. A larger cloud formed and fell to the pavement as he shoved against the car door with his shoulder, leaving only a portion around the side mirror still attached to the hinges.

"Damn it, DK." Diego shouted from the back of the car. "What the hell is wrong with you?"

"Insurance ain't gonna cover that," Thandi pointed her finger at him. "You gonna have to pay for that yourself."

"Screw you." Daiki pushed past them and stormed for the hotel entrance. He raised his hand, energy swirling around it, but the automatic doors opened in time.

Thandi and Diego chatted behind him, but he ignored them. He didn't care what they thought. Erin was his, the mother of his child. And she wasn't about to leave him for someone hiding behind the President.

Javiera stood behind a small wet bar, three bottles of liquor propped on top. Her eyes grew wide as Daiki strode up to her. He pointed to the bottle of bourbon. "Double."

She retrieved a glass from the stack and poured from the

bottle. A few drops splashed out of the glass as Daiki grabbed it off of the cocktail napkin she sat it on.

"Give me the keys." Daiki downed the drink, then made the glass vanished from his hand. Glittering dust flittered to the floor.

"No, Daiki." Thandi flicked a finger at him again. "She's gone, done left you long ago. You just ain't got that through your mutant head yet."

He took a step toward Diego, then felt heavy. Gravity pulled at him, unable to lift his feet. He glared at Diego as he struggled to lift his arm.

"Give me the damn keys."

"Can't do it, dude. Can't let you go up there."

Green-black energy formed around Daiki's hand, then flew at Diego's hip. His jeans vanished, allowing keys and coins to fall to the carpet. Diego stepped backwards, surprised at the attack from Daiki.

The gravity pull on Daiki lessened, and he rushed toward the car keys. Diego kicked at the keys. Daiki tossed another ball of negative energy. Diego's leg swung up in front of him and he fell onto the floor.

Thandi screamed. "His foot! You dusted his foot." Blood shot out from Diego's ankle, spraying the carpet and keys.

Daiki lost sight of the keys as he reached for them. Everything around him went black. He reached outward, unable to see his arms or hands. Bringing his hand together, the glow of an energy ball the size of a beach ball breached the darkness. He pushed outward with the energy.

Two women screamed, then glass shattered, followed by metal and plastic crashing, then silence as the darkness faded and the room reappeared.

Thandi and Diego lay huddled together on the floor, the popcorn maker on top of them. A section of the continental breakfast equipment was missing. Water and juice poured from the refrigerated drink machine.

Daiki flicked his fingers outward and the popcorn covering the car keys vanished.

"Don't wait up." Daiki said as he left the hotel.

Even as the breeze blew into the car past the missing doors, Daiki's anger grew hotter as he sped through the valley toward the turnoff for Mendoza's residence. Fueled by co-workers attacking him and the thought of Erin leaving him, he reached up and the sedan became a convertible.

Swerving onto the asphalt drive, Daiki tossed a large energy sphere at Gate #1. One soldier jumped clear, but the negative energy caught the second. The molecules that were the post, guard shack, and soldier floated away, stirred by the wind created by the rest of Daiki's car.

The lighting in the house went from normal white to red. Lani shot upright in her seat, eyes wide, staring straight at Adam. "Put in your earpiece, damn it." She scooted to the end of the bench seat and waved for Troy to join her.

Adam stood up as well, reaching in his pocket for his earpiece.

"… mutant insurgent… passed the gate… gate dissolved… man down…"

Adam pointed at the President. "X-ray Zulu, sir. Inside the safe room now. Erin, you too."

"What's going on?" Erin asked as she moved her chair away from the table.

"Sounds like DK."

"Adam?" Antonio stood steadfast, but Adam glared at him.

"Oh, hell no. We have this." He pointed to Lani. "Plus, I have air support."

"Well, at least get me a gun." Troy asked.

"Follow me." Antonio said, hand on his shoulder as he led him down the hallway.

"Adam, I need to go with you. He's here because of me." Erin said, looking Adam in the eyes.

He hesitated, then agreed. "This will not end well for him. Are you ready for that?"

She swallowed hard, then nodded. "Yes."

"Can we go now?" Lani said over the comms system.

"Okay, okay. Go two hundred up, circle around, and give me a report. I need to confirm how many and where they are." As soon as Lani took to the air, Adam keyed his comms.

"All personnel, we have air support from Captain Knight. Don't shoot the purple glowing thing. Also, two additional personnel on my position."

There were no sirens or other indications of an attack on the President's home, just the change in lighting. Adam knew that any staff members still in the house would move toward the center of the building to the elevators that would go five floors down to a bunker. There would be four agents with Antonio. Being the head agent and 'mutant blocker', it was Adam's duty to lead the team against the XZ intruders.

Adam held the front door open for Troy, who came running down the hall. He keyed a control inside the doorway, then stepped out. He heard several loud clanks as metal gates fell down on the inside.

Adam smirked at Troy, holding an assault rifle in one hand and stuffing several clips in his pockets.

"May be overkill, but not running out of bullets this time." Troy said as he walked past Adam.

"Take position straight down the path. Erin, to Troy's right. I'll be on his left."

The trio took up a position on the far side of the water

fountain in the circle drive, Troy kneeling, rifle up. Erin stood five feet to his right, Adam the same to the left.

Several steel masts were being raised around the compound, stadium-style lamps illuminating the area. Adam grimaced, knowing that all of Los Alamos could see the lights and would know something was going on. Phone calls would stream in to the switchboard at any moment.

The sound of the car warned them he was close. Adam steeled himself against what was about to go down.

"Gate Two breached." Lani radioed in. "One vehicle, one passenger. Stopping the vehicle."

"Careful, Lani. He has Disintegration ability."

The sedan cleared a corner, the bright headlights blinding Adam. Erin flinched when a brilliant beam of light streamed downward, followed by an explosion and a flash of red and yellow at the ground level.

"Anything in your radar?" Troy asked.

"No, he's out of my range. I can only pick up you and Erin."

Troy pulled his face from the butt of the rifle. "Excuse me?"

"Ah, later." Adam pointed down the road.

"Vehicle stopped. Passenger rolled clear. Looks like—" Lani's transmission stopped.

Adam reached to key his mic, but the sound of handgun fire erupted to his right. Soldiers and Secret Service agents were firing at someone down the road. In the bright lights of the dozen masts, Adam could make out a cloud of dust next to Daiki Kobayashi as he strode toward them.

"He's stopping their bullets," Adam said. He took a step forward. "He's still out of range."

Troy waved his hand at Adam. "Stay back. Don't get in front of me."

Daiki weaved his hands in front of him. A glowing ball of

green and black energy formed and flew toward the soldiers. The front line dodged the globe, but it struck someone in back. A cloud of dust particles formed where the soldier had stood.

"DAIKI!" Erin shouted.

Daiki's head snapped around, finding her and Adam. He whirled his hands again, another ball of decay forming. His hands went forward and the energy globe launched. Adam and Erin fell to the pavement. Clearing Troy's head, the globe struck the marble fountain. Water sprayed up and out from the water pipe, two feet of the fountain severed off the top.

"He's still to far away," Adam said. He stood back up. "We need to get him closer."

"He's dangerous enough from way back there." Troy muttered.

"You want me to take him out from here?" Lani asked, circling overhead.

"No." Adam glanced at Erin, knowing she wasn't on the comm link. "Just nudge him this way."

"Gotcha. Moving him forward."

Beams of purple-white light flashed downward, behind Daiki. The mutant ran away from the laser, wildly tossing small globes into the sky.

"Erin." Adam pointed to the spray of water. "Distract him."

Erin reached with a hand toward the fountain. The foot-high gush of water coalesced into a snake, jumping into the air and arching toward Daiki. As the water splashed down on him, it vaporized into a fog.

"Damn." Adam exclaimed. "Lani, disable him."

Three spheres of light dropped from above, each striking Daiki in successive order. He fell to his knees.

"Now." Adam shouted. Troy shot at Daiki, the first bullet finding its way to flesh. The second and third turned to dust a foot away. Leaping from his position, Adam ran toward the mutant, but at an angle. He knew he had to leave a clear shot for Troy. Adam didn't need to hit Daiki, just get close enough.

As he closed in on Daiki, he saw him raise his arms. A green globe formed in front of him, then blinked out. Two bullets whizzed past Adam, impacting Daiki in the upper torso. The concussion knocked him onto his back.

Lani landed a few feet away from him, purple energy glowing around her fists. Two Secret Service agents ran to them, handcuffs and suppressor in hand. When Daiki was securely detained, the glow vanished from Lani's hands.

"Is he dead?" Erin walked alongside Troy, her arms wrapped tight around her.

"No, but he'll need medical attention quickly." Adam stepped to her, extending his arm so she could move closer to him. She hesitated at first, then fell in to him.

The agents lifted Daiki by the shoulders and drug him away from the courtyard, other soldiers standing ready to receive the captive.

"Damn, girl." Troy pulled the magazine from the rifle and cleared the chamber. "You really know how to show a guy a good time."

"Report!" A deep voice bellowed from the front door of the mansion.

They all turned, the President standing at the doorway, fists at his hips.

Adam turned to look at the President approaching. "What the hell are you doing out here? We haven't secured the area."

"Must be." Antonio announced. "You're already congratulating each other."

"Sorry, sir." Erin held her head low as she released her hold on Adam.

Antonio looked at Adam. "Status report in five minutes in my office, Agent Knight. Ms. Murphy, a word." Antonio turned on his heel and walked back inside the house.

"Yes sir," Adam replied. He patted Erin on the butt, pushing her to go. Watching her walk away, he knew he had to get back to work. He turned to face Troy and Lani. "Okay, reports."

Antonio's feet were heavy on the tile floor as he stormed through the foyer for his office. Erin rushed to keep up with him. He stood at the door, waiting for her to enter before closing it behind her.

"What the hell was that all about, Ms. Murphy?"

"Sir, I can explain."

He approached her, his hand in front of her face, his thumb and index finger nearly touching. "I'm about this close to naming Mutant Defense Foundation, a terrorist organization. And you know what that will do."

"It will destroy everything we've been working toward, sir."

Antonio waved his hand through the air. "Wipe it all away, erase all chance of peace and harmony between us and the humans. It will be just like the last four years never happened."

Agitated, he wanted to implant fear into her. A quick look at her and he wasn't sure if he hadn't done so already. Antonio deepened his breathing, calming his nerves, forcing his own emotion down.

"I don't know what your plans are, but they best be on hold until tomorrow. Understood?"

"Yes, sir."

Antonio swung the door open. Adam was there, waiting for his turn in the hot seat.

"Good night, sir." Adam exited the President's office and pulled the door closed behind him.

Erin ran to Adam's side as he moved into the central foyer. She fell in under his arm, hugging him. "What did he say?"

"We will hold Daiki under sedation down at a secure section of the Los Alamos Hospital," Adam explained. "Later, he'll be moved to the Ultra-max prison south of Colorado Springs."

"Will he get any kind of hearing?" Erin stayed as his side as they joined Lani and Troy, waiting in the rec room. Lani laid stretched out on the three-cushion sofa, Troy perched on the sofa's arm at her feet.

"Normally, I would say yes. However, this is an attack on the Presidential residence using extraordinary methods. There are some extenuating circumstances."

"There will be hell to pay if the press gets a hold of this." Troy crossed his arms, frowning.

"Too late about that. Nothing alerts the media like the stadium lighting on the mountain top or the Los Alamos police going on alert and heading out here. Barrett is crafting something to send out now. DK's name will be left out of the report, and that he is a mutant."

"County sheriff's radio is still buzzing," Lani interjected, "trying to keep reporters out."

Adam glanced down at Erin. "If we're leaving first thing in the morning, we'd better get some sleep."

"Got it." Lani rolled upright, then pushed herself off of the sofa. "Shut eye." She moved to Erin, and they touched cheeks. "G'nite."

Troy dropped on to the center sofa cushion. "This my couch for the night?"

Lani waved her arm for him to follow. "Come on, Army. Yours is down here."

"What about me?" Erin gently put a hand on Adam's chest. The warmth of her touch soothed him.

"We have the Blue Room. Just down here."

"We?" Erin asked in a whisper.

"Presumptuous of me." Adam's face blushed. "Your security profile said you were single."

He gazed down into the eyes he recalled from years ago. There was no way of hiding his increased heart rate from her. "I can have Ms. Alvarez make another—"

"No, this is good." Her hand slipped off of her chest and she stepped down the hallway. Adam calmed, but his heart rate remained high.

They walked down the hall, hand in hand. Opening a powder blue painted door, Adam let Erin enter first. Sensors raised the lighting in the room to a soft illumination. Painted powder blue, the place was large. A king-size bed stood in the center of the back wall, a small kitchenette to the right, bathroom to the left. Erin's brand-new suitcase stood at the foot of the bed.

He walked over to the bathroom door, waiting for Erin to join him. Dual sinks, a big tub, a large shower. The sink had bathroom stuff already on it between the two sinks—toothpaste, razor, and two toothbrushes, one still in a plastic wrapper. A wet towel hung from the rack at the side of the shower.

"Is this your room?"

"When I'm here with Mendoza. He said it was his room when he was growing up before he went to Berkeley."

Adam stood side of the bed. Erin stayed next to him. There was a calm, a familiarity between them. Still, Adam felt excitement, with Erin showing her mettle in the mutant combat outside, and being with her again, alone.

Erin looked past him at a phone charger sitting on the bedstand.

"I see you still sleep on the left side."

He motioned over his shoulder. "Close to the bathroom."

Adam looked into her eyes, but wasn't sure what he was seeing. Had too many years gone past?

Erin touched him on the cheek. "Don't worry. You know I would have said something earlier."

Any tension he had flowed away with her touch. He pulled her into his arms and kissed her. She responded in kind.

Erin's arms turned watery and slid between their bodies, separating them. He released his tight grip on her, ready to step away until she reached up to his shirt and unbuttoned it. Pulling it off of his shoulder, she gasped. Her fingers ran over his chest muscles.

"You didn't have these in college."

Her touch tickled him. He recalled lying next to Janice, the slight physical interaction they had. They had shared a bed twice on Air Force One, but only slept. The small three-high bunk gave little space for fooling around. Adam shook his head, clearing the vision from his mind.

He focused on Erin's shirt. Gathered the material along her ribs, he slid it up over her head. His eyes glided over the opalescence of her bare breasts, glistening, changing in color to the emotions she felt. Adam continued on down, undoing her jeans button and squeezing his thumbs inside the waistband.

"Wait, I have to tell you…"

He wasn't waiting, sliding her jeans and underwear off of her hips and guiding them to her ankles. Adam removed her sandals, lifting each leg out of the jeans, now on the floor. His eyes journeyed up her legs, pausing at the thin scar of a C-section delivery.

"That wasn't there in college either." Adam sat back on his heels.

Erin's hands moved over the scar, hiding what he had already seen. Her skin turned to a more-human tanned color. Adam felt her embarrassment. He stood up, his nose bumping against her lowered forehead.

"I didn't have time to tell you. I had complications in the last trimester. She came three weeks early."

"Your husband's?"

"He left me before she was born. Her name is Ariel."

Adam kissed Erin's forehead, then ran his nose down past her temples, to her cheeks.

"A little mermaid?"

"I don't know if she carries my mutant genes or not. I haven't tested her yet."

Adam dabbed her under her chin to raise her face, her lips to his.

"I would love to meet her."


Erin rolled over onto her right shoulder and opened her eyes. Adam was on his right side also, his left arm above the thin bedspread. She laid there for a while, listening to his breathing and the occasional snore. They had fallen asleep in each other's arms. Now, with a gap between them in the king-size bed, she remembered how he would roll over in bed instead of rotating in one spot.

Confident he was asleep, she slipped her legs out from under the sheets and walked over to a cushioned chair for a thin lace robe. She guessed that Ms. Alvarez had staged it there for her.

Padding across the room, she found her cell phone and headed for the bathroom. Erin looked back to check if Adam was still asleep. Tilting her head as she watched him sleep, a touch of jealousy swept past her. Remembering how his face lit up when he mentioned the Secret Service agent he worked with in Russia, then his face again when he saw her C-section scar. A different look, although he tried to hide it.

Fighting a creaking hinge, Erin closed the door before turning on the light. Pulling the robe aside, she sat on the toilet. The seat was warm. Wiggling on the cushy seat, she tapped the screen of her phone.

She wanted to check her messages first, looking for anything from her babysitter, but she saw the red indicator—a missed phone call and a voice mail. The time stamp on the call was three hours ago, not long after Adam and she arrived at Antonio's estate. The phone number was not in her contacts, which was why she missed the call. Erin tapped the 3-second message and brought the phone to her ears.

The voice was Daiki's. "Coming after you."

Erin swiped her finger across the screen, deleting the message.

She closed the phone app, then went to the messages. Expecting more, there were only two messages.

**Thandi:** *At the hospital. Diego's right foot missing at the ankle. DK dusted it, then left. U better hide.*

Erin swiped across the screen, deleting the message.

The second was photos from Jeanine, the babysitter. Ariel got

Jeanine to open the box of her favorite puzzle, the 100-piece puzzle of a leopard in among tree leaves. Something most three-year-old don't do. She does well though, getting the leopard finished before her attention span vanishes.

Still in the message app, Erin scrolled to a previous message from three days earlier, then tapped the button to send a reply.

**Erin:** *Had trouble with old boyfriend. Actually help secure my spot. M played along, as expected. See you tomorrow.*

The corridor took a slight turn to the left, toward the servant's area. Lani stopped at the first door past the turn.

"I present to you, the Rose Room." Lani turned the knob and let the door swing wide. The room brightened. The wallpaper was in neutral colors with faint vertical pin stripes. There was a small bathroom to the left and two queen-size beds farther down the wall, across from the dresser and wide-screen TV.

Their bags were sitting on the foot of each bed, Lani's closest to the bathroom.

"I feel like I'm at a Marriott." Troy walked down the length of the room, checking behind the curtain.

"Pretty much. Not much of a view, but better room service. Adam said Antonio's grandfather was a US senator and used to get lots of visitors from Washington or even Mexico. They would stay here instead of in town."

"Yeah, I noticed there wasn't much in town."

Troy glanced around at the three paintings on the wall. Each featured roses as a central theme. "The rose room. Now I get it. I was expecting pink walls."

Lani unzipped her pack and pulled out her overnight bag. As she walked behind him for the bathroom, she giggled. "You should see the pearl room."

She closed the bathroom door behind her and sat the bag

down on the counter. Spreading out its contents, she grabbed her brush and worked the rats out of her hair, whipped around by the wind during her surveillance flight around the complex.

"So, what's the scoop on Erin?" Troy asked. "You haven't mentioned her before."

"She's Adam's girlfriend from college."

"Yeah, I got that much."

"There was an anti-mutant protest in town one time. She and Adam tried to protect a group of mutants being harassed by humans, and she got shot. Her mom and dad moved right after that, taking her with them."

"So, she's in Mutant Defense Foundation now."

"Guess so. Or what will be left of it."

"You want the bed next to the window? I rarely get up much at night."

Troy kept on talking, but Lani tuned it out. As she drew the brush through her hair, she stared at the face in the mirror. Her eyes stared back at her, looking deep inside herself.

They had talked at length. Actually, she talked and he listened. And tried to not yawn. When one sneaked out, Lani yawned in return. She climbed into bed and he had his turn in the bathroom. And a sink covered with her toiletries. It brought back memories of Jackie, his ex-wife. Red curly hair draped off of her shoulders. Bitchy attitude. Not a fond memory. But these were not Jackie's stuff. He knew that, and it made a difference.

Lani was already asleep. He made his way around her bed and crawled into his. When his eyes had become adjusted to the darkness, his ears picked up on Lani's breathing. Her soft, sensual breathing.

The frame of the queen-size bed squeaked loudly as Troy rolled over. He pulled the pillow over his head to block the sound. It wasn't right; he told himself. She was a work partner, and she had a boyfriend. Which she didn't love cause he loved another.

Squeezing the pillow tight against his head, he considered whether smothering himself would help.

He told himself to think about something else. Anything. Like what Adam said. He hadn't a chance to talk with Adam about *picking up* him and Erin. Did Adam think he was a mutant? He'd never been tested. Since no extraordinary power came around in his teen years, his family assumed he wasn't. That was because Dad didn't want to find out.

The sheets on Lani's bed shuffled. Troy opened his eyes in time to see her bed empty, her finger tugging at her underwear, the door to the bathroom closing. He tossed, turning away.

He tried thinking about the Iranians from the attack on the Atlantic Fleet Headquarters. Then about the Russian Commander and her destruction of the detention facility, along with two hundred mutants, minus those that escaped. Then he remembered fighting off the Russians, Lani standing close beside him. Shoulder to shoulder.

Her bed squeaked as she got back into bed. It sounded like a call to him.

Jackie, his ex-wife, came to mind. Perhaps to break the taunt of Lani's breathing.

Inhale. Exhale. Inhale. Exhale. Each of her breaths, soft, calling. He preferred a freight train rumbling through the room. He buried his face into the mattress. Nothing helped.

Tossing the sheets aside, Troy climbed out of bed. He untwisted his pajama pants, then pulled on his t-shirt as he plodded for the door.

Five steps out in the hallway, Troy regretted not having any slippers. Sweaty feet on the ceramic tiles sent chills up his spine.

Not like he even owned a pair of slippers. He had to borrow the pajama pants from a Secret Service agent. Didn't own a pair of them either.

At least the chills were distracting him from his thoughts of Lani sleeping a short distance from him. Plus the thought of her pregnant with a dip-shit boyfriend. Her words, he reminded himself. He hadn't actually met Marc, but he sounded like a loser from the conversation they had on the *flight* from his house tonight.

With the subdued lighting in the hallway, it was still bright enough to walk about. Troy wondered if he was the only one awake.

A voice just ahead down the hallway said otherwise. A male voice, deep sounding. It wasn't the President's voice.

Troy found himself in the main foyer of the house, doorways leading off to the kitchen, dining room, and the great room where a cable news channel was playing in silence on the big screen television. He could see the President sitting in the recliner, holding a cell phone in front of him.

"You're sending her to talk with Addison." The deep voice said.

"Yes. I think they are entitled to know the truth, finally." Antonio replied.

"I'm not sure that was a good move, but it is already done."

Troy moved to get a glimpse of the phone's screen. It was black.

Antonio turned his head slightly, then tossed the phone onto the table next to him. "Troy, come on in."

"Sorry, sir. Hope I didn't interrupt a trade negotiation or something."

"Definitely not a negotiation. Just another skeleton, another reason to not run for re-election." He waved at the television as he reached for the remote. "Not like these fools would let me win, anyway."

Troy smirked as he sat on the arm of a chair. "What's the cliché? Fool some of the people some of the time."

"Yeah, something like that."

Antonio kicked the leg section down on the recliner and moved to the edge of the seat. "What about you? Who are you trying to fool?"

Troy's eyes went big, his mouth gapping open. "Sir?"

The President smiled as he put his elbows on his knees, clasping his hands. "You forget, I'm an empath. I know what you are feeling."

Troy moved from the arm to the cushion, dropping his fists in his lap.

"Son, I've had my eye on Lani for a long time. Ever since Adam came onto my detail. Closer since her graduation from the Air Force Academy. Been kind of a father figure, but from a distance."

Troy felt his hands and feet getting sweaty again.

"Always wanted the best things for her." Antonio went on.

Troy's stomach tightened, churned.

"She's not there yet, but I think soon enough, she'll find the right person."

Then a calm came over the agent, a sense of tranquility, relaxation. He yawned.

"I think you'll do fine now. Come see me next week."

The President sat back in the recliner and turned the television on, adjusting the volume up just over the sound of Troy's snoring.

Tires squealed, then car bumpers crashed, as they tried to avoid the woman that abruptly appeared in the crosswalk. Blinded by the car lights, Doris staggered out of the crosswalk and onto the curb. Reaching for the palm tree, she leaned against it with one hand, the other planted hard against her temple. The drivers were shouting at her, standing in the street, while inspecting the damage.

Doris' face scrunched into a hateful stare. *"Get in your cars and drive away!"*

The two drivers walked straight to their cars and drove away as best as the vehicles would allow them. A couple walking out of a pharmacy on the street corner dropped their sacks and walked stone face down the sidewalk and climbed into an SUV five spots down. They barely missed being struck by a car coming toward them as they pulled out onto the street.

Doris caught sight of herself on the monitor as she entered the pharmacy, the camera catching her in all of her glory. Disheveled hair, drywall dust making her gray Rolling Stones t-shirt look white and her jeans more faded than before.

"God, I look terrible. Almost like I belong in here."

Each step she took was pain, each movement of her head or

arms was pain. Doris wasn't sure if even blinking wasn't pain. She made her way back to the dispensary counter, pausing for a moment to check out the wine bottles in the cooler.

Three people stood in line and two more sat in the waiting area while a single clerk worked the register. Doris's brain screamed again, telling everyone to leave. The crowd walked away like mindless zombies. The clerk moved away from the counter also, but Doris caught him and brought him back.

"What do you have for pain meds?"

"Do you have a prescription?" The man asked.

"Prescription? Do I look like I have a prescription?"

"Ma'am, I'm sorry but…"

Doris reached out mentally, grabbing his attention. His eyes grew wide, his mind vacant.

*"Give me something for pain."*

"Can you rate your pain, on a scale of one to ten, ten being the…"

"Twelve."

The clerk stepped away from the counter to the back shelves. Doris heard a woman talking with the man, the conversation turning louder, becoming shouting.

"What are you doing? You can't give those out."

Doris connected with him again, looking through his eyes. A young blonde stood at his side, beating him on the arm as he poured a handful of light green tablets into an orange tube. The pharmacist reached for the bottle and the clerk pushed her away, knocking her against an office chair and onto the floor.

The clerk snapped the lid onto bottle and handed it to Doris. "Take one every six to eight hours as needed, with water. Do not drive or operate any machinery until you know the effects. Do you have questions for the pharmacist?"

Doris poured three tablets into her hand, then stashed the

bottle in her pant pocket. "No questions. Thanks."

As she passed the coolers, Doris opened the door and grabbed a bottle of white wine. She couldn't twist the cap off of it, so she headed for the front. A clerk behind the photo section stepped up to a counter.

"Ma'am, are you okay?"

*"Open this."*

"You need to pay…"

*"OPEN IT, NOW."*

The man took the bottle, twisted the cap off, and handed it back.

"Thank you." She dropped the pills in her mouth and washed them down.

Doris moved toward the exit. The doors automatically opened, but no one passed through.


"Well, Maurice, that should move the Marlins a game closer to Washington, won't it?" Michael asked.

"But still in last place, sir." The Home Health Care tech nodded. He glanced at his watch. "Time for your evening medication."

Michael spun the wheelchair away from the television to face Maurice. "Yes, I guess it is."

Maurice took one step from the couch when Doris appeared out of thin air in his path.

"Holy…" The tech put a hand to his chest, trying to catch his breath. "Where did you come from?"

Silently, Doris staggered off to the kitchen.

"Television off." Michael spoke a command for the TV controls, then maneuvered the wheelchair after her. As he turned into the kitchen, he saw Doris, the bottom of the bottle pointed high into the sky, wine seeping past her lips and down her cheek and neck.

"Look what the proverbial cat drug in," Michael said. "Must have been a rough night. Did he ride you hard?"

Doris lowered the bottle and stared at him. "Don't start with me. This is all your fault."

"Somehow, I don't see it that way. I was doing just fine until you took one of those to her head."

She sat the wine bottle down on the counter and reached into her pocket for the pills. Emptying the contents into her hands, they poured into the sink as she collapsed onto the floor.

Michael pressed the chair's control level to back the chair, getting a full view of her. He sighed, letting her lay there. He considered leaving her, but then Maurice would complain. "Maurice, I need you."

"Yes, Michael?" The man jumped again at the site of Doris on the floor. "Oh, my." He stepped to her and touched her on the neck, checking for a pulse. "She's alive, but her pulse is weak. Should I call the EMTs?"

"What are the pills in the sink?" Michael asked.

The tech picked up a pill, then the bottle. "There's no label on the bottle, but I've seen these before. If she took even one of these with wine, she'll be out for most of the day tomorrow."

Michael's voice was but a whisper. "Now that's a shame." A grin crawled across his face as he made room for Maurice to walk by. "Time for bed."

Saturday, June 24<br>Present Day

A foul smell stirred Doris. Breaths fell against her face. Dog breath. Something licked her nose.

"Sparky!" Doris grimaced at the dog's attention. "Go away."

She opened her eyes, and the brown ball of hair panting on her face moved. She tried to roll out of bed, but couldn't. Nothing moved, her arms, her legs. Her eyes opened wide, fear rushing over her. Blinking repeatedly, she noticed that the room was different. Michael's wheel chair sat at the side of the bed. Next to it, a bed stand held a glass of water and a photo of Antonio, Michael and her from their college days in Berkeley. Beyond all that, a mirror on the closet door, reflecting the body of Michael Clarke.

"Oh, shit. I'm in Michael's body. How the hell did he get past my mental defenses?"

Doris thought about last night. Most of it was fuzzy. She recalled taking Lani to Marc's apartment after Michael almost flew off in the pilot's body. Then Lani thanked her by blasting her and Marc against the bedroom wall. Marc stayed with her for a while. Last, she remembered the Fifteenth Street Pharmacy and picking up some extra-strength pain meds. The damn pain pills. And wine.

"MICHAEL!" Doris screamed. "Get your ass back in here. Get MY ass back in here."

Michael's wheelchair held a digital tablet propped up in the seat. The digital tablet came to life, a video launched on the screen. Doris saw her face appear, smiling, moving around while she tried to position the tablet.

"Surprise! Good morning. Or it most likely will be when you watch this video. Hope you can see it, wasn't sure about the angle." Her voice had a slight British accent to it, not as strong as Michael's normal articulation.

The video paused, then started again. Doris was now wearing a different shirt.

"I must say, it has been some time since you and I have mind swapped. I like how you've been keeping yourself fit." She moved her head around, twisting her neck. "Damn, what did you do to yourself last night? It feels like they ran you over by a bus. Teleport to the wrong street corner?"

"Screw you, Michael." She wanted to flip him off, but Michael's arms wouldn't move.

"Anyway, after my jaunt around in your *friend's* body, before you bashed us on the head, I felt alive again. How is she doing? Wish I could spend some time in her body again instead of this old thing."

The screen jiggled, the background behind Michael-turned-Doris moving quickly. The great room wall became balcony and the glow of the sun about to rise.

"That sense of freedom, along with being able to actually feel, made me want to step out. You know, while I was in her mind, I learned what she knew. Boy, you pissed her off. She thinks you had something to do with the explosion that killed her father. You recall, the one that should have killed me."

The scene changed. Doris' body sat on the white loveseat.

"That explosion would have killed me also if you hadn't pulled me out. And instead of healing me, you confined me to the damn chair which you will enjoy today." An evil-looking smile grew across Doris's face. "I hope you remember how to operate the controls."

Doris slammed her head—his head—against the pillow. "You asshole. You just wait til you fall asleep tonight."

The view changed to show Michael's body, tucked in under the blanket with Sparky laying snuggled by his left arm. Then it switched back to Doris' face.

"Now don't worry. I've arranged for Maurice to come by to feed you and keep you clean. Oh, and for the dog walker to come and take Sparky outside twice a day. I know how much you hate the smell of dog urine."

"Since our mutant powers are tied to our body's DNA, you could mind swap with whoever shows up. Maurice is Mind Shielded, of course. You made sure of that, bringing someone I couldn't swap with. A word of warning: I had Sparky trained to swap back with me whenever you teleported back into the flat with him, or rather me, on your arm. So if you swap with him, you may find yourself stuck as a four-legged bitch until she wants to swap back. Oh, and I requested that anyone who comes in be XZ-negative. For your safety."

"And to make it harder for me to come after you, asshole." She knew what he was doing, making sure she wouldn't escape while he was off in her body.

"Maybe it will be that black fellow, the one that loved giving sponge baths."

"Oh, good grief." Doris rolled her eyes. Michael's eyes.

The scene changed again. She wore her Air Force uniform again. At the balcony table, the sun shone on her face, a breeze blowing her hair.

"Good bye, Doris. I know I only have today, since falling asleep forces us to swap back. Just so you know, I'm off to follow up on Lani's investigation. And if I find out you played a part, well, I won't have to worry about swapping back to a paralyzed body if it stops breathing. One last thing, I've programmed this recording to delete. Again, for your safety."

On the video, Doris' face blew a kiss and waved before ending the recording. The screen went blank.

"MICHAEL!" Michael's voice coming out. Tears ran down from the corners of his eyes.

Sparky lifted his head, sniffed, then jumped off the bed and ran to the balcony. There, Doris sat. She finished her cup of coffee and placed it on the saucer. Next to the saucer was a printed page from a contacts list. The name at the top of the page read: *Dr. Lauren Thornburg.*

Folding up the page and stuffing it in her shirt pocket, she stood up, smoothed the wrinkles out of her skirt, and disappeared.

The hallway was dark, darker than Michael expected it. As her eyes adjusted to the dark, the ceiling lights blinked on, blinding her. Michael shielded his eyes. Doris' eyes. He stood in a lobby area, a wide hallway running left and right, a doorway marked *Ladies* before him. Next to it, a glass display case with plaques and trophies. A sign on the wall above read:

*446th Airlift Wing, Joint Base Lewis-McChord*

The reflection in the glass was of an old woman. He sighed. Her body was old. Then again, his body back in Miami was old as well.

He cast out a mental search for anyone around, finding only a single airman walked down the hallway, shuffling his feet, phone in hand. Making himself *mentally invisible* to the airman, Michael watched as he approached. Assault rifle slung across his back with a shoulder strap, Michael assumed he was military police, but couldn't tell from his uniform. He had no clue about British uniforms, let alone American. He used the airman's inattentiveness to his advantage. He bumped into Michael, his phone knocked from his hand.

"Oh, sorry, ma'am. I didn't see you there." The airman bent down to pick up his phone, stuffed it in his pocket, then adjusted the rifle against his back.

"Last night's ballgame?"

The airman looked back at him, a look of surprise on his face. He snapped to attention, staring over Michael's left shoulder. "Yes, ma'am. Sorry, ma'am. Won't happen again."

Bloody hell, British accent. He reminded himself that he was an American now. Michael brought a fist up to his lips and coughed. "Good. See that it doesn't. Now, tell me where your administrative office is."

"Yeoman's office is down that way, second hallway on the left, ma'am."

Before he could say anything more, Michael took the direction given. He brushed his hand across the name tag on his left breast. "Colonel Doris Kutcher," he muttered, Doris' feminine voice coming through. "Have to remember who I am. I'm not Michael Clarke anymore. Not today."

Lights blinked on down the dark corridor as she turned the corner. Michael checked the signs stuck on each door as he passed them. When he found one marked Administration, he paused. The thin vertical window was frosted and dark. Michael turned the doorknob. It didn't open. He rattled it a few times. It didn't budge.

"What the f...?"

He glanced at her watch and realized the time. Saturday, 8:10 AM on the east coast. Three hours earlier on the west coast.

The view of the office came into focus as he teleported across the locked door. The room had several desks on the other side of a counter and a short swinging gate. The lights in the room blinked on as Michael stepped past the gate and wandered around, glancing at any paperwork on the desks.

Clicking sounded, and the locked door swung open. A man dressed in a grey t-shirt and jeans walked in and closed the door behind him.

"Dammit, Jonesy." His mouth dropped open, and he attempted to snap to attention. "Oh, sorry ma'am. I thought you were the MP."

"Clearly, I am not."

"Yes, ma'am. I mean, no. Airman O'Donnell, ma'am. Can I help you?"

"Yes, please. I'm looking for an Airman Statler."

A look of confusion came over O'Donnell's face. "I don't recognize the name."

O'Donnell moved away from the door and around the countertop to a desk. Michael wheeled a chair beside him and sat down, crossing his legs. The airman tried to be inconspicuous as he glanced down at her knees. Michael coughed to clear his throat, and the yeoman grabbed the mouse, moving the cursor about the screen. "S-t-a-t-l-e-r?"

"Correct. As I understand it, they transferred her from Thayer."

O'Donnell's expression changed from confusion to sadness. "Thayer Air Force Base, up in Alaska? Colonel, I'm sorry, but I recall now. Airman Statler, Kira, right? Died last year, around Halloween when she was first transferred here."

"Excuse me?"

After a few more clicks, the name appeared along with other details.

"Yeah, here it is. Car accident out on I-5. Happened right after she got here. Guess she wasn't used to Interstate highways, coming from Alaska and all."

Michael shook her head in disbelief. "No, I'm sure Dor… ahh… I'm sure someone's mistaken." He brought a hand up to his chin and stroked it. The lack of whiskers caught him off-guard and brought him back to the moment. "Is there any information about where the body was taken to, or next of kin?"

The yeoman pulled a pink sticky note out of the dispenser and wrote an address and phone number.

"Here's the phone number to the base. It's all I have, ma'am. Only person listed as next of kin is Major Marc Black. Not sure his relationship to Kira."

A smirk came across Colonel Kutcher's face as he accepted the pink paper square. "Oh, I know him. Since you're in the system, there's another number I need you to look up for me."

He gave a second name, also at Thayer. The airman wrote it down next to the first.

Michael looked around, grabbing at his breasts then his butt cheeks. He cursed at himself for forgetting to bring Doris' purse. It would be too risky going back for it now.

He looked at the airman and peered into his mind. "Do you mind if I have your phone?"

O'Donnell stood up and pulled a cell phone from his pant pocket. "The code is 32DD." He blushed.

"Thanks. You can ask Jonesy if he's seen it later. And forget that I was here and about Airman Statler."

"Yes, Colonel."


*A black curly-haired labradoodle bumped against Captain Henry Bordeaux, trying to knock him over. He swatted at the dog, but the dog only took it as play and bumped him again, from behind this time. Henry swatted at the dog again when an insect buzzed past his head.*

The noise grew louder, and he climbed out of his dream. His three-year-old son laid beneath the blankets between him and his wife, Carly. The child twisted in bed and kicked out, striking his father, barely missing his groin. Henry groaned and rolled over.

His cell phone buzzed again.

He swung his legs out from under the blankets and grabbed it. Groggy, he said, "This better not be a drill."

"No drill, Charger. Real deal. This is Doris Kutcher."

Henry dropped the phone, and it bounced to the floor. "Shit."

"You okay?" His wife asked, looking over her shoulder.

"Yeah, just someone from base. Go back to sleep."

He reached for the phone and padded on the wood laminate floor as he made his way out of the bedroom. Closing the door behind him, he brought the phone to his ear, his brown hair matted up like a mohawk.

"What the hell do you want? Something happen to Marc?"

"Oh, your buddy Marc is just fine. Sorry to bother you at home like this. How's the weather in Alaska?"

"Cold, just like you." He stepped farther from the bedroom, dodging the toys spread out on the living room floor. The room was in a soft shadow, the day-long sun filtering through the darkening shades. "What do you want?"

"Charger, my dear. No reason to be mean. Just looking to get in touch with my granddaughter. Her number doesn't seem to be working, and I don't know her new address."

"And you know there's a reason, right?"

"Really, now. You can't keep holding that Colonel Kilpatrick situation over my head."

"Can and will."

Henry heard Doris sigh.

"Charger. Henry. This isn't about you or Marc. This is about that young girl he met last year. Lani Knight. You remember her?"

"Same event, and for the same reason."

"Captain Bordeaux, look. I'm here at the Pentagon with Airman..." Doris paused. "... Airman O'Donnell and he's helping me process your transfer request to Afghanistan. Now I know how that will disrupt your family, what with your two children and all."

"Don't you f—"

"Oh, trust me, Charger. I can and I will."

"Hang on." Henry brought his phone down and went to the Contacts app. Scrolling through the list, he came across a listing for Joe's Pizza. Memorizing the info, he read it back to her.

"Thank you, Captain Bordeaux. I'll see that they delete this transfer request. Have a wonderful weekend. And if you get a hold of Kira before I do, just remember, Afghanistan is such a lovely place this time of year."

Henry lowered the phone from his ear. "Bitch."

Faintly, he heard a voice from his phone. "I'm still here."

He pressed the button to end the call. "Unfortunately."

The skies were clear and bright, and the breeze was warm. Michael realized he was out of place, dressed in an Air Force uniform in residential Lakewood, Washington. A jogger and her dog passed him as he glanced at the airman's phone to verify the location.

Michael stepped toward the front door of the address Charger had given him. He shook his head, sad at the lack of grass, or anything green on what should be the front lawn.

Just as he reached out to knock on the aluminum screen door, the main door opened. Kira let out a yelp at the sight of someone at her doorstep, stumbling back a half-step. Michael noted she had a purse slung over her shoulder and keys in hand.

"Hello, my dear. Going somewhere?"

"Grandma. Hi." Kira stepped outside and pulled the front door closed. She leaned in for a hug. "I'm on my way to work."

Michael noticed how attractive Kira was. He stood back and

looked at her. She wore a white pressed button-down shirt, black skirt, and matching high heels, her soft brunette hair back in a single ponytail.

Kira did a once-over on her grandmother as well. "So, what's with the Air Force uniform?"

"Well, I went to McChord to find you, but you weren't there."

Kira looked confused, tilting her head to one side. "Grandma, I thought you knew. I'm not in the Air Force anymore."

Michael dipped his head, faked a sniffle to hold back tears. "I need a favor. Can we talk?"

Kira looked at her watch, then huffed. She opened the door and pointed inside. "Sure. Let me call Bobby and let him know I'll be a little late."

The living room of the small two-bedroom house was trashed. Beer cans and flattened pizza boxes littered the floor. Ash trays were full of cigarette butts and other rolled and smoked substances. Clothes were tossed onto the back of chairs.

"Seriously, you live like this?" Michael asked.

"Grandma, it's not that bad. It takes a lot to keep me from shaking the house down."

Michael took two long steps to Kira and grabbed her head. Palms pressed against her temples, reaching deep inside Kira's mind, searching, Michael found the center of her powers. Vibration energy.

"Control," Michael whispered. "You must learn to control your energies."

Kira's eyes rolled back in her head. She convulsed, her knees wobbly. A glass ashtray on the table vibrated. Beer bottles on the kitchen counter rattled then fell over to the floor. The beaded curtain hanging from a hallway frame waved back and forth.

"Kira, is that…?" A voice called out from behind the beads, and a man appeared. Long black hair and multiple tattoos across a bare-chest, the man looked as if he was sleep-walking.

Kira's arm stretched out toward the man. A wave of vibrational energy pushed out, flinging the beads wildly, tossing the man against a wall. His head and arms waved all about until his chest collapsed inward, and he fell to the floor.

The energy wave lessened and Kira's eyes blinked as she focused on Michael. Her forehead furrowed, then relaxed.

"Michael?"

Michael grinned, loosening her grip on Kira's head.

"I need you to help me, to work with me in my quest."

"Okay." Kira shrugged, then glanced over at her boyfriend, blood streaming down from his nostrils and tear ducts. She waved at him, blowing him off. "No loss. He was a loser anyway." She looked at her grandmother's face. "What can I do for you?"

Michael's grin widened. He tugged at his skirt. "First, point the way to a clothing store. I need to get out of this uniform."

Searching through Doris' memories for Marc's home, the most recent was his bedroom. Michael wasn't too surprised, knowing of her penchant for doing what Michael and she had rarely done, and not at all in the past four years. Holding hands with Doris' granddaughter, the bedroom came into vision, including the huge body-shaped indentation in the drywall.

"That must be why she needed the pain meds." Michael reached out and dabbed the broken plaster.

"Damn," Kira muttered. "Who did that?"

"The fox, my dear. And we are the hounds"

Voices spoke up in the other room. Michael raised a finger to his lips to quiet Kira. Kira stepped back, giving Michael an unobstructed view of Doris's body in the full-length mirror hanging on the back of the bedroom door. Sporting a dark sage shirt unbuttoned down to her push-up bra and tight-fitting jeans over flats, Michael cocked his head, admiring the view.

"Even for an old broad, she has a good body." Michael twisted, getting a view of Doris' butt.

Michael opened the bedroom door and stepped into the living room. White plastic sheeting hung from the curtain rod, fanning inward as the wind blew through the missing balcony door and a section of the wall in Marc's apartment. A wide screen TV sat on the floor, huge spider-web cracks running across the glass. Marc stood next to a man, clipboard in hand, facing the sheeting.

"So, you want the same door as what you had here? Won't be a big deal. But fixing the wall, inside and out, will tricky. Patching the exterior siding will take some doing, trying to match what's still there."

"Hey, lover." Kira waved, walking over to Marc. "Doing some remodeling?"

The two men turned to see Michael and Kira.

"What? Kira?" Marc stood stiff, his arms hanging down as Kira hugged him tight. When she stepped back, he couldn't help but look her over. She was wearing a black rock band t-shirt over jean capris and white athletic shoes. He liked what he saw, remembering the time they were together in Alaska.

"Marc, dear. Sorry to intrude." Michael walked over to the contractor and offered a hand. "Doris Kutcher. I'm a close friend of Marc."

"Sorry, I… forgot… that you were here," Marc introduced him."This is Kevin Donovan."

Kevin's mouth was agape as his eyes traveled up and down the length of her statuesque figure. He mumbled out a 'hello' as he shook her hand.

Marc guessed that he was up to her usual tricks of putting thoughts into peoples head, making them like her when they really shouldn't.

"Right, well." Marc slapped Kevin on the shoulder, pulling the man's attention from her cleavage. "Work up those numbers for me and let me know when you're ready to start."

"Ahh, yes, sir. Like I said, I have to get with the property manager to see what he wants for the exterior."

Nudging the contractor toward the front door, Marc glared as he passed her. Closing the door, he turned, an index finger extended, ready to take her on. He found Kira in the room, holding the plastic sheeting open, inspecting the damage.

"Sweet. Who did this?" Kira asked.

"Lani." Marc replied, glancing around.

Kira let the plastic fall. "Who?"

Marc ignored her. "What the hell do you want, Doris?"

Michael was taken aback. "Aren't you going to ask how I'm feeling?"

Marc looked away. "I don't give a f—"

Michael lashed out at him, catching him off guard. His hand grabbed him by the throat and slammed him into the wall. Michael pushed into his mind. *"Don't even think about ghosting away."*

Behind Michael, Kira stood ready, her fingers curled, the air vibrating around them. Marc latched onto Michael's arms, struggling to pull them from his neck. His grip held strong, finger nails finding purchase in his skin. Doris' face turned red, veins popping out around her temple and her neck.

Michael stared deep into Marc's eyes. "Tell me what you know about Ann Arbor."

Marc squirmed under her grasp. "Doris, I… don't…" He gasped for air. "… know what you're…" Another gasp. "… talking about."

Michael placed his free hand against Marc's face, reaching inside his mind to find the cognitive area. Michael's face replaced Doris's.

Marc's eyes went wide. He struggled harder at Michael's arms, then lost control of his muscles. Marc's hands fell to his side.

Kira stepped beside her grandmother. "Don't fight it, man. She's a mean bitch, ya know."

"Doris said you had a part in the explosion, asshole." Her voice was deeper, masculine, a British accent slipping out. "You know, the one that almost killed me."

"Michael… I can… I can explain."

Michael pulled back and tossed him across the room. He landed sprawled out on the floor, coughing and wheezing as he gulped air.

"You bloody well start before I have Kira vibrate the whole bloody building down on us."

Marc climbed up onto the couch. He could still feel a presence in his mind, knowing Doris—or rather, Michael—could dig the information out of him.

"I got a call from someone, really deep voice. He told me to go to Ann Arbor. To stop the explosion."

"Deep voice?" Kira asked.

Michael's hand reached up to his chin, stroking a missing beard. "Why would he…?" His voice trailed off. "What else did he say?"

"Just that someone wanted to kill Professor Knight, blow up the building, and that I should stop it."

Michael towered over Marc, his arms crossed. "And you obviously failed. Keep talking."

"I searched the Engineering building top to bottom. In the basement, I saw someone pushing gas bottles into the furnace room. When I went in, the guy had a phone strapped to one bottle. Gas was already spreading through the room. I grabbed the phone and left the room. I must have ghosted through something in the room, making the furnace kick on."

Kira sat down next to Marc. "Who was the guy, with the bottles?"

"I don't know, but I know who might."

Michael took a deep breath. "And?"

"My dad told me about a photo he saw, of me in the hallway

outside the furnace room. Dad was at Camp David, with the President. The Chief Justice was there as well."

"The guy who ran the investigation?" Michael rubbed his chin again. "And a client of Aquarius Group. Now isn't that odd."

*Saturday, June 24*
*Present Day*

From outside Adam's jeep, Lani and Troy watched as a business jet landed at the Los Alamos airport. The white plane taxied toward the terminal and powered down.

"Uncle Allen is a commercial pilot, partner with two other guys." Lani said. "Has his own business and planes. They fly oil executives from Alaska to Seattle then on down to Texas."

"You're a pilot, your father was a pilot, and now your uncle."

"Yeah, Adam was the only one without the urge to get sky-borne. He's got a lot of Mom in him—a protector instead of a flyer."

The hatch on the jet popped out and fell open. An older gentleman climbed down the stairs, waving at them. A worker from the terminal came out to meet with the pilot.

A bit of sorrow hit Lani's heart, seeing a man so similar in looks to her father. Three years older than her father, it seemed like Allen was always around for special occasions—birthdays, holidays, school plays. Mom said he stopped coming around as often after her father died.

Lani knocked on the hood of the Jeep. She glanced over her shoulder, Adam engrossed in the photos on Erin's phone. "Yo, lover boy."

Adam put a hand on the top of the steering wheel, a single finger extended out. Lani giggled.

Allen handed the airport worker a card, then headed toward the Jeep. Lani ran to meet him.

"Uncle!" Lani squeezed him tightly as they hugged.

"Lani." His deep voice vibrated in her ear. "So good to see you again. How you doin'?"

"Good. How about you?"

"Oh, you know me. Always high, in the sky." Allen glanced over her shoulder. "Who's this?"

She stepped back a bit. "This is Troy Thornburg, a co-worker."

"Pleasure to meet you, sir." Troy reached out to shake hands with the elder Knight.

"Nice to meet you too, son." Allen touched Lani on the shoulder, then stepped away from her. He reached out to Adam, and they shook hands, then hugged. "Adam! How you doing?"

"Just great, Uncle Allen."

"Please, just Allen. We're all over twenty now."

"Okay." Adam looked to Erin. "This is Erin Murphy."

"Nice to meet you." Allen offered a hand, but Erin moved in for a hug also.

"I've heard so much about you."

"All lies, even the parts that are true." Allen turned and motioned to the jet. "Let's get y'all inside, and we'll get airborne."

"Mind if I take the second seat?" Lani asked.

Allen grinned. "I was hoping you would."

Erin and Adam led the way into the plane. Lani paused as she entered, seeing the layout. A chill ran down her spine. It was the same as the jet they flew in a few days ago.

She startled when Troy touched her in the small of her back.

"You okay, Air Force?"

Lani looked up over her shoulder at Troy. "Bad feeling, that's all.”

She got comfortable in the co-pilot seat. Going over a clipboard, she was half-way through the pre-flight when Allen closed the door behind him and sat down. He went over some idiosyncrasies of the jet. They made short work of the process and were airborne in no time.

Lani flipped the switch for the PA. “Ladies and Gentlemen, the captain has turned off the fasten seat belt sign. However, we always recommend keeping your seat belt fastened while seated. Meanwhile, please sit back, relax and leave the flying to us. Thank you.”

“You’re a natural at this,” Allen said. “I could use a third pilot, if you ever leave the Air Force.”

She blushed. “Thank you. That means a lot.”

“You always had your father’s knack for flying.”

“You seem to do pretty well if you’re looking for another pilot.”

“Just an airborne taxi service, really. I hear from your mother that Adam has a good gig going with the Secret Service.”

“Yeah, he lives in Mendoza’s back pocket, going wherever the President does.”

“Will he stay on after the election, since Mendoza’s not running for re-election?”

Lani tilted her head. “You know, I’m not sure. He works for the Secret Service, not Mendoza, so he’ll still have a job come January.”

“What’s in Helena, Montana, that has you flying there, if you don’t mind me asking?”

“Chief Justice Addison,” Lani said. “He has information about the Explosion that wasn’t in the report.”

She waited for a reaction. At least he isn’t trying to discourage us from investigating. That’s refreshing.

"Your father had concerns about the Conference, you know."

"Like what?"

"Just some fears that someone might sabotage it somehow. I told him he was just being paranoid. But I asked someone to snoop around."

Lani raised an eyebrow. "Anyone I might know?"

"My boy, Joe, your cousin? His brother-in-law, Marc Black."

"Ahh…" That bastard. "He ever say what he learned?"

"Nah, never saw him again. Figured he either didn't go or died in the explosion."

"Interesting. Adam and I may have to look him up when we get back."

The two-lane blacktop turned into fourteen miles of gravel road, weaving its way between the 500-acre ranches with barns at least as tall as the two- and three-story homes they hid behind. Lani sat in the back seat of the rental car, behind her big brother. Troy sat next to her, listening to the conversation in the front seat.

"You'd be surprised how smart she is." Erin exclaimed. "Ariel's only three years old, but she's learning to read by herself. Still basic stuff, though she's finished all the first-grade books I could get my hands on."

"Wow. Is she active?" Adam asked.

"Oh yeah. Runs all over the place. My house backs up to a wooden area. She's always exploring."

A humph slipped out of Lani. Over a two-hour flight from Albuquerque to Helena and she's still gloating over the young child.

Lani whispered to Troy, "And then when she was three…"

Troy leaned in close. "You going to be like that?"

She shook her head, slowing. "Oh, hell no. I am not ready for that life yet."

"Not ready for a little Lani running around the place?"

"Can you imagine me flying at eight months pregnant? Some

football team would have me circling the stadium on Sunday afternoons with a banner attached to my ass."

Lani caught Adam's eyes in the rear-view mirror when Troy laughed out loud.

"What are you two joking about?"

"Oh, nothing." Lani shuffled in her seat. "You keep hitting these bumps in the road, making me have to pee again."

"It was terrible," Erin said, looking over her shoulder to Lani and Troy. "I couldn't go more than an hour with no bathroom. Especially when Ariel kicked me in the bladder."

Lani sighed again, then gasped.

A large two-story home, or what used to be a home, looked like it took on a tornado and failed. It scattered lumber across the one-acre trimmed lawn. The walls had collapsed outward, and the roof had dropped on the interior of the house. Bricks from the top third of the chimney littered the area, and the remaining section stood tilted. The barn, five hundred yards toward the Missouri River, stood unscathed from whatever destroyed the residence.

Troy pointed through the windshield. "What the hell happened here?"

Adam stopped the car halfway down the long driveway from the road. Everyone got out, not venturing far from the car. Lani lifted into the sky, circling the area at one hundred feet.

"Adam!" Lani shouted from above. She swooped down to his side. "There's a beeping alarm inside. Someone may still be in there."

Everyone ran to the edge of the debris. Adam circled around to get his bearings on the house. "Where at? It could take us all day to dig through all of this."

Erin raised a hand. "I think I can help with that." Erin pulled her shirt over her head and tossed it to Adam. She unbuttoned her jeans. "This is a new power I developed while I was carrying Ariel. It was the reason I had to deliver early."

"That's some power." Troy mumbled. Lani glared at him, punching him hard on the shoulder. Troy shrugged.

Erin's body became fluid, liquefied. A human-shaped glob of translucent aqua-blue gelatin stepped out of the jeans, also handing them to Adam. She tugged at her bra and panties, pulling them through her body. Adam grabbed those as well.

Erin's pulpous body climbed onto the wreckage, looking for an opening into the interior. Moving as an intelligent ooze, she slithered away, flowing behind lumber sticking out from under shingle-covered plywood.

"Okay, that will take some getting used to." Adam mumbled, running a hand across his face.

Troy nodded. "You gotta admit that's sweet."

"Almost makes you wish you were a mutant, huh?" Lani nudged him.

"Well, I don't know about that."

"Found someone!" Erin's voice filtered up through the debris. "He's alive."

The trio waited for more info, then Erin's watery head stuck out from under the roof where she had disappeared. Her head turned back to flesh as the rest of her flowed out of the hole. An arm formed out of the translucent glob, pointing to her left.

"He's over there. Lani, can you cut through wood with your light beams?"

"Like cutting through hot butter." Lani lifted upward and floated toward Erin as she oozed across the shingles.

"There are stairs right here, so if you cut along here…"

Erin waved her fleshy arm in a semi-circle. A narrow lavender beam shot from Lani's fingertips, striking the roofing material. The spectrum shifted darker, a plum color, then to a deep purple.

Wisps of smoke flittered up as her laser cut through the material with ease. A section of the building shifted, the balance of the weight changing. Adam jumped toward Erin, but her fluid body moved with the roof, unfazed by the motion.

Troy reached out and grabbed at a section of the roof now freed by Lani's laser cut. Adam joined him and together, they found what looked like a staircase leading down.

"Come on." Erin's body plopped into the hole, and she flowed downward. Troy jumped in behind her.

"Hello?" Someone shouted from inside the razed home.

Erin and Troy crawled down the stairs and into the basement of the demolished house. An older man, bald and chubby, sat against the outer concrete wall in the remains of a storm safe room. Something had cracked a lens of his glasses.

"Chief Justice Addison? Are you okay?"

"Who are you?" Addison flinched when Troy reached out to him.

"Sorry, sir. Troy Thornburg, NSA. We're here on behalf of President Mendoza." Troy reached into his jean back pocket and flashed his ID.

Addison relaxed and nodded. "Ah, good. Tony said you might be here. Could have been an hour earlier though."

"What happened here?" Erin asked.

"A few of your friends stopped by for a visit." Addison pointed at Erin's liquefied body. He poked a finger into her abdomen, then removed it and checked to see how wet it was. "Say, that's a cool trick."

"Thank you, sir. Let's get you upstairs."

Erin led the way up the stairs, Troy following up behind the Chief Justice. At the top, Adam and Lani introduced themselves as Addison made his way to the surface.

Erin gathered her clothes from Adam and slid them through

her fluid flesh. Covered, the gelatin form solidified back into her usual opalescent self. "He said this was not weather-related."

"Sir?" Lani raised an eyebrow.

"A man and two women. The older woman said her name was Doris, said she was friends of you two. She kept asking about the investigation around the President Taylor explosion. Wanted to know who caused it. I explained that everything was in the report."

Chief Justice Addison sat down on the pile of wood they pulled from the house earlier. He ran a hand over the top of his head, smoothing down the random strands of hair.

"They threatened to kill me, the man saying he could pull my heart out. I stood my ground, told them I've lived a good life. So they tore my house down instead, with me stuck in the middle."

"Lani, if it was Doris, who…?"

"Marc." Lani's voice was as cold as her expression.

"What about the other woman?" Erin asked.

"Kira. She's Doris' granddaughter and Marc's cohort from Thayer Air Force Base. She has vibrational energy."

Adam looked out over the collapsed building. "That would explain how did they knock the house down."

"It was the younger girl," Addison put his hands outward, pointing down. "She held her hands out and the place shook. Felt like a California earthquake. I fell into the basement and made it to the panic room. Lucky it didn't catch fire from the propane."

"Fatima's clue?" Lani whispered.

"Clue?" Addison asked. "What clue?"

Lani repeated the line. "There is an unseen servant, one that plotted against your president, one that wanted your father to die. One that could go places and open doors without notice."

Addison sighed. "Seems like you know a few things."

Lani shrugged. "All we have are puzzle pieces that don't quite fit together. We were hoping you had a few of the missing parts."

"I wasn't truthful with them." Addison put a hand on his knee and stood. "They asked about what we found during the investigation, anything not in the report. The report was complete, mostly."

Lani cocked her head aside. "Mostly?"

"The report mentioned a damaged hard drive, from the security computer. What wasn't in the report were the photos recovered from the drive. Copies of the photos are downstairs."

"Where?" Adam asked.

"Inside my safe, down in the basement." Addison pointed down the stairs as they came up. "Down there, near where you found me."

Adam stepped toward the staircase, but Erin grabbed his arm. "It's way too narrow for you. Best let Lani and me go."

"Alright. Be careful." Adam said, a concern on his face.

"Don't worry, I will." Lani spoke out, pulling Adam's attention to her.

Adam rolled his eyes. "Whatever."

Lani led the way down, her hands providing the light. Erin and the Chief Justice followed close behind. Back in the basement, they climbed around wooden beams, floor joists, and furniture that had fallen through the collapsed ceiling.

"She did a good job on the house. I'm surprised you made it to the safe room." Erin's fluid body split in half, allowing a string of electrical cable to move through her.

Addison touched Lani on the shoulder, then pointed passed her. "There."

"Damn." Lani gave a heavy sigh as she saw a rough-cut square log beam standing diagonally across the front. "Sir, you'd better get back upstairs, in case the house drops more on us when I cut this."

While the Chief Justice climbed clear, Lani assessed the situation, the beam to cut, where to cut, what it supported. "Okay, to get the door open, I have to remove this piece here." Lani moved her hand across the wood. "And all of that will shift."

"Then maybe I should do this." Erin touched her on the shoulder and Lani felt her body wiggle. Her arms glistened, the light she was projecting reflecting up into her liquified flesh.

"Wow. Cool." Lani giggled.

"Yeah, not so cool when you have an eight-month-old trying to get out."

"Ready?" Lani asked over her shoulder as she faced the wooden beam.

Erin nodded. "Ready."

Lani created another lavender ray of light, adjusting it to deep purple. The wood didn't cut as easily as the roof did, so she adjusted further. The solid ray became translucent as she shifted farther down the spectrum into the ultraviolet range. Wisps of smoke appeared as the laser cut through the wood. The support snapped, and the house pushed down. The flooring above them dropped close to their heads. Other supports changed position as well.

"Hey! Whoa! You guys okay down there!" Troy shouted from above.

Lani looked down at her body and saw a piece of lumber sticking down into her neck and her chest. She stepped forward, away from the wood. Her body regain rigidity as Erin released her grip on her.

"You guys okay?" Adam shouted from above again.

Lani shouted upward, "Yeah, we're fine."

Erin dropped a piece of paper into Lani's hand. "Here's the code. Sixteen digits, too many for me to remember."

Lani raised an eyebrow at the sudden appearance of the paper, but didn't ask. Tapping in the numbers, there were a series of clicks, then she tugged at the handle. It turned with a final click, and the door popped open.

"He said it was on the top shelf."

Lani looked over her shoulders, then whispered to Erin. "Cover your eyes."

Erin mouthed 'okay', then brought her hands to her face. Counting to five, Lani released a flash of light energy, three thousand lumens—brighter than most flood lights—from her entire body. Returning to her soft light glow before the flash, "All done."

"What was that for?" Erin asked.

"Just checking for ghosts."

Lani tugged at the handle on the safe, and it swung open. Papers and boxes slipped out to their feet.

"Did you find it?" The Chief Justice shouted.

"Think so." Lani shouted back.

"Manilla envelope, with the words *Engineering Building* on it."

Erin allowed her arm to solidify and sifted through the files that fell out. She handed a 9x11 envelope to Lani, then placed the rest take into the safe and closed it.

"Got it." Lani shouted upward. Liquified, Erin moved with ease through the rubble while Lani climbed between beams and wires.

Before raising above the roofline, Lani collected energy around herself. With no constant communication with Adam or Troy, there was no way of knowing what they may find when they reached the top. The men stood at the top of the stairs, ready to help them up and out of the debris.

"Are we clear?" Lani whispered to Troy.

He shrugged his shoulders. "Sure. Paranoid much?"

"Remembering an old motto from my gaming days—only the paranoid survive."

Troy laughed. "Nah, we're good. I did a circle around the area while you were down there."

The group stepped clear from the collapsed house and walked toward the barn and the rental car. In the shade of the mid-day sun, they gathered around Chief Justice Addison as he opened the envelope.

"These photos came from a security system for the building the President and your father was in." He pulled out two photos and handed them to Adam. Lani moved to his side and glanced over his arm.

"Oh, shit." Adam mumbled. He handed photos of a man in a hallway, encircled with purplish electricity.

Troy faced Lani and Adam. "Know anyone who can create portals like that?"

In unison, Adam and Lani spoke a name. "Billy."

"Who's Billy?" Addison asked.

Adam crossed his arms. "We need to get to him before Doris does. But I don't know—"

"I can get us there. Come on." She stepped away from the group, motioning for Adam to join her.

Troy handed the photos back to the Chief Justice. "I'm coming with you." He ran to them, swinging an arm around Lani.

"Going to be faster than our Russia trip, gentlemen. Buckle up." Lani keyed her phone. *"Northwest Control, Knight Seven Three Four personal. Rapid ascent to angels fifty, then tracking…"*

A blast of wind blew dirt and dust up around Erin and Addison as they launched into the sky.

Erin watched a contrail develop behind the trio as they flew off to the west.

"I put the tracker on her waist." Erin said to the open air. "Is it working?"

"Yes. Working well." Marc faded into view, standing next to her, smartphone in hand. Erin could make out a map of the western US and a blinking dot showing Lani's location.

She looked toward the space toward the barn. "Adam didn't seem to know you were here."

Doris's body appeared next to Marc. "He has a limited range, about fifty yards. A common limitation, in my experience."

Kira stepped out of the barn and joined them. "Where is she headed?"

"West coast, over Oregon right now."

"Hawaii," Doris said. She turned to face the Chief Justice. "Leonard, thank you so much for your help with this."

Addison reached out and took her hand, kissing her knuckles. "My pleasure, Doris. For all you've done for me in my career, temporarily destroying my house was the least I could do."

"Temporarily?" Kira asked.

Addison released Doris' hand and turned to face his demolished house. In an action that took two minutes, he moved his arms in an arc from right to left. The roof lifted off the ground, walls became rebuilt, stone and brick flew back into place. When his hands completed the arc, the house stood fully restored.

Doris's mouth hung open. "Amazing."

Addison looked back at her. "Sure I can't offer you a drink before you go, maybe a 'j' or two? Like old times, down in Berkeley."

"You're much too kind, Leonard. But I need to see this through."

"Very well. How about you, my dear?" Addison looked to Erin.

Erin grinned from ear to ear. "Well, they left me a car. And my babysitter is good through the weekend."

Addison waved his hand. "Good. Send for DK and your daughter, we'll go camping down by the Missouri."

Erin shook her head, sighing. "Daiki won't be joining this weekend. Not for a while anyway."

Marc flipped the app off and slid the phone back in his pocket. "Michael, they stopped on Oahu, North Shore area."

"Just what I thought." Doris said. "Thank you again, Leonard. Erin, excellent work." She motioned for Kira to stand beside her. "Come, let's go rattle another house."

Marc and Kira stepped over to Doris, reaching out for her hands. Doris nodded to Addison as the trio vanished.

Erin pulled her phone out of her back pocket. She scrolled through the Contacts app, finding the letter K, then pressed the number to call. "They're on their way."

"Both groups?" A deep voice asked.

"Yes. Leelee has a full house right about now."

"Good. Flying back then?"

"No, sir. Not today." Erin ended the call, then put her arm around the Chief Justice as they walked toward the house.

Energy flowed through Lani, energizing and exhausting her simultaneously as she drew in the solar radiation above her and transformed it into the force to push the three of them through the sky. Determination fueled her, pushing her to get to her mother before Doris could, and to find out how Billy could be behind her father's death.

They were halfway to the edge of space, the curvature of the earth was visible all around them. The terminator—the separation between day and night—was ahead of them, the sun behind them. Lani usually felt at home here. Today was not one of those days.

Troy moved, testing the grip she had on him. "And you're not concerned about Space Command?"

"They know it's me." Lani gave a bitter response. "I have a tracker on me, as do most of us."

"Us who?"

"Mutants with high-speed flight ability."

"And just how fast—"

"Mach 15, just shy of ten thousand miles an hour, at an altitude of fifty thousand feet." Lani felt him staring at her, another question forming. "An app on my phone relays everything to me.”

“Does she know we were coming?” Adam asked.

“It’s 6:30 am local.” Lani said after a quick check. “I called several times via sat phone, no answer.”

“Then she must be sleeping in.”

“She does every day.”

“How do you know that?”

“I call or visit at least once a week.”

This time it was her brother staring at her.

“Look, you’re just so damn busy with Mendoza. She gets that.”

“Bring me up to speed,” Troy spoke up. “What did you guys learn back there?”

“Billy.” Lani answered.

“A friend from college, a mutant,” Adam explained. “He can create portals, miniature wormholes, through which he or anyone can move.”

“Okay. That was him in the photos. But why?”

“Best to let him explain,” Lani said. “We’re here.”

The protective force field shifted from ultraviolet to purple, then to a soft lavender. The ocean breeze blew at their clothes as the bubble vanished. They were a thousand feet over Oahu’s northwest coast and dropping fast. At an altitude of one hundred feet, Lani slowed their descent to that of an elevator. They touched down on Mom’s back lawn between a pair of flower beds.

“And we’re back on earth.” Troy announced.

“Mom!” Lani mentally unlocked the electronic lock on the door as she ran for the house, Adam fast behind her. Nearly flinging the aluminum exterior door off its hinges, she turned the knob to the wooden door and bounced off of it.

“What the f—”

Adam pointed at the deadbolt. “Looks new.”

Lani glared at him. "And she usually answers the door before I get to the door." She banged hard on the wood. "Mom!"

"Chill out, Lani. We're the only mutants here." Adam said. "Just us and Mom. And Billy." Adam's face turned red, grim. "The hell, he's upstairs with Mom."

"Oh, yeah. Forgot to tell you about that." Lani did a double-take at Adam. "Wait, you can detect Mom?"

"How do you think she knows when someone's at the door before they knock? And when she would sneak up on us?"

"I figured that was just her doing that mom-ninja thing. You never said anything."

Adam shrugged. "I thought you knew. Dad did."

"Well, of course Dad would. Hell, I do come from a family of mutants." It all made sense. Her mom always had that ability to be there standing, watching when you had no clue how long she had been there.

"Someone's coming," Troy said, a face to a window.

The door clicked and swung open. Leelee stood in front of the door, her long wet hair clinging to a red silk robe with oriental dragons and designs around it.

"Good morning, my dear." Leelee held back a yawn. She threw her arms out at the sight of Adam, wrapping them around him. "Adam, my boy. Come in. Have you eaten breakfast yet?"

"Mom, are you okay?" Adam asked. "Is anyone here?"

"Billy is here. He stayed the night, watching late night TV again."

"Yeah, I know he's here. I mean anyone else."

Leelee shook her head, glancing over at Troy. "You must be Troy."

Troy walked over from the window and stood behind Lani. "Ms. Knight, hello. Troy Thornburg. I work with your daughter in Washington."

"You went with them to Russia this week. Nice to meet you." She stepped away from the door and waved them in. "Please, everyone come in."

"Why did you get a new lock on the door, Mom?" Lani led the group into the house.

"Well, Billy thought it would be a good idea, so he had a second one put in yesterday afternoon." Leelee walked into the kitchen and grabbed the teapot off the stove and went to the faucet. She turned the water on, filling the pot.

Lani glanced at the refrigerator. The hula girl was missing.

"Mom." Adam moved to his mother's side. "We need to talk."

"Hey, Lani." Billy walked into the room, wearing only pajama bottoms, drying his hair with a towel. "Adam, dude! What's up?"

He laid the towel around his neck and raised his arms to hug Adam. Adam walked to him and swung a right hook, connecting hard with his jaw. Billy's legs gave out, dropping him to the floor. Adam stood over him, fists curled, biceps flexed.

"Adam Makoa Knight!" Leelee shouted at her son. She darted around the counter and slapped Adam hard on the arm. "What the hell are you doing?" She pushed him aside and knelt down to Billy, looking at his face.

"It's ok, Leelee. I suppose I deserved that." Billy touched his jaw, testing the forming bruise. She tried to help him stand, but Billy waved her away and stood on his own. Adam stepped forward, and Leelee stepped between him and Billy.

"Adam, sit down. Now!" She pointed at the kitchen table.

Troy leaned over Lani's shoulder and whispered. "Let me guess, unexpected roommate?"

She turned to whisper back, her lips brushing his cheek. She flinched, then leaned forward, rubbing her nose against him. "Nothing gets past you, Mister Obvious."

Adam stomped to the back side of the table and pulled a chair out. Lani plopped next to him to his right. Billy sat opposite of Lani with Leelee next to him. Troy took up the neutral spot at the end of the table, his back to the living room.

"Mom," Lani started the interview. "We saw a photo of Billy downstairs of Dad's classroom."

"I don't know what photos you are talking about." Leelee held her hands under the table. So did Billy. Lani put a hand on Adam's arm, his hands flexing in and out of a fist.

"Ms. Knight," Troy spoke up. "Some people are on their way here. Someone willing to kill to find out the answer."

"And we know you did it," Adam said. His words were flat, without emotion. "I know you meant to kill Dad."

"Someone gave us a clue, Mom. That's why we went to Russia." Lani laid her hands flat on the table. "The person said there was someone who wanted to kill Dad. She said it was someone that could go places and open doors without notice. That's you, Billy."

"That could be your boyfriend, Marc," Leelee said. "He can do that, right?"

"It wasn't him, Mom. He was there, but he didn't do it."

"Ms. Knight," Troy interjected. "Why would you want to harm your husband or President Taylor?"

"Why do you think it was her?" Billy put his hands on the table, his right hand in a fist in his left palm. "No one accused her of—"

"We saw photos, damn it," Adam said, his voice raising as the anger built up, pointing a finger at his friend. "You walking through one of your portals, pushing hydrogen bottles into the boiler room, downstairs of the Engineering building."

"Billy, you didn't have a motive. You were just doing what you were told." Lani interjected. "Mom, it couldn't have been against the President. You're one of the most unpolitical people we know. It had to be because of Dad. What was he doing that would make you want to kill him?"

Leelee pulled a tissue from a pocket on her robe and wiped at her eyes. Billy stood up and grabbed a box of tissues on the counter behind him.

"Because he was making those horrible things." Leelee sniffled into a tissue.

"The halos?" Adam asked.

Leelee's eyes had a puppy-dog look to them as she gazed at her son. "Yes, and he used you to do it."

Adam was taken aback. "I don't know what you mean."

"He used those studies he made of you, when you were younger. When Lani was getting her powers, and you could stop her."

"You mean at the University?" Adam asked.

"Remember?" Lani nodded. "I had just learned to fly, and he recorded you blocking me? Mom shaved your head real close, and you had those wires all around your head."

"Why would you want to harm Dad because of the halos?"

"Because someone could use them against you or your sister," Leelee explained. "Because they could hurt you."

"But where does the unseen servant part come in?" Troy asked.

This time, Lani pointed a finger at her Mom. "Concealment. You can hide in plain sight. Who were you working for?"

Leelee turned and pointed to the backyard. "Someone's here."

Lani shook her head. "No time for distractions, Mom…" She turned to look out the open door. Three people stood near the edge of the beach, walking toward the house. "Shit."

"Everyone, take cover!" Troy shouted.

Michael didn't recall having been to this place, but it was vivid in

Doris' memory. Recent memory. Just last month, in fact. He couldn't recall all of what they said, but it was about their observations on Lani. They had been spying on her, using Marc. That interested Michael, but it didn't matter now. It was Leelee's involvement in the explosion that nearly killed him that was foremost in Michael's mind. It was time to knock on the door and invite themselves in.

He put a hand on Kira's back. "They know we are here. Time to make an entrance."

The young woman took a step forward, her arms out in front of her. The space before them rippled as force energy made its way toward the house. The multiple waves of compressed air boomed as they struck the wood, brick, and mortar, thrusting it inside.

Michael smiled. "Good girl."


The material that was the exterior wall scattered into the house. The force continued inward, pushing against everyone inside. Billy created a portal, sending much of the debris out the opposite end of the wormhole, located twenty feet behind them in the living room. Adam took the brunt of the remaining wreckage full force, knocking him and Lani onto the floor.

Troy stared out the enormous hole in the wall as he readied a handgun. "Three contacts, forty yards and closing."

Adam struggled to his feet. "One telepath, one ghost, one vibrational."

Purple glow bathed the room as Lani super-charged. "Doris, Marc, and Kira. One helluva trio."

"The telepath can teleport as well. I'll block her. You can have the rest."

"Leelee Knight!" Doris shouted. "It's me, Michael Clarke. I'd like a word with you, if you don't mind."

"Like hell," Billy said. Tossing his arms in front of him, a ring of blue-purple electricity formed on the ground around the attackers. Gravity took hold, and they fell into the black interior of the ring.

"Billy?" Lani stepped passed everyone, then floated out onto the lawn. "Where'd they go?"

Billy climbed over the foot-high remains of the wall to stand beside her. He pointed up and out over the ocean. "About a mile out and up."

"Holy…" Troy muttered.

"She's a teleporter," Lani announced. "She'll be back. We better be ready."

Leelee moved between Billy and Lani, motioning out. "Too late. Here they come."

Two bodies appeared prone a foot off of the ground and fell hard, almost bouncing in the grass. Adam's training kicked in, moving him to stand in front of his mother and sister. Troy dropped to one knee, handgun taking aim.

"Where's Kira?" Lani asked.

Billy jumped backwards as the Knight family members doubled over. A massive stabbing pain shot through their minds. Lani fell to her knees, her hands raised to her temples. Through the agony, she heard Troy's handgun discharge; the bullets passing through the translucent bodies of Doris and Marc.

Doris's voice was weak as she commanded Marc. "Screw talking. Kill the mom."

Marc's eyes went blank as he stood, becoming solid. He reached to his back and withdrew a handgun. Troy fired, striking Marc in the shoulder. Lani pushed out with a broad blast, knocking Doris and her puppet tumbling backwards.

"Adam!" Leelee shouted.

Lani turned to see her brother slumping to his knees in front of her mother, then falling face down in the grass. She leaped off of her knees, landing at Adam's side. Rolling him over, a blood stain formed around a tiny hole in the center of his shirt. Lani put an ear to his chest.

Marc sat upright, tossing the handgun aside. "What… what happened?"

"Asshole!" A brilliant green and purple glow erupted around Lani, engulfing her and those around her. She pointed her index finger at him, releasing a pencil-thin beam. The beam sizzled as it struck Marc in the forehead. He slumped over, laying on Doris's unconscious body. No blood exited the cauterized hole in his skull.

Anger fueling her, aurora energy continued to swirl around Lani as she stood over Doris. Troy pushed against her, keeping her hands away from the telepath.

"Lani. I can't stop you, but are you sure you want to kill her too?"

"She needs to pay for what she's done."

"Yes, but she called herself Michael. He is to blame, not Doris. Will you be killing Doris *and* Michael, or just Doris?"

Lani pushed him away and returned to her brother. Leelee knelt at his side, Billy beside her, comforting her.

"Call NSA Honolulu. Screw the halos. We're going to need three sedation kits."

"Three?"

Lani crossed her arms, glaring down at her mother. "William Watson, Leelee Knight, you are under arrest for the murder of Zach Knight and Holly Taylor."

Michael blinked several times. He groaned, trying to raise a hand to his head. Then he sighed, seeing the ceiling fan circling above him, the tassel hanging from the ball chain swirling underneath.

"Bloody hell."

Michael found the sensor on the ceiling with his eyes and winked. A chime sounded in the great room. A young, dark-skinned man walked into the room. Grabbing onto the door frame, he leaned into the room.

"What is it now, Michael?"

"Has Dr. Thornburg called yet?"

"Yes. She said she would be here tomorrow morning."

"Excellent." A wide grin grew on Michael's face. "We can finish this later."

*Tuesday, July 4*
*Present Day*

The music of a marching band rolled over the hill from somewhere in Arlington, clashing with the sirens of an ambulance. Troy figured the combination of heat and humidity claimed another victim in the Independence Day crowds in the nation's Capital. He stood in the shade of a tree along Eisenhower Drive in Arlington National Cemetery, hands stuffed in his jeans pockets. US Air Force markings painted on the car shined behind him. The driver sat inside the running sedan, the air conditioner fighting against the 105-degree heat index.

Samira leaned against a tree, her left arm in a black nylon sling over her white t-shirt. The doctor at NSA hadn't released her back to full duty just yet, only half-days to start with, and desk work only.

"What are you going to do if she goes to prison?" Samira tried to cross her arms, but the sling kept getting in the way.

Troy looked at her like she had a third eye. "What do you mean? For killing a mutant who just killed her brother? It was in the line of duty."

"You weren't exactly on a mission."

"An assignment, sanctioned by the President."

Samira let out a humph. "Speaking of."

The Presidential limo and its two-car entourage crept around the bend and stopped behind the Air Force sedan. A Secret Service agent got out of the lead car and walked back to the middle car to open the door for the President.

Antonio buttoned his jacket as soon as he stepped out of the limo. Beads of sweat formed on his forehead. He nodded to Troy and Samira as he approached them. Troy stepped away from the sedan and met the President halfway.

"Mr. President." Troy saluted.

Antonio waved off the salute, then pointed at the young woman standing in grass fifty yards away. "How is she doing?"

"She's good, still processing Adam's death and her mother's involvement in all of this."

They stood side-by-side, watching Lani.

"Court-marshal?" Troy asked. "For excessive use of force?"

"For Lani? Nah. She'll get a hearing, but I'm sure they see clear to releasing her."

"With some Presidential encouragement?"

"Advice from the Commander-in-chief." Antonio held up a fist and they fist-bumped.

"I think I'll reassign her for a while. Give her a mission to focus her mind on during the pregnancy."

"Hopefully nothing to do with Ann Arbor."

"No, no." Mendoza spoke his head. "Something well suited to her skills."

"Oh?" Troy raised an eyebrow. "Any hints?"

"Well, she loves to fly. I'll just leave it at that."

Troy caught the hint. Time to change the subject. "What about her mother?"

"She's being held without charges at the moment."

"Shit's going to hit the fan if the world finds out." Troy sighed.

"Not all secrets need to be revealed today."

"Understood, sir. Understood."

Antonio took a step onto the grass. "If you'll excuse me."

Troy returned to the shade tree as the President walked toward Lani.

Samira cocked her head. "Well?"

"No prison orange, from what I gathered."

"That's good. Would hate to see her sharing a cell with her mother."


Arlington National Cemetery was a quiet, humbling place. The pattern of small, white gravestones pleased the OCD in Lani. The smell of the freshly cut green grass also pleased her until it teased her sinuses. Or that's what she blamed the sniffles on.

The gravestone before her was blank, which annoyed her. Only a paper card with a name identified the remains in front of it: Adam Knight. The stone to the left was a familiar one. She had stood in front of it many times in recent years. She read the words once more, though she knew them by heart.

*Major Zach Knight*
*USAF*
*Loving husband, father, patriot*


"What inscription are you going to put on Adam's?"

President Mendoza approached Lani from behind. She knew he was in the area. The Secret Service radio frequencies were one of her favorites to listen in on.

"I thought about something like 'protector of democracy,' but that may be a bit much."

Lani pushed a tissue under her dark sports-style sunglasses. She wore her blue and green camouflage Airman Basic Uniform.

Antonio pulled a handkerchief from his breast pocket and

wiped his brow. "When is your hearing?"

"For unnecessary use of deadly force and killing the father of my child?"

Antonio raised an eyebrow. "Yes, I suppose that would be that one."

"Sorry." Lani hung her head down. "They set the hearing for tomorrow."

"How are you feeling?"

"Better."

"I'm glad to hear."

She could tell he was being sincere, but having never married or being a father, she wasn't expecting a lot of sympathy from him. Lani thought that was strange, considering his mutant ability to implant and control a person's emotions. The complete revelation that the American President was covertly a mutant still blew her mind. It was obvious now why he kept Adam so close to him.

Lani looked up, gazing across the field to the other grave markers. "Thank you for arranging for this plot. I wasn't sure if Secret Service would get the honors."

"The law gives permission to lay to rest children of military here. I've reserved the next spot over for you." Antonio waved to the other side of her father's grave.

Lani smirked. "Don't be killing me off so soon."

"Oh, don't worry." He chuckled. "I'm sure I'll be needing your help from here on out. More than ever."

"Yes, sir. Ready when you are. Depending on the hearing, of course."

"I'm sure the judge advocate will see clear to release you. Take as much time as you need. I'll see that NSA know."

They stood in silence for a moment, in quiet contemplation.

"You just missed Erin." Lani said, not looking away from the gravestone. "She seems to do pretty well. All things considered."

"Mutant Defense Foundation has already reached out to me, asking for a few minutes at the White House. I may work them in, probably at the end of July. Let things settle down in her organization first."

Lani turned to look at Antonio, squinting at the sunlight. "You know, when I was in Michael's body, I saw some of his memories."

"Oh?" Antonio raised an eyebrow.

"You, Doris, and Michael sitting in a restaurant booth. You were eating pancakes."

He sighed. "Berkeley, a long, long time ago."

"He wanted to hate you, but you wouldn't let him. You wouldn't let him love Doris either, even after you left them."

The President crossed his arms. "That was a long time ago."

"Yes, sir." Lani turned around, facing the vehicles. She saw Troy and Samira at the rear of her ride, chatting with one of the Secret Service agents.

"The Vice-President has me going to Michigan for a campaign rally next month, ahead of the convention." Antonio put a hand on her shoulder blade. "Come see me next week. We'll talk about some ideas I have."

"Thank you, Mr. President."

He nodded, stepped back and away from her. Another tear came to her as she watched him walking away, alone.


Antonio waved to Troy and Samira as he approached the armored limo. An agent opened the door for him. He gave a long look back at Lani before getting inside. He unbuttoned his jacket and tapped on the window between him and the driver. The car jerked as the driver put it in gear.

Passing the gravestone and small monument for President

Taylor, he felt his phone buzz. He grimaced when he saw the caller.

"Yes, sir?"

A deep voice was on the other end. "Well?"

"There was some memory transfer, yes. But I don't think it will be a problem."

"You had better see to it."

"Yes, Grandfather."

ABOUT THE AUTHOR

R.G. Bisig has been reading X-Men and Legion of Super Heroes comic books since what seemed like the beginning of time. Or at least it was for him.

Soon after the release of "The Empire Strikes Back", he wrote his own version of Episode VI on a typewriter on board the USS Hammerhead. Sadly, it wasn't what George Lucas had in mind.

After a tour in the US Navy, he went on to be Dungeon Master for several D&D groups. His scenario "Busy Night" for the Living Verge RPGA community debuted at the 1998 GenCon gaming convention.

R.G. Bisig lives in Columbia, Missouri.

This is his second book, a sequel to GUST OF WIND.

www.ingramcontent.com/pod-product-compliance
Lightning Source LLC
Chambersburg PA
CBHW051438190726
48289CB00001B/250